*Time is the most fluid med*
*humans are its most rep*

# THE THIRTEENTH MONTH

There are rules for traveling:
*A mage must never go forward.*
*Keep the secrets of the order in all times.*
*And never, ever travel during the thirteenth month.*

Born into a powerful mage family, Narine Anahid Khoren is a time traveler whose life is constantly in flux. Since committing to the order of the Seba Segal at fourteen, she's spent her life traveling through history, trying to make a difference and sacrificing her life in the present for one jumping through the past.

But while the world in 2071 has moved forward, the ancient order of the Seba Segel has become ever more archaic. The secret sect, founded by astronomer priests, has passed its magic to thousands of generations, perfecting the secrets of divination and time travel while also amassing power, influence, and riches.

Change is on the horizon, and some in the order would do anything to stop it. When one of the highest laws of mage travel is broken in the thirteenth month, Narine, her friends, and one unsuspecting professor will have to scour history to set the timeline right.

*The Thirteenth Month* is the first book in the Seba Segel series, an all-new time-travel fantasy series by ten-time *USA Today* bestseller Elizabeth Hunter, author of the Elemental Mysteries and the Irin Chronicles.

# THE THIRTEENTH MONTH

## SEBA SEGAL SERIES
### BOOK ONE

## ELIZABETH HUNTER

Recurve Press LLC
PO Box 4034
Visalia, California 93278
USA

*For my mothers*
*Joyce &*
*Sereke*

# AUTHOR'S NOTE

Since the beginning of the modern era, Ethiopia has used a calendar unique in the world. Based on the calculations of Annianus of Alexandria—who set the incarnation of Christ eight years before a later calculation used by European calendars—this difference appears to set Ethiopia eight years "behind" the Gregorian calendar used by much of the world.

Despite modern pressure, the Ge'ez calendar has remained constant. Both civil and religious in nature, it is used for business, government, and everyday life, and because Ethiopia has resisted all attempts at European colonization, it was never forced to give up its unique way of marking time.

The Ethiopian calendar consists of twelve equal months of thirty days and one month that is unique. Consisting of five or six days, the thirteenth month is a time of celebration and anticipation marking the end of the rainy season and the beginning of new life.

It is a time to reflect, meditate, and transform.

# CHAPTER I

*Addis Ababa*
*Capital of Ethiopia*
*2071 Ethiopian Calendar/2079 Gregorian Year*

It was the sound of tapping that finally woke her. Narine had been drifting in restless sleep all night, listening to the familiar songs coming from the church, which floated over the rooftops and through the twisting cobblestone streets of Addis Ababa before the dawn of Pagume.

"Narine." Genet's voice from the hallway made her open her eyes.

Narine rolled toward her bedside table, tapping on the sleek digital assistant sitting in its charging port. She saw the hour flash against the wall and rubbed her eyes to urge them to wake.

"I'm coming," she called to Genet.

She threw a heavy woven *gebi* over her shoulders and slid her feet into slippers before she walked from her bedroom. Then she made her way down the hallway and out the side door of the house.

The old compound in Sidist Kilo was surrounded by a

high wall covered in vines, and a spreading mango tree dominated the open space where Genet kept a large vegetable garden.

Genet and her housemaid Samira were preparing the bath, pouring a liter bottle of holy water Genet had retrieved from the church into a washbasin already halfway full.

They waved her over to join Gelile, Genet's eight-year-old daughter, who was leaning against the compound wall and yawning.

The light was blue grey, and the songs from the church were clearer now. Genet pointed to the wooden stool and Narine unwound her gebi, the cotton wrap that was keeping her warm in the chilled air, handing it to Samira.

Her goddaughter's eyes were wide and blinking as Narine stripped down and sat on the old wooden stool by the washbasin, her pale skin appearing almost blue in the predawn light.

Narine closed her eyes and tried to relax, but Genet's murmured prayers, the holy water, and every regret from the previous year washed over her with the bathwater, stealing the breath from her lungs as her body locked from the cold.

The water soaked her hair, her neck, her chest, and her back, flowing from the roots of her dark, curling hair to her feet before sinking into the earth where her family had planted their roots over one hundred years before.

Tears came to Narine's eyes, but they were hidden by the water Genet poured over her head. *I can't keep going like this.*

A flash of memories hit her, one after the other, like waves beating a rocky shore. A thread of blood spreading through the travelers' pool, her mother's hissed whisper, and the kiss of a knife against her skin.

Genet continued to pray as Narine rubbed the holy water over her arms and shoulders.

*I can't keep going like this.*

The fine scars that crawled up her left arm all the way to

her elbow were a testament to her vocation and her magic. She opened her eyes and glanced at Gelile, who watched her with unwavering focus.

Narine remembered watching her mother the same way Gelile watched her, as if her adult body was a riddle for her childish mind to decipher. Her mother's arms had been marked by elaborate scarification, a curiosity to the uninitiated and a testament of power to those in their order.

The water bit her skin with its cold sting, but her lungs loosened and her mind and heart settled. She tried to release it all to flow away with the water.

The guilt.

The uncertainty.

The doubts that plagued her mind.

The next year would be different. Somehow she would set things right.

Genet whispered prayers over her, kissing the top of Narine's head.

She didn't deserve Genet.

The bath, the prayers, and the predawn waking were rituals, but they were born of a faith that had anchored Narine's ancestors for over a thousand years. She knew better than the average human that time changed everything. It was far more fluid than the water Genet poured over her head.

But this? This did not change.

The earth beneath her feet. The sky above her. The sun rising in the east and the early-morning prayers of the priests. The afternoon call to salat ringing from the mosque and the smell of roasting coffee and frankincense calling her home.

These things were the frames on which her life was woven.

In a world that shifted constantly, Pagume did not change.

Genet finished her prayers in Ge'ez, the language of the old liturgy. "In the name of the Father and the Son and the Holy Spirit, amen."

"Amen," Narine repeated.

"Amen." Gelile's sleepy pout turned into a whine. "Ema…"

Genet set the pitcher next to the washbasin. "You're next."

The stern woman pointed to the stool as Narine stood and reached for the gebi that Samira held open for her. She slid her house shoes back on, the dirt from the garden sticking to the damp soles of her feet.

Narine clutched the wrap tightly around her body, goose bumps spreading over her skin. She watched in silence as Gelile stomped over to the basin, took off her nightdress, and hung her head back. "It's cold."

"It's not that cold."

Narine didn't agree with Genet, but she said nothing, exchanging a glance with Samira, who was holding back a smile.

Gelile continued her childish rant as she sat on the bench. "Samira doesn't have to take a bath."

"Samira is Muslim." Genet took the bonnet from Gelile's hair and lifted the pitcher of holy water. "She has to bathe for many things, but not for Pagume. Where is your heart? Would Maryam be pleased by your complaining?" Genet's arch look silenced her daughter. "Thank you."

She poured the water over Gelile's narrow shoulders, the child's dark brown skin glowing soft gold as the water and the dawn light combined. The little girl froze and her back straightened, but she didn't whine again.

Narine watched her goddaughter receive the ritual bath, then took Genet's place to bless the woman who was—in every way but blood—her sister.

Samira took Gelile and wrapped her in a thick towel, rubbing her arms and legs as Narine spoke the first prayer of Pagume over her sister. The holy water poured over Genet's round shoulders and smooth arms, falling over her soft belly and sturdy hips, hitting the ground and sanctifying the living earth.

When Genet's husband had been alive, he had been the one to offer prayers in his deep, soothing voice and bless the women he watched over, but Teddy was gone, lost to the mundane tragedy of a bus accident when Gelile was only three.

Genet leaned her head back, silently asking for Narine to soak her thoroughly. Her eyes were closed and her lips moved in prayer.

Narine finished the water, tipping the basin to the side and pouring the last into Genet's hair. She leaned over and kissed her sister's forehead. "Amen."

"Amen."

As the basin was put away and the sun rose in the east, Narine let out a relieved sigh, grateful for the reprieve Pagume offered.

For the next five days, she would have to take freezing cold baths every morning with an enthusiastically praying Genet, but at least nothing about the world would shift. For the next five days, the timeline would rest.

The thirteenth month had begun.

WHILE IT WAS A HOLIDAY FOR MOST OF THE COUNTRY WITH neighborhood festivals, light shows in Sheger Park, and bright yellow daisies adorning the shops and skytrains, Narine was still expected at work.

She gulped down the breakfast of *chechebsa* and tea before she dressed in dark pants and a close-fitting black shirt, stuck her freshly charged AI assistant in her ear, and drank a quick cup of coffee Samira had prepared in the living room.

Alerted by her personal assistant, the house AI greeted Narine as she was reaching for her zip-bike helmet.

"Good morning, Narine. Today is the first day of Pagume

and the sixth day of September in the World Calendar. Would you like to hear the news headlines for today?"

"No, thank you. Forecast only." She grabbed the sleek fiberglass helmet and paused to hear the weather report.

"There will be rain this afternoon at approximately one o'clock. Would you like to send commuting alternatives to your assistant?"

"Nope. I won't be driving during the rain."

"There is a knot of traffic under the skytrain overpass in Arat Kilo Square. Would you like commuting alternatives?"

A knot of traffic wouldn't be an issue on her bike. "No, thank you."

She was almost out the door when her niece stopped her.

*"Akeste!"*

"Yes?" Narine kissed the top of Gelile's head and hugged her shoulders. "Enjoy your holiday. I really need to go, *mita.*"

The little girl looked up with a dimpled smile. "Will you bring me a present tonight?"

Narine narrowed her eyes. "For what?"

"Because…" The girl fidgeted with the end of her braid. "Ah… I didn't cry this morning."

Narine knew she could easily find some trinket for her niece at the holiday markets in Shiro Meda. There would be hair clips or a flower garland or digital wristbands that would light up and delight the girl. "Are you going to complain about your bath tomorrow or be very, very good for your mother?"

Gelile considered the sacrifice. "I'll be very good. Very quiet. And I will pray all day today."

"Don't make promises you can't keep."

"Okay. I will pray today though." She walked over and hung on to Narine's arm. "Please get me a present?"

*"Eshi,* I'm going to call your mother and check this afternoon before I leave work, and if you've been helpful to her and Samira, I will bring a present." She put on her helmet

and adjusted her assistant to link with the speakers. "You do not get a present for praying."

"Thank youuuuuu." Her niece kissed her hand. "You're not making a jump today, are you?"

"It's Pagume." Narine finally walked out the door. "No one travels during Pagume."

Gelile followed her out to the front step and watched as Narine walked to the concrete-block garage covered with solar cells. Along with the household batteries, the garage contained an antique diesel Land Cruiser Teddy had fixed up, a small electric car they used on rainy days, and the practical electric all-wheel crawler that could be programmed to drive anywhere in the city.

The morning was crisp, sunny, and the dense clouds that marked the rainy season had started to finally break apart before the New Year. Narine would take her favorite form of commute, her zip bike.

She unplugged the bike from its charger and glanced at the dusty workbench that hadn't seen love since Teddy had passed. Genet's brother occasionally came by the compound to fix things in the house, work on the solar cells, or use Teddy's tools to tinker with his antique Volkswagen, but he was the only one to use them.

She rolled the bike into the yard, passing more solar cells mounted on the old stone walls, and patches of vegetables that Genet and Samira grew to supplement their fresh-food allowance.

Narine's house was a twentieth-century relic in a city that had grown up and out as the population of the capital had surged in the past fifty years. Still a spreading, single-story wooden house with a large garden around it, the property was dwarfed by modern mansions that had been built as the area transitioned from a middle-class neighborhood to a wealthy enclave for the upper class and international professionals. Their neighbors came from Addis, Lagos, Bombay, Shanghai, and Rio, a mélange of cultures that was a testament to the future of the African capital.

In the distance, the skyscrapers in the financial district dominated the skyline, and a concrete skytrain overpass was blocked by a soaring row of eucalyptus trees. As she pushed her bike to the front gate, a car of early-morning commuters whooshed overhead, the clack-clack of electromagnets the only audible evidence of their transit.

Narine's compound had been in her family since her ancestors had moved from Armenia to Greece to Addis in the 1920s. As she was the only powerful mage of her generation who had remained in the capital city, the property fell into her care. There were three houses within its stone walls, and while Narine lived in the largest one, she was rarely alone. She always had cousins coming and going along with family friends from Europe, Asia, the United States, and other parts of the continent.

Genet and her daughter lived in the second house, and the third—more like a cottage—was kept for guests, visiting relatives, or the occasional traveling mage.

Narine couldn't imagine living alone. People—mundane or magic—were exhausting as a rule, but the lack of them was worse. Too much silence left her with more time to think.

She pushed the bike down the path toward the metal gate where Samira was already pulling back the door.

"The Chen family just got a new automatic gate," Samira said. "It links with the house assistant."

Narine nodded. "Is that so?"

The girl gave her an innocent shrug. "It has security built in. It would probably be much safer than this one."

"And it doesn't squeak when you pull it open?"

The girl gave her a brilliant smile. "You don't have to pull it at all."

"But if we had a modern gate, how would the whole neighborhood know when we were coming and going?"

Samira rolled her eyes. "Have a beautiful day, Akeste."

"Make sure Gelile helps in the garden today before she goes to play." Narine put on her gloves and flipped down her visor before she mounted her bike. "I'll send a message when I'm on my way home."

"I'll make her pull weeds."

"Perfect."

Narine rode through the gate and into the narrow alley-way, winding through the market stalls that were already bustling as vendors swept the cobblestones and propped up the metal shades that folded down at night. Over the stalls, solar-powered electric notice boards flipped between news headlines and advertisements for the latest assistants, zip cars, or new takeaway food stalls.

INDIA EXPANDING SOMALI SHIPBUILDING HUB.

CITYZIPPASSES ON SALE FOR THE NEW YEAR. BUY AHEAD!

BETO'S BRAZILIAN BARBECUE; NEW BRANCH IN SARBET.

The flashing ads and headlines followed Narine down the alley along with the scent of boiling coffee and cooking oil. Familiar sights and smells greeted her as she maneuvered her bike through the pedestrian-crowded street.

Men and women on their way to work or heading to holiday markets stopped at the stalls on the corner, chatting over coffee or buying crisp *sambusas* or beef empanadas before they started their day. A few familiar faces greeted Narine, but the city was waking and the sun was crawling higher in the sky. It was the beginning of the holiday season, and everyone had somewhere to go.

She left the side streets and merged onto the main road, weaving between the automated crawler traffic that congested under the skytrain overpass before she whipped around the traffic circle and sped up as she passed Addis Ababa University.

ELIZABETH HUNTER

When Narine was riding, she was just another commuter on her way to work. She could be anyone or no one. She wasn't a third-tier mage of the order, she wasn't the scion of House Kayl, she was just a twenty-eight-year-old woman on her way to work. She breathed in the morning air still tinged with the scent of rain from the night before.

Narine passed the lion monument and pointed her bike north, passing the university gates on her left, scattered government buildings, and the countless blue-and-white electric minibuses that ferried residents to their work at the foreign embassies or the always-expanding government compound near Entoto.

Pagume also marked the beginning of the tourist season in the country, so in addition to commuter traffic, tour buses filled with Chinese, Brazilian, and Indian visitors crowded the roads in the museum district, and the scent of food carts drifted across the road as eager vendors catered to the tourist crowds.

While much of the world had to supplement their supply of natural foods with manufactured nutrients because of climate change, Ethiopia continued to have a thriving fresh-food economy, which made it popular as a tourism destination for those eager to taste natural meats, fresh fruit, vegetables, and spices.

Narine tried to slow down as she passed the crowded intersection, but a tall man with a beard, sunglasses, and an orange backpack nearly stepped in front of her before she could swerve around him.

He stepped back from the traffic just in time but yelled after her, "Hey, watch it!"

Narine paused at the light and looked back at him, surprised by his rudeness and his English.

She hadn't been the one stepping into traffic.

"Watch where you're going!" The man looked like he'd

10

spilled something hot. He was holding a paper cup and shaking his hand.

Narine narrowed her eyes behind her visor. The man might be Ethiopian, but he sounded American. Perhaps he was one of the numerous diaspora who had returned in the previous decades to invest in the burst of economic activity that energy and agriculture had brought.

A skytrain passed overhead with its familiar clack-clack-clack, and a woman with a Syrian accent yelled out the window of the minibus she was driving. "Don't you see the light? Move!"

Narine turned away from the American and focused on navigating the road without holding up traffic.

Minutes later, she pulled off the main road just before the American embassy, bumped over the pedestrian walkway, and guided her bike through quiet backstreets until she wound past a city park and approached the gates that had guarded the order's Addis headquarters for over 175 years.

It was a lush, wooded compound a world away from the bustling city that had grown around it. As large as an embassy, it contained offices, libraries, residential dwellings, meditation rooms, and constellar temples.

The sign on the stone wall of the heavily guarded compound read SOCIETY OF ETHNOGRAPHY, GEOGRAPHY, AND ETHNOLINGUISTICS.

In reality, the compound housed the largest and oldest branch of the Seba Segel.

THE HEDGE MAGE AT THE DOOR HELD UP HIS HAND BEFORE SHE could enter. "Vocation?"

He spoke in English and was dressed in formal white with the red trim typical of order guards. Hedges were the security arm of the order, powerful mages born with magic that could build barriers and sense incursion. They were trained with martial precision and the first layer of protection around any order compound.

Narine was wearing no uniform and had her helmet tucked under her arm, her riding jacket open, and her messenger bag banging against her hip. She could tell this hedge was new to the order when his eyes lingered on her face. He was probably from one of the northern observatories where foreigners weren't as common.

"Good morning." Narine answered him in Amharic and managed a smile despite his frown. "Are you new in the city?"

"Vocation?"

That was it? Narine felt her delicate bubble of morning peace waver.

The solemn hedge nodded at Yìchén, a senior alchemist who had worked closely with her mother, developing the new console for the traveling chamber.

The scholar adjusted his glasses and pulled a lanyard with a clear ID card from inside his jacket, spilling tea on it as he held it out. "*Ech*," he muttered in Amharic.

"Dr. Mǎ." The hedge glanced at the ID card covered in tea. "Good morning and welcome." He waved at the alchemist to enter the building.

"Thank you." The doctor adjusted his glasses. "Oh, good morning, Narine. A peaceful Pagume to you."

Pagume was always a time of rest for travelers. "Thank you, Dr. Mǎ. Good morning to you too."

The alchemist gave her an absent wave and walked into the building. Narine turned back to the hedge. His stoic expression hadn't changed.

"I'm Narine."

He was tall and lithely built with closely cropped hair, deep black skin, and a wide mouth that might have been expressive if it ever moved.

"I work here. Narine Anahid?"

The hedge didn't move or crack a smile. Granted, his entire purpose in life was protecting the compound, but the mage at the gate had already greeted her by name, exchanged family niceties, and shown her where to park. She was clearly not a stranger.

"Your vocation?" the guard asked again.

"Seriously?" She pulled up the sleeve of her jacket to reveal her traveling scars. "Anything else?"

The man glanced at them, then back at her face. "I need to see your identification card."

So the new guy went solely by the book. When she was younger, she would have approved. Now it was just annoying.

"Right." Narine set her messenger bag down and placed her helmet beside it. She unzipped her biking jacket and peeled it off, revealing her black shirt underneath. She unzipped a narrow pocket in the seam of her jacket and retrieved the bent, plastic-coated card with her name, vocation, and ID number on it along with her picture.

Narine Anahid Khoren

Traveler-3

4-Tr-2043EC.

Her name was hers, her mother's, and her grandfather's names as they were the most dominant powers in her parentage. She was a traveler of the third tier, and her ID number indicated she was the fourth traveler mage born in the year 2043 in the Ethiopian calendar.

The Seba Segel was meticulous about records, and this hedge seemed like the type that thrived on organization. It was no wonder he was guarding the Addis compound when he looked younger than Narine.

He examined the card, handed it back to her, then nodded. "Sister Narine, my name is Brother Mesfin. It is nice to make your acquaintance."

"Great." She clutched her card between her teeth and tried to gather her bag, her helmet, and her inside-out jacket in her arms. "So I'll be seeing you around?" she muttered around the card.

He nodded. "As the stars will it."

So he was a traditionalist. "It's nice to meet you, Mesfin."

Narine held on to her belongings with both arms and pushed the door to the front office open with her shoulder. From the lobby, the headquarters of the order looked like any of the hundreds of random charities, research organizations, and academic institutions that dotted the city.

On the wall behind the front desk, there was a giant map of the world with Addis in the very center and SEBA SEGEL branches marked with stars in Zanzibar, Peru, New Zealand, Indonesia, Costa Rica, and Iceland.

One might wonder what the Society for Ethnography, Geography, and EthnoLinguistics was doing in a fairly homogenous region of the world like Iceland, but that was because linguistic studies were only a cover for their true mission.

"Good morning, Sister Narine."

She adjusted the bundle in her arms as she walked. "Good morning to you, Sister Njeri."

She shot a quick smile at the older woman at the front desk who had transferred from Mombasa three years before and quickly made herself indispensable to the order. She was tall, broadly built, and had a crown of silver-threaded braids that fell to her waist.

Though Njeri had been born to a mage family, her power was nonspecific, which meant that she was magic sensitive but not powerful. No one would ever say the woman lacked authority though, not without risking the wrath of administrative persecution.

"There's a message waiting in your office."

Narine frowned. "From who?"

Njeri shook her head. "Not for me to know. It was delivered from the safe yesterday after you'd left for the day."

"Right."

Every order had a safe where messages across the timeline could be guarded and opened in a future time. Because travelers weren't allowed to jump into the future or anywhere within their own lifespan, the safe was the only way for mages from the past to send messages forward. It was also only accessible to a particular sect of archivist mages who released each safeguarded letter at the exact time and place specified by the sender.

Narine headed to the left and made her way through the mostly empty building to her office, where she found an envelope on her desk with a red seal, her name, and the date.

*Narine Anahid Khoren*
   *1ST PAGUME 2071 EC*

She didn't recognize the handwriting, but she recognized the paper, and a sense of dread fell over her morning like a cloud covering the sun.

She broke the wax seal that had remained unmarred in the safe and opened the letter, a missive written on a faded journal page dated the year 1920. Across the faded writing, there was only one sentence, written in bold black ink: *THIS CANNOT CONTINUE.*

Narine froze, her hands clutching the note.

She knew who had written it, but why?

She was trying to process the reason for the cryptic note when she felt a familiar shiver at the back of her neck.

At first it didn't register. The cold, creeping sensation was what every traveler felt when the timeline shifted. It was a shiver she'd felt since she was twelve years old.

But no.

No.

The letter fluttered to her desk with a whisper, forgotten as the shock of realization hit her.

Today was the first day of Pagume.

Her mind rebelled at the thought.

Time travel was forbidden during the thirteenth month.

Those precious five days were the only time when fixed points on the timeline—the tasary—could be altered, so travel was completely taboo. Wars had been fought over it. Mages had been murdered and travelers had been lost to their native timelines to prevent it.

Narine tried to think of an explanation for the impossible, but the tremor at the base of her skull didn't lie.

History had been altered in the thirteenth month.

# CHAPTER 2

*Six years before…*

N arine watched her mentor from the side of the room as he drank tea with the mage elders of House Mkisi and an envoy and diviner from the island of Tanzania. The meeting room was a lavish hall in the Mkisi castle, located in coastal Mombasa.

The building itself was a three-story edifice of pure white plaster with arches and balconies decorated with elaborate fili-gree stonework, surrounded by towering palms. The breeze from the warm Indian Ocean swept through each room, cooling the tiled floors and wafting the scent of plumeria and salt through the air.

Abdi and Narine had jumped back to the late nineteenth century two days before, and Abdi had been deep in confer-ence since yesterday morning.

The mages sat on traditional low couches that lined the walls of the hall and drank tea served with trays of fresh fruit and date candy. Narine sat along the edge of the room with various clerks, servants, and seconds, all listening in on the conversation between the traveler mage from the future and heads of the two most powerful houses on the Swahili coast.

While Narine was a third-tier traveling mage of an ancient Armenian house who had been with the order for eight years, when she accompanied Abdi on missions like this one, she recognized how much she had yet to learn.

"I want to thank you for your hospitality to my student and myself." Abdi nodded deeply at his host. "Narine and I have been very comfortable here."

"Travelers of the Seba Segel are always welcome in Mombasa." The head of House Mkisi was broad shouldered and round faced, a powerful hedge mage named Khamis who had dominated the conversation the previous day. "Especially those from the most ancient order."

The head of House Mkuu had remained in Zanzibar but had sent his second, Syed, an alchemist who was also married to their most prominent diviner, a woman named Aziza who was dressed in deep royal blue.

The sultan of Zanzibar had ruled Mombasa for decades, but there were new threats emerging from Europe. The mages of the Seba Segel in the region needed clarity on where power shifts would take them.

"The British takeover is all but assured without intervention," Syed said. "Our diviners have seen it."

"Our diviners have seen the same," Khamis said. "The elder council here in Mombasa sent a letter forward far enough that we hoped a prudent course of action might present itself."

"And the Addis council received your missive from the safe room and sent me," Abdi said. "Though I doubt I'm going to give you news that will please you."

"It will happen whether we want it or not," Syed said. "That is what you're going to tell us, isn't it?"

The silence after his question was heavy.

Abdi had to weigh his words carefully. The mages of the

past wanted answers, but travelers of the Seba Segel were limited regarding what information they could share about the future.

"Options have been considered," her mentor began, "and interventions already attempted, but according to the reading of the Tibeb, the takeover of Mombasa is tasary."

The verdict fell like a stone. To deem something tasary was to say that a turning point in history was fixed. The Seba Segel might attempt to subvert it by magic, but time would inevitably shift and twist to bring about the outcome they were trying to avoid.

Abdi continued. "I cannot tell you the exact date—"

"Within the next five years." Aziza, the diviner, spoke in a quietly resonant voice. "The British will take Mombasa within five years."

"The diviners of House Mkuu are wise and known for their accuracy in my time and yours." Abdi left it at that.

"And interventions have been attempted?" Syed was not pleased. Though the question asked had only been about Mombasa, a foreign power on the Kenyan coast meant a precarious situation for the sultan of Zanzibar.

"Multiple times," Abdi assured him.

Narine knew from her own family that every old order house wanted to remain close to power, and according to what Abdi had told Narine, House Mkuu had spent money and influence to remain close to the sultan. A loss of the sultan's power meant a reduction in their own influence and status within the order.

Her mentor continued. "If you would like our archivists to examine the Tibeb and suggest negotiation strategies for the mage houses in Mombasa and Zanzibar to use with the British, that can be arranged."

Khamis nodded. "That would be appreciated. We look forward to your continued input as we navigate this change."

The elder of House Mkisi was trying very hard to hide his

reaction behind a veneer of dispassionate diplomacy, but it was impossible not to notice that he was pleased.

The most ancient order of the Seba Segel was formed to read the stars, navigate time, and provide human leaders with advice that would precipitate the most beneficial outcome for the greatest portion of humanity. It was a purpose designated when the first mages had learned the secrets of divination and time travel.

But as within any organization, power and influence often became a purpose of their own.

Abdi stood with the other senior mages and exchanged polite greetings, farewells, and gratitude for their hospitality. He also promised to return with a course of action for the order that would maintain their mission and guide the inevitable political transition they were facing.

Moments later, Abdi left the room, catching Narine's eye as he left so she would follow him.

Narine nodded at the two mages she'd been sitting with, both young men with evident hedge power, and followed her mentor.

"That went well," she said. "Didn't it?"

"It went as well as can be expected when you tell a people they're about to be ruled by a foreign power."

"House Mkisi was not unhappy."

"You read the situation correctly. The political power in Mombasa has rested in Zanzibar for too long from their perspective, and they have made connections with the British. House Mkisi will rise in power when the Europeans take over." He kept his voice low. "They have been very savvy in their political dealings."

"So the order will maintain influence with the new government," Narine said. "That is the priority, correct?"

"It's the priority of the order," Abdi said. "Correct."

Narine noticed the careful answer. "We are of the order."

Abdi glanced to the side as he walked down the open-air

corridor that would take them to their guest quarters. "We are."

"So the ebb and flow of human governments should be secondary to maintaining the influence of the Seba Segel."

"That is true," Abdi said. "But for what purpose?"

"To do the best we can for the most we can."

Abdi offered her a smile, and she felt the internal glow of his approval. "Remember that as you grow in power, Narine Anahid Khoren, scion of House Kayl. The power the old houses accumulate is to be used for the good of the world, not hoarded like a prince hoards wealth."

"Yes, Abdi."

Her own house had once advised princes and queens, but war and genocide had driven House Kayl from Armenia and taught them a kind of humility. They had found refuge for generations within the Seba Segel of Ethiopia, but they were considered minor—if important—political players, more useful for their ability to produce travelers than anything else.

Narine had taken vows with the order when she was only fourteen and been working ever since, sometimes as a messenger, often as a spy. Rarely had she been given her own assignments, though Abdi had suggested her for missions more than once.

"Do you think after this jump—?"

"I have no idea." Abdi's smile was as gentle as the hand on her shoulder. "We shall see, Narine. You have done well, and your understanding of negotiation grows every day."

*Addis Ababa*

NARINE ROSE FROM THE TRAVELERS' POOL, FEELING THE PULL of magic that wanted to keep her submerged. She eased away from time's power as Abdi surfaced in the water beside her.

Both were wearing the pale linen tunic and loose pants standard for travelers.

The room was dim, and the dome over their heads was midnight blue and sparkling with artificial stars set to specific coordinates. A faint smell of frankincense wafted through the humid air.

"Welcome back." Elder Kebret was standing along one wall, waiting for them to return. "Brother Abdi, Narine."

She nodded and looked for someone—anyone—with a wrap or a warm towel or gebi.

"Elder Kebret," Abdi said. "I didn't expect to see you so soon."

Narine wished she'd been able to keep the luxurious red-trimmed caftan she'd worn in Mombasa, but keeping mementos from jumps wasn't encouraged. She'd come back with nothing but the clothes on her back, and seeing Elder Kebret standing there, she was grateful.

"You were both right on time." Calla was the archivist in charge of setting their jump that morning. She walked from behind the sleek black console that calculated and set the constellar coordinates in the traveling chamber. "How did everything go?"

Narine climbed out of the pool and let Abdi answer. Her mother was always quick to jump in with an answer to everyone, but Narine had taught herself to wait and let her mentor speak first.

"It went well." Abdi's voice was matter-of-fact. "Is Muna around?"

Calla laughed. "Just outside the door, waiting for you. She said you were going to want to talk to her when you got back."

Abdi glanced at Kebret. "I'll have time to talk in a few minutes, but let me check in with Muna on something."

Kebret patted Abdi on the shoulder. "Of course." He turned his attention to Narine. "And Narine. Did you learn anything new?"

She chose her words carefully. "I always learn something new with Brother Abdi."

Kebret was a hedge mage who took the security of the order seriously and, according to her mother, had his sights set on the chief elder's seat on the council. He was judgmental, abrasive, and he hated Anahid Khoren.

Narine did her best to avoid him, but when she couldn't, she always made sure to defer to her teacher in some way. Abdi was a mage from the Southern Mage Clans and was seen as a neutral and wise arbiter among the often-squabbling political houses of the capital. Narine's mother had personally asked Abdi to mentor Narine.

"Well done." Kebret patted her shoulder awkwardly. "Keep that learning spirit and you'll surpass your mother soon."

Narine glowed with pride. There was no greater compliment, and she could admit it. She did everything she could to distinguish herself as an individual, which was not an easy task with a mother like Anahid.

Elder Kebret walked out of the traveling chamber, following Abdi's path, leaving Narine damp and shivering in the near-empty room.

"Aida!" Calla called for her own apprentice. "Get Narine a towel, will you?"

"Already grabbed one."

The young archivist walked over with a towel to wrap around Narine, the assistant in Aida's left ear buzzing as the microscreen came down and images flashed. "Sorry—ignore that. My mother keeps sending pictures from their holiday in Iceland to the family chat, and every time my screen pops, more transmit through." She slapped at her ear. "*Sleep.*" The assistant seemed to wilt as it folded itself away. "The drying tube is available if you want it."

"Stellar." Narine took the towel anyway. She was starting to shiver with cold and exhaustion.

They'd returned minutes after they'd left, but Narine was still exhausted. While she could spend days in the past, the traveling window was set in the present and only moments would pass before her return, leaving her body and internal clock out of sync with the rest of the world.

She clutched the towel around her and walked out the side door of the traveling chamber where a plush ready room was waiting.

Every mage had different rituals before and after a jump, and Narine was no different. She liked to take her time meditating, she wanted incense in the chamber, and she didn't take anything modern near the pool.

Partly because the travelers' pool was heated and the humidity in the chamber tended to be bad for electronics. She kept all her electronics in her locker and didn't touch them until she was dried out and dressed.

Right now though, she wanted music.

"Computer, play Addis morning mix."

"Streaming Addis morning mix, local speakers only."

A thumping beat hit the speakers in the locker room, and Narine felt the music brushing away the last cobwebs that clouded her mind after a jump.

She glanced over her shoulder and saw Aida was still with her. "So how is your morning going?"

"Good." Aida perched on a stool near the drying tubes. "Have you seen your mother today?"

Narine punched in a code that opened a pale yellow locker where her personal items were kept. "What did she do now?"

Aida's eyes went wide. "Nothing. That I know of. I was just... making conversation?"

"With my mother, you never know."

There were strict rules about how long travelers could stay in the past, how far they could go, when they could travel, and Narine's mother, Anahid Khoren Madlene, had pushed the boundaries of most, if not all, of them.

Travel to the future was one of their most serious taboos and probably the only one Anahid hadn't broken.

Probably.

Narine left her locker open, hung up her towel, and jumped into the warm vortex of the drying tube that used a combination of heated air and directed jets to dry a person and their clothes in minutes. It was the same type of tube that the city pools used, but the order's machine was twice as fast.

Entertainment screens were built into the walls, already streaming the videos that accompanied the music playing through the speakers. Narine glanced at them, then closed her eyes and focused on the music and the warmth of the wind.

"Did you hear something about my mom?" Narine could still hear Aida while she was in the dryer.

"No, but I was over in the archives this morning—you know how everyone gossips over there—and I mentioned that I was assisting you in a jump today, and they asked if it was your mom or Abdi you were going with. They seemed surprised it was with Abdi."

"My mom has been pushing the elders to let me go on missions on my own."

Aida shivered a little. "It's hard to imagine being alone so far from— Not that you're far… I mean, I guess you are?"

Narine smiled. "We were just in Mombasa a few minutes ago. About two hundred years ago."

"Oh my God." Aida's voice went high. "Did you see the ocean?"

"It was *beautiful*." Narine closed her eyes and pictured the vivid deep blue and a clear horizon. "Like you only see in the past now."

Like most of the East African coast, Mombasa had adapted to the changing climate even after Iceland developed the carbon-capture technology that finally stabilized the warming planet and Indian companies had made it accessible to the world. The oceans were still recovering. Beaches at certain latitudes were often too warm to enjoy.

"So is it true that third-tier mages can take people with them on time jumps?"

Narine popped her head out of the drying tube. "Where did you hear that?"

Aida shrugged. "Where else? Archives gossip."

Narine glanced around the room, but there was no one there but the two of them. She put her finger over her lips and nodded.

"Really?" Aida whispered. "So you can—?"

"Shhh." Narine shook her head and returned to the tube. "Don't ask me things I can't tell you. It's not like archivists share all their weaving secrets with the rest of us, is it?"

All the different mage orders of the Seba Segel could be cagey about their magic. Diviners had an obvious job interpreting the stars and predicting future events, but hedge mages were notoriously closemouthed about their methods of protecting order facilities and people. Archivists were vague about the extent of their power and how they interpreted the Tibeb. And alchemists? They were the kings and queens of disguising magic in new tech.

"Anything else the subject of gossip over at the archives?" Narine asked.

"Just the usual about everyone's love lives and the latest microdrama."

"What's popular at the moment?"

"There's this period drama with really gorgeous costumes from Iran that everyone is talking about. We can't figure out how they do the embroidery. Half the weavers are convinced the show hired mages to do it."

Narine shook her head. Archivists: obsessed with fiber.

She glanced at the clock on the wall, realized that it was lunchtime, and her stomach growled in alarm.

She was hungry and it was lunchtime on the Thursday

before the Easter holiday, which meant it was fasting time for everyone at her family compound. If she wanted meat, she wasn't going to find it at home. "I want to get out of here for lunch," she said. "Join me?"

"Sure." Aida tossed Narine's clothes into the drying tube. "Get dressed. We can take my crawler."

LIKE MOST CITY DWELLERS IN ADDIS, AIDA DROVE AN ELECTRIC crawler over a zip bike or manual car. She had a new model, elongated and cushy with comfy benches, an open floor plan, sliding doors, and roof windows that could retract on sunny days.

"Jump in!"

The crawler was painted verdant green with gold and red trim. Flashy, but it was still a crawler. They reminded Narine of bread loaves, and they were just about as fast.

They were, however, highly practical, and since Narine didn't feel like driving after her jump, she ducked and climbed into the green crawler. Her body had lived three days in the past and come back minutes after she'd departed in the present. It didn't know what time it was supposed to be.

Her hair was mostly dry, so she stuck her assistant in her ear.

From the moment the tiny computer went live to the moment Narine turned her off at night, the assistant would be listening to every word Narine said and tracking her movements for cues about what she might need or ask. It was both convenient and annoying, and no one in the modern world seemed to have a problem with this except political extremists, traditionalists, and Narine.

She tapped the assistant in her ear. "Ana, wake up."

It was the pervasive surveillance that had prompted Narine to name it Ana, after her mother.

"Good morning, Narine."

"What are you in the mood for?" Aida touched the crawler console and it came to life.

Something modern. Something fresh. "Maybe Brazilian?"

Her assistant chimed in. "There are seven Brazilian restaurants within walking distance. Would you like directions?"

Aida nodded. "That sounds good."

Narine put her assistant on mute. "Meskel Square food stands?"

"Perfect." Aida set the console to drive them to Meskel Square and the countless pop-up kitchens that filled the city center during midday.

In the decades since the massive hydroelectric system was built, Addis Ababa had become even more international as climate refugees had flooded inland from the African coasts. Descendants of those who had emigrated in the twentieth century often found their way back to the city with abundant economic opportunities and a stable climate. And new immigrants from economic investors like India, Brazil, and China had become more and more common.

With its abundance of fresh water, cheap electricity, and investment from the Pacific Quad countries of Japan, India, South Korea, and Australia, Ethiopia had become a clean-energy vanguard, leading to a burgeoning economy and colossal agricultural growth.

Food was abundant in the city center, with local green markets a constant fixture and pop-up restaurants and take-aways as common as coffee stands and electronic billboards. In the late twenty-first century, fresh food like that was a luxury to everyone in the world.

They swept under the skytrain overpass and pulled into the underground parking center. Leaving the crawler in the autovalet, they walked up and into the square where vendors and holiday markets were starting to set up.

"You just moved here, right?" Narine glanced to the side as she saw Aida taking everything in.

"Yes. My family in Alexandria is pretty traditional; I lived at home during my training."

"But your dad is in Addis, right?"

"He is. The city still surprises me every day." A skytrain passed overhead, the clacking of the magnet lift the only audible sign of commuters passing. "You've lived here your whole life?"

Narine nodded. "It changes fast though."

"Is all this new?" Aida motioned to the food vendors.

"Not this part. This has been around since my mom was a kid. But did you know there used to be no lights at all in this intersection?" She turned and pointed to the five roads leading into Meskel Square, the center of the modern city. "There used to be just petrol cars and buses. All the minibuses were petrol. All the cars."

"Can you imagine the traffic?" Aida shuddered. "And the smell. I hate it when people manually drive. They're the number one cause of accidents, you know."

"Are you sure? My mother tells me it's zip bikes."

Aida laughed. "No, not zip bikes."

Narine spotted a familiar face eyeing her from the line for the Jamaican restaurant. She took Aida by the hand and herded her away from the area.

"What?"

"Uh… kind of an old boyfriend but kind of not."

"Not an old one or not a boyfriend?" Aida was craning her head to look.

"Stop!" Narine took her hand and pulled her along. "He was just for fun. Not our kind, but he has beautiful eyes."

Aida's eyes went wide. "You've dated regular people?"

"Don't let it get around—my mother's head would explode." Narine played things very conservative at work, but she realized this was the first time she'd taken young, innocent

Aida anywhere outside of order activities. "I enjoy men of all kinds. Mages. Order-adjacent men. *Normal* men."

She liked normal men best of all. They were so blissfully unaware of all the ways time could screw up their lives. "How about you? Have you met anyone since you've been here?"

Aida's cheeks went a little rosy, and Narine had to poke at her. "I'll take that as a yes."

"You can't say anything."

"Who is it?"

Now Aida's cheeks were on fire. "Have you met Tadesse Girma?"

"You're interested in a traveler?" Bad bet, she wanted to warn Aida. Baaaaad bet.

The only traveler she'd ever known to have a successful relationship was Abdi. By nature, traveler mages were suspicious, aloof, and difficult to connect with.

Forming relationships was difficult when you knew that if the timeline shifted, the person you loved could be written out of history, leaving you devastated by their memory until you forgot them completely.

Which was just another level of loss.

Knowing all that, it still wasn't any of Narine's business if Aida was into a colleague. She didn't know Tadesse all that well. He'd been transferred to Addis recently, and they hadn't worked together. Maybe Tadesse Girma wasn't jaded like Narine. Maybe he'd be more like Abdi with a partner.

"Tadesse seems cool." Narine was aware she'd gone silent for a long minute. "I was trying to remember if I've heard about him dating anyone since he moved here, but I don't think so. He's new to the city too; he did his training up in Bahir Dar. He's nice. You should ask him out."

"I don't know." Aida drifted toward a Thai noodle stand. "All the older archivists say that it's better to date a hedge or an alchemist."

"They're probably not wrong." God knew she was a fan of

alchemists. They were so… inventive. "But I will say that Tadesse seems like a very nice guy. If you're into men, you probably couldn't find better."

Narine was into men. She spotted a beautiful one who looked Latin American at a food stand and got in line. Within moments, she was chatting with him in his broken Amharic and English, laughing as she waited for her beef kabob.

Her assistant buzzed her ear. "Can you excuse me for a moment?"

The beautiful Brazilian smiled warmly. "Of course."

She stepped away, keeping an eye on Aida, who was watching a band play near the steps leading up to the holiday market, and tapped on her assistant. *"Abet?"*

"Narine, it's your mother." Her mother was speaking Armenian, which meant she was talking family business.

Narine switched languages without a second thought. "What is going on?"

"You've been approved for a jump tomorrow. A solo job."

She blinked. "What?"

"A solo jump, Narine. It's a simple assignment, but it's important." Her mother's voice was vibrating with excitement. "Abdi assured the elders you were ready for this, and you are."

She felt someone touch her arm. It was the Brazilian chef with her tray of kebabs. She smiled and took the food, but inside she was vibrating with excitement. "This is good."

"This is excellent. It's long past time for you to be given the responsibility," her mother said. "Don't work too late today; I want you ready for tomorrow."

"I'll be ready."

# CHAPTER 3

*Addis Ababa*
*2071*

Tadesse appeared in Narine's doorway seconds after she'd stuffed the mysterious scroll in a drawer. "Did you feel that?"

"It wasn't just my imagination?" Narine knew it wasn't.

"What is going on?" His solemn face showed the barest hint of panic. Tadesse was a few years older than Narine and a darling of the elders. Anything that Narine did poorly— particularly anything political—Tadesse took in stride.

"I don't know." She walked toward him, keeping her voice low. "Is that coffee? I need coffee."

"You're thinking of coffee when—"

"I need a moment." She held up a hand to stop the flood of words she knew was about to erupt. "And you do too." She stepped out into the hallway and looked to the left and the right. The rest of the order was going about their business, subdued as it was because of the holiday. "Think, Tade."

He was a natural mage. Like a good number of mages in the order, he'd been born to a mundane human family in

Gondar with no known link to the Seba Segel. Yet even with humble beginnings, Tadesse's power, discipline, and skill had moved him up the hierarchy with speed. While Narine might have old family connections, Tadesse had better political instincts by far.

He took a deep breath. "The rest of the order knows nothing."

"Exactly. This could be… minor."

She knew it wasn't. Traveling during Pagume was the greatest taboo travelers had, as forbidden as traveling to the future. There was only one reason to travel during Pagume, and that was to change something on the Tibeb that should never be altered.

"We're the only ones who've felt anything change," Narine said. "For now we should keep it that way."

A change to the timeline during Pagume hadn't happened in centuries, and the last one started a war. Narine still remembered stories her mentor had told her.

The Second Mage War had ended over five hundred years before, and it had disrupted world events beyond repair. Empires had waned before their time, uncontrolled migration had been spurred, and several human wars had been set off by a power struggle within the Seba Segel.

"Telling anyone before we know more could spark panic." She nudged him to the side and walked toward the inner courtyard. "That's the last thing we want."

Only traveler mages knew when history altered, and they only remembered it for a time. Eventually their minds would adjust to the new reality as a form of survival. New memories would form and others fade.

While Narine remembered timeline shifts, after a while her mind would reset, the exact memories would blur, and it would be impossible to remember the details of what had been lost. It was time's reprieve, the only way a traveler could survive without losing their grip on reality.

Narine continued herding Tadesse toward the courtyard and the smell of freshly roasted coffee. "Until we can figure out what's changed and speak to the elders, we say nothing."

"We don't know where or when—"

"Of course we don't." Even as she said it, she doubted her own words. The letter was sitting in the top of her desk drawer, and its arrival couldn't be a coincidence. "This might have to do with another chapter of the order entirely. Just because we felt it in Addis doesn't mean it originated in our territory."

Tadesse followed Narine as she walked through empty corridors. "We need to call the elders."

"They're going to know soon enough. Abdi will tell them something changed."

Her mentor had long moved past teaching students and had become an elder on the council, the first elder of the Addis Ababa council to be born from a free clan and not from an old house. His elevation marked a turning point in the political makeup of the Seba Segel around the world.

He was also the wisest man Narine knew. Abdi's father had been named for the first traveler of his people, and Abdi was also one of the foremost experts on the Second Mage War. If anyone would know what to do, it would be Abdi.

"Right now let's get coffee. I think better with coffee." Narine moved through an arched doorway and into a brightly lit atrium at the center of the circular building. A garden with hibiscus flowers and glossy coffee plants thrived under the care of Kidist, an aged diviner who had rooted herself at the compound and rarely left.

"You know, I was actually a little happy this morning." Narine kept her voice low as she sat on a low stool and nodded at their hostess, who was dressed in a bright white traditional *kemis* trimmed with diviner's blue and golden-yellow flowers sewn in to celebrate the coming new year.

Kidist poked the coals on her charcoal brazier and picked

up the clay *jebena* to make more *buna*, the traditional dark coffee that Ethiopians drank throughout the day. A large bowl of popped corn sat in front of the low table where coffee cups were displayed.

"You?" Tade grabbed a handful of popcorn and sat next to her. "In a good mood?"

"Mostly. Then I drive here, nearly run over an American on Entoto Road, and get hassled by the new guy at the door like I'm still a trainee."

"The new guy is Mesfin, and the elders in Bahir Dar were very eager to promote him."

*Of course they were. He's a complete tight-ass.* "He reminds me of me when I was young and obnoxious."

Tade offered her a rueful laugh. "He's not like any Narine I remember."

"My mother would be thrilled to hear that."

Oh, how the tables had turned. Whether Narine liked it or not, she grew more like Anahid every day. Secretive, irritable, and fed up with order bullshit.

He sat forward and rested his elbows on his knees. "Have you heard anything from her?"

"No." Narine rubbed her hands together to chase the last of the morning chill away and hide the trembling that wanted to take over her body. She couldn't think about her mother that morning. Not after the note. Not after the shift.

Tade lowered his voice. "What are we going to do?"

"After we drink some coffee, we're going to find Abdi."

Everything in the world changed with time, except the Seba Segel.

New governments rose and fell. New powers surged forward. New antagonists were born.

But the Seba Segel was a venerable order, dominated by ancient magical families around the world who could trace their lineage back to the original astronomer kings. When a new power rose, the goal of the order was to rise with it.

*To do the best we can for the most we can.*

She'd believed that naively as a child. Now she clung to the old motto like a talisman.

Tadesse said, "Abdi's probably not in the compound today."

Narine nodded. "I think most of the elders are home for the week. We might need to go to his house."

"You know where he lives?"

She gave him a look. "Of course I do."

"Right." Tadesse smiled a little. "Those convenient family connections."

"Please." She shook her head. "Don't pull that. Besides, Abdi is a Southern Mage."

"They're just like an old family now."

"Hardly."

Natural mages like Tadesse were born from mundane humans every year, but the majority of the Seba Segel were born into common mage families or free associations like the Southern Mages or the Somali Clans. And those in power mainly still hailed from the aristocrats of the order.

Because in a constantly shifting world, there was stability in the archaic.

Kidist brought their coffee in small cups with sprigs of the sweet herb *tenadam* on the side. She also brought the bowl of popcorn over, and Narine reached for a handful as she took her first taste of the coffee. The dark chocolate sweetness of the brew came to life with the addition of the herb. Narine sipped and closed her eyes, trying to find some balance within the chaos of the morning.

Tade drank his buna in one searing gulp and set down his cup. "You're right. We should go; Abdi will know what to do."

She looked at her fellow traveler and marveled at his even temperament. He looked troubled and determined, but he threw corn in his mouth and kept a placid expression on his face.

All the while, Narine felt like her sanity was balanced on the edge of a knife. The letter from the safe was burning in the front of her mind. The time shift felt surreal—even more surreal than normal. She wanted to let out a scream and run around the atrium, shaking everyone and asking them if they realized how bad this might be.

She sipped her coffee deliberately.

The astronomer mages of the ancient world were so old that not even their own history books knew when the first star had been read or when the first mage discovered the secret of traveling through water to visit other times. The Seba Segel had been built on an intricate fretwork of rules and taboos passed down for thousands of years.

Changing history during Pagume was the highest form of taboo.

Because while time was fluid, chaos was unlimited. Her kind didn't try to keep order within the timeline because Time was a river swollen with the weight of past, present, and future, as powerful, destructive, and fecund as the Nile.

On the banks of that river, the Seba Segel plucked stones from its bed—reading the stars to predict the future and going back in time to bring greater order where they could—trying to shore up the edges or release the pressure to prevent destruction and havoc.

"Narine?"

She closed her eyes, and Tadesse fell silent.

Often minor changes were all they could accomplish. The tasary were immovable threads that kept the Tibeb together. Changing a single one of them could cause ripples that might overturn an empire, if not something far worse.

Kidist walked over and held her hand out for their cups. "More rain is coming," the old woman said.

Narine blinked. "Are you sure?"

Kidist's eyes met hers, dark and unwavering. "The season isn't over."

"It's almost the new year."

Kidist glanced up at the clear roof where splatters of rain were tapping and clouds had moved over the sun. She was an old woman, a respected diviner of House Abay who had never married or had children. When Kidist spoke, Narine had learned to listen.

"The skies keep their own calendar, Anahid's daughter." The old woman straightened and turned to Tadesse. "More coffee?"

He was already handing his cup back to Kidist. "I'm finished, but thank you, Sister." He glanced at Narine. "I had a thought. Before we talk to the elders, we should go check the archives."

"The archives?" Kidist smiled. "Or one archivist in particular?"

Tadesse didn't rise to the bait. "The archives. Narine and I have some research to do."

Narine and Kidist exchanged an amused glance. "Yes," Narine repeated. "Important research."

THE ARCHIVES OF THE SEBA SEGEL DIDN'T CONSIST OF endless corridors of books or collections of scrolls or tablets. Though there was an extensive reference library in the diviner's temple, the order's true record was kept in over five thousand rolls of intricately woven fabric that made up the Tibeb.

While the other chapters around the world kept written records, only the most ancient order in Addis Ababa kept the Tibeb, a woven account of the timeline in all its intricate beauty. The threads for the sacred weaving were spun of cotton and silk by trainee archivists while each shuttle of the loom was cast by a master weaver.

Each year a new weaving was started, and each year the

old one was stored in a vast collection of rooms that started on the first floor and went deep into the earth.

Narine and Tadesse walked out of the sprawling building that branched around the front of the compound where the travelers and hedges kept their offices and practice rooms. They walked through the compound gardens, walking around the diviner's temple with a vast planetarium built inside and meditation rooms for the mages working there.

Past the temple, the compound branched again. To the right were the three-story laboratory, greenhouse, and reading rooms of the alchemists, and to the left was the five-story, open-air building that housed the archives.

Their building was perched on a hill at the back of the compound, which sloped down toward a narrow river. Soaring cedar trees shaded the terraced building where thread spinners sat in the open air, enjoying the light rain that fell over the verdant gardens where a bounty of flowers grew. The flower garden was both beautiful and practical as most of the dyes for the Tibeb threads were sourced directly from what was grown on the grounds.

The archivist mages in Addis were constantly in communication with chapters of the Seba Segel all over the world, so while mundane human archives might be quiet and sedate places, the order archives in Addis Ababa sounded more like a trading floor where men and women shouted in languages from all over the world, the heavy thunk of the looms worked day and night, and music floated over the chaos.

Today that music was a new electronic album by a Senegalese group that was blasting on every channel and club around the city.

Narine grimaced. "That song is going to live in my brain for the rest of my life. I'm going to have to go back two hundred years to escape it."

"Someone played it on a speaker in the skytrain the other day, and I thought the rest of the car would riot."

"Everyone over the age of seventeen is sick of it."

Tadesse shrugged. "Except the weavers."

She sighed. "Except the weavers."

While most of the order offices were empty for the holiday, the archive building was as noisy as ever. History didn't pause during New Year, so their weaving continued.

While music was welcome in the archives, artificial intelligence and assistants were not. Narine had never seen a microlens flipped down among the archivists while they were talking to each other. Their attention was solely on their tasks and their interactions with each other. It made them some of the most popular mages in the order.

Which meant they always had the best gossip.

In addition to the weaving of the Tibeb, archivist mages also produced more practical and decorative scarves and wraps for different vocations in the order. White robes for the elders, deep blue robes to shroud the diviners, and neat red scarves to identify hedges. At formal events, travelers usually wore ceremonial robes in green and archivists wore sunny yellow that brightened every room. Most of the alchemists kept their white coats for formal events, sometimes brightened with a burnt-orange sash.

The constant weaving kept the trainees busy and was a good place for them to practice their craft as only the most skilled weavers were ever allowed to touch the loom of the Tibeb.

Batches of freshly dyed thread were hanging along the terrace as they approached: bright yellow dyed from the annatto seed, red from the cochineal bugs, soft brown from ground coffee, and softer orange from marigolds. The drying thread made the entire building appear festooned with banners dancing in the breeze.

It was so different from the quiet, whispering halls of the travelers that Narine often cursed the day of her birth. It was rare for any traveler to celebrate their birthday. They were all during Pagume, and it wasn't a time for revelry.

She glanced at Tadesse. "Do you ever wish you were born with a different power?"

He stared up at the archives. "Sometimes ignorance would be bliss."

"Yes."

They climbed the stairs to the first floor, glancing at the terraces they passed to see who was working that day.

"Do you see Aida?" Tadesse was craning his neck, but between the flapping cloth hanging along the building and the bundles of colorful thread, it was difficult to see inside the buildings.

"We can ask inside." Narine might be friends with Aida, but Tadesse was in love with her. "Just calm down. Have you considered—I don't know—asking the woman on a date?"

Tadesse shot her a horrified look. "You're teasing me about my dating life? Now?"

"The world doesn't stop because there's a hiccup in the timeline." Narine faked nonchalance because it was the only thing keeping her from screaming. "Ask the woman out."

"Not right now, Narine." Tadesse climbed the stone steps that led from the pathway through the compound up to the archive doors. "What are we going to ask them?"

"Let's just talk to Aida. If a tasary has been altered, it would be visible. It would look like a knot or something."

"You think?"

"I think." She really had no way of knowing because she'd never seen a warp in the Tibeb. Probably no one alive ever had. "Aida is a senior weaver now; she should know what to look for."

Tadesse pulled the door open and held it for Narine to walk through. While technically Narine was senior in experience, Tadesse was older and frankly, everyone liked him more. They'd get better information if he asked.

Tadesse walked up to the reception area and smiled at the two older women who were spinning thread while they chatted in a mix of Amharic and Oromic.

One was using a smooth spindle carved from fine dark wood that dangled at her side until a callused hand rolled it along her thigh, letting the weight of the wooden knob rotate as the cotton thread grew fine and strong between experienced fingers. The new thread wrapped around a bobbin, and the hypnotic process started over again.

The other was using a newer wooden spindle, pressing her foot in rhythm with the staccato tempo of her Gamo accent.

Another woman joined them from a tablet, her face flickering from the virtual screen display that floated above the table. Her assistant captured her face as she worked, sending it to the display so she could work alongside her fellow mages even from a distance.

"Sisters, good morning." Tadesse greeted them in Amharic and put a hand to his chest, offering each of the women a friendly smile. "How are you today?"

"We're well, Tadesse Girma." One woman exchanged a sly glance with the woman on the screen. "How are you?"

"I am well, thanks to God."

"And your family?"

"Healthy and well, Sister."

"And your health?"

"I am ever blessed, Sisters. Thank you. And how is your health?"

It went on for three rounds back and forth, and Narine hung in the background, nodding, smiling, and responding when appropriate.

By the look on the older women's faces, they knew exactly whom Tadesse was there to see, but they'd make him jump through all the hoops they threw out anyway. That was the way of things.

"Sisters, is Aida Mikel in the building today?"

"She's in the garden." One of the sisters winked at Narine. "Did you need to speak to someone in the archives?"

Of course they did. Why else would a traveler visit their building? But then, Tadesse didn't want to speak to just anyone, he wanted Aida.

As did Narine. She knew Aida more than any other archivist and knew she could be discreet.

Narine stepped forward and took Tadesse by the arm. "We'll find Aida in the garden. Thank you, Sisters."

Low laughter followed them down the hall and through the double doors that led outside.

Tadesse looked around. "So far nothing seems different."

"Not yet."

"But there's no way of knowing."

"Aida will know if there was chatter this morning. We're in gossip central, remember? But keep in mind we just felt it."

It had been less than half an hour since the first buzz of awareness had hit them, and so far nothing about reality seemed different.

Of course, that was the point of the tasary, to keep a steady timeline. The path of the river would remain unbroken, and that was because fixed points existed. While the mages might make minor tweaks, the greater path of history could never be altered.

"There she is." Tade lifted a hand and waved. "Aida!"

A tiny woman with a cap of curly brown hair stood up in the garden, carrying an armload of bright yellow flowers. Aida's mother had been an Egyptian archivist and her father an Ethiopian hedge. The mix of features gave her a distinctive beauty that garnered attention everywhere she went.

"Tade!" She smiled and walked over to them, shaking a spray of water from her head. "And Narine. Are you both working today? I thought everyone except us was home. Isn't Pagume supposed to be your time to relax?"

"Just working a little," Narine said. "I had some mail to

answer." Narine looked at Tadesse. "What *are* you doing here? I thought I was the only one coming in."

"Brother Desta wanted me to come in and write his reports."

Narine rolled her eyes. "He's supposed to do those himself."

"But why when he has AI and me?"

Aida smiled. "Well, I'm glad we're not the only ones working." She walked under the terrace. "The first Meskel flowers are starting to come up, and I wanted to grab some before the rain started coming down hard." Aida held up the bright yellow blooms. "In a week, the hills will be covered."

"Kidist says the rain isn't over," Narine said.

Aida lifted her shoulders in a shrug. "But can the rain stop the flowers?"

"True." She kept her voice low. "Tade and I came by because we need to speak to the elders about something, and we wanted to check with you first. Don't say anything to the other senior weavers, but has there been a… fault in the Tibeb this morning?"

Aida frowned. "What do you mean?"

"A change."

"Of course not."

"In the timeline," Tadesse said. "A… warp. A knot. Anything."

Aida still looked confused. "What are you talking about?"

"We felt it about half an hour ago." Narine kept her voice quiet.

Her eyes went wide. "Wait, today?"

Tade and Narine both nodded.

The weaver clearly didn't want to believe it. "There must have been something residual from before the holiday."

Tadesse shook his head. "Not possible. All sanctioned travel is cut off three days before the thirteenth month begins.

Everyone is supposed to return to their own time to prevent anything like this happening."

"So…" Aida clearly didn't know how to wrap her brain around the idea. "There are always changes to the timeline. You know that. The Tibeb fluctuates, and even the most gifted archivists can't detect alteration. Only travelers remember the difference, so alterations work themselves into the larger pattern."

"What about a tasary?"

Aida shook her head. "Tasary can't be altered."

"Except during Pagume."

Aida had to force the words out. "Except during Pagume."

Narine asked, "Would there be evidence?"

"In theory—" Aida cleared her throat. "In theory, of course. If a tasary was altered, there would be some visible evidence of the change."

"Like what?"

Aida dropped her voice and pulled them to a far corner of the garden. "I think it's technically called a warp. Not a warp like that part of the loom, but a warp like a distorted pattern. Again, it's impossible, but if it happened, we would be able to see it." She shook her head. "But that's impossible."

Narine nodded. "We know."

"I don't understand."

Tadesse kept his voice low. "We don't understand either, but we felt it happen half an hour ago. That's why we're going to the elders."

Narine could see when the idea of the impossible registered.

Aida froze. "Are you saying…? What are you saying?"

"Check the Tibeb." Narine urged her. "Be as discreet as possible; we don't want to cause a panic."

Aida visibly swallowed. "If what you're saying is true—if it's possible—the warp would only be visible if the tasary that was altered occurred this year."

"If it was in another year?"

"It would still appear, but Narine, we're talking about five thousand rolls of weaving to go through. Tens of thousands of meters. If what you're saying happened really happened, then the rules don't matter." Narine dropped her voice to a whisper, every bright expression of her face turned grim. "Do you know how many tasary are in each year? Hundreds. There are hundreds of fixed points in every year. Multiply that by five thousand—"

"I know." Narine put a hand on Aida's arm. "But we don't know if any of this is even important yet. We know *something* changed. That someone traveled during Pagume and changed something, but we don't know what or if it's important. That's why we asked you to check."

"But be discreet," Tade said. "That's why we came to you. We're going to speak to Abdi right now. He should be able to give us better—"

"Who?" Two lines appeared on Aida's forehead. "I don't think you should take this out of the order."

Narine froze. "What are you talking about?" Everyone knew Abdi. "We're going to the elders. We're going to talk to Abdi."

Aida understood immediately. "I'm sorry, Narine, there's no elder named Abdi."

Narine's heart dropped.

"There's no one in the Addis compound with that name," Aida continued. "Whoever Abdi was in the previous time, in this one, he doesn't exist."

# CHAPTER 4

*Six years before*

Narine checked her clothing before she walked into the travelers' pool. She was going back to a time where dresses were more conventional for women, but in water, skirts were a killer. To do her best to fit in, she'd donned loose linen pants, a long tunic, and of course taken off all her jewelry, including her trusty assistant.

The lights were dimmed and the traveling chamber was filled with calm music and the faint sound of lapping water from the pool.

Abdi was next to the console, checking constellar settings with Calla.

"Narine." Calla's voice was low and easy. "Everything is ready when you are."

"But no rush," Abdi said. "We can go over everything again if you want."

She took a deep breath and set her mobile assistant on the desk next to her backpack. Then she rolled her shoulders and let out a long breath. "No, it's fine. I'm ready."

While a week would pass during her journey in the past,

her return would be only moments after her departure in the present. It was her first solo journey; everything had to go right.

"Who did the calculations?" Narine glanced at her mother, who was sitting in a chair in the corner of the room and furiously typing on her assistant.

"Muna," Abdi said. "I asked her personally."

Anahid added, "And I checked her work."

*Of course you did.* Narine managed not to roll her eyes. Never mind that Muna was one of the most skilled star readers in the order. Her mother still checked the diviner's work as if she were a schoolgirl.

Anahid Khoren Madlene was a third-tier traveler mage, and before Narine had been born, the only third-tier traveler working for the order in Addis. Narine's grandfather had left Addis years ago and retired to the mountains near Odzun in Armenia, where his ancestors were born, leaving Anahid the head of House Kayl in Addis, a title she wore with arrogance and more than a little ambition.

"Do you want to use the toilet before you go?" her mother asked. "You're going to a rural village in the 1920s. They won't have plumbing." Anahid's hair moved as she texted, because whether it was over text or in person, Narine's mother spoke with her whole body. The dense cloud of dark brown curls that she picked into a sculptural crown towered over her head, giving the tiny woman nearly an extra foot in height.

No one would miss her when she walked the halls of the order.

Narine watched her mother, determined to be the mature professional. "It's fine. It's hardly the first time I've had to live on my own in a place without plumbing, heating, or electricity."

Anahid looked up for a moment. "That year in Dorze was good for you. You needed survival skills."

"Can we debate that when I get back?" Narine took deep breaths, in and out, preparing herself for the pool.

Anahid shrugged and turned back to her furious texting. "It's not a debate."

Narine kept herself from baring her teeth. She was twenty-two and had been an experienced traveler for eight years, and yet her mother could make her feel like a foolish child with one shrug. It was maddening.

"Narine, why don't we go over your instructions again?" Calla came from behind the console and stood beside the travelers' pool with a clipboard in hand, reviewing the trip brief as Narine stepped down into the water. Aida was beside the console, watching everything Calla did.

Abdi stood beside the pool, reviewing everything they'd gone over that morning in his office. "Remember, Lake Ziway is far south of where the massacre happens, but Muna is convinced that the message should be transmitted to the elders of this particular village and not one in Gondar or in Addis."

"Right." Narine nodded. As Abdi had taught her, what the diviners saw in their visions sometimes didn't seem to make sense, but all of the Seba Segel had to recognize that the stars were wiser than the mages.

"It will probably make sense once you're there," Anahid muttered. "It could be that there's a particular person—"

"Mother." Narine's patience snapped. *"Ayo, Mama."*

Anahid raised one eyebrow but said nothing else.

"Ziway." Narine cleared her throat and kept her eyes on Abdi. "So Amharic and Oromic?"

"You're going to the islands; it will be Amharic and Zay."

"Zay?"

Anahid muttered, "Semitic language group related to Gurage."

Narine pursed her lips and kept her eyes on Abdi. "Got it. I can speak some Gurage."

"You'll be fine." Abdi reassured her. "Zay is the most

commonly spoken language on the islands, but the mage village there will speak Amharic since it's a mixed community."

Narine knew the jump would take little out of her. It was routine. She was going to a similar geographic region and to a place where she would speak the language. This was an excellent solo jump.

She needed to travel to a village in the past, transmit a message to the elders there so they could avert a massacre in the north, then go home. It was similar to jumps she'd made countless times with Abdi or her mother.

She was even arriving during the same time of year as her native timeline. It was Holy Week, a festive time to visit.

Narine took a deep breath, waded into the travelers' pool, and took a small curved knife from her belt. "Any other information I'll need?"

Abdi shook his head. "You're ready."

Anahid spoke from the corner, her eyes still on her messenger. "Start with whatever elder council is in charge and go from there."

Narine bit her tongue and looked at Abdi, who only smiled. "Yes, Mother."

Aida caught Narine's eye roll and pressed her lips together to stop the smile.

Anahid added, "Calla will check the Tibeb when you return. Remember, if she doesn't see an alteration in the outcome after the first trip, you can always go back."

Travelers could never go to a time they'd already been. Nothing horrible would happen if she tried to travel during her own lifetime or one where she had visited, her magic simply wouldn't work. But she could go a day later, a week later, or a year before. As long as there was never two of herself in the same time, Narine could make the jump.

She tied back her hair in a neat bun, pinning it in place so it wouldn't blind her in the water. The dome above her lit up as Calla and Aida finalized the coordinates of the jump into the console and the stars over Narine's head shifted in alignment to the exact place they would be in the early 1900s at the latitude and longitude of her destination.

"Ready when you are," Aida said.

Narine waded into the pool, her nose detecting a hint of olive leaves and rosemary rising from the water.

The silence moved beyond the surface and into the profound as Narine closed her eyes and whispered the first spells that would bring her magic to life.

The magic on her lips was spoken in Ge'ez, the language of the Seba Segel, invoking the power in her blood and the magic that connected her to the past while asking the water's permission to slip into its depths and swim against time's current.

She waited for the smell of sandalwood and musk to hit her nose.

The second she sensed the burgeoning power in her body, she felt for the series of raised marks on her arm, carefully placed her blade, and made a clean cut along her forearm, just above her wrist, letting the blood drop and spread into the water.

A sacrifice was always necessary for the magic to be accepted.

She plunged beneath the surface.

Her eyes were sealed shut as time took her; her breath froze in her lungs. Narine could feel the transformation like a sizzle along her skin. The whole of her body and mind dissolved in a shower of stars as she was pulled into the current of eternity.

*Ziway, Southern Ethiopia*
*1920*

SHE GASPED FOR BREATH AS HER FACE BROKE THE SURFACE OF the water. The sound of singing from the church at the top of the hill greeted her like a mother's ululation, and she felt her racing heart settle.

Traveling, as much as the Seba Segel had practiced it, was not a science. It was a combination of ancient wisdom, intricate astrological reading, and pure blood magic. So while Narine knew she was supposed to arrive in Ziway just before Palm Sunday, the sound of the Hosana Mezmur that marked the start of Holy Week was a welcome confirmation that her magic and Muna's star charts had been correct.

She dipped under the water again to slick back the hair that had come loose from the pins, and her feet touched thick lake mud. The water was cloudy with silt but smelled clean and vegetal, hardly the worst place she'd ever landed.

She heard a shout in the distance and the sound of bleating sheep. Someone had spotted her.

After wiping the water from her eyes and mouth, she swam toward the folded rocks jutting into the water of Lake Ziway, home to a remote Seba Segel outpost on the Zay Islands. As she made her way toward the shore, Narine sent up a silent prayer that the instructions from the archivists had been accurate and her appearance wouldn't raise alarms in a mundane human village.

While a European face wasn't something that stopped traffic in modern Addis, she was 150 years in the past and Ethiopia was hardly an international crossroads. She would likely be the only white face on the island.

She reached the rocks and hoisted herself out of the water only to realize that her legs were caught in fine fishing nets that had tangled in her linen pants.

Two men ran down the hill and reached out their hands to help her from the lake.

One shouted something at a shepherd boy who had run to see the excitement. He spoke a language that had to be

Zay, and the only word Narine recognized was *farenji*. Foreigner.

The two men hoisted her out of the water, and one of them set to the nets, grabbing a curved knife not unlike her ritual blade to cut the tangle from her legs.

The younger of the two patted her shoulder and switched to Amharic. "You're bleeding. Do you understand me?"

"*Eshi.*" Narine responded in Amharic and squeezed his hand. "*Arifnew, abati.* I am not hurt; I am a traveler."

The older man deftly cut through the knotted lines. "It's blood for the sacrifice, Yohanes. I think she is fine." He looked up and smiled, revealing a brilliant white smile with one missing tooth in the front. "I'm Abel; this is Yohanes. We're fishermen here. You're not the first traveling mage I've dragged out of the lake, but it's been a long, long time."

Narine smiled. "Did you have to use a net for the last one?"

Abel laughed and released the last of the fishing lines. "I did not. Are your legs cut? You speak good Amharic for a foreigner."

"My legs are fine." The question was unspoken but familiar. "My family isn't Ethiopian, but I was born in Addis."

Abel nodded. "I see."

"I am Narine Anahid Khoren, traveler mage of the Seba Segel." She tried to sit up straight. "Are there any other travelers in this time and place?"

"No." The old man sat back on his heels. "As I said, it's been a long time. I was young the last time we had a traveler come to this place. We definitely would have heard if another one was around."

Narine nodded. In an out-of-the-way place like Ziway, she wasn't surprised.

The men didn't ask what year she came from, and Narine didn't offer, conscious of the rules Abdi had drilled into her memory.

Narine flexed her legs and examined them. "My legs are fine; it's just my arm that was bleeding." The neat red line from her blade had already scabbed over and joined the others that reached just past her wrist. "See? It's healed now."

While some travelers chose to give themselves elaborate patterns or decorative markings when they offered their blood during the traveling rite, Narine did not. Her scars would be economical and organized, a visible record of her travels and not an artistic or family statement like her mother's.

"The mages will come now." The young man, Yohanes, threw a heavy cotton gebi over her shoulders. "You've come at a very holy time, Sister. How long will you be with us? Will you be here for Easter?"

The traveling rite specified two points on the timeline, the astral alignment when and where the traveler went back in history and the alignment when they would return. The points were fixed and could not be altered once the spell was cast.

Narine shook her head. "I'll only be here for a week, but I will enjoy celebrating Palm Sunday with you." She glanced at the boy running down the hill from what looked like a village in the distance. "The people in the village…?"

"This island was once a resting place for the Ark of the Covenant," Yohanes said. "The people here honor the Seba Segel. You won't face any danger here."

Abel rose and reached a hand out to help Narine to her feet. "Welcome to the islands of the Zay, Sister Narine. The sun, moon, and stars of this place welcome you."

NARINE SAT ON A LOW WOODEN STOOL AND REACHED FOR A piece of injera from the woven *mesob* in the center of the room. The tall basket was layered with injera and *wot*. It was the fasting season, but her hosts had provided a feast of flatbread, fish, and spicy vegetable stews appropriate for the Orthodox diet.

A woman was roasting raw coffee outside as the elders of the mage village gathered to talk with Narine. The smell of roasting coffee and berbere spice filled the round meeting-house at the top of the hill.

"Sister Narine." Her host, Chief Elder Samuel, leaned forward with eyes that missed nothing. "How is the food?"

"*Betam konjonew*. So good." She reached for another piece of fish that had been stewed in a spicy mix of peppers, onions, and berbere. "No one can compete with the fish from Lake Ziway."

The man across from her smiled. "Even in your time?"

"Even in my time, Brother." Narine looked around at the group that had gathered that morning when she arrived. So far the village had been hospitable, if a little surprised to receive a time traveler from Addis.

Typical for the era, there were more men than women on the elder council, though her sister mages were well repre-sented in the compound. The diviners and archivists she'd met in the outpost had been mostly women, but there was a large hedge presence—possibly because tensions in the surrounding countryside were heightened—and hedges were commonly male.

"The treaty you speak of," Brother Samuel continued. "We have heard of it. The empress does not trust the Italians."

"Neither does Ras Tafari." The woman named Tigist was young—maybe only thirty years old—but she was an elder and a female hedge. She had been directing the girls serving the meal; now she turned her attention to Narine. "My brother is correct that they are suspicious of the overtures from Italy, but from what we have heard here, the Seba Segel's current influence only stretches to Zewditu's court, while it is the young prince who is making decisions on foreign policy now."

Narine listened carefully as the elders of the village debated around her, washing her hands when a serving girl came by with a basin of water.

"He will take the crown within the year."

"I think it will be longer than that."

"Two years maximum."

Narine knew exactly when the new emperor would take control from his aunt, but she could say nothing.

Samuel said, "According to my connections in Addis, the order has tried to make inroads with Ras Tafari's advisors, but he sees the Seba Segel as a relic of the past."

From the tone of his voice, Elder Samuel might have put more stock in his connections than Narine would.

Tigist lifted a hand. "I think we should focus on the reason our sister mage has traveled from her own time. If the elders in Addis have found this prediction compelling, we cannot ignore it."

The archivists who studied the past in Narine's time had identified a thread in the Tibeb that led to a conflict on the Sudanese border that would eventually take hundreds of lives. After consulting with the diviners, the archivists determined that the massacre was not tasary and preventing it would have no adverse consequences in the greater timeline.

*To do the best we can for the most we can.*

Narine had been sent back with the message that the crown prince should be tougher on the British during treaty negotiations. If the prince listened to the Seba Segel, that massacre could be avoided and over two hundred lives saved.

"The British have retreated from Ethiopia for now, but they haven't given up their ambitions." The man who spoke wasn't a hedge like Samuel or Tigist. His name was Gideon, and he was a Kenyan alchemist who was sitting on the council since two of its regular members were traveling for the holiday. "They never do."

Brother Samuel pursed his lips. "Gideon, we all know how you feel about the British, but we're speaking of the Italian treaty right now."

Gideon watched Narine with an intensity that felt unnerving, and she hadn't seen him smile once. "The British will not give up their ambitions because they've been shamed by an African prince."

The man who answered Gideon was a hedge named Ger, a tall, regal mage from Sudan. "We are not speaking of the Nile or the British now. The problem is the Italians." Dressed entirely in white, he was a striking figure and would have caught Narine's interest if she hadn't already been introduced to his two wives.

"The problem is the British," Gideon countered. "The Italians are nothing."

"The Italians are the ones threatening our sovereignty," Samuel said.

"Look deep enough," Gideon said. "It's always the British."

"That may be," Ger said. "We have both seen what the English have done to our countries, Brother Gideon, but today we are speaking of the Italian threat."

Narine sat silent, biting her tongue.

Knowing the future and not being able to share it was a special kind of torture that all travelers had to learn to survive. As much as Narine wanted to warn the Ethiopian government about the horrors the Italians would eventually bring to the country, she could only say what the elders of her time had instructed her to share.

She couldn't warn them of the invasion that would happen in 1935. She couldn't warn them about the chemical attacks that would kill tens of thousands of civilians. She couldn't sound the alarm about the Second World War that would engulf the globe. She couldn't go back and warn her own people of the genocide that would push her family from its ancestral home and make Armenians refugees all over the world.

Travelers knew the bloodstains of history but could do little more than offer bandages to press against the wound.

*It could be worse.* Her mother's voice popped into her mind. *If we didn't exist, it* would *be worse.*

The village elders were debating how the Seba Segel should advise the empress and the crown prince, and Narine was wondering if they could even manage an audience with the crown prince. When she'd gone on diplomatic missions like this with Abdi, they had always spoken to those in direct power.

*Sun and stars, why was I sent* here?

Narine offered one final piece of advice. "Brothers and Sister, I cannot tell you what to do with this information, I can only tell you that the Seba Segel should advise the crown to push back hard on the British and negotiate with the Italians."

Brother Samuel knew that the message had been delivered. "Sister Narine, thank you so much for your time and effort to bring us this message." He looked around the room. "I am sure that we can deliver this message to the capital and the right ears."

Gideon narrowed his eyes. "Why only push back on the British?"

Narine swallowed the frustration and kept her face neutral. "I have said all I can."

Gideon stared at Narine. "She knows more."

"But I can't say more." She met his accusing stare and didn't flinch.

Narine was young and this was her first solo jump, but Gideon wasn't the first mage who had challenged her to break the sacred rules that governed travelers. Far more persuasive tactics had been tried on her and failed.

"No one will know." Gideon raised an eyebrow. "Convince us, Sister Narine."

*Impertinent man.*

"I have shared all that I have been instructed to share." She folded her hands and set them on her lap. "The mages of your time must use their own judgment on how to advise the empress."

Brother Ger put a hand to his chest and inclined his head. "The future will be as the stars will it, Sister. We thank you for taking the risk to come here." He looked around the room. "Brother Samuel and I shall consult with the hedges in the capital and share this with them."

"Thank you, Brother Ger."

The peace treaty wouldn't last, but Narine knew why she couldn't share its eventual demise. The Italian occupation of Ethiopia was tasary—it couldn't be stopped—but the damage the Italians would eventually inflict on the Ethiopian nation would be mitigated by the treaty, leading to Ethiopia's continued independence after the war.

And that would change everything about its fate.

"Sister Narine." Tigist smiled at her. "Would you take some coffee?"

"Yes." She let out a breath, thankful for the distraction. "Thank you."

SHE SPENT THREE MORE DAYS AND NIGHTS IN ZIWAY, ENJOYING the ceremonies of Easter week, celebrating with the people of the village, and enjoying Zay hospitality. She was also half-eaten by mosquitos, but that was hardly a rarity for Narine. Mosquitos all over the world and in every time seemed to love her.

The community was a close-knit group of two dozen

mage families along with the ordinary Zay people who lived in the other village on the island.

Tigist proved to be a wise and amusing companion, a female hedge who understood what it felt like to be out of place among her own people.

Samuel was the wise elder of the community and her host. As a guest of the order, she stayed in his family compound with him, his wife Lidet, and their seven children.

Ger, his wives, and his children were the only Muslims on the island, but they were welcomed at all the community celebrations and seemed content to live in a Christian mage village. One of the wives was Sudanese, and the other was Ethiopian. Between them, they were raising ten children.

Gideon, after the elder meeting on Monday night, had disappeared. Tigist told Narine that he preferred his solitude at the medical clinic he ran just outside the village. He hadn't been raised Orthodox but in the tradition of the English Anglicans in Kenya. Most of the ceremonies the village celebrated were foreign to him.

Other than Narine, Ger, and Gideon, all the mages on the island were Ethiopian, and the majority of them were Zay.

"It's unusual, isn't it?" Narine was having dinner with Tigist and her husband Daniel the night before she would jump back to her time. "To have so many mages in one community? The Zay people are not a large group."

Daniel was another hedge, warm and easy with a smile. "It is unusual, but you have to remember that the Ark rested on the islands at one time. It is a place of great spiritual power. Almost all unions here—even mixed ones—produce powerful children."

Tigist added, "There are many great alchemists and diviners in this place. The sky is very good for star observation, and the flora here is excellent for herbal medicines."

"And hedges." Narine sipped her coffee. "I don't meet many female hedges, even as much as I travel."

Daniel laughed. "Neither had I, but I don't think it's the island's magic at work there. Tigist and I are both from the north. I was assigned to Ziway ten years ago."

"And I came five years ago," Tigist said. "Then I met Daniel." She smiled at her husband. "People did question a woman as a hedge, but they have come to be accepting."

Daniel winked at her. "Who could deny my wife's skill with a knife?"

Tigist's cheeks turned a little pink. "He flatters me. I am more a strategist, less a warrior."

"Both are essential to the order." Narine set her coffee cup to the side. "So have any travelers been born here?"

Tigist's smile froze. "Not in many years. The elders here encourage people not to bear children during Pagume."

While traveling mages could be born at any time, the chances were far greater during Pagume, a fact that her family had used over the years to enhance the power in their clan.

"I see." Narine could see that her hosts were worried she would be offended, but she wasn't. "It's fine. Ziway is far from the only community that discourages it."

As the sole mages to remember fluctuations in the time-line, Narine knew travelers could be disruptive. Many close-knit communities felt relieved when no travelers were born.

"Are you…?" Tigist shook her head. "I shouldn't ask."

Narine shook her head. "You can ask me anything. If it's not something I can tell you, I won't answer." She loosened the collar around her neck. The fire, the food, and the coffee had combined to flush her cheeks.

"The astral sign on your arm." Tigist nodded at the mark on Narine's right arm that marked her power. "I've never seen a traveler's mark that prominent."

"Ah." She smiled. "Well, I am the daughter of two mages with traveling power, and my mother's father was also a traveler, as was his mother."

Daniel's mouth fell open. "You are a fourth-generation traveler?"

It was more like nine generations, but Narine just smiled. "Obviously my people don't avoid bearing children during Pagume."

In fact, her ancestors considered a child born during Pagume, the thirteenth month, to be the most desirable. Her clan had even been known to induce labor if a pregnancy was near term. A child born during Pagume wasn't guaranteed to have traveling power, but it was far more likely.

As for why her family was so obsessed with producing travelers, her mother had never explained it, not even when Narine had asked. She felt the tip of exhaustion bearing down on her. She was also starting to feel the effects of travel and meeting so many new people. Her body was aching and her head felt cloudy.

"Tigist, Daniel, the food and the coffee were so good, but I'll be leaving tomorrow, so I should get some rest." She rose from the comfortable cushions on the ground where they'd been drinking coffee. "I don't want to get home and be exhausted."

Though she'd spoken a little more with Samuel and with Ger, Narine knew that the Seba Segel here would do what they would.

She wanted her first solo mission to be successful, but she had a feeling she'd be coming back. She had no idea why the diviners had determined that this small village was the place to leave the message about averting a massacre. Hopefully when she came back, they'd send her to the capital.

"I'll walk you back to Samuel's," Tigist said. "Daniel, can you ask the girls to clean up please?"

"Of course." Daniel rose and offered her a warm hand. "Sister Narine, it has been a pleasure. May the stars align again."

"Thank you." She squeezed his hand, knowing she'd probably never see the man again. "I appreciate your hospitality; may it be a blessing to your family."

Tigist led her out of the house and into the darkness. She could hear the water lapping against the shore as they walked along the path that ran along the lakeside.

"I admire you," Tigist said. "It must take so much courage to go to places where you will be foreign."

"I was born foreign." Narine blinked, but her vision was swimming. "In a way."

"What do you mean?"

"I was born in Ethiopia, but I'm not…" Her mouth felt dry and hot. "I'm foreign everywhere."

"Narine?"

Tigist's voice sounded as if it came from a great distance. Had the woman walked away from her? She turned to look for her new friend, but the world around Narine spun, she stumbled, and everything went black.

# CHAPTER 5

N arine and Tadesse took their lunch outside the compound that day. With all the tumult in the timeline, Narine craved the press of mundane human energy. She wanted to be surrounded by people and their smells and joy and vivid life.

It was the first day of Pagume, but nothing felt like a holiday.

She and Tadesse left their vehicles at the order and caught a skytrain south to find lunch at a small Syrian café in Arat Kilo that served chicken kebabs and burgers.

Narine watched the city rushing below, the blue-and-white minibuses, the zip boats speeding up and down the river, the rushing skytrains floating over the hills on their magnetic cushions, all ferrying people from one side of the city to another even as the skies opened up and the rain started to fall again.

From the riverbeds to the sky, Addis Ababa was bursting with holiday preparations. Sleek, modern fashions were mixed with traditional dresses and braids. In the days to come, Addis would become a mosaic of people from all over the country and tourists visiting from around the world, eager to witness the New Year festivals, shop at the markets, and eat abundant natural food.

Her assistant chimed in her ear. "You have a message from Jamila Sahid."

"Archive."

Usually she'd be planning a holiday trip to Harar around this time, so she knew why Jamila was calling. Narine needed to speak to her best friend, but not until she knew what was happening.

*Anahid would know what to do.*

But Anahid wasn't there, and it was entirely her mother's own fault.

Her mother shouldn't have been playing in the timeline; Narine needed her in the present. She wanted to turn back the clock and pretend none of this was happening. Pretend there was no message burning a hole in her desk drawer. Pretend that Abdi was home with Fatima and his grand-children.

It was just another reason to resent the woman who birthed her.

"Narine." Tadesse touched her arm and nudged her toward the open doors as a flood of passengers descended on the cafés and shops of her neighborhood.

"I don't understand how Abdi can't exist," Narine said. "He was a traveler. He was born during Pagume. Doesn't that make his birth a tasary?" She had always assumed that mages of her own vocation were safe from the fluctuations of time if they were born during Pagume.

Tade countered with logic. "Maybe not all births during Pagume are tasary."

"But most of them are."

"Then that must be what we felt," Tadesse said. "Someone eliminated Abdi from the timeline."

"But why?"

They walked to the café and sat in a corner, ordering their

drinks from a screen at the table. Minutes later, a server brought a bottle of Coke and an ice-cold mineral water. Narine poured half of the cola in two glasses, then filled the rest of the glasses with the water.

The café was packed that day with a mix of people typical for the neighborhood. Business owners speaking a mix of Amharic, English, and Chinese pointing at floating screens with glowing numbers scrolling across them. Students taking lunch near the library, their lenses flipped down to watch a video or chat with friends. Groups of mothers meeting with children in strollers and watching as they played in the garden behind the café.

Narine kept her voice low, though nobody was paying attention to them during the busy lunch rush. "If Abdi's birth was tasary, it would happen no matter what. History would conspire in some way to bring him into existence. How many times has the order tried to stop individuals from being born? King Leopold? Hitler? Hastings and Columbus? They always end up being born no matter what."

"I realize that, but Abdi was not Leopold."

"Obviously not, so why would anyone want to eliminate him from the timeline?"

Tadesse didn't have any more answers than Narine did. "Maybe it wasn't intentional. Maybe whatever change happened altered Abdi's fate accidentally."

It was possible, but Narine had a hard time imagining that the foremost expert on the Second Mage War just happened to be eliminated from the timeline at the exact same moment a taboo like this was broken.

The door to the café opened and a tall man with a short beard walked in. Narine stared at him. She knew him. Was he a mage? How did she know him?

"Narine?"

She pointed her chin in the direction of the man who'd

walked into the café and lingered by the door until a server came up to him.

"*Selam.*" The man greeted him in accented Amharic.

"Uh... sorry." He broke into English. "Do you speak—?"

"Of course." The server responded in lightly accented English. "Please choose a table. Anywhere you like. You can order from the screen."

"Who is he?" Tadesse asked. "Narine?"

She shook her head. "Where do I know him? Are there any mages visiting from the US right now?"

"Not that I know of. He could be Ethiopian." Tadesse looked again. "Or part Ethiopian maybe."

"But he sounds American."

"So he's diaspora." Tade turned and put his back to the man, who had taken a seat in the opposite corner from them. "How do you think we should approach—?"

"The American I almost ran over!" Narine snapped her fingers. "I knew I knew him. That's the guy I almost ran over this morning."

And he was far better-looking than she'd registered at the time. The American was tall and broadly built with medium brown skin, a full beard, and dark hair twisted at the tips. He lifted the menu the waiter brought him and took reading glasses from the messenger bag on the bench next to him.

"Narine?"

"Sorry." She blinked and looked back at Tadesse. "I'm glad I didn't run him over."

"Excellent. I'm glad I don't have to turn you in to the traffic police."

Something about his calm, collected professionalism made Narine want to poke him. "He's much better-looking than I remembered."

"Fascinating. I don't think your handsome American can help us with a possibly disastrous change in the timeline during the thirteenth month and the disappearance of our mentor."

"Maybe he could. Maybe I should tell him that my friend and I were born into an ancient order of mages who manipulate history for the common good. He might find it interesting."

"He might!" Tade lifted one eyebrow. "Or he could call the hospital to report an insane woman roaming the streets and trying to mow over foreign tourists with her zip bike."

Narine glanced at the man again. He'd pulled out a laptop and was typing away. "He doesn't look like a tourist. Maybe a businessman or something."

"So the authorities will take him seriously and lock the crazy farenji Ethiopian away."

She leaned her elbows on the table and rubbed her eyes. "I'm feeling pretty crazy right now, Tade."

"Yeah, me too." He reached over and squeezed her wrist. "We need to figure out a way to approach this with the elders. Elder Kebret will be the biggest problem; I think he'd eliminate traveling altogether if he could. God knows he considers it overused and would rather focus on fostering connections with the current political elite."

Narine was listening, but her eyes kept drifting back to the man in the corner bench.

He was almost *too* good-looking. Was he an actor? A musician? She considered trying to point her assistant in his direction and sneak a picture of him to show Genet and Jamila, but she decided Tadesse would probably notice.

He was still talking about the possible world-changing disaster, which was far more important than a handsome man at a café.

Narine's brain was on overload and she was starting to fixate. Only instead of fixating on a temporal thread or a constellar position, she was fixating on the stranger. That was the only reason her eyes kept going back to the man.

She needed to be alone to process everything that was happening and figure out a way to fix it and bring Abdi back, but to do that she needed Tadesse to shut up and let her think.

"I think that Hawa will be in our corner," he said, "but she might be out of the country right now. Kebret always takes diviners seriously. God knows what Dr. Majid will say. He'll want reports. Lots of reports. He'll probably be in favor of some kind of exploratory committee. He loves those."

The American had paused in his typing to take off his fitted wool jacket as the room grew warmer. He folded it and placed it neatly on the chair across from him, then unbuttoned his sleeves and rolled them up, ready for a serious session of typing.

Damn, he had beautiful forearms.

"Narine, are you paying attention?"

She looked back at Tadesse, then glanced over his shoulder where a server with two plates was approaching. "Sorry, I think I'm hungry. The food is here." She took her assistant out and set it to the side as her AI paged her with another message from Jamila. "We should eat, then talk."

"Fine."

Narine stood as soon as the plates were down. "I'm going to wash my hands, but go ahead."

She passed by the hygiene stations at the front of the restaurant and walked to the toilets and the sinks in back, looking for a moment of quiet. That direction also led her past the American, who glanced at her as she walked by, then continued typing on his computer. Narine's eyes fell to his well-muscled forearms, and she nearly tripped when she saw the distinctive pattern of marks on his left arm.

The man glanced up and frowned. "Can I help you?"

Narine barely managed to force out a strangled "sorry" before she turned the corner and hid on the other side of the wall in near-darkness.

She looked down at her own forearm and the eight dark

circles that marked her. To most people, they appeared like nothing more than a scattering of freckles, but unlike normal birthmarks or moles, they would never fade, and if she cut them out, they would only grow back. They had appeared on her skin at birth, a sign that her parents' machinations and planning had been fruitful.

Those eight spots were the mark of a traveler. The mark of the river goddess and the guardian wolf.

The exact same marks that were on the stranger in the café.

# CHAPTER 6

*The Island*
*1920*

N arine woke to the sound of water lapping against stone.
Her body ached and her skin felt crusted with sweat, her joints unused.

She rolled toward rhythmic thumping that paused. There was a shifting sound and a mildly familiar voice that disturbed her senses.

"You're awake, so you'll live."

She forced her lids open to meet a pair of intense dark eyes rimmed with lush lashes. Angled eyebrows, straight nose, severe mouth.

Gideon.

She wanted to speak, but she couldn't seem to make her mouth move.

"Sleep." The hand on her forehead was disturbingly gentle. "You still need to rest. You almost died."

She opened her mouth, but nothing came out.

"Malaria. Not the worst case I've seen, but not mild

either." The corner of his severe mouth lifted. "Sleep. Your fever is better."

She slept.

NARINE WOKE TO THE SOUNDS OF RIOTOUS BIRDS. HORNBILLS were yelling at each other in the trees outside while finches sang. Something was pecking on the thatch roof above her, and the leather straps of the bed creaked as she sat up.

The floor of the clinic was pounded earth, and the walls had been smoothed by hand. It was a traditional round structure with stacked stones outlining the foundation of the house and a thatch roof overhead. Herbs of all kinds hung from the rafters, and wooden shutters had been pulled back to let in light.

Four single beds populated the open room with a large desk and worktable placed near the open door. Alchemist equipment—glass jars, clay pots, a mortar and pestle—was neatly lined up on the worktable along with two large books. There were hooks on the wall with medical equipment hanging from them. An old stethoscope, what looked like a blood pressure cuff, and a white apron.

There were many windows in the building, and they were all open. Through the nearest one she could see the waters of Lake Ziway, and a fisherman paddled his way across her view, his back straight as he perched on his wooden raft.

*When was she?*

Narine's heart began to race, and she forced herself to her feet. Her legs felt wobbly and unused. Her feet were sore, and there was a heat rash over most of her body. She ran a hand down her arms and felt the cotton shift brush against her legs. Everywhere the cloth touched her skin, she ached.

She walked to the door and stepped outside, the ground soft beneath her feet. The sun had warmed the rocks of the threshold, and she braced herself in the doorway to get a sense of where and when she was. She reached for the magic that was her constant companion and could not find it.

"You're awake."

Narine turned and saw a man sitting on a bench that over-looked the water, writing in a journal. He looked up, and it was the first time she'd seen him smile.

"How are you feeling?"

"I'm still here."

He swung his legs over the bench and faced her. "It was questionable for a time, but you're tougher than you look."

His Kenyan accent sounded musical to her ears, at odds with the severe persona he presented.

"You're Gideon."

"And you're Narine Anahid Khoren, traveler of the house of Kayl, which I assume is one of the old houses, but I've never heard of it. You were speaking in a language I don't know." His eyes narrowed. "And I know many languages."

She leaned against the doorway; it was an effort to remain standing. "Probably not as many as I do."

He smiled and switched to beautifully accented English. "I like your arrogance."

"It's not arrogance." She was slightly out of breath, but still she answered him in English, which she spoke as fluently as Amharic and Armenian. "I just don't make myself small for others' convenience." Her heart was beginning to race. "I'm still here."

"You mean in 1928?"

"Nineteen what?" She nearly fell to her knees.

"Sorry. Nineteen twenty." He rose and walked toward her. "Don't panic, I was thinking in the European calendar."

Her head started to swim. "Why?"

"Because it was the first one I learned," he muttered. "I'm not— What are you doing?" He put a hand under her elbow.

"I just saved your life, and you want to make yourself collapse?"

"The water." She swallowed hard and reached for the ceremonial dagger that wasn't on her waist. Why wasn't it on her waist? A traveler was never to take her dagger off. "I need to get to the water." She could find a thorn or a sharp rock perhaps. "Where is my knife?"

*Where is my magic?*

She was on the verge of tears. She whispered spells under her breath, reaching for the power that had been her surest friend since she was six years old, but it was gone. She didn't even feel a whisper of her normal strength.

"Narine, you're not going anywhere." Gideon nudged her back inside the house. "You've had malaria for two weeks. You need to rest."

She let out a rough cry. "No."

"It's not the end of the world," he said. "They won't even notice in your time. You'll wait until you're better, and then you'll go back."

"You don't understand." She'd missed her window. She'd been traveling since she was fourteen years old, and in eight years of travel, she'd never missed a window. And for good reason. Missed windows led to travelers lost in time. "What did you do?"

"I saved your life." He sounded irritated. "Should I have thrown an unconscious, fever-bound woman in the lake and hoped she didn't drown before she traveled back to whatever time she came from?"

"2065." Narine was near collapse again. That was the only reason she could think that it slipped out. She felt empty. Hollow. "Forget that."

"Oh yes, no problem. I often forget things on command. I'm known for it."

"I would like your sarcasm better if I wasn't going to be stuck here for a year."

"It's not sarcasm; it's thinly veiled contempt of a world that hates me." He was helping her back to bed. "What do you mean, a year?"

"Traveling window. It's set…" She was already so tired. "It's set in my native time based on annual… I can't change it here; I have to wait until the stars are back in alignment the same way at the same time…" She was out of breath.

"And that takes a year?" He clearly didn't have much experience with travelers. "Well, I'm sorry, but I wasn't going to risk your life by tossing you back in the water when you were delirious. Welcome to your new home for the next year, I suppose. Now get some sleep."

Had her magic abandoned her? Would her power return when the stars realigned? She'd always felt a thread of it in any time she jumped, like an anchor line leading her back home. Why hadn't anyone warned her that she could lose her magic if she stayed too long in the past? Would it come back? It had to come back.

She was lost. So lost.

Abdi had told her what to do if she missed a constellar window, but he'd emphasized that she should never miss her window. The consequences could leave her lost in time.

Gideon moved around the building, opening the windows and closing some of the others. "I want to keep the air moving so you won't stew in your own sweat, so stay covered up so you don't get worse. You still need to sleep."

"Gideon."

"What?" His voice was acid, but his hands were gentle as he laid her back in the bed.

"I'm sorry." Narine reached up and touched his hand. "Thank you for saving my life."

His eyes softened. "I'm a doctor, and I'm extremely good at what I do."

She tapped her finger on his cheek. "Arrogant."

"Yes. That was arrogance."

She sat on the bench that overlooked the lake, awash in the sounds and the silence of the world around her. There was no traffic, no hum of electricity in the air or clack-clack from the skytrains. There was no honking from the river taxis or clever songs from the street vendors. There was no music, no blaring adverts or news blasts.

There was wind over water, birds, and sheep bleating in the distance. And no magic in her bones.

Narine hated it.

She missed her zip bike, her bedroom, and chewing khat with Jamila. She missed modern plumbing. She didn't miss the social channels online, but the world without music or entertainment programs felt eerily quiet. She was disconnected. Uninformed. Adrift.

And weak. Her power had always been her shield, but in this place it had been stripped away. Narine felt exposed in a way she'd never been in her entire life. A naked child, a creature with no shell.

She could already hear the condemnation from her mother and the quiet disappointment from Abdi.

*Your first solo jump and you miss your window.*

Time hated her.

"Is it very different?"

Narine looked over her shoulder and saw Gideon leaning against a massive southern ficus that grew on the edge of the lake. Its roots reached up and formed a natural bench where village boys came to fish.

"You mean is Ziway different?"

"Is everything different?"

She gave him the simplest answer. "Yes."

"So in your time... the future." He looked into the distance. "Is Kenya—?"

"You know I can't tell you specifics."

"Is it free?" He asked anyway. "Are we free of them?"

"I can't tell you that."

"We are." Thinly veiled anger. "We must be."

Narine looked over the water, shifting her focus to the lake, the same lake she'd visited as a child many times to bird-watch with her father. "This place might be the same. I've never been to the islands before." There were a few isolated places she visited that had remained mostly untouched by modern life. Perhaps the islands were one of those. "I might have to go back and look when I get home."

"To 2065."

She turned and looked at him again. It had been a week since she woke up, and she was becoming accustomed to his moodiness. "You really do need to forget that."

"I haven't told anyone else." He leaned down and tossed a pebble in the water. "You won't get in trouble."

"That's not why you need to forget it."

"Why then?"

"Because if you don't, every moment of knowing me will be shadowed by dissatisfaction."

"It is already, Narine." The corner of his mouth turned up in a wry smile. "Don't flatter yourself."

"Ha!" The laugh was unexpected. Maybe she would come to enjoy his humor. "Why did you leave Kenya?"

He glanced at her, then looked back at the water and threw another stone. "I was working at the order headquarters in Mombasa, and I angered the wrong people. I needed to leave."

"And your elders sent you here?" Going from a city post in Mombasa to an isolated island in Ziway could only be a demotion.

"Yes, they did." He bowed his head a little, though nothing about his expression was humble. "I am a servant of the Seba Segel."

"You came to Ziway to be a doctor?"

"This community needed one." Another stone tossed. More ripples in the lake. "I believe the council in Addis made a request for mages with medical training. They had alchemists, but no one with any formal degree. The outpost is large enough now that it became necessary." He looked east and pointed to the largest island on the lake. "People come from the mainland and the other islands when they need medical treatment. It's a service the order can provide for the humans while still remaining isolated."

"Is that why the clinic is outside the village?"

The building was situated on a stretch of land that jutted out into the lake, and Gideon lived in a cottage behind it. To one side were grasslands dotted with acacia trees where boys grazed their sheep, and on the other side was a small bay where fishermen launched their boats and larger vessels from other islands docked.

"Yes." The corner of his mouth turned up. "Of course, I'm not exactly one of them, am I?"

"One what? You're an alchemist."

"But I'm not Zay. Or Ethiopian. My Amharic is barely passable, and none of them speak English. You speak better Amharic than I do."

"It's my first language."

Gideon smirked a little. "Interesting."

Narine looked at the clinic with its neat white paint and bright green shutters on the windows. The mages of the village had taken care to make it beautiful as well as functional. "It's a beautiful spot, but it could get lonely after a while."

"I don't mind the isolation."

Narine didn't know him well enough to understand if he was lying to her or himself. She looked into the distance where a dark cloud was approaching and changed the subject yet again. "The little rains are coming."

"I like the rainy season here," Gideon said. "Concentrated. And there's less flooding than at home. Kenya has two rainy seasons."

"One around now and another that starts after the new year, right?"

"The Ethiopian new year, yes." His eyes narrowed. "You think in Ethiopian time."

"Travelers think in the traditional calendar. It's how we're trained." For Gideon, raised in a European colony, the new year would start in January. For Narine, Ethiopians, and most mages, it started at the end of the rainy season in the rest of the world's September.

"Hmm."

She looked at him. "Do you come from a family of alchemists?" Some families like Narine's had strong power over generations, but most common mage families were mixed, and Gideon spoke like a common mage.

"No." He shook his head. "They were not powerful at all. My father is a clerk in Nairobi. I was found by a hedge when I was six."

Narine was surprised. "You're powerful for a natural mage."

She could feel his magic when he treated her. He made no show of dampening it, and her magic had abandoned her. She had no shields at all.

He smiled a little. "Is that a compliment?"

"It's an observation. People act like power only builds over generations, but one of the most powerful diviners I know is a natural mage."

"People in Mombasa think power is concentrated in the old families." He raised an eyebrow. "Like yours."

"That's one viewpoint."

"But not yours?"

Narine shrugged. "My best friend was born into a very old house, and she has almost no magic. Power isn't predictable."

But it could be guided. Narine's mother was the queen of that.

"You were lucky." Narine picked at the hem of her dress, twisting the threads of raw cotton. "To be found and trained when you were young."

"Was I?" He raised an eyebrow. "I suppose I was. The order educated me. My parents were confused but grateful."

"Do you still see them?"

He shook his head. "As long as I write, they're happy. They're simple people; they wouldn't understand any of this." He tossed a last stone into the water and turned to Narine. "You're feeling better now. Have you thought about where you want to live for the next year? You can't stay here."

Tigist had already come to the clinic and offered her a room in hers and Daniel's compound. It was the best offer Narine could hope for. It wouldn't be acceptable for a single woman—not even a farenji traveler—to live alone in the village.

"I'll be staying with Tigist and Daniel."

Gideon nodded. "Good. The elders won't want you living on your own."

"I wouldn't want to live alone." She looked around. "Times like yours are not conducive to independent living."

Narine had spent enough time in the past to know how much work survival entailed. Teff had to be grown and ground and made into injera. Vegetables would need to be tended, seeds saved, and food preserved. Animals would need to be raised and slaughtered. There were no stores to buy clothes and no restaurants to grab a bite to eat.

Thank God she was on an island and knew how to fish. Other than weeding a garden and the basics of cooking, it was about all she'd be able to contribute as far as food for the village.

Clothes washed by hand. Houses cleaned by hand. Water

drawn from the lake every day. The running of a compound was a full-time job in this period.

Narine missed her kitchen. She missed her autowash and her sonic shower and the kebab place on the corner.

She really missed her toilet.

Gideon had given her a bag of herbs to take every day that was supposed to help her digestive system adjust to the new environment. It helped a little, but she still struggled, and life with digestive issues was even more fun when modern plumbing didn't exist.

"Tigist and Daniel are from the north," Gideon said. "Will you be comfortable with them?"

He was trying again to figure out where she was from, but after eight years of traveling, Narine was an expert at dodging questions.

"I will be more than comfortable with anyone generous enough to offer me a home."

She smiled and saw the glint in Gideon's eyes. He knew exactly what she was doing, but luckily she amused him.

Narine was keenly aware she was in a time and place where men ruled. While mage houses had always leaned toward the more egalitarian, they were still dominated by men, even in her own time. A hundred and fifty years in the past? There was no question she would have to watch her tongue.

She couldn't mouth off to the elders. She couldn't take off on her zip bike and roam the streets of Addis. She wasn't going to live in a compound ruled by women like she did at home.

Narine was going to have to learn silence, patience, and temperance without losing who she was as a person and without her magic.

*You are Narine Anahid Khoren of House Kayl. Your father is a diviner of House Vana. You were born in the year 2043 of the Old Calendar. You are a third-degree traveling mage of the Seba Segel, ninth in your line of power. You were born in Addis Ababa, Ethiopia. You have no siblings and many cousins. You are the godmother of Gelile, the adopted sister of Genet, the daughter of Anahid. Your best friend is Jamila Sahid of the house Rajab. You are a mage of the old order in Addis Ababa, your mentor is Abdi Mulenah of the Southern Mages.*

She would have to repeat this information to herself over and over for the next year. She would have to write down everything she could remember about her time, repeating it like a mantra so her mind didn't fall into the timeline where she was and her magic didn't abandon her.

And if she could make it a year, she would find her way home.

# CHAPTER 7

The second day of Pagume was about to dawn, and tapping on her door woke Narine again. She ignored her flashing assistant and threw her gebi over her shoulders before she wandered out through the kitchen and to the side of the compound where Genet, Samira, and Gelile were already waiting for their baths.

Her goddaughter was a grumpy lump sitting on a stool and pouting, but Genet was already pouring another bottle of holy water in the bath. Samira was whispering to Genet and stirring the water with a long stick.

Narine took her place on the bench, still half asleep, and crossed herself as the frigid water began to trickle down her neck. She clutched her hands together, her thumb moving to worry a rough traveler's scar at the side of her left wrist. Unlike the other neat cuts, it was twisted and gnarly.

Her lungs seized as the water reached her back; it stole her breath.

*Her chest was burning.*

*Fire in the water. It ripped through her abdomen and up her back.*

*She had to reach the surface, but she couldn't move and a voice at the back of her mind whispered to let go. She tasted the blood in her mouth.*

*Sink.*

*Sink into the darkness.*

Narine forced out a harsh breath and opened her eyes as Genet's prayers reached her ears. She saw the sky turning to an opal with drifting clouds scattered along the horizon. It would be a clear day today; the rainy season was finally ending.

One more day. They needed one more day of rain.

*Archangel Rafael, give us one more day.*

Genet was finished. Narine made the sign of the cross, then rose and made way for Gelile.

The little girl took the yellow flower clip from her hair and clutched it in her hands, glancing at Narine to show her brave face as the water touched her neck.

Narine had nearly forgotten the small gift she'd promised her goddaughter after the chaos and surprise of yesterday's revelations, but a vendor near the library caught her eye before she arrived home empty-handed. The bright yellow flower clip for Gelile's hair had been exactly what the girl wanted, and she'd fallen asleep with it perched on her head.

After Pagume baths were finished, the women walked back in the house, Samira going to the kitchen to prepare breakfast while Genet, Narine, and Gelile dressed for the day.

After she'd dressed, Narine sat at the table in the wood-trimmed dining room and stared out the arched window into the garden while Genet sorted through the house messages on the living room screen.

There was cabbage ready to be harvested, and green mangoes were hanging on the tree. Between the vegetables and the fruit trees, they would all have plenty of fresh food to eat even if there were ration cutbacks after the holidays.

"I don't appreciate you enough."

Genet turned and looked at Narine. "What's wrong?"

"Nothing. There has to be something wrong for me to appreciate everything you do to keep our home running?"

Genet sat at the table with her. "It's my home too. What's going on?"

Narine shook her head and blinked back tears. "Nothing. I miss your mother." *I miss my mother.*

"I know you do."

She wiped her eyes with her wrist. "That's all. Even after four years, I miss your mom."

"And your mom."

Narine shrugged.

"You know she wasn't dealing with my mother's death well." Genet's voice was soft. "You know she didn't intentionally go missing."

"But she didn't care enough to be cautious." Narine sniffed and cleared her throat. "She knew we both needed her after Aster died, and she was still reckless."

"Narine, what is going on?"

"Nothing."

"Stop." Genet raised a hand. "I know you."

She stared at her sister with watery eyes. Genet's family was mundane, but they had been working for and with Narine's family for generations. Genet wasn't powerful, but she understood the dynamics of the order and knew how to keep a secret.

*There were so many secrets.*

Narine closed her eyes. "You can't say a word."

Genet shrugged. "And who would I tell?"

"You know other mage families, Geni."

"And I ask again, who would I tell?"

"Fine." Narine lowered her voice. "There was a timeline shift yesterday."

"What?" Genet frowned. "During Pagume?"

Narine nodded.

"I thought that wasn't allowed."

"It's not."

"So there is a rebel among the mages?" Genet shook her head. "It was bound to happen eventually. I'm amazed—"

"No, it was not bound to happen. The last time someone traveled during the thirteenth month, a massive war broke out, every attempt to fix the problem failed, and the timeline shifted so drastically that fixing it would have killed even more people than leaving it alone."

Genet's eyes went wide. "What—?"

"It's a long story that happened in the sixteenth century, but the lesson is that travel during the thirteenth month is forbidden for a reason because now Abdi is gone."

Genet frowned. "Abdi who?"

Time's cruelty left bitterness on her tongue.

Genet had been to Abdi's house countless times for meals, parties, and holiday celebrations, but in her sister's reality, the man had never existed.

"Abdi Mulenah." Narine's throat swelled with suppressed tears. "Fatima's husband."

Genet frowned. "Fatima is married to Kamil."

It made Narine want to scream, but she knew it was the way of time. She'd allowed herself to depend on Abdi because he was a fellow traveler; she'd thought his birth was inevitable, so she'd foolishly assumed that he would always be with her.

Anahid's voice whispered in her ear: *Time is the most fluid medium in the universe, and humans are its most replaceable element.*

Narine dashed angry tears from her eyes and nodded. "Now she is, Geni. But yesterday, for me, he was here. He was my teacher. He was an important elder."

Genet reached out and squeezed her hand. "I'm sorry, Narit."

She nodded and blinked back tears. "I should go. Tade and I are meeting with the elders this morning. We need to figure out who traveled and when it happened. We can't do anything about it until the new year, but if we can narrow down when the change happened, we might be able to reverse the damage."

If Abdi *was* a tasary, the change that wove him out of history should show some kind of evidence.

*This cannot continue.*

Narine touched the scar on her wrist again and remembered the words scrawled on the letter hidden in her office.

She might not have understood everything, but at least she knew where to start looking.

Narine and Tadesse met in the hallway outside the Elders' Chamber. Both of them had performed the baths needed before an audience with the elders and dressed themselves in undyed linen robes, covering their heads with green travelers' shawls and wearing colored sashes around their waist that indicated rank. All travelers wore green to indicate their connection to water and the sacred river. Triangles and stars were woven in with gold thread, and the years of their traveling were embroidered with silver thread.

"The elders will be just a few moments," the hedge in the anteroom said. "Thank you for waiting."

"Of course."

While Narine was over a decade younger than Tadesse, her traveling years were longer. And while fourteen years of service would have ranked her as a senior mage in most branches of the Seba Segel, in Addis Ababa, she ranked below Tadesse.

Reckless.

Overconfident.

Arrogant.

These were only some of the labels that had been applied to Anahid's daughter after a once-promising apprenticeship under Abdi ended. Coming from a prominent mage family and gifted with a childhood of power and potential, Narine had become a disappointment to the elder council at the ripe age of twenty-two, which was why Tadesse, with two years less experience than Narine, was considered the senior mage.

His eyes were fixed on her sash and the abundant silver. "You know I think it's unfair."

"Why?" Narine straightened her shift and attempted to straighten the knot in her sash. It always bunched up under her fingers. "You're a better traveler, Tade. You follow orders. You're more persuasive with councils, and you never deviate from the diviners' suggestions."

"You're more powerful than I am, and everyone knows it."

"Yes, but you didn't disappear for a year without explanation." She gave up on her knot. "They really don't like that."

Tade shook his head slowly. "It was six years ago. Do they still——?"

"I ignored their summons for a full year; they will never forget." She shook her head. "Don't worry about it; it's not your problem. I don't resent you. Don't ever think that."

His mouth settled into a firm line. "You know I should do the talking when we go in there."

"Of course." She inclined her head slightly. "Have you heard from anyone else? No one has contacted me from other chapters. You?"

"I called Touma in Cairo, and I'm waiting to hear back. I haven't heard from Binyam, but I know he's visiting family this week. Yosef and Salama called from Zanzibar, but according to the travelers I've talked to, they felt the shift, but they haven't noticed any changes where they are."

"So it's local."

"That's what it seems like so far." He straightened when the hedge opened the door and gestured for them to come in.

The Elders' Chamber of the Seba Segel resembled a round throne room with seven intricately carved chairs raised on a low, circular dais that surrounded the room. Junior mages had the benefit of always looking up at the elders. It created a dynamic of supplicant and benefactor that was highly intentional. It was also one of the reasons Narine had always chafed at visiting to give reports.

Tadesse, tall and regal with neat locs falling to his waist and stylized traveling scars that ended just below his left elbow, looked up at the elders with an open countenance.

Narine tried to keep her expression from settling into what her father lovingly called her "resting bitch face."

"Blessed elders of the Seba Segel, wise mages of the East, heirs of Basenater and the twelve, we thank you for your attention during this holy month."

There were five mages around the room and two empty seats. Narine's eyes fell on her mother's seat, and for a moment she couldn't look away.

Four years and nothing. Not a word. Not a messenger from the future. Not a letter in the safe. Nothing.

Most of the five mages in the chamber that morning were familiar to Narine. There was the chief hedge, Elder Kebret, his wrinkled face set into a permanent scowl; taking the traveler's seat in Abdi's place was the politically savvy traveler Desta of House Zuria in the south; and Issa, a senior weaver from Uganda, sat tall in the archivist's chair.

Sitting in the alchemist's seat was a friendly, round man with a pleasant smile. Narine had never seen him before.

And finally there was Yosef, a traveler from a future whom none but the elders could know.

Wait.

Narine tried to catch Tadesse's eye.

Why was Yosef still there?

It wasn't unheard of that a traveler took an elder's seat in Addis. While it wasn't accepted in other Seba Segel orders around the globe, the East African seat was the original of the seven and held the most sway. Having a traveler from the future was considered wise even if he or she could only share limited information.

Narine wondered why Yosef hadn't returned to his native time, but she didn't have the standing to ask. Was Yosef's presence what had caused the time shift? Or had he stayed in their time because he knew it was going to happen?

So many questions and no answers.

The traveler was an enigma. He was clearly from the Horn of Africa, his light brown skin, dark curly hair and large, deep-set eyes typical of the region, but his accent was impossible to place and his mannerisms were a mystery. He wore every emotion on his face, but those emotions often didn't match the mood of the room or the topic at hand.

Who he was and when he came from remained a constant mystery.

Yosef spoke before Tadesse could present their request. "There is a fault in the Tibeb."

Every eye in the room swung toward him.

"Impossible," Issa scoffed. "There are no mistakes in the sacred record."

"Explain yourself, Yosef." Kebret frowned.

"In my yesterday, Abdi Mulenah sat in that seat, and today it is held by Desta of House Zuria." Yosef's eyes landed on Narine. "Your mentor?"

"Is gone."

"And do you know Elder Kamil Muhamed?"

"His face is new to me." Narine kept her voice quiet, but even as she looked at the man who sat in the alchemist's seat, scattered pieces of memory fell into place in her mind.

Kebret turned to Desta. "You knew of this?"

"I felt the shift," Elder Desta said.

Yosef cocked his head. "And yet you did not bring up this change when we gathered."

Desta frowned. "I was going to, Yosef. You didn't bring it up either."

"Indeed I did not."

"Until now."

"Yes."

Elder Kamil cleared his throat. "As I am new to the travelers on the elder council" —scattered laughter rang around the room— "let me introduce myself."

Narine knew him even as she didn't. As he spoke, new memories filled her mind.

Kamil was an alchemist and a prolific joke-teller. He and Fatima had three children and fourteen grandchildren. He was a natural host and opened his home to any traveling mages.

Within moments of seeing him, she knew him. Tadesse would have the same experience. It was the life and the reality of travelers. People were there and then they weren't. Friends could disappear in an instant if the timeline shifted. Homes that had been established could be gone, and over a matter of days their memory would fade away until nothing was left.

Reality, for Narine, was always in flux.

"...so the incidence of this change must be investigated, but of course nothing can be done in the thirteenth month," Kamil concluded. "The taboo of Pagume must be respected."

"Of course we can't travel," Tadesse said. "I would never suggest that."

Despite her training, Narine was tempted if it meant that Abdi would return. She closed her eyes and tried to fix the memory of her mentor in her mind so she would not forget him quickly.

"Write down everything you know."

Narine opened her eyes, and Yosef was staring at her.

She met his penetrating gaze. "Elder Yosef?"

"Only a day has passed; your memories are still intact. Write down everything you know about Abdi and his life. You've done it before. It will be useful in discovering what has happened." Yosef turned his eyes to Tadesse. "You come to us with a request."

"I do," Tadesse said. "We do. Narine and I would like permission to investigate the archives for the warp. We believe Abdi was tasary; there should be evidence of his disappearance in or around his birth year."

"You want permission to investigate this… change," Kebret said, "but there is nothing to be done about it."

"Nothing to be done?" Desta cocked his head. "A member of our order has disappeared during the sacred month—a man whose birth was likely a fixed point in history—and you want to do nothing? This is a major breech of protocol."

"None of us has forgotten the Second Mage War." Issa spoke for the first time. "But there is no proof that this wasn't an isolated incident. Has a president or prime minister died? Has a conflict started? How far has this ripple been felt?" She looked at Tadesse. "Well?"

Narine and Tadesse exchanged a look.

"As far as we can tell," he said, "it has only been felt locally. Fellow travelers on the continent felt the time shift but have not seen any affects so far."

"It could have been an accident. An oversight. A missed traveler's window," Issa said. "We have no evidence that this will lead to greater complications."

"A question." Kamil leaned forward to grab the council's attention. "Could it have been a traveler out of time who changed something unintentionally simply by being there?"

"If you're looking at me," Yosef said, "don't. I was not the cause of this shift."

"I think the point is that we don't know," Elder Desta said. "Yosef has confirmed that there is a fault in the Tibeb. That means that a fixed point has shifted. Any fault must be investigated."

"It may look effortless to those with different vocations" —

Yosef looked amused— "but our kind do not *accidentally* fall through time. All travel must be intentional."

Kebret looked at Yosef. "Do you know when this warp occurred?"

"Not specifically." The traveler spread his hands. "I concur with these two. They should start looking around the time of the missing traveler's birth."

Issa nodded. "Good. Investigate it, Tadesse. You are welcome in the archives, and the brothers and sisters of the Tibeb will assist you."

Kebret glared at Issa but said nothing more. An elder had spoken.

"One more thing." Yosef leaned forward and put his elbow on the arm of his curved chair. "Narine has something else significant to share."

She looked at the strange traveler and narrowed her eyes. "How—?"

"The American you saw yesterday." Yosef nodded. "Tell them."

# CHAPTER 8

"So Tade gets to investigate this time breach and I have to hunt down a tourist." Narine tore off a piece of injera and folded it around a bite of lentils spiced with berbere. "Can you believe that? I understand that they want him to lead the investigation, but they won't even let me help?"

Aida looked amused. Her mouth curled as she took another bite of greens from their shared plate at the shiro house in the Old Airport neighborhood. "What do they want with the American?" Her eyes shifted to the side for a moment. "Hold on."

She was listening to something from her AI. After a few moments, she took her earpiece out and set it on the table beside them. "My mother again."

"You clearly didn't have your ear pinched if you left your assistant in at the dinner table." Narine remembered the quick sting like she was still ten years old. "What was it?"

"Nothing important." Aida looked flustered. "The American?"

The smell of spicy berbere and rich ginger and turmeric filled the air in the shiro house. Low tables were scattered around the room, tucked in every corner while old jazz music played from invisible speakers built into the walls.

"They want to know who the American is. Why is he in Addis? Is he powerful? Did someone send him? It's like they think someone is pissing on the corner of their house or something. I mean, even if he is visiting from the US, who cares?"

Aida sipped an orange soda. "You know, it's a holiday week. You'd think you'd be happy you get to snoop around the university and look for a handsome American instead of spending the time unrolling very long bolts of old weaving."

Aida's house was within walking distance of the restaurant, so Narine had met her at the minibus stop and walked with her to the restaurant before the archivist had to return to the compound to assist Tadesse.

"This fault is going to be within the past hundred and fifty years." Narine took another piece of injera. "I know it."

Aida frowned. "How do you know?"

Narine met her eyes and held them. "Trust me?"

Aida's eyebrows went up. "Do you think this has to do with—?"

"I don't know, but start looking around 1920. Between that date and Abdi's birth—"

"How old was he?"

"Seventy-eight or -nine I think."

Aida hummed. "So… 1920s to turn of the century. I'll start looking there and think up some reason to tell Tade."

"If you find the warp, then after Pagume is over either Tade or I can go back and put things right."

If that was even possible.

It had to be possible.

Aida said, "I think that, with time, the warp will become unmistakable."

"What do you mean?"

"Think about history being a river, right?" Aida moved a potato to the middle of the plate of injera. "Here is a tasary.

This is part of what holds the river on course and gives the Tibeb its structure." She put carrots around the potato, arranged beans behind it. "That tasary holds this section of the river in place. If you take it away" —she took the potato and fed it to Narine— "all these other pieces fall apart." She pointed to the rest of the vegetables she'd arrayed around the potato.

Narine nodded slowly. "So there will be some kind of warped area or knot, but until the tasary is repaired, it's going to keep messing up the pattern of the Tibeb."

"I don't think you can *repair* tasary. Once they are altered, they are altered. All you can do is mitigate the effects and contain them."

Narine nodded. "Try to get the threads back on the right track."

"I suspect what looks like a knot right now will slowly get bigger and bigger because that tasary was holding the pattern."

Narine stared at their plate. "So you keep looking. You're going to find it."

Aida lifted her eyebrows. "Oh, I'm going to find it."

"Good. Because as long as I can remember Abdi, I'm going to try to get him back." Narine stared at the plate of injera and vegetables. "I think I'm done eating."

"Good. So tell me more about the American. He had a travelers' birthmark on his arm?"

"The American is old news." She decided to poke Aida a little. She had no desire to talk about the American. "I'm more interested in you and Tade working together."

"What are you talking about?" Aida was suddenly very interested in the green beans on the plate. "Have you tried the *fasolia*? It's really good."

"Yes, I love fasolia almost as much as you love Tadesse Girma."

Aida tossed a balled napkin at Narine. "Shut up."

"Never. It's been five years since you dated and broke up with the man without reason."

"Did Tade tell you that?"

"You've never dated anyone else seriously, and I know you're both hung up on each other, so clearly the breakup was a mistake."

"Narine, this is none of your—"

"Go to a concert. Go dancing. You both like that electronic music from South America. You're perfect for each other, but all you do is make moon eyes at each other during meetings."

Aida's cheeks turned pink. "Tade is Orthodox."

"And you're Muslim. But really you're agnostic, so why is this even an issue? You'll pick a religious tradition and raise your kids in it. Then they'll decide on the opposite when they're grown anyway."

"It's not that simple."

"Why?"

Aida's mouth settled into a firm line.

"Oh come on, Aida. Like you don't know my secrets?" Narine stared at Aida.

Her friend's expression softened. "I don't like to talk about it because my family is like yours."

Narine leaned back in her chair. "I know your dad is from an old house."

"And so is my mother, but do I ever go to Alexandria for visits? No."

"So you're closer with your father."

"Because he's not part of my mother's" —she waved her hands— "political scheming."

Narine narrowed her eyes. "You mean marriage?"

"Yes." Aida sighed. "I never wanted to talk about it because I don't even like thinking about it." She kept her eyes on the plate and took another bite. "I like my life in Addis. I love my friends here. I love the weather and the freedom. I don't want to leave."

"Is that why you and Tade broke up?"

"The short version, yes."

"Do they have someone arranged already?"

"My mother is interviewing candidates in Dubai right now. That's probably what her last phone call was about. Last year it was London. The year before was Singapore. It's the third year they've been trying to match me. My dad has been putting them off, talking about how important my work here is, but I can't avoid it forever."

Arranged marriages were far from the norm in most of the modern human world, but in old mage families like Narine's and Aida's, it was still considered the most desirable way to maintain bloodlines and consolidate power. Narine's parents had an arranged marriage, as did her grandparents, as did most of her more powerful aunts and uncles. Marriages were carefully planned to produce powerful children and create information and wealth networks that would benefit the Seba Segel and the old families.

Even though the past fifty years had produced more mages from human families than any other time in history, the practice—particularly among old families—continued.

"Tell them the golden boy of the Addis Elder Council is in love with you. They can't argue with that."

"If I wanted to marry you, they wouldn't have a problem with it," Aida said. "Other than the fact that we couldn't produce children."

"Damn biology." Narine waved at the girl making coffee.

"*Damn* biology." Aida caught the coffee girl's eye and held up two fingers. "But who is Tade's family? Where does he come from? If he had powerful bloodlines, that would be one thing even if he didn't come from money. But the rest of his family is human."

The server came by and took the rest of their plate away, leaving the table clear for coffee and popcorn.

"I think Tade's family does have money though."

Aida waved a hand. "They don't care about that. It's about the power."

"So… ignore them. That's what I do anytime my family tries to marry me off."

"It's not the same with me," Aida said. "I'm an only child, and none of my cousins are very powerful. Your family throws travelers and diviners like it's as common as curly hair and brown eyes."

"In my family it is." She curled her lip. "Of course, my mother would say it's all the years of carefully planned marriages." She sighed. "Maybe ask Yosef to tell your mother that he's seen your magnificently powerful children with Tadesse. If it's coming from the future, she can't argue with that."

"Oh yes, I'm sure that's why Yosef's elders sent him back to our time." Aida rolled her eyes. "To help me with my love life."

Narine leaned forward and whispered, "Your love could change history—you never know."

Aida stared at her, and Narine saw the beginning of tears in her eyes. "I wish I thought things could change. That they could really change."

*They can.*

She wanted to say it, but the words stuck in her throat because wasn't she in the same boat as Aida even if she didn't have an arranged marriage in her future?

Serving an order her family was bound to.

Hiding so much of her past.

Shoring up the river of inevitable time.

Dragging others into a world where nothing remained certain, not even your own existence.

*I wish I thought things could change too.*

99

Narine cleared her throat. "I wish I could help you and Tade. Looking for this man seems like the least important thing in the universe right now."

"What do the old diviners say?" Aida's smile was sad. "The stars are wiser than us, Narine."

The girl came by and set down a burner of frankincense, a bowl of fresh popcorn, and two strong cups of coffee. She put two scoops of sugar in each cup, then left the incense and popcorn at the table while Narine and Aida drank their coffee.

"Right." Narine picked up her cup. "The stars are wiser than us."

# CHAPTER 9

*The Island*
*1920*

That morning, Narine woke up to the same sound she'd heard every morning since she'd come to the island two months before: rain pounding against the thatched roof of her house and a persistent drip in a bucket she'd placed near the door.

She stared at the thatched roof and tried to imagine she was in her bedroom at home.

Narine had thought she knew what life was like when you didn't fit in. Growing up with a European face in Addis Ababa meant that she often stood out in crowds. It meant that people —mostly in rural areas—stared at her. It meant that strangers talked about her in front of her face, not knowing she'd grown up speaking the same language.

But life on the island was even more alienating.

As a visiting mage, she was granted a degree of deference, but people still looked at her with suspicion because she was a traveler. There were stares and whispers when she went to gather water or visit the meetinghouse with Tigist.

Narine wanted to contribute to the household where she was living—she didn't want to be a burden to Tigist and Daniel—but everyone assumed she was ignorant. So as soon as she settled into the small room where she'd be living for roughly the next year, she started to clean.

Narine was a poor gardener and was hopeless when it came to butchering animals, but she was her mother's daughter and she knew how to clean.

She washed the clothes for the compound. She spent hours every day going back and forth to the lake to gather water and boil it so she'd have something safe to drink. The last thing she wanted was to survive a bout of malaria just to die from cholera. The alchemists did their best to create vaccines for common strains of viruses, but there was no way to protect against all strains in all times of history. They'd tried, but they inevitably failed.

The day before, a boy who'd come to deliver bread to Daniel and Tigist casually knocked over a water jar and ran off with a careless "Sorry!"

Narine had to walk down to the lake to fill it again.

She dragged herself out of bed and went to empty the bucket into her water jar. At least this much rain would keep her from having to walk down to the lake twice a day to fill jars for the compound.

"Narine?" There was a quick tap at her door; then Tigist rushed in, a heavy wool wrap over her head. "How are you feeling?"

Bored.

Frustrated.

Cold.

"I'm fine." She sat on the edge of her bed. "It's fine. Do you need help with anything?"

"No." Tigist sat on a low stool across from her. "I was going to roast coffee—do you want some?"

"Sure."

"And there's spinning to do." Tigist smiled. "Nothing magical, just the regular kind. Have you ever learned?"

"No." Narine's interest was piqued. "Spinning cotton thread?"

Tigist nodded. "I invited a few women over from other compounds. There's not much to do in the rain, so we spin. I'll teach you if you want. It would give the others a chance to get to know you too."

The traditional spinning technique that women practiced in the country hadn't changed much over the centuries. It produced a thick, nubby thread that was used for everything from traditional dresses to the heavy gebi that Narine's godmother had given her when she was a child. While Narine had seen spinning done in the archives, she was a traveler and had never practiced it herself.

"Sure." She nodded. "I'd love to learn."

After all, there wasn't much else to do.

Tigist departed while Narine dressed in the cotton shift she'd been wearing most days. Around it, she wound a thick woven belt, then tied her hair up before she wrapped it. It was dry on the ends, and she found herself missing the oil she used to massage her scalp at home. She missed the woman at the salon who trimmed her hair and gave her luxurious hot-oil treatments. She missed pedicures and warm drying tubes after a shower.

She sighed. There was nothing to be done about it. She simply had to survive. Her hair should be the least of her worries.

Narine shoved her feet in the boots she'd used to travel to Ziway instead of the sandals that would sink into the mud. The feel of firm leather surrounding her feet grounded her, bringing sharp memories of splashing through rain puddles in Addis and climbing the steps of the national library with Jamila the day after she bought them. They'd given her blisters before she broke them in.

Jamila. What would her best friend think of this adventure when she returned to her time? Technically, Narine wasn't supposed to share her jumps with anyone but her mentor and the elders, but she always told Jamila because she knew her best friend kept her secrets in a vault.

She missed Jamila. She missed Genet. She missed her entire annoying family.

Narine threw a heavy wool wrap over her head and walked out of the house and toward the glowing doorway where others were gathering. Tigist had invited the women to sit in the large front room where Narine had joined her and Daniel for coffee before she fell ill. She could already hear the friendly chatter from across the yard.

"Narine!" Her host called to her in Amharic and waved her inside. "Come in. The fire is already lit; it'll be warm soon."

She entered the front room, and immediately the friendly voices she'd heard from outside fell silent.

Five women smiled at her and nodded, but they didn't speak. One of the older women turned to a teenage girl and spoke in whispers in a language Narine didn't understand. The other two busied themselves taking bundles of clean washed cotton from woven baskets and grabbing various instruments they needed before they organized themselves into a kind of assembly line in Tigist's front room.

"Let's see." Her new friend walked back into the room. "I think we're all here. Maryam, Deborah, and Samri, this is Narine. She speaks Amharic."

The tension in the room lifted slightly as the women nodded and smiled at her.

"Hello."

"*Tena yistilin.*"

"Welcome."

The women murmured their greetings but did little more than shoot curious glances at Narine as they busied themselves with their work. The girls with them said even less, but their smiles were warm and their eyes were curious.

Tigist patted her shoulder. "Let's start with you combing the cotton before we spin it. Does that sound good?"

"Sure." She nodded. *"Eshi."*

She settled in a corner of the room, sitting on a stool near Tigist, watching her friend expertly comb cotton into smooth, fluffy piles just like the teenage girls did. After a few moments of watching, Narine reached for the combs and took over the job from Tigist, who was happily chatting with each of the women, drawing them into conversation about their children and their homes.

Narine sat and listened, trying to make herself as invisible as possible while she watched the girls across from her work. Her job was to comb the raw cotton fibers into a smooth, soft bundle free of any husks or bits of cotton scrap or seed.

When the combers had created the clean piles of cotton, the spinners would pick it up, twist the end onto a carved stick, and roll the long end along their leg to twist the fibers into thread. This single long thread wrapped around the stick in a slowly growing ball until the woman created a sphere a little larger than a lemon before sliding the ball of cotton off the spindle and starting again.

It was rote, meditative work made faster by the flying stories, wise opinions, and scattered laughter of the women around her. Once she'd made herself quiet and listening, the women opened up to Tigist and a wealth of information came flying at Narine.

One of the women was worried her husband's back injury wasn't healing.

Another woman shared that her newly married daughter was dissatisfied with her house and her mother-in-law.

Another was irritated that the herb she'd been taking to stave off pregnancy had failed and she was pregnant again.

Advice was given to the mother about her adult daughter,

and various stories were shared—good and bad—about experiences with in-laws. And the woman with the injured husband was encouraged to press the man to see Dr. Gideon and make sure there wasn't a more serious problem.

Various ideas were thrown around about how to deal with the unwanted pregnancy, but in the end the woman was resigned to a sixth child. Her husband would hire another girl from the village so she could fulfill her archivist duties for the order after the new baby arrived.

It was utterly common talk that Narine might have overheard in Addis when she was growing up, in Zanzibar two hundred years before, or in Pasadena when she visited her father's family there.

Slowly the women seemed to grow accustomed to Narine's presence; a few even ventured to ask her about her family or her home.

"How do you find our village?" One of the women asked with a slight smile. "Is it very different than where you come from?"

Narine smiled. "I was just thinking that women talk about the same things everywhere."

The women in the room laughed.

"Children," Narine said. "Work. Husbands. Family."

"The inability of the elders to repair the roof in the weaving room." The woman with the new pregnancy rolled her eyes. "Hedges only think about politics."

"Hey," Tigist said. "I am a hedge. And an elder."

"You know what I mean."

"This is the first I'm hearing about the leak," Tigist said. "I'll ask Daniel to fix it when he returns from the city. I'm not climbing on that roof in the rain."

More laughter, and Narine had to blow a curl of hair out of her eyes when it fell into her face.

"I want to see your hair." The woman with the injured husband was closest to Narine. "Let us see it."

"It's a mess." Nevertheless, Narine unwound the cloth she'd tied around her curls. "I just wrapped it because I haven't done anything but wash it since I've been here."

"One of my younger daughters has your same hair." The woman with the newly married daughter smiled at Narine. "Darker, but the same kind of curls."

Narine touched the ends. "What do you use for oil here? My scalp is so dry."

"Butter." Tigist touched Narine's head. "You need some. Everyone here uses butter."

"My mother does that sometimes, but my godmother uses..." Narine frowned at the flickering memory. "Sorry, the opposite. My mother uses oil and my godmother..." She didn't remember what Aster used. "I've used both."

Hadn't she?

She frowned at the memories flashing in her mind. She was on the floor and it was wood. Oil rubbed onto her scalp. Then the floor was earthen. The floor was wood again, and the tang of fermented butter hit her nose.

The floor was earthen, and the oil smelled of roses and olives.

The floor was wood, and butter covered her head.

No, the opposite. Oil and wood. Butter and earth.

Wasn't it?

Her heart began to race. It had only been a couple of months. It couldn't happen yet. It was too soon.

"Narine?" Tigist was staring at her. "Are you feeling well?"

"Sorry." She blinked and looked up. "Sorry—it's been a long time since I thought about this." She stood up. "Excuse me for a moment."

Quiet murmurs followed her out the door. She must miss her family. She was tired from the work of the village. She might have a husband or a lover in her time.

Narine knew they had no idea how precarious her mental state really was.

Her mother had warned her about this. A traveler who spent too much time in the past would slowly become absorbed in the timeline, forgetting her own time and place, mixing the reality of their time and the past.

It was the gift and the curse of their magic. While time travelers were able to adapt to shifting realities without losing their minds, that same flexibility could turn against them if they spent too long in a foreign time.

*Does the fish know the water any more than we know the air?*

The reality where a traveler found themselves became their reality if enough time passed, but Narine had thought it would take longer for confusion to set in, especially since she didn't feel her magic working.

Forgetting your time was how travelers were lost to time, losing bonds of family and order. Losing everything if they lingered too long in the past.

For Narine to survive a year with her memories intact was going to be a challenge. She had to focus, and she had to be able to recount her past and make it real. She could journal, but paper was hard to come by on the island.

*You are Narine Anahid Khoren of House Kayl. Your father is a diviner of House Vana. You were born in the year 2043 of the Old Calendar. You are a third-degree traveling mage of the Seba Segel, ninth in your line of power. You were born in Addis Ababa, Ethiopia. You have no siblings and many cousins. You are the godmother of Gelile, the adopted sister of Genet, the daughter of Anahid. Your best friend is Jamila Sahid of the house Rajab. You are a mage of the old order in Addis Ababa, your mentor is Abdi Mulenah of the Southern Mages.*

She repeated it every morning like a mantra, but it wasn't enough. What else could she do?

She could find someone trustworthy to share her memories and reality with.

It was forbidden, but if Narine wanted to survive a year without losing track of her identity, she might not have any choice.

But who?

GIDEON STARED AT HER. "WHAT YOU'RE TALKING ABOUT IS forbidden."

"I know that." Narine sat across from him on the roots of the ficus tree, hoping she wasn't making a terrible mistake. "But if I'm going to last a year in this place—"

"Why wouldn't you last? You're healthy. We're not living in prehistory, Narine. There is sanitation and cooked food. No war is threatening—"

"Do you know any travelers?" She kept her voice low even though they were sitting on the lakeside near the medical clinic and no one was around them.

He was silent for several moments before he answered. "I don't know any well, no."

She nodded. "We're not like other mages."

"What does that mean? I know you're not like other mages. Obviously not all of us can travel to the past."

"It's more than that."

He crossed his arms over his chest. "Tell me."

No one seemed to question Narine and Gideon's time together. It was as if the entire compound allowed that the two outsiders would bond. In fact, Tigist had even asked Narine if a romance was happening with Gideon, which was a rumor Narine quickly quashed. The last thing she needed was people watching her interactions with Gideon like the morality police.

"Travelers..." How to explain? "Time shifts, Gideon. Things change, and it's not unusual for us. Usually it is only noticeable in the details. Minor shifts like someone has a different job one day to the next or a restaurant that was on one corner doesn't exist or has moved to a different location."

Gideon nodded slowly. "I understand what you're saying."

"And obviously there are set points in history that cannot be changed—things that are tasary—which is why wars still happen and the world isn't a utopia."

He huffed out a bitter laugh. "Is that what they told you? What makes you think the Seba Segel would want utopia?"

Narine blinked. "Our purpose is to enlighten the world and guide its leaders."

"Is it? Or is the order's purpose to amass power for a few at the expense of all the common mages that keep things running for them?"

Narine shook her head. "Maybe you feel like that now, but—"

"So has that changed in your time?" Gideon crossed his arms and leaned against the tree. "The Seba Segel is egalitarian in your time? All mages are equal?"

No. Narine knew that wasn't the reality even if that's what some elders gave lip service to. "You're talking about internal politics, and I'm talking about the greater good."

"I'm not talking about politics; I'm talking about purpose."

Narine was confused. She'd never heard anyone speak so disdainfully of the order, not even her mother, who was known to be rebellious. "You're talking about *my* purpose?"

"The purpose of all of this, all of *us*." He looked at the horizon. "If the diviners can really see the future and the archivists the past, and if travelers can go back in time to divert violence and war, why is there any war at all? Why is there violence? Why not stop genocide and slavery and theft?"

"Because we cannot change set points."

"Why not?"

Narine sputtered. "It has been tried. Chaos happened. Wars happened. More died by trying to thwart the Tibeb than would have died in the original timeline. That's what the Second Mage War was about."

"Then what is the point of travel, Narine? Why attempt to

change any past?" He turned back to her, glaring. "What is the point of *you*?"

Narine didn't have answers for Gideon's questions. He was asking things she'd never heard before, and he made her feel like a foolish child. "I... I'm sorry, I made a mistake coming to speak to you. I should go."

She rose and started to walk away, but Gideon grabbed her arm.

"I'm sorry." His voice was softer. "That was unfair. You are following your training, the same as the rest of us."

She turned and looked up. "You're saying that we do nothing. That the order has some secret agenda, but you are part of that order. You know we do the best that we can for the most that we can."

"I know..." Gideon struggled for words. "I know that's what you've been taught. I know that the intentions of many are good, but on most days it doesn't feel like it's enough."

She frowned. "A tiny pebble can start a ripple that breaks a mountain."

His smile was amused. "Who told you that?"

"My mother."

"So it was wisdom you were taught, not wisdom you learned."

"All wisdom is taught."

He shook his head. "I don't need to be taught that stealing a farmer's land is wrong when his family will starve without it. That should be evident to anyone with eyes and a mind of their own."

"You're talking about a specific situation. Mages are trained to think about the big picture. About universal truths."

"Universal truths have consequences."

He was speaking in riddles, and Narine was trying to hold on to her sanity. "What do you want from me, Gideon?"

He let go of her arm. "From you? Nothing, I suppose. Tell me how travelers are different."

Narine didn't want to, and yet she couldn't think of anyone else.

Tigist was trustworthy, but she shared everything with Daniel. And Narine didn't know who Daniel trusted. Ger was solemn and serious, but he was also aloof and patronizing. Samuel was eager to hear anything Narine had to say, but she knew he shared everything with other mages of the order.

So there was Gideon. Private, severe, sarcastic, and arrogant. He didn't treat her like a child or an oddity.

Narine took a deep breath and let it out slowly. "First, you have to promise me that whatever I tell you about my time—about the future—you will not share with anyone. Ever. Not a mentor, another elder, a lover, a wife. No one."

He narrowed his eyes. "I can agree to that."

"The reason I'm telling you is that travelers adapt to the time, not time to the traveler. If something changes in the timeline, eventually our minds adapt to that reality. We recognize the change at first, but over time—"

"Your brain becomes accustomed to the new reality. The new environment." He nodded. "A survival mechanism."

"Exactly. It's one of the reasons we have set times to arrive and depart the past. The magic we use requires it, but the other reason is that if we're in the past too long, we lose our grip on our native time."

He cocked his head. She was a curiosity now. "Would that be so bad?"

"To be stuck here?" Narine barked a laugh. "Yes, Gideon. I'm not a fan of everything in modern life, but it would be very bad for me to be lost to the timeline. I have a family. I have people who love me and depend on me." *I have magic.* Some instinct warned her to hide her weakness. "I miss… plumbing, dammit. I cannot stay here, and I don't want to."

The flash of hurt was so quick, Narine almost thought she'd imagined it, but Gideon's next words confirmed what she'd seen.

"I don't think we're that backward here in the past, are we?"

"I'm not saying that. Modern technology is secondary at best." But what she would give for running water. "I told you, I have family. I have people who love me. My sister just had a brand-new baby! This time is not my home."

He pursed his lips, stuck his hands in his pockets, and nodded. "Okay, tell me. I promise I won't share with anyone what you tell me about the future."

She touched his arm. "Thank you."

Gideon shrugged. "I'm a scientist. I might have questions. If I'm going to keep you sane, I think it's only fair that you answer some of them."

"I'll answer what I can, but if you ask me about DNA therapy or artificial intelligence, I'm not going to be able to explain much of it."

He frowned. "DNA?"

"Never mind. Better you not ask because again, I can't explain it to you." She closed her eyes. "I'm going to tell you about my life. A lot of it will probably be boring because… Well, life is boring. But the telling will help me remember."

"Fine." He walked back to the ficus tree and sat down, his hands folded loosely in front of him. "Tell me, Narine. How did a European girl come to be born in Addis Ababa?"

She sat across from him and met the intense gaze of the man she'd chosen as her confidant. "It's 1920 here. Five years ago, the head of my family arrived at a refugee camp in Greece, and since then, he's been assigned to the order in Athens."

"What drove him from his home?"

"War." Narine hesitated. "Genocide."

Gideon nodded. "So your family is in Greece right now."

"And before this year ends, mages from the order in Cairo will reach out to the head of House Kayl and tell him that because of his family and the antiquity of his clan, he has been accepted to the mage order in Ethiopia as an apprentice mage."

"Head of house to an apprentice mage in Addis. A reduction in status."

"It doesn't matter; he will accept. An honor like this will not have been extended to an outside traveler—even one from an old family—until this year."

"Why him?"

"Because according to our records, our family has produced more travelers than any other in Seba Segel recorded history. Our genes seem predisposed to time travel, and there are skills that travelers in my family have that are uncommon. Extra, if you will."

"Like what?"

"That isn't important."

"I doubt that." He narrowed his eyes. "Very well. What's his name?"

"My ancestor? Also not important."

Gideon would likely be able to figure out who it was, even without a name, if he tried. She was hoping he wouldn't try.

"He will move to Ethiopia this year, and in a few years, he will marry a young woman that his family has chosen for him, another refugee from our country. She will move to Addis in the future, and eventually my grandfather will be born there, then my mother, then me."

It felt remarkably good to share the information, and the previous confusion in her mind died down. It was a little like the satisfaction of sorting cutlery in a drawer or graphing a star chart. Her mind thrived on the temporal organization; she would have to be careful not to share more than necessary. In this state, she could be an open book.

"So five generations."

Narine nodded.

Gideon narrowed his eyes. "And you're still white."

"Define white. Once upon a time, that was a very muddy classification."

Gideon frowned. "Not in my world."

"Because you come from a British colony," Narine said. "But if you're asking, I have mostly European blood. A little bit Persian. A little bit mixed from the United States."

"But in all your family's time in Addis Ababa, none of them married Africans?"

"Most of my family did if they were old order families." Narine shrugged. "Just not my parents for whatever reason. Most of my cousins have some Ethiopian or Sudanese blood, but I don't."

"That's unusual."

"What part?"

"Arranging marriages like that."

She shrugged. "Not among the old families."

"Even in rural places, children born in the order don't usually have arranged marriages."

She smiled. "If you knew more old order families, you'd realize it's common among them."

"And you?"

Narine frowned. "What about me?"

"How old are you?" For the first time he looked amused. "They haven't arranged your marriage yet?"

"No!" They had tried. "I'm only twenty-two."

"Younger than I thought." He crossed his arms over his chest. "Who taught you how to travel in time? Who was your mentor?"

"Most of what I learned came from a very wise traveler from the south. But unofficially, my mother and grandfather taught me a lot."

Gideon caught on quickly. "Because of the… unusual traits."

"Exactly."

Narine took a deep breath and let it out. Gideon was

staring at her like she was a curious specimen he wanted to dissect. It was unnerving, but at the same time, she was even surer she'd made the right decision.

Gideon was greedy for knowledge, and he wouldn't be quick to share it. He didn't gossip, and he didn't trust easily. The man was possessive enough that he'd consider Narine's life and history his own research project, and he didn't seem like the type to welcome collaborators.

Sharing with Gideon had cleared Narine's mind. She was sharper and her memories were crystal clear. The words of the spell that would take her home were sitting in the front of her mind, and nothing about them was muddled or cloudy.

She had to get back to her own timeline if it was the last thing she did. If that meant baring her life history to Dr. Gideon Marangu, so be it.

# CHAPTER 10

*Addis Ababa*
*2071*

The third morning of Pagume, Narine maneuvered her zip bike through Bole Mikael and around the mosque to the street where the khat dealers sold their wares. She kept her helmet on, but the regular vendors recognized her, shouting and pointing as she weaved through traffic toward Jamila's truck.

It was a clear morning; so far there wasn't a cloud in the sky. Rain on the Archangel Rafael's day was good luck, but that morning didn't look promising for rain.

The woman she was looking for was sitting on a round wooden stool, idly popping delicate green leaves in her mouth while she chatted with one of the girls who ran from the large delivery van behind them to the table where a small crowd of buyers were examining the fresh green leaves they could purchase.

The skytrain whooshed over them, clack-clack-clacking as it propelled shoppers toward the holiday markets in Meskel Square while beneath the shade of the overpass, holiday crowds more interested in relaxation than acquisition jostled to find the best leaf.

The entire strip north of the mosque in the Bole Mikael was devoted to khat shops. Permanent vendors occupied the east side of the street, often with open-air khat houses built behind them. Electronic music poured from the establishments, and mobile vending machines carried trays of steaming tea and cold, sugary sodas up and down the street from one khat house to the next.

On the opposite side of the street, temporary electric carts were set up in a green space under an arching row of jacaranda trees planted in an attempt to hide the concrete overpass. Falafel and kebab vendors with their electric pushcarts trolled up and down the row. Peanut sellers roasted the treat over portable grills and waved down passing cars. Delivery boys ran from carts and shops to vehicles idling at the curb. Cash and electronic currency rained.

Jamila Sahid's khat was brought in fresh every morning via air transport from Harar and was known to have a delicate, bright flavor and a mild *merkana*, the buzz that came from chewing the leaves.

While khat had always been traditional in parts of the country, prosperity and modern convenience had spread its use in the capital city and the southern parts of the country as more and more workers enjoyed half-day shifts that left hours to waste with merkana and conversation.

Raised voices from the khat houses debated everything from the price of coffee and the latest football scores to the most recent news from the African Union meeting or the latest foreign investment or electronic currency scheme.

Parliament. That's what Genet called the khat houses. The common citizen's parliament.

Sitting like a colorful oasis in the busy market, her friend's table was crowded with those willing to pay the higher prices for Harar khat.

Jamila Sahid was a stunning woman who looked younger than Narine, though they were born the same year. Her hair was styled in a mass of intricate braids and a mustard-yellow headscarf wrapped loosely around her face, covering most of her hair and her shoulders. Her glinting gold assistant was perched in her ear, decorated with tiny rubies, and a discreet viewing lens was flipped forward as she watched market numbers race across the screen.

She wore a small fortune in gold on her fingers and a brilliant blue dress woven through with sparkling thread. While Jamila sat on a humble stool nibbling on green leaves and drinking a cold Mirinda orange drink, it was clear that she was the one directing the flurry of activity and constant exchange of cash and electronic currency.

She watched Narine park her zip bike, arching an eyebrow when she took off her helmet and shook out her hair.

"You should braid it."

Narine walked toward the woman who'd been her childhood partner in crime.

Often literal crime.

"I'm not going to be *that* farenji." Narine walked over, set her helmet on the empty burlap bags behind Jamila's stool, and pulled up another to sit next to her. She switched to English so *everyone* in the market wouldn't overhear their conversation. "How's business?"

"Business is good." Jamila watched the girls working the table with a keen eye; she flipped her viewing lens back. Her girls handled cash with one hand and electronic transfers with the other. All of them were Harari girls dressed in the bright clothes typical of their city. All of them had sleek black assistants in their ears.

They were dressed to stand out in the crowd, all chosen by Jamila for their intelligence and business sense. One of the girls wore a pink hijab, another wore green trimmed with silver, another was dressed head to toe in purple satin. All of them cast kohl-lined eyes toward Jamila if they were unsure of a price a customer offered.

Jamila lounged among the hubbub of the market, picking at her bundle of khat and giving the girls a slight nod or a subtle shake to direct the bargaining.

She kept her eyes on the table as they talked. "I have some mismar for you in the truck if you want it."

Narine sighed at the lost opportunity. "I don't have time to chew today. I have to find an American."

Jamila pointed to a group of tourists half a block away. "There's a whole group of them right there. Just arrived on a tour bus. Take your pick."

"Very funny."

"Have you very conveniently managed to lose the assistant I bought you again?"

"No." Narine pulled it out of her riding jacket. "I just don't like it when people can contact me all the time."

"Who has your contact besides me and Genet?" Jamila rolled her eyes. "You know you need to keep it on you. There are reasons. Wear it please?"

"I'll consider it."

"Why do you need to find an American?"

"Not any American. A particular American who's working at the university. At least I'm pretty sure he is."

Jamila cast her eyes to the side. "Order business?"

"Of course."

Jamila knew all about the order. She came from a powerful family but hadn't been born with any significant magic herself. It never seemed to bother her, likely because being born with only minor divination power had allowed her to chart her own course in life as soon as she left school. She'd created a thriving khat business along with some shipping that wasn't as strictly controlled and taxed as the khat.

If Narine needed to find anything, hide anything, or move anything without the mages or the human government knowing about it, she came to Jamila. And if Jamila needed Narine's right arm, she'd give it to her without question. Their loyalty to each other was unquestioned after years of friendship and shared secrets.

"How's your family?" Narine asked.

"They're all good. My mother wants me to get married."

"Again?"

She shrugged. "She's a romantic. You know how she adores my father. She thinks I'll eventually find the right one if I keep trying."

One of Jamila's girls held up a bundle of fine green khat with tender stems and shouted an unreasonably low price.

Jamila glared at the man in front of her table. "I know you don't mean to insult me, Demeke," she shouted in Amharic.

The man looked sheepish, then pulled out his wallet with a fat stack of birr fresh from the bank.

Narine managed to hide her amusement. "So she wants you to get married again. The first two husbands weren't enough for her?"

"She says that I work too much to be a good wife, and if I cut back and treated my husband as something more than an employee to order around, I'd probably have more success."

Narine agreed with Jamila's mother but wasn't going to say it. "To be fair, you work more than anyone I know."

"Isn't there an American saying about one black kettle pointing at another one?"

"Do you see me marrying anyone?" She glanced at her friend. "No. I know I'd make a bad wife."

"Fine." Jamila cut her eyes toward Narine. "I do have other priorities besides work."

"And how is the golden boy?"

"Doing well." Jamila's voice was softer. "You got the pictures I emailed?"

"Yeah." Narine's throat tightened at the memory of the happy, smiling boy laughing in the courtyard of Jamila's flower-filled compound in Harar. "He's as beautiful as always."

Jamila smiled. "Samson the sunshine baby."

Narine smiled and slid her arm around Jamila's waist to give her a side hug. "Thank you."

"For the pictures?"

"For everything."

Jamila returned the hug and let her arm rest around Narine's waist. "So why did you come see me today if you're not going to buy some of my green gold?" Jamila caught her runner's eye and motioned her over. "You want some tea?"

"I'd love some."

Jamila held up two fingers. "You just come for a talk? How's Geni? Is Samira happy?" She had been the one to send Samira from Harar.

"She's doing great. Everyone is doing well. Genet is teaching Samira how to make berbere from scratch. Gelile is ready to go back to school."

"She takes after her mother and not her auntie then."

"You and I never worked at school because we never had to. Geni didn't grow up the same way."

"True." Jamila's attention was caught by another one of her girls, and she gave the young woman a sharp nod. "We both knew our destiny from a young age."

Narine leaned back and surveyed the table, the crowd, and the loaded truck behind Jamila. "Who knew that smuggling rebuilt mobile assistants into school would lead to all this?"

"Me." Jamila shook her head at another customer. "I did. I made good money with those pieces of junk."

"Yes, you did." It had been enough to buy a used car by the time they graduated. "Our plans for the New Year," Narine said. "They might be interrupted."

Jamila's eyebrow arched up, and she leaned away from Narine. "You need to come."

"I want to, but I don't know—"

"The *family* would be very disappointed if you didn't come."

Narine's mind was fixed on the message in the letter she'd received days before.

*This cannot continue.*

"I don't know if it's safe." She reached over and picked a sprig of her friend's khat, whispering about the note in Jamila's ear. "It might not be a good idea."

"Did he find out? How could he find out?"

Narine nibbled on the khat. "I don't know that he has, but I don't know that he hasn't either. You know how the gossips in the order flap their tongues."

There was no way he'd have been able to…

No.

Better if she didn't even let her mind go there.

"I'll try my best to make it." Narine stood and brushed off her pants. "But I'll message you if I can't. I should go."

Jamila pointed to the girl who was scurrying back from the tea shop. "Your tea."

"I'll stay for tea, but then I need to go, Jamila." Narine felt the weight of expectations bearing down on her. "This week has turned out more complicated than usual."

The American was at the library again, wandering through the Amharic fiction section and perusing the shelves. Did he speak Amharic? What she'd overhead so far didn't sound fluent. It wasn't an easy language for foreigners to learn, especially with an entirely different writing system than most European languages.

But there he wandered.

And he was coming closer.

And he was walking toward her.

Damn. Narine looked down at her notebook, then started

gathering her things as the American approached. She was just about to stand and escape the third floor when she heard a pleasantly low voice whisper in English: "Where have we met?"

She had to look up to meet his eyes. "Pardon me?"

He crouched down next to her, and the scent of his cedar-tinged cologne teased her senses.

"I know we've met. I keep seeing you around, and you look so familiar."

*Probably because your magic is subconsciously attuned to other mages.*

She could feel it now that he was close. If Narine had to describe it to another, she wouldn't be able to. It was simply knowing. This man—this foreigner—was powerful. Quite powerful, but in an untamed, free-flowing way.

It was delicious. Between his scent and his magic, she wanted to curl up in his lap and purr.

She had to play it off; this was the opening she'd needed, and she had an assignment from the elders.

Narine put on a thoughtful expression. "You know, you do look familiar. Do you work for the university?"

He smiled, and it was devastating. "Is it obvious?"

"You're from the United States, aren't you?" She glanced at the book in his hand. "But you speak Amharic?"

"This?" He held up a historical fiction novel. "No. I wish. I'm working on it, but this is more... aspirational than realistic."

His humor was disarming, but she could see their whispered conversation was drawing annoyed attention from others on the floor.

"I was just about to go get a coffee," Narine said. "Would you like to join me?"

There was the devastating smile again. "I'd love to." He stuck out his hand. "I'm Jacob Martin."

*Yacob. A good Amharic name.*

"My name is Narine."

She gathered her things, and he followed her down the central curving walkway of the national library. They headed toward the door, stealing glances at each other until Narine was distracted by a security guard waving them back.

"Sir! You cannot take the book," the guard hissed in Amharic.

"The book." Narine put a hand on his arm. "*Ykirta*," she told the librarian. "He's not from here and didn't know." She looked at Jacob and spoke in English. "You can't take the books out of the library. It's not for lending."

"Oh right!" Jacob glanced at the hardcover book in his hand. "I'm so sorry. *Ykirta*. I didn't realize I still had it."

The librarian tsked, but she didn't seem too annoyed. Her eyes were already scanning other patrons as they exited the building. "Make sure he doesn't forget again," she muttered to Narine. "This is the third time."

Narine smiled. "I'll remind him. *Ameseghinalehu*."

"*Chigur yelem*." She waved them away and turned her attention back to the students rolling in from the university.

"There are so many kids here." Jacob spoke in English as he watched the groups of teenagers arriving. "Isn't it a holiday week?"

"Yes, but national exams are coming up right after New Year, so the more diligent students usually take the free time to study." Narine walked outside the building and looked up at the massive pillars that outlined a perfect, sunny blue sky.

"Nice to have the clear day, isn't it?" Jacob hoisted his backpack over his shoulder and—now that they were out of the library—popped a sleek silver assistant in his ear. "I was getting pretty tired of rain."

Narine looked at him. He was pale for an Ethiopian but pale in the way that office workers and old priests were pale. "You don't get much sun, do you?"

He smiled. "Is it that obvious?"

"Your melanin is looking a little starved for light."

"I grew up in Seattle, so…"

"It's really cloudy there, isn't it? That makes sense. Your family is Ethiopian right?"

He smiled and looked at the ground. "They're not actually."

"They're not?" She frowned. The man had to be Ethiopian. Or at least part. If he wasn't from Ethiopia, his genetics had to originate in the Horn of Africa. "Eritrean?"

"It's complicated."

Huh. Well, that wasn't what the elders would want to hear, but—

"I was adopted." It burst out like he hadn't been planning to say it. "I never knew my biological parents. Sorry, too much information."

"No." She started walking toward the church, waving at him to follow. "My mother said it used to be very common for international adoptees to come back to Addis, looking for family. I didn't know it still happened though."

The adoption angle explained a lot but left Narine with even more questions. Mage families didn't give children up by choice. They were taken by the order at times, but they were never given away.

"I wasn't born here or anything, but I did a genetic profile and it showed that my father was Ethiopian, so I've been thinking that I should…" He shook his head. "Sorry. Too much information again."

"Are you thinking about looking in the genetic database?" He wasn't likely to find answers if his father was a mage. They never volunteered genetic information, not even after disasters.

"I'm considering it."

Narine had more questions than answers after speaking with Jacob. His parents were unknown, but mage children were rarely born outside a clan. Surely his parents would have had extended family. Was he a natural mage born with that much power? It was possible but not typical. Tadesse was the most powerful natural mage Narine had ever met, and this man's untrained magic felt more powerful than Tadesse's.

"So you came to Addis looking for birth family." She watched the foot traffic around them, noticing how people moved out of their way for the man next to her. He was a sizable presence, and he didn't seem aware of how crowds reacted. "That's understandable."

Jacob shrugged. "It's a secondary goal. I'm mainly here to teach a class at the university on the First Harlem Renaissance."

"Oh cool." Narine stopped on the sidewalk and looked up. "I love that. So you're a history professor?" Poetry, books, music, and art were more interesting than science to Narine. "It seems like most visiting professors are scientists of some sort or another. I've never met one who teaches history."

"I teach literature actually." He smiled. "I was teaching in London last year. Paris the year before that. I wrote a book a few years ago that got just enough attention that it let me land guest professor gigs internationally, so I figured I'd take the opportunity, you know?"

"That's smart. I'd travel like that if I could." *Instead of crawling backward in time to defuse political situations or gather information.* "That's a great opportunity."

Jacob pointed to a café across the street. "Do you know that place?"

"Yes, good macchiato. You want to go there?" Narine gauged traffic, grabbed Jacob's arm, and started across the street, barely missing an electric minibus that roared around the corner.

"Fuck!"

"You get used to it," Narine said. "They'll swerve around you."

"Will they?"

They were standing on the median, waiting for traffic to pass as a crowd gathered next to them, chatting on their assistants and sneaking glances at the two foreigners speaking English.

"Is Seattle a walking city? I know London is. What about Paris? Where else have you lived?" She was jabbering, but she didn't meet many international travelers in the human world. Most of the people she knew were from the order.

"London is definitely good for walking, but you have to take the underground trains a lot. And the river flooding can be a problem certain times of the year. Seattle... not so much." He followed her when she crossed the street. "Bikes. There are lots of zip bikes."

She looked at him with a smile. "I love zip bikes."

"I saw your helmet." He nodded at her backpack where her motorbike helmet was dangling.

"It's parked over by the library. I'll go back for it later." She unwound her scarf as they stepped into the heat of the café. "Do you like pastries? I'm going to order a croissant." She motioned to a table in the corner. "Sit. I'll order this time, and you can get the next."

NARINE WAS STARING OUT THE WINDOW AT THE CLOUDS gathering over the hills.

"I like that you assume there will be a next time."

She blinked and looked back across the table. "What?"

Jacob's full lips curled into a smile. "You said I could get the coffee next time."

"Ah." She shrugged. "I mean, of course I'm going to have coffee with you again. I don't meet many handsome literature professors at the university from Seattle who worked in London and Paris."

He sipped his macchiato. "You make me sound way more interesting than I actually am when you put it that way."

"You're not interesting?"

"There's no way to answer that question without coming off as a bore or a bragger." He sat back and crossed his arms over his chest. "I appreciate the handsome though."

"It's the truth." Narine watched him. He wasn't a thin man; he had some meat on his bones and a broad set to his shoulders. She could tell he was the type who liked a beer and a full meal more than a protein shake before his morning run.

Not that he was fat. He wasn't, but something about him was... generous. He kept his assistant in his ear, but he hadn't brought the lens down once.

"You are handsome," Narine said. "And you don't strike me as a bore or a bragger; I think you're very interesting."

"I think you are too." Jacob smiled. "You're far bolder than most of the people I've met here."

"That's the American side coming out. My father is American. Ethiopians are very warm people, but most tend to be reserved when you first meet them. At least here in Addis. I was more reserved when I was young." At least at work she had been. "Now I'm old and don't care as much, I suppose."

"What was it like growing up here as a foreigner?"

"I'm not a foreigner." She smiled. "I'm an Ethiopian citizen. I suppose I could get American citizenship if I wanted it."

"Does your father live here or in the US?"

"The US. I've been to visit a few times. He lives in Pasadena."

"Southern California is beautiful."

"Crowded though. The weather is pretty good."

Jacob laughed. "Only someone from here would call weather in Southern California 'pretty good.' It's paradise compared to Seattle, especially now that the temperature is creeping down."

She sipped her warm macchiato. "Seattle sounds cold."

"It is." His face glowed when he spoke about his home. "But I love it anyway. I love the rain. I love hiking in the Cascades. There are ferries and skycars that run all over the city. It's beautiful right now. I was just video calling my parents last night."

Professor Jacob Martin had enjoyed a happy and secure childhood. People who did had a settled quality about their face that Narine envied. Despite being separated from his birth family, he knew that people loved him. He had work that he obviously enjoyed. He likely had friends that mattered to him.

Narine should stand up, walk out of the café, and forget that she'd ever met him.

She should tell the elders that she'd been mistaken and the man didn't have power. The minute he tapped into it and cast his first spell, he'd be flung into her world, living in a constantly shifting reality, never being able to depend on anything or anyone. Always living in fear that the ones he loved could be woven out of existence by a single twist of time.

"So?"

She blinked. "So what?"

"What was it like growing up here?"

"Uh…" She frowned. She wasn't used to small talk. Most of the people who knew her already assumed they knew everything about her. "It was good. There are so many things to do in the city, and it's very safe. I think my sister—well, kind of adopted sister—and I were taking our zip bikes all over the city when we were ten or so? It's a great place to grow up."

"And you never felt out of place?"

"Not really. Not like my mother or my grandparents did. Addis is so international now. I have neighbors from all over the world."

"Where do you live?"

"Not far from here." She motioned in the vague direction of her neighborhood. "And you? Did they get you an apartment?"

"A house actually. Well, a house in a compound near Old Airport."

"I have a friend in that neighborhood." She waved for the young man clearing the coffee cups to take theirs and motioned to ask for the bill. "And have you made friends at the university?

"Yes, but I'm still trying to figure out where we've met." Jacob leaned his elbows on the table. "I know we've met."

"You've probably just seen me around the college. My office isn't too far from there."

"And you work for an NGO?"

Narine nodded. "It's the same one my mother worked for. A foundation that studies linguistics." *And messes up people's lives.*

How could she keep him away from the order? She couldn't deny he was powerful; Yosef had brought him up, so clearly something about Jacob was known in the future. Could she convince them the American wasn't suited for order work? She'd never heard of a traveler starting mage rites in his thirties. Other magical disciplines? Yes. But not traveling.

Maybe that would take the elders off the poor man's tail.

"This is the place for it."

Narine frowned. "For what?"

"Linguistic research. With all the languages and cultures—"

"Yes." She nodded. "Yes, we do a lot of... translation. Language and cultural preservation. Targeting the smaller ethnic groups. That kind of thing."

"What's it called?"

"Segel." She cleared her throat. "Uh, the Society for... Ethnography, Geography, and Ethnolinguistics."

"Interesting." He frowned. "I don't think I've ever heard of it. Do you guys attend many conferences or—"

"No. We pride ourselves as being more behind the scenes if you know what I mean. We try to connect directly with decision-makers in different governments." At least that part was true.

"That's good though, right?" He leaned back to let the server clear their coffee cups and plates. "Leaves more money for research."

The waiter put the bill on the table and Narine grabbed it before Jacob could. "I told you, remember? You can get the next one."

He smiled. "So can I get your contact?"

"Complicated." Narine had an assistant, but only Jamila and Genet had her number. She had a contact number with the order and the home AI. She was reluctant to give out her office number to a regular human—even one with power—and the home AI seemed too personal. "I don't have a mobile contact, but I can give you the one to my house. The AI can take a message if I don't answer."

He smiled. "You have an assistant in your ear."

Oh right. Damn it, Jamila. "That's only for work though. I'm not allowed to make personal contacts on it."

"How do you exist without a personal assistant?" He seemed more amused than irritated. "Do you carry cash everywhere?"

"I do." She smiled and picked up her bike helmet. Sometimes she carried gold bullion, but that depended on what time period she was traveling to. "How about you? E-birr only?"

He tapped the assistant in his ear and smiled. "Electronic funds do make international travel pretty seamless." He cleared his throat. "So how does your... Boyfriend? Girlfriend? Partner? Significant other? ...get ahold of you? Should they need to, of course."

Narine smiled and felt a long-neglected buzz of excitement. "Very smooth."

"Yeah? I mean, you barely even noticed that, right?"

"It was very subtle, yes." She wanted to laugh. She wanted to cry. "I just have the house AI and of course my contact number at work, but that's not for personal use. So if my best friend, my goddaughter, or my housekeeper—who are the only ones who live with me" —the corner of her mouth turned up— "if they need to get ahold of me, they just knock on my door."

"Right." Jacob opened his jacket and fumbled with a card on the inside. "I have a card since you can't transfer me your information."

"See?" She took his card and felt her heart break. "Paper still works."

She couldn't keep him away from the order because she wouldn't be able to keep away from him herself. *Damn you, Narine. Damn you.*

"I'll message you from my house AI when I get home," she said. "That way you'll have mine too."

He stood and held out his hand for her to join him. "Promise?"

"I mean, if I don't, it will be very awkward when we inevitably run into each other again, right?"

"There's no way we could avoid each other in a city of only twelve million people."

"A small town really." She grabbed her backpack before she headed toward the door.

Just as they reached the threshold, the skies opened up and the rain fell down with a crash of thunder shaking the air. Narine didn't hesitate.

Like the other patrons in the café, she walked outside, holding out her arms and letting the rain soak her.

It was the third day of Pagume, Rafael's day, and the water from the heavens was holy. She spread her arms, lifted her face, and let the rain baptize her.

*Bless me, Rafael. Forgive me.*

*Forgive me for pulling him into my world.*

She turned her eyes to Jacob, who was standing in the doorway of the café.

He was watching the residents of the city laugh and pull each other into the rain. Others filled empty water bottles or buckets with the rain. It would be used for morning baths, blessing the sick, or adding to injera in the coming weeks.

Narine held out her hand.

He cocked his head. *Really?*

She nodded. *Yes.*

He hesitated for a moment, then secured his backpack, tucked his assistant inside his jacket, and walked into the water.

# CHAPTER 11

*The Island*
*1920*

"You're spending a lot of time with Gideon." Tigist glanced at Narine as they hung damp clothes on a rare dry morning in the middle of July.

"I think because we're both outsiders here, you know?" Narine had been in the village for nearly three months, and she felt as if she was finally getting the rhythm of life. "I don't have any plans for a romance, Tigist."

Tigist smiled and continued hanging clothes. "You know people will gossip."

"Let them." She shrugged. "They have to have something to talk about."

Since her afternoon spinning cotton, women were friendlier when they went to wash clothes by the lake. They smiled instead of stared. The elders were still dismissive, and Narine was beginning to think that the single mission she'd been sent to accomplish—preventing the massacre of a village in the north—was a hopeless cause.

The diviners had told the elders to send a traveler here, to this spot.

Why?

Why not Addis? Why not the seat of power? Narine had been taught not to question the wisdom of the order, but she was starting to wonder if this lost year of her life would have any meaning in the end.

Tigist threw a large sheet over the line. "I was the subject of gossip too. It's normal for new people."

"You're from the north?"

Tigist nodded. "I grew up in Gondar; my father was a hedge. When I first came here? Things felt so different."

"There's a big compound in Gondar, right?"

Tigist nodded. "It was the main seat of power before Menelik founded Addis Ababa. The diviners lived in Bahir Dar, and the order lived in the capital. Both my parents worked there."

"Your mother?" Narine reached for one of the dresses that Tigist had found for her. She had two now. One to wear and one to wash. "Was she powerful too?"

"She is an archivist—a really beautiful weaver, as was her mother. My grandmother worked in Taytu's household, if you can believe that."

"That's very impressive." Empress Taytu was one of the most famous regents in Ethiopian history, wife and counselor to Menelik the Second. A powerful political thinker, she was known as Menelik's enforcer within the court. Taytu had retained very close ties to the Seba Segel.

"But I got my power from my father." Tigist's strong shoulders flexed in the bright morning. Her arms were bare and her hair was loose. Both of them had taken showers that morning and washed their hair. They were hidden behind compound walls, affording them privacy while their hair dried.

"And you?" Tigist asked. "You said you received your power from your mother's side?"

"I did." Narine tossed another *netela* over the drying line. "But she got hers from her father. Power isn't concentrated on the female line in my family."

"It is in some of the families here." Tigist's eyes danced. "It drives some of the elders crazy."

"Really?" Narine smiled. "It shouldn't. The scroll of Karsudan says that the power of the Seba Segel knows neither male nor female. It is granted by the heavens, and since the stars know no human form, power must be respected above sex." It was one of her mother's favorite teachings.

"Oh yes. That is the teaching here too. The teaching" — Tigist met her gaze with a level stare— "not the practice."

"I see."

"Do you?"

Narine nodded. "I wish I could say that all barriers of sex had finally been abolished in my time, but sadly it's not so."

"Well, I can be glad then to be married to a man who thinks of me as his partner and equal, not his servant." Tigist shook her head. "Too many powerful men here still have that human mentality."

Narine thought about Daniel, currently out fishing with the other men in the village, and wondered if he'd be happy to hang clothes and fetch water. She was thinking not, even with all his egalitarian leanings.

But she said nothing. Tigist appeared happy, and this wasn't Narine's home. Her own father had moved back to the United States when it became evident that Narine took after her mother's power and not her father's divination.

Had she taken after her father, her parents would have tried for another child, but as their union was intended to produce a powerful traveler, Narine fulfilled their purpose. As soon as her power was tested, her father had left for the United States.

That left Narine to be raised in a female-dominated compound with little male presence or authority. She wasn't accustomed to men dictating what she did or how she lived her life. It was a foreign idea, but one she knew she'd have to live with for the next nine months even if it left a sour taste in her mouth.

"What about you?" Tigist asked. "I know you can't speak in details about your time, but do you have a husband or a partner?"

"Husband? No. Partner? My mother would say I have too many."

Tigist's eyes went wide. "What does that mean?"

Narine knew casual sex would definitely be taboo, so she laughed. "My mother is very old-fashioned. She would arrange a marriage for me if she could."

"Oh, I see." Tigist nodded. "Yes, most mothers here would do the same. They don't even want their daughters *talking* to boys when they're young. Especially if they have power. They only want them to study until they have some status in the order."

"My mother thinks the same way. But I'm sure she'll start trying to arrange a marriage for me soon."

And Narine would be having none of it.

It wasn't that she didn't like men. She did. Her mother would say she liked them too much. Of course, her mother had little to no sexual appetite as far as Narine could tell. Her closest relationship was with Genet's mother, Aster, and Narine had long ago given up trying to understand their dynamic.

Narine, on the other hand, hungered for the physical. For sensation. She enjoyed the thrill and pursuit of sex, whether it was a quick explosive affair with a visiting mage or a deliciously drawn out flirtation that led to nothing more than lingering looks and stolen kisses. Sometimes the denial of satisfaction was as delicious as giving in.

She reached down to hang a heavy blanket that would come in handy when the rainy season ended and colder weather hit.

Narine was already thinking about a year alone in bed with no one to keep her company. Not ideal, but less ideal was forming any kind of attachment to a man in the past. She'd known of travelers who had love affairs with mages outside their timeline, and it always ended badly.

Narine didn't need the complication.

"Tell me more about Ger." She walked over and took some of Tigist's washing to hang. "He's very handsome. Maybe he's looking for a third wife."

NARINE FOUND HERSELF WRAPPED HEAD TO TOE IN A COTTON gebi and sitting at the base of the ficus tree at dawn. Her back rested against a large protruding root, and her fishing line dangled in the water as the aching love and hate of silence battered her mind.

She didn't know what to do with the quiet of the island. It was too slow. Too deliberate. Too empty. Life was busy and exhausting, but Narine felt like an algorithm starved for data.

Not enough people.

Not enough noise.

Not enough life.

There was no traffic she could weave through, no chattering news at the corner market stall, no electric billboards flashing news and entertainment gossip, and no digital assistant in her ear, reminding her of appointments, meetings, and where the traffic was snarled on Bole Road.

To make up for the lack of traffic, Narine focused on the riotous clamor of the birds flying over the lake. Swarms of them swung down to feed on insects while a pair of fish eagles hunted in the distance. There were egrets wading along the shore and pygmy kingfishers clutching the reeds that grew high on the edge of the water.

Egyptian geese honked in the distance, and a massive pod of white pelicans floated in the shallows, scooting to the right, then the left as they fished.

She heard a splash in the water to her left and started. She set her fishing pole into the twisting roots by her feet and wrapped her gebi closer around her as she turned to see who it was. Probably village boys getting in a quick morning swim before the day began.

Gideon surfaced and he quickly swiped a hand over his face, clearing the water from his eyes before he stood and found his feet. Narine couldn't look away from his defined shoulders, arms, and stomach. Underneath his formal clothes, the Kenyan doctor was a beautiful man. His skin was medium brown and glowed with red undertones in the dawn sunlight; shining drops of water beaded on his broad shoulders.

He walked to the edge of the lake and grabbed a thick bar of soap, then proceeded to lather his body, the water riding low on his hips and just barely protecting his modesty.

Narine tore her eyes away and lifted her gebi to hide her face. There was no way to leave her perch in the ficus roots without being extremely visible, so her best bet was just to hide her eyes, look the other direction, and pray that Gideon didn't notice the figure wrapped in bright white cotton.

"Narine?"

Yeah, that was never going to work.

She poked her head out. "Sorry. I was fishing."

He immediately switched to English. "Did you——?"

"I'm not looking." *Anymore.* "If you want to stay in the water, I can leave."

"It's fine." He dipped his head back, washed the soap off, then climbed out of the water. "I'm a doctor; I'm not particular about modesty."

*Well, if you don't care...* Narine peeked over her wrap and watched him climb out of the water. His legs were long, lean, and muscled. His butt was tight and round. His penis was impressive, especially considering he'd just been in the lake.

She tried not to stare, but it was difficult. It had been months since she'd taken a lover. Gideon was an attractive man, and she wasn't blind.

He wrapped a towel around his waist, and the corner of his frustratingly impassive mouth turned up. "Did you get a good look?"

"It's only fair. You saw me naked."

"Ah yes, the seductive beauty of the feverish malaria patient." His expression was droll. "I was transfixed by your heat rash."

"It's clearing up nicely, thank you for asking."

He broke into a smile. "How is your life, Narine?"

"Honestly?"

"I am not usually interested in polite small talk."

"My memory seems to be more stable, so thank you for that." She stared out at the lake while Gideon dressed. "I'm very bored."

"Yes, the island must be very quiet to you."

She poked her head up again. "You're not offended?"

He frowned. "Narine, I'm from Nairobi. You think I feel at home here? It's a tiny village on a small island in a huge lake. There are more hippos than people."

Narine shuddered. "Don't remind me."

"There's no modern plumbing. No cars. No music clubs or bars." He shrugged. "I don't know what else you're used to, but I can assume those things."

"Yes." She put her head in her hands. "Can you believe that I miss traffic?"

He smiled a little. "Can you believe I miss public houses?"

"Everyone likes a good pub, Gideon."

"So many interesting injuries," he mused. "I once repaired

a knife wound that was in the shape of a lightning bolt. Two dozen stitches."

"I can't relate any interesting injuries, but I miss..." She sighed. "I just miss home, I guess. I never know what to expect, but it's more familiar than this. And I'm a traveler. I'm used to going places where I'm uncomfortable. You're not precious about modesty? I'm not precious about cultural differences. When I travel, I have to be ready for anything."

Gideon finished buttoning his shirt and walked over to sit on the root next to her. "When did you start?"

"Traveling? I was fourteen." Gideon didn't need to know this was her first jump on her own. He'd probably make fun of her.

He stared. "You were a child."

"A child who was raised by travelers. The magic is as natural to me as breathing." She cleared her throat. "When I was young, I always went with my mother or my teacher."

"Hmm."

"But being here. Being... stuck." She shook her head. "I hate it."

"That all sounds normal to me." He frowned. "Have you spoken to Tigist about this? You know she's not from the village either."

"I don't want to offend her. I don't want her to think she's a bad hostess or that I'm unhappy in her home."

"But you don't worry about offending me?" His dark brown eyes were amused.

"I don't think you get offended by much."

"I am offended by everything." He stood, braced one arm on a low-hanging branch of the ficus, and looked out over the lake. "I am offended by the world as it is. So I suppose that makes any small offense you could offer very minor in comparison."

Narine didn't know what to say to that. She sensed a well

of anger in Gideon that she couldn't explain and she didn't want to examine too closely.

He glanced at her from the side. "The time will pass quickly. Eight more months now? It will pass in the blink of an eye."

IT WAS ONE THING TO OFFER ADVICE TO A MAGE COUNCIL, then leave and find the result of your effort in archival records in the future. It was quite another to be in the village when the hedges returned and told the elders that the crown prince hadn't given them an audience.

"What?" Narine dropped the grinding stone in her hand. "He wouldn't even speak to them?"

Tigist leaned on the doorpost and shook her head. "I told you, our influence is with the empress, not the crown prince. He's a modernist."

"But he has to understand..." She fisted a hand in her hair, tugging on the strands hard enough that she made her head ache. "There are things that cannot be changed. Tragedies that we have to live with because... we don't know."

"And probably we will never know the reason." Tigist dragged a stool over and sat next to her.

Narine felt young and angry and impotent. "I am not telling you anything you don't know already."

Tigist's eyes were kind. "We all struggle with this. We are bound in the order to help humanity, but there are limits to what we can change."

"But this... This can be changed! The event is not a tasary. The diviners saw that changing this event wouldn't lead to any negative results in the overall timeline. The advice I gave them could prevent..." She rubbed her temple. "I can't tell you anything more."

"I promise I will send a letter to my father and my mother.

Both of them have relationships within Empress Zewditu's household. If there is a chance we can grab the ear of the prince, we must. The Seba Segel has advised the royal family of Ethiopia for centuries, and we will do everything in our power to protect them now." She patted Narine's knee. "Don't give up. No treaty has been finalized yet."

Tigist rose and left Narine to grinding while she called for the serving girl to fetch more water for the wash. There was a fire burning in the middle of the compound and a clay jar of heated water was already steaming.

It was a harsh reminder that while world events happened in the far distance, in this reality, Narine was grinding barley.

*What is the point of you?*

Gideon's words accused her while at the same time, Narine battled the arrogance of knowledge.

She knew that the crown wouldn't last the century and that modern democracy was coming for the ancient kingdom of Ethiopia. The elders here didn't know.

She knew it was imperative that the Seba Segel gained the ear of the future emperor if they were to have any sway over events that would eventually engulf the world in war. The elders didn't know.

She knew.

They didn't know anything.

*The river of time humbles the proud and lifts the humble.* Narine could almost hear her mother whisper in her ear. *Time is the most fluid medium in the universe, and humans are its most replaceable elements.*

Time would flow as it wanted, and nothing—not a failed traveler, not a bout of malaria, and not the stubbornness of a prince—would stop its inevitable flow. Kingdoms would rise. Others would fall. Territory would be conquered and victors would exploit the spoils of war.

Thus it had been.

So it always would be.

*The Tibeb reveals the truth. Everything is pattern.*

She closed her eyes and picked up the grinding stone again. Smack, push, scrape, repeat. The grit from the barley and the stone filled the air and caught in her eyelashes. She blinked and watched the dust and flour floating in a beam of light that angled from a high window.

*The patterns of time are like the currents of the ocean. We float on them, but we do not control them.*

In the distance, Narine heard chanting from the church. The priests were getting ready for the service of Medhane Alem, and they'd been singing all day. Their voices faded in the distance, snatched by the wind, and in their place the voice of the serving girl tending the fire rose, her clear song filling the afternoon air.

# CHAPTER 12

*Addis Ababa*
*2071*

N arine was officially tired of the cold baths.

It was the fourth day of Pagume, and while usually she'd be able to relax and enjoy the steady days of the thirteenth month, this year everything had been thrown into chaos. She'd lost Abdi, received an unwelcome message from the past, and been forced to lure an unsuspecting professor into the twisted world that was her reality.

She let out a rough breath when the water Genet was pouring over her head reached the small of her back. A shock of memory hit her.

Pain shooting up her spine.

*"You can do this, Narine!"*

*Her throat was raw from crying.*

"Narine?"

She opened her eyes and Gelile was staring at her. "Akeste?"

She wiped her face, grateful for the water that hid the tears. "Your turn, baby." She stood and reached for the warm wrap that Samira held out, then took her place beside Genet, speaking the prayers of her mother, her grandfather, and countless ancestors as Genet spoke the blessings in Amharic.

*You can do this, Narine.*

"I can't do this." Narine sat at the kitchen table and drank a cup of tea. The sky was clear again, but the air was chilly. "This man has a good life, Geni."

"But the order already knows about him." Genet patted Samira on the shoulder after checking on the stew she was heating for breakfast. She grabbed a large cup of tea and sat across from Narine. "That means that he's meant to be found by the Seba Segel. You can ease that transition or leave him alone and confused."

"He has friends. He has family. Parents. Maybe a family here too. If he's not from mage blood——"

"But think, Narine. He probably is. His parents probably wanted to raise him in the order but..." She shrugged. "Something happened."

Narine bit her lip. "I hadn't thought about that."

"By bringing him in, you may be doing exactly what his parents would have wanted. And finding the order may be his only chance to find his birth family."

"Fuck." She whispered it in English because Genet didn't have a casual attitude to profanity around the girls. "This poor guy. He buzzed me last night."

"On the house number?"

"Yes."

Genet raised an eyebrow. "And you answered?"

"I sent a message back. I didn't feel like talking."

"Is he handsome?"

Narine threw up her hands. "Why do people keep asking me that?"

Genet smiled. "You've got kind of a… look."

"So?"

"You've cut yourself off from relationships for years now. You changed after that jump. It's not healthy to be so alone."

Genet knew Narine had spent a year in the past and come back changed. She didn't know everything, but she knew that and she wasn't wrong.

Narine shrugged. "I have my reasons."

"I know you do, but I'm your sister." Genet sipped her tea. "I still get to give you a hard time."

Narine smiled. "Fine."

"So is he attractive?"

She rolled her eyes. "I… suppose."

"That's a yes!" Genet's smile turned into a grin. "Maybe this could be fun."

"There are reasons for my celibacy." The dull pain that lived in her heart pulsed, just a little. "I like him, Geni. I don't want this life for him."

Genet sighed. She had no illusions about the order that Narine served. "They're going to pull him in whether you want it for him or not. Tell him the truth and let things fall where they fall. Sooner is better. Take him to the museum."

"Why?"

"Because he's not going to believe you at first."

Narine pursed her lips. "He's not a scientist."

"But he is an American. In my experience, they're not very keen to believe in magic."

"I don't want to be doing this." She threw up her hands. "Any of this. There are people who do this, and I am not one of them! I want to be helping Tadesse bring Abdi back. He hasn't given me any progress updates, and I'm worried the elders are telling him not to tell me anything about the investigation. And why would that be? What do they know that I don't? All of this feels very…"

Genet frowned. "What?"

"Targeted. Abdi was *my* mentor, but they've cut me out of investigating what happened. Tade usually collaborates with me, but he's avoiding me."

"Narine, it's only been three days since all this happened. Only two since he was given the assignment. Maybe Tade hasn't made any progress yet."

"If we don't know where the warp occurred by the new year, the chances of reversing it—"

She stopped herself. Tasary were fixed points. Once they were altered, they could never be set back in place unless you broke the Pagume rules *again*. Aida said the only option was to mitigate the warp that had occurred and make the damage less.

Genet frowned. "It can be reversed?"

"No." Narine rubbed her temple. "No, but we can lessen the damage. We can try to correct things. That's what they did after the Second Mage War."

Dammit, she wanted Abdi back. He was the expert, the one who knew everything; he was also the only one who could tell her .how to deal with the letter or what it might even mean. What this warp meant and why anyone would risk death to change a traveler's birth.

Genet's eyes were kind. "In all your years in the order, have you ever seen someone brought back who was woven out?"

"Yes." Not often. "It's possible. Maybe not likely, but…."

Genet nodded. "Possible."

"Yeah."

"Has any other change happened?"

Narine shook her head. "As far as I can tell, the only change to the timeline was Abdi's disappearance."

"That's strange, isn't it?" Genet narrowed her eyes.

"All of this is strange."

"But why risk a taboo as strict as the prohibition of Pagume to remove one person from the timeline?"

Narine shrugged. "I can't figure it out."

"There has to be more."

"I agree, but I can't see it yet."

"I remember what your mother always said about traveling." Genet sipped her tea and stared out the window. "A tiny ripple can turn into a wave."

"That's why I need to talk to Tade."

"I understand that, but today you need to tell your professor that life as he knows it is about to change. I have a feeling that the longer you put that off, the worse his reaction is going to be."

She stuck her assistant in her ear before she left the house and maneuvered her zip bike through the morning market, dodging mechanized laundry deliveries and bread carts, waving to her neighbor having coffee at the stand near the main road.

She tapped her assistant. "Ana, wake up."

A soothing voice with a faint Chinese accent sounded in her ear. "Good morning, Narine. Today is Friday, September ninth. You are located in Addis Ababa, and the weather today calls for clear skies and a high temperature of seventy-one degrees Fahrenheit. It looks like you're headed to work. Would you like traffic conditions?"

She wanted to swing by the order and check on Tadesse before she tracked down Jacob.

"No." Traffic was what it was. It wouldn't be too bad on a Friday during Pagume.

"Would you like to hear your stored messages?"

Dear God in heaven, no. "I need you to contact Jamila."

"Do you want to contact Jamila at her house or on her mobile assistant?"

"Mobile assistant please." There was no way Jamila would

be at home at this hour. She was probably on the air transport from Harar with her khat.

"Contacting Jamila Sahid."

A drift of classical music played in her ear until she heard a small chime and Jamila answered. "You better not be contacting me because you're canceling the holidays. Where is your face?"

"Not all of us keep our lenses down all the time." She lifted her right foot and merged into traffic on her bike.

"By the memory of my grandmother, Narine, why are you such a Luddite?"

"You know the answer to that. I can't talk long, I just wanted to let you know I am keeping the spy on me should you or your mother need to contact me."

"Are you worried about the letter? What else is going on?"

Narine couldn't give her specifics. "Just... if anything strange happens, call me please."

"You sound strange."

"It's a strange week. I have to go."

"I'll be at the market later if you have time."

"Bye." She tapped on her ear and ended the conversation. "Ana, silent mode."

"Understood."

The assistant went silent, but Narine knew it was still tracking her as she swung around the traffic circle and headed toward the university.

She turned in to the gates of the order only a moment later, her ID card already in her hand for the uptight guard Mesfin.

He examined her credentials as if he hadn't seen her the day before. "Good morning, Sister Narine."

"Brother Mesfin. I see that the stick is still firmly implanted in your—"

"Narine!"

She turned toward the shout as Mesfin's eyebrow went up. Elder Kebret was striding toward her.

"A word in my office," he snapped.

She nodded at the elder, then turned to take her ID card from Mesfin, who could barely suppress his smile.

"I see you." She pointed at his face. "That's an expression, and I'm fairly sure there's a rule against hedges having expressions. Especially amused ones."

The corner of his mouth twitched. "Have a productive day, Sister Narine. I wouldn't want to keep you from your meeting with idle conversation."

"That was almost a smile," she whispered. "That means I'm winning."

She shoved her ID card back in her jacket pocket and walked past Njeri with a wink. She made her way to the end of the hall where the hedges had their offices, past the elder's secretary, and into his office.

"Close the door."

Narine did so, keeping her gaze on Kebret.

"You haven't brought the American in yet."

Narine took a seat even though Kebret was standing at his desk. "No, not yet."

"Do you have a problem with your assignment?"

"Of course not. I am a servant of the Seba Segel. I simply want to make the introduction to our ancient order in the most positive way possible to ease the transition of this new mage into our company."

Kebret narrowed his eyes. "Was it your mother?"

Narine kept her expression blank. "I don't know what you mean."

"Was she the one who taught you how to be so apparently respectful even when you chafe at proper authority?"

Was it her mother? In a way. Narine had perfected the art of subversive compliance in her mother's house. "In what way have I shown disrespect, my elder? Tell me and I will correct it."

"Get out of here. Just remember, your family name can't protect you forever. The memory of Anahid Khoren will fade in time."

Narine stood. "If there is anything else I can assist the elder council with, please make sure to contact my office."

She walked out of Kebret's office, through the courtyard, and back toward the traveler's offices within the order.

The flashing light on her desk told her messages were being stored. She tapped on the light, and a talking head popped out of the machine.

"Narine!" A friendly voice with a German accent greeted her. "It's Cyril Ranulf from Berlin. There's been... I've heard some rumors about changes happening this week, and I may have some information for you."

Narine glanced at the time.

"Call me when you can, and if I don't speak to you before the New Year, have a wonderful holiday, okay?"

The face disappeared, and Narine's mind was racing.

Berlin? What was happening in Berlin?

NARINE SNEAKED DOWN TO THE SECOND BASEMENT LEVEL where the early twentieth-century Tibeb was kept. She spotted Tade and Aida at a library table with a four-meter bolt of weaving spread out.

She approached the Tibeb with reverence, knowing the power it took to create it and the wisdom it contained. Within the Tibeb, births and deaths were recorded, the diviners' predictions and the travelers' journeys were marked. Wars and conflicts, celebrations and victories, all were recorded in the intricate threadwork that only the archivists were trained to interpret.

She sat at the end of the table and kept her hands away from the Tibeb. "Tell me you've found something please."

Aida looked up with a small frown. "We found a conflict in South Africa that could likely be avoided with mage intervention and we've made a note of it for Tadesse to bring to the elders, but as far as Abdi's birth, we've found no visible warps in the year he was born."

"He was born in the Bale region," Narine said. "I'm not sure exactly where."

Tadesse nodded. "We've looked, but nothing was noted by the archivists at the time. The birth of a traveler is always noted, Narine. In this Tibeb, Abdi was never born."

How was it possible?

"Keep going back and maybe check a few years ahead too," Narine said. "Maybe his birth was delayed somehow. Maybe more was going on than we realized. Maybe I had his age wrong."

Aida cast pitying eyes in her direction. "Narine—"

"Check again." The minute Pagume passed, she was going back to Abdi's birth year and going to Bale. Something had happened to her mentor. Someone had considered him a threat so insurmountable they'd kept him from being born.

"Tade, can I talk to you?"

Tadesse said something quiet to Aida, then walked over to join Narine by the stairs.

"Hey," he said. "I know you're frustrated, but—"

"Are you getting pushback from Kebret?"

He frowned. "I mean, a little bit but nothing much. He thinks this isn't as big a deal as we're making it."

"And doesn't that seem strange to you?" she whispered. "Kebret is usually manic about the rules and order protocol. He's nearly fanatical; it used to drive my mother crazy."

"There's no proof your mother is dead."

"As far as I'm concerned, she's lost to the timeline. I don't have a lot of hope on that front, and that's not the point. The point is that everyone should be as freaked out about this as we are, but no one seems to be taking it seriously. There should be swarms of archivists in this room, every one of them looking at the Tibeb to find that warp. A change was made to the timeline in Pagume, an act that has led to two different mage wars—"

"Those wars were worldwide though." Tade spread his hands. "Those were time breeches that were felt all over the world. This one was only felt on this continent and in Arabia."

"I got a message from Cyril in Berlin."

Tadesse shook his head. "Cyril?"

"Redheaded traveler. Not from a big house. Great football player."

"Oh!" Tadesse's eyes lit up. "He visited a couple of years ago for that conference."

"He left me a message. Didn't say much but asked for a callback."

"So something is happening in Berlin too?"

"I don't know, but maybe whoever did this is smarter than the other mages who have tried. Maybe they're starting small. They're trying things out. Testing the waters. And if they can get away with traveling this time, making this change, they'll keep going. They'll figure out a way to keep doing this until they accomplish…"

Tadesse's eyes were wide. "What? What do you think their aim is?"

What was the goal?

"I don't know." The letter hiding in her desk tickled the back of her brain. "Something we're not seeing yet."

*This cannot continue.*

What couldn't continue?

She knew who had written the note, but not when or why, and she couldn't answer any of those questions until after the thirteenth month.

"Where is Yosef?" Narine asked. "I need to speak to him."

155

She needed to find out what he knew about this breech. He was the one who'd told her there was a warp. How had he known and when had he felt it? The mysterious traveler seemed to come and go as he pleased, dipping into and out of their time over the past year with no clear directive, dropping cryptic clues that had driven Abdi up the wall.

Until Abdi wasn't there.

"Yosef disappeared sometime last night. He didn't use the travelers' pool, but he's not in the compound."

"Damn it." And Narine couldn't travel forward even after Pagume was over. Travel to the future was possible, but it was ridiculously risky, which was why it was forbidden.

The past was known.

The future hadn't been written.

"Narine, just give me a little more time. Give *us* a little more time. Aida and I have only been looking for a couple of days. We will find the warp."

"You're right." Narine patted his arm. "I'm being impatient, and I'm sorry."

Aida piped up from across the room. "I can hear you. If you're really concerned about keeping those sneaky travelers' secrets, just letting you know my ears are very good."

Narine smiled.

"What are you doing right now?" Tade lowered his voice. "I know you're not assigned to this, but Aida and I could use your help."

Narine raised an eyebrow. "And you're willing to risk the elders' anger by including me?"

"We both know that you'd have more luck giving Aida clues where to look. You know Abdi's life better. They only did this because of… you know."

The incident.

Narine sighed. "Unfortunately, Elder Kebret is already asking about the American and why I haven't brought him in yet. I have to meet with Jacob Martin and turn his life upside down."

"Right." Tadesse shook his head. "We'll keep looking."

Aida spoke again. "There are a few archivists I can bring in if I need the help, Narine. We'll find the warp. Go do what you need to do for the elders."

"Good luck," Tade said. "I don't envy you one bit."

# CHAPTER 13

*The Island*
*1920*

N arine heard the banging on the gate from her bed. It was night and clouds drifted across a full moon. The predawn air was heavy with the scent of rain.

Daniel must have answered the banging because Narine heard his voice along with another low male voice urgently exchanging words. A few moments later, someone tapped on her door.

Narine wrapped a heavy wool blanket around her shoulders and rose from her bed. She walked to the door and opened it to see Gideon on the other side.

"What time is it?" She rubbed her eyes.

"Tigist mentioned in a meeting that you had medical experience." His face was grim.

"Not much. All travelers have to take basic—"

"It's more than most people here. Can you come?"

Narine blinked. "Gideon, you're far better trained than I am. I don't know anything you don't about treating sick people."

"Can you *assist* me? My regular nurse is visiting her mother off the island, and the midwife in the village just sent a boy to fetch me because a woman is dying. Can you assist me, Narine?"

She felt a twisting discomfort in her gut, but she nodded. "I'll do what I can."

"That's all I ask." He pulled the door shut, and Narine ran to her room to get dressed. She walked out to the yard moments later to join Gideon, who was talking with Tigist near the gate.

When he saw her, he opened the gate and departed, not waiting for Narine to catch up. Tigist handed her a bundle that she grabbed before following Gideon out the gate.

Narine was nearly running after him so she didn't get lost. She was thankful for the full moon, but she still tripped over and over again as she rushed to keep up with the doctor.

He took the footpath along the ridge of the hill and then down to the other side of the island where the human village was situated past the church. He walked down through narrow streets, past rocky outcroppings and arched acacia trees until he came to an isolated house on the edge of the town.

A group of men were sitting outside the house around a low fire. There was a quiet murmur of conversation from the men, but from inside the house, there came no sound. No cries, no moans of pain. Nothing.

Gideon didn't stop to speak to anyone, but he ducked under the low doorway and Narine followed him.

She smelled the blood immediately. There was a woman lying on the floor, her back leaning against a stack of baskets and some blankets, angled to allow her to give birth. She was pale and her eyes were staring at the wall. Another young woman sat at her side, holding her hand and wiping the sweat from her forehead.

A midwife was holding a baby wrapped snugly in a swaddling cloth. "The child is healthy, but she wouldn't stop bleed-ing." The midwife shook her head. "I told her husband to call the priests."

"How long has she been bleeding?" Gideon was angry. "You're just sending for me now?"

He crouched down by the woman, his knee dipping into a bloody cloth that lay at her side. More blood-soaked cloths were between her legs, and Narine could think of nothing to do except kneel on the woman's other side. She gripped the woman's limp hand and whispered an incantation her mother had taught her for healing.

*It won't work.*

Her magic was gone, but the incantation came anyway.

"I'm going to give her an injection that might help with the bleeding." Gideon tossed up the woman's dress, revealing a stomach that still appeared pregnant. "Did the afterbirth deliver?"

"Partly." The midwife was rocking the baby, shaking her head. "She was a rebellious girl."

Gideon nearly shouted at her. "That has nothing to do with her medical condition!" He withdrew a long needle and syringe from his bag and swabbed the woman's belly.

His tone might have been angry, but his hands were gentle. He glanced at Narine and spoke in English. "Check her pulse."

She didn't have a watch to time it, so Narine put her fingers at the woman's wrist, then another at her own neck to compare. "I can feel it, but it's slow."

"If I'd been able to give her this injection earlier, it would have helped more, but I'll do what I can." His hand smoothed the woman's hair back from her forehead, and he glanced at the young woman at the mother's side. "Auntie," he said in halting Amharic, "you will need to find a nurse for the baby. Your sister is very sick."

*Your sister is dying.*

Narine didn't say it, but it was nearly impossible to imagine this woman could survive. Her eyes were open, but as the needle went into her womb, she didn't even flinch.

The woman beside Narine scrambled to her feet and walked out, whispering something to the midwife about the wet nurse.

"Boil some water," Gideon said. "I'm going to try to push the rest of the placenta out; then we'll try to bathe her womb."

"Bathe it?"

"Boiled hot water. Go." He withdrew the needle and started to gently press on the woman's abdomen. He muttered something in a language Narine didn't recognize.

She went outside to boil some water, hoping it would be enough to save the woman's life.

It was not.

"She would have lived if they called me earlier." Gideon stared at the water as the sky turned from deep blue to a lighter azure touched by the blush of dawn.

They'd spent two hours with the woman before she let out a final breath and closed her eyes. Gideon had tried his injection, then bathing the woman's uterus with hot water douches intended to make the organ contract.

They succeeded in delivering the last of the placenta and the bleeding slowed, but it never stopped. Eventually the blood looked more black than red. The woman's heart stuttered, then stopped.

"You did everything you could do." Narine sat on the roots of the ficus and stared over the water. The cries of the woman's sister had been low and aching. The husband was silent, staring at the small child who had taken his wife. "Childbirth is dangerous."

"The lack of education is appalling," Gideon spat out. "I've told the midwife to bring women to the clinic, but she ignores me."

"Most women want to be at home." Genet had just given birth at home. Of course, Narine's niece had been born under the supervision of a midwife who was connected to the hospital via voice assistant and AI. If something had gone wrong, emergency air transport could have had her at a hospital in minutes.

"That's backward thinking." Gideon was glaring at the horizon. "Backward rural thinking that leads to death and disease. These people have no concept—"

"These people?" Narine raised an eyebrow.

"You know what I mean," he muttered. "Country people. Uneducated people. People who don't see the value in education or progress or civilized—"

"Whose progress? Whose civilization?" She raised an eyebrow when he shot an angry look at her. "I'm not saying you're wrong. They should have called you sooner. But to make one woman's arrogance a… judgment against an entire village is wrong. She might have died in a hospital too. She might have died of something completely different in a hospital because of a superbug or a careless physician or malpractice."

He narrowed his eyes. "You're speaking of the future. You said you were only going to tell me things about your personal life."

Narine blinked. "I'm speaking very generally. We don't have everything in the future figured out. Women still die giving birth. It's rare, but it happens. And in the process of… homogenizing knowledge around the world, we've lost things too. Traditional cures that might still be effective or adapted to modern use. Just because something is modern doesn't mean it's better."

"Says the woman who is desperate to leave this backward time."

She thought about grinding grain while powerful men decided the fate of the world. "Would you want to be a woman in this time?"

"Would you want to be a natural-born mage in this order with no family connections? Stuck in a backward village because you angered a powerful idiot?"

"Is that my fault or your own? Your arrogance—"

"Has kept me from withering in a world that hates me."

Narine didn't know how to respond to that.

"And I have good reason to be arrogant. Have you performed surgery? Have you ever had to prove yourself to a room full of people convinced you're inferior because of the color of your skin? Then had to go back to an order that considers you inferior because you weren't born into the happy accident of an aristocratic house? I had to be twice as good as any of my classmates. Three times as superior as other alchemists. And I still ended up here."

Narine stood and faced him. "I don't envy you those experiences or the racism you were forced to endure, but think of who you're insulting when you judge an entire group of people by one woman's stubbornness."

His eyes bored into her, swinging between anger and sadness. Narine saw the soul-deep frustration. And the pain.

"I'm sorry, Gideon." Narine blinked back tears. "I'm sorry that Haben died."

"Haben?"

"That was her name. Haben. She named her baby Biruk before she passed."

He stood over her, his body tense and his hands shaking. Narine put her arms around his waist and hugged him. Hard.

His shoulders relaxed, and he brought his arms around her, returning her embrace. She felt his racing heart calm, and his arms held her tightly as she rubbed soothing circles on his back.

He was angry because he cared. He was angry because the world didn't value Haben's life the same way that he did. He was angry for good reasons, and Narine admired his passion.

Gideon sighed and rested his cheek on the top of Narine's head. "Thank you for assisting me."

"I didn't do much."

"You did what you could, and you remained calm and caring with her family. That helps more than you know."

"Her sister was heartbroken; I think they were very close. At least she'll be there to raise the baby."

"The father should raise his child."

"That father was in shock. And he was young." Narine patted Gideon's back. "The village will come together. That's what villages do."

His arms relaxed but stayed around Narine, and the embrace that had been intended to comfort slowly became something... more.

Gideon's fingers slid over her spine, and his thumb brushed the sensitive skin at the small of her back. Narine shivered and he pulled back, searching for her eyes. He cocked his head, watching her.

Narine felt exposed, far more naked than Gideon had been when he'd bathed in the lake the morning she saw him. His eyes pierced her armor, leaving her heart racing and her body hungry.

She wanted him. There was no getting around the fact. He was passionate and intense. He was alive in a way that drew Narine like a moth to a flame.

Gideon leaned down and pressed his mouth to hers. Narine let out a soft sigh, and he took the kiss deeper, delving in to taste her mouth. His arms tightened and lifted her against his body.

He was so strong.

The firm muscles of his chest pressed against her breasts and she clung to him, throwing her arms around his shoulders as he devoured her mouth in a devastating kiss that left her head swimming and her body on fire.

His hands were firm on her backside, bringing her hips firmly against his. He lifted her and pressed her against the trunk of the tree, caging her with his arms.

She pulled her mouth away with a gasp. "Gideon."

He pulled back, his mouth still open and his eyes wide. "This is a mistake."

Narine shook her head and he dropped her. She landed on her feet, nearly falling over as he backed away.

Gideon looked away, opened his mouth, then closed it.

Without another word, he walked to his house, leaving Narine breathless and alone.

DAYS TURNED INTO WEEKS. NARINE HAD BEEN IN THE VILLAGE for months, and the heavy rains were still pouring down. The footpaths turned to mud, and the men kept close to the shore when they cast their lines, wary of the lightning that struck the water during storms.

Narine stayed in her room most days, cooking porridge in the mornings, keeping the house as clean as the constant mud allowed, and reading whatever she could find to read. She found old newspapers in Amharic, some Italian books in the order's library, and a solid collection of medical journals in English that were probably Gideon's.

She didn't see the alchemist, who had isolated himself at the clinic since he was dealing with two children who'd contracted what was probably pneumonia a week before.

She hadn't told Tigist about the kiss or about what had happened after the woman in the village died. Her friend was saddened by the death but not shocked. Women died in child-birth. Children died of fevers.

Even within the Seba Segel, this was the reality of life. Tigist and Daniel's own child had passed the year before. They didn't speak of it; the baby was with her ancestors in the heavens, and her soul would be reborn one day if the stars aligned to bring her back.

Among the mages—even those who followed different human faiths—it was a common belief that souls taken early from the river of life might be returned one day if they hadn't fulfilled their potential. No soul was ever destroyed, even if it was woven out of the timeline.

It was the one thing that comforted Narine when she'd lost friends to time's whim. The soul that she cared about wasn't gone, and it might have even been reborn in another she would meet someday.

"Narine?" She heard Tigist's voice in the courtyard. "Are you awake?"

She'd been nodding off while she paged through old news-papers, but her friend's voice woke her up. "Come in. I'm awake."

Tigist opened the door and popped her head in. She looked excited. "I have good news."

"Oh?" Narine straightened and rubbed her eyes. The door brought in cold air, and she tucked her blanket closer around her body. "What is it?"

Tigist brought over a stuffed leather pillow and sat next to Narine's bed. "Letters just arrived from Addis; my mother wrote me." She pulled a folded paper from her woolen wrap. "She's an archivist, remember?"

"I remember." Narine roused herself when she realized the news must have been about the treaty and not village or order gossip.

"I wrote to her when you first arrived, and she was disap-pointed when she heard that the elders here had not received an audience with the crown prince."

"I have a feeling they didn't push for one though either."

Tigist nodded. "I think you're probably correct. But my mother writes to me that she has spoken directly to the empress, who has convinced her nephew to give my mother an audience. My mother is a weaver but is also a very learned woman who has traveled and speaks multiple languages. Her mother worked in Taytu's household, remember?"

"I remember." Narine sat up. "What does that mean? What are you trying to say?"

"Empress Zewditu convinced her nephew that it would be wise for him to hear my mother before the negotiations with the British and Italian parties continue." Tigist looked up from the letter. "She would like to hear the instructions from your elder council directly."

Narine scrambled to sit up. "She wants to hear from me directly? Am I going to Addis?"

"It would be faster to send Daniel." Tigist glanced at her. "You likely wouldn't travel as quickly as he could go on his own. But if you can write her a letter this afternoon, Daniel could leave in the morning."

"What have the elders here said?" Narine thought of Abdi's many lessons; she was cautious about stepping on toes. She also had to live here for many more months.

Tigist shrugged. "Do I need to inform the council if I send a message to my mother?" Her eyes were dancing. "My correspondence—and whatever that correspondence includes—is no business of the council's."

Narine threw her arms around Tigist. "Stellar!"

Tigist laughed a little. "What?"

"Never mind." Narine scrambled out of bed. "Let me find some paper. I'll get the letter written right now." She looked at Tigist. "How long will it take Daniel—?"

"With the rain, it will take him at least four days, but my

mother writes that her meeting with the prince isn't for another week, so the message should make it to her in time."

Narine walked over to Tigist and gripped both her hands. "Thank you."

Tigist squeezed Narine's hands back. "I know you're frustrated here. I know that you feel like your world right now is very small. But I haven't forgotten you, and neither have the stars. All this has happened for a reason, Sister. Never forget that."

# CHAPTER 14

T he Modern Museum was poorly named, because though the mode of exhibits ranged from immersive interactive displays to 3D videos to holograms, the subject matter was Ethiopian history and culture. The museum was a companion to the Ethnographic Museum that had long been curated by the university and was now housed in a new building not far from Unity Park and the Museum of Science and Technology.

Tour groups and families with children crowded the interactive displays, but Narine and Jacob bypassed them to visit the Ethnographic Gallery where a series of moving portraits by Yatreda, a prominent artists' collective, was displayed.

"Wow, these are beautiful." Jacob admired the moving photographs, some of which had been adapted into three-dimensional holographs and digital sculpture. "These are recreations?"

Narine nodded and wound through the display. "Menelik and Taytu. King Lalibela. The Queen of Sheba. Tewodros and his family. The royal guards and of course..." Narine came to stop at the digital sculpture of a beautiful, fierce woman holding a torch. "Yodit."

Jacob came to stand next to her. "She destroyed the Aksumite kingdom, right?"

"That's what the legends say." Narine turned to him and smiled. "Don't piss off Ethiopian women. A lesson for all time."

Jacob smiled and nodded down the hall. "Should we keep going?"

"Let's." The digital sculpture she wanted to show him was at the end of the hall, a collection of four figures that moved and looked around in simulated firelight, standing on a stone floor and offering homage to a toddler who stood with his arms outstretched in blessing.

Wrapped in priestly white garments, one knelt next to a glowing chest of gold, another held out a shimmering orb filled with myrrh resin, and still another offered a carved wooden chest filled with frankincense.

"What is this?"

"The Seba Segel." Narine forced the words from her mouth. "Americans call them the Wise Men or the Three Magi. Some think they were kings. In reality, they were ancient astronomer priests who visited Yeshua in Bethlehem."

Jacob crossed his arms over his chest, and the corner of his mouth turned up. "Not like any nativity scene I've seen."

"He wasn't an infant when they reached him. They left from their kingdom when the star appeared in the sky. It took them two years to get to his birthplace. The diviners had predicted there would be a revolutionary born in Judea who would change the world, but they didn't have precise coordinates until the star appeared." Narine walked slowly around the three-dimensional projection. "Of course, there were more gifts and more than just the three of them, but this display nods to the familiar story in the Bible."

Jacob glanced at her. "So is that all considered fact in Ethiopian history? They really believe all that stuff happened like it says in the Bible?"

Narine looked at him with a frown. "Why wouldn't it be?"

"I mean—"

"The Seba Segel were not Christian, though Christians honor them. They came from different faiths. Moon worship, Zoroastrianism, Mandaeism. This was the first recorded appearance of the order in written history. I was taught it was the first allowed to be written because it was a warning to future mages to be wise when giving advice to a ruler. There is debate whether the massacre of the innocents was folklore or fact."

Narine looked up to see Jacob staring at her. She looked around the polished marble hallway, which was silent except for the quiet narration of the museum AI offering information in Amharic and English.

The man was incredulous.

"You don't believe me." Narine smiled. "Completely understandable."

"It's just that the Bible… I mean, it's stories, not history, you know?" He narrowed his eyes. "I'm kind of surprised you believe all that stuff."

Narine held back a smile. This might be more fun than she'd anticipated. "It seems crazy, right? I mean, even if you believed that astronomer priests existed—like they do now in the Orthodox Church—do they really know what's going to happen in the future?" She leaned closer. "Could they really have predicted the birth of a revolutionary who would change world history on the scale of Yeshua of Galilee?"

Narine walked around him, circling the digital rendering. They had used actors for the holographic sculpture, and they were closer than most artistic renderings, but they were still actors. "They didn't look like this." She cocked her head. "I mean, one of them is pretty close, but he was much shorter."

She glanced at Jacob. "That's one thing you learn—the first time you really experience the past—almost everyone was shorter in history."

Jacob was looking around the hall, his eyes wide. "Narine—"

"It's the first time all young travelers want to visit when we first learn our magic. We want to visit the magi because the story is so famous. Even though there was a whole company— like, thirty diviners plus hedge guards because they thought it was going to be a royal visit, you know? Not a little boy in a stonemason's house."

Narine strolled out of the gallery and toward another wing where a virtual reality program was guiding visitors through the tunnels that wound through the ancient churches of Lalibela. Jacob was walking behind her, his face a mixture of fascination and mild horror.

"You know," he said, "maybe it would be better—"

"Give me a chance to explain, okay?" Narine turned and walked backward, leading him into a hallway where a series of photographs documented the archaeological expeditions that had been conducted in Lalibela. "Keep in mind, I was a little younger when this picture was taken and my hair was a lot shorter."

Jacob blinked. "What are you talking about?"

Narine took his hand, weaving their fingers together so he couldn't escape. "Jacob." She pressed her finger to his lips. "Look. Listen. I promise I'll explain everything."

He followed her, probably more out of concern than belief.

Narine stood in front of the large photograph that she'd been foolish enough to pose for. In her defense, at the time she imagined it would end up—at best—in a dusty library some- where and definitely not blown up to cover nearly half a wall in a modern museum.

"Most young time travelers were fascinated by the three

magi." Narine stared at the edge where she'd stood so many years before. She'd taken off her shoes; Lalibela was holy ground. She could still feel the cool stone beneath her toes. "I was fascinated by Lalibela. This was my fifth trip back in time." She pointed to her picture, then looked at Jacob. "I was twenty then, but I'd been traveling in time for six years."

Jacob was silent, his eyes darting between Narine's face and her picture on the wall. "It... I mean, the resemblance is uncanny."

"That's because it's me," she whispered.

He was shaking his head. "This is... a mother or cousin or—"

"This picture was taken over a hundred years ago. My mother wasn't even born yet." She let his hand go and rolled up the sleeve of her right arm. "I'm one of the Seba Segel, Jacob. That's really me, and this birthmark here" —she showed him the constellation on her arm— "is the mark of the time traveler. The same mark you have on your arm."

Jacob was staring at her arm, his eyes getting wider and wider.

"We've followed the stars since before the pyramids were built. The sign of the river goddess marks us from birth."

He shook his head. "That's a coincidence." He held his forearm in his hand. "That's just..."

"You're not imagining this, Jacob Martin. When you roll up your sleeve and compare your birthmark with mine, you're going to see the exact same pattern." Narine touched his arm. "Because you're a time traveler too."

Jacob hadn't taken his eyes off his coffee. "This isn't real."

She frowned at him, wondering if she should have tried to take him home instead of to a private café not far from the order headquarters. "I'm sorry. Most of us grow up knowing all this stuff."

He took a deep breath and let it out slowly. "Let me see your arm again."

"Sure." She pushed up her sleeve for the tenth time and held it out so Jacob could hold his arm to hers. "Do you want to take a picture?"

He hadn't worn his assistant since the museum when he'd taken the thing out of his ear in the men's toilets and marched out of the lobby with Narine in his wake.

Jacob took the slim black assistant from his pocket now, pointed the lens at their side-by-side arms, and pressed a small button.

"There," Narine said. "You can examine it at home later."

"Time travel isn't possible."

"It isn't for mundane people, no. And other kinds of mages have tried, and it is not successful. They just end up half-drowned. It's just our kind."

He stuffed his assistant back in his bag and rested his head in his hands. "Explain this to me again. Like I'm an idiot."

"You're not an idiot. You were under the impression that you lived in one world when you actually live in another. It's hardly surprising that you're shocked."

"Narine."

"Fine." She leaned forward and dropped her voice to barely over a whisper. "You were born with supernatural power into an order of humans who retained or developed skills that set us apart from mundane people. It's both a spiritual and a magical practice, and it encompasses many different world faiths."

"So it's… evolutionary. Archaic human traits that were passed down and retained in some people."

He was really struggling with this. How did intake specialists deal with this? Of course, most intake specialists were dealing with children. "It's partly evolutionary."

"So it's not magical."

"No, it's definitely magical."

"But you said diviners like the Three Wise Men—"

"Three Magi or Three Mages is more correct. Or Seba Segel."

"They interpret stars. Like… astronomers."

"Yes." Narine nodded. "To determine future world trends. Predicting the future is magical."

Jacob rubbed a hand over his face. "What were the other…" He waved his hand. "You know, the other… things."

"Things?" Narine was able to keep her eyes from rolling. Barely. "There are diviners who interpret stars to determine future trends and events." She held up a finger to count. "There are alchemists, who are kind of like magical chemists. Archivists, who keep and interpret the Tibeb, which is how the order records history; travelers like me and you, who can travel through time; and hedge mages, who are the martial arm of the order and keep us all from being hunted down and experimented on."

He stared into her eyes. "And you are not suffering from any psychotic breaks or severe mental illness?"

"I am not. I mean, I probably have anxiety, but I'm so used to it at this point—"

"Magic isn't real." He closed his eyes. "Magic isn't real."

"Says the man born in a time when a magical voice speaks into his ear and assists him through daily life like an electronic servant." Narine picked up Jacob's assistant before handing it to him. "Through most of world history, many things that mundane people call magic now are considered science."

"Like astrology?" He was incredulous. "Alchemy?"

She shrugged. "I mean, I'm not sure what I can do to prove it to you if seeing my face in a picture from the early twentieth century doesn't work."

"How does anyone travel through time? It's impossible."

"Actually it's a process of very detailed star-mapping

combined with specific magical spells and a blood sacrifice that takes place within a water-gate since water is the element most analogous to time."

His eyes went wide. "You practice blood sacrifice? What kind of fucked-up—?"

"On myself." Narine pulled up her left sleeve where the neat scars from her travels lined up like rows leading up to her elbow. "It has to be your own blood for the magic to work."

"Oh." He had the grace to look embarrassed. "Sorry. I thought you were saying… Never mind."

"You thought I was slaughtering chickens and throwing their guts into the bath?"

He shook his head. "None of this is real. You say that I'm a traveler, but I'm thirty-four, Narine. I've never experienced anything magical in my entire life. Whatever power you say I have—"

"You have it, and I'm going to tell you something now that's going to prove it, and suddenly a lot of things about your life are going to make sense." She took a deep breath and knew that this revelation was going to break his brain more than any other, but it needed to happen.

It had to happen.

Narine caught his eyes and stared intently into them. "You remember things that other people don't, Jacob."

His face went blank. "What are you talking about?"

"You meet people who know you well, but you have no memory of them. Eventually you remember, and then you feel like an idiot because of course." She waved a hand. "You've known them for years. But when you first meet them…" She shook her head slowly.

Jacob's expression didn't change. "Everyone forgets things sometimes."

"Yes. That's true. But you haven't forgotten, because you remember a different reality." Narine kept going. "You have vivid memories of friends doing things that they don't remember at all. You remember a different name for a colleague at work. You could have sworn that lady from the history department was married to John, but her husband's name is Mark."

The expression on his face changed. Just barely. A crinkling frown that flashed between his eyebrows. "That... that's something that happens to everyone."

"Not like you." Narine sat back and tried to make her voice as soothing as possible. "Eventually your brain adjusts and you realize that of course you'd just forgotten, but it's a little like déjà vu, isn't it? You remember the forgetting even when the details fade."

Jacob was shaking his head. "That's... That's not—"

"It's because your brain recognizes fluctuations in the timeline even though you've received no training and don't practice magic. But you recognize those little fluctuations. Because you're a born traveler, you can't help it."

"So you say." He reached out and carefully lined up the paper napkin next to the placemat. He smoothed the napkin out, then aligned his water glass and his coffee cup. "What you're telling me is not proof of any—"

"You remember people who aren't there. At least, you do for a while, and then the memories fade and you don't really know why."

"Narine, what you're describing is called false memory. Things you're sure you remember correctly that just aren't real. Another term for it is the Mandela Effect, and it's—"

"Mundane people call it that, but it's a modern term. And I believe Mandela did die earlier in one timeline. There was an assassination attempt, but we stopped the plot from going forward."

Jacob opened his mouth, then closed it and crossed his arms over his chest. "It's normal."

"It is normal." She leaned forward. "For you, it's very normal. Because you're a mage and a traveler. Your memories are not false and they never have been. Your parents and your teachers probably called you forgetful—called you imaginative if they were being nice—but you're not forgetful."

He swallowed, and she could see the beginnings of belief dawning in his expression.

Narine kept going. "You don't remember less, Jacob, you remember more. You remember the possibilities of a time that wasn't meant to be."

He blinked, and it was as if a light switched on behind his eyes. He believed her.

And he was confused.

"What do you want from me?"

THEY SAT ON STONE BENCHES UNDER THE TREES, LOOKING AT Kidist Selassie, the Holy Trinity Cathedral where worshippers came and went in silence, paying respects at the cathedral or visiting one of the prominent grave markers that surrounded the church.

A light mist was falling on them as they sat, and Narine pulled her raincoat more closely around her figure. She adjusted the white scarf covering her head and glanced at Jacob, who was staring at the church with an intent expression.

"You know, Ethiopian churches are always supposed to have a garden or forest around them." Narine broke the silence. "To represent the perfection of Eden."

"That's beautiful."

"They also became seed arks." Narine glanced at him. "Especially in the north where there was so much deforestation, sometimes church forests were the only natural forests left. So when climate change reached its peak and the country was desperate to reforest the north, they would get seeds and plants from around the local churches. And generations later, the mountains are healing themselves."

Jacob was still staring at the church. "So the church forests were like the Seba Segel? Preserving the knowledge of the forests so they could be replanted in the future."

Narine shrugged. "It's not the best metaphor."

"It's not bad."

"Coming from a literature professor, I'll take that as a compliment."

They sat in silence as more worshippers poured in around them. It was lunchtime, and workers from the area—the few still working during the holiday—came to pray or simply to enjoy the silence around Kidist Selassie. Churches and mosques were the only places in the city that remained untouched by technology. There were no electric billboards or mechanized delivery trucks. People tucked their assistants away, and no one brought out screens except to capture the occasional picture of a child or an elderly parent.

"Faith is magic, isn't it?" Jacob's eyebrows were furrowed together. "What else is faith than looking beyond our own experience to accept that there is something greater than us? And yet, of the billions of people in the world, something like eighty percent of them believe in a higher power of some kind."

Narine smiled, thinking of Pagume and the prayers she offered every morning. Thinking of Genet's uncanny ability to cut through the bullshit of life to see higher truth and the anchor she'd run to when her own life had shattered.

"Yes." She nodded. "Faith is magic. And it's also ritual and practice. It's not a bad parallel for the order, I guess."

"What's the purpose? I mean, I know you said that they preserve knowledge, but what's the purpose of the time travel and the divination and... all that stuff?"

"The magic stuff?"

He shrugged.

"To do the best we can for the most we can." Narine glanced at him, then turned her face back to the church. "That's what my teacher used to tell me. You've heard it said that nature abhors a vacuum? Well, so does time."

"What does that mean?"

"Think of a river, Jacob. Think of the Nile. Nothing is going to stop it; it's too powerful. In the end, the river will always reach the sea, will always reach its end, no matter what we do to it." She held up a hand. "And we can't drain time like humans drain a river, so please don't make that argument. I did when I was a child and my mother smacked me."

"Lovely."

"She wasn't." Narine looked at him. "She isn't. But she was wise and she was powerful. We're shepherds, Jacob. River tenders, if you will. The Seba Segel can't stop the river, and often we can't even change its course, but maybe sometimes we can convince the king to shore up a riverbank to protect a town." She swallowed hard. "Maybe we can… divert a flood from doing the most damage."

He nodded slowly. "So you can't stop history, but you can make it a little better?"

"The wise men went home another way," Narine said softly. "No one talks about that, and it's the most important part of the story. They told the king about a prince's birth, but then they didn't return to give that king the child's location."

Jacob frowned. "And according to the story, because of that, the king killed all the boys in that village."

"But Yeshua and his family escaped. His life was tasary—a fixed point in time."

"And the other boys?" Jacob asked. "The ones who died?"

"Their lives were not." She could see the horror on his face. "Time is powerful, not kind."

"But if you're a time traveler, why not go back and fix it?" Jacob asked. "Why not fix everything? Why not stop the wars? Stop massacres? Stop colonization and imperialism and repression? I understand that natural disasters or plagues are always going to happen, but can't human disasters be stopped?"

It was the most fundamental argument of their kind. And the most frustrating.

"The order has tried to stop many things in the past. The birth of tyrants. The colonization of the Americas and Africa." She took a deep breath. The answers were so... unsatisfying no matter how many times she gave them. "Wars that ravaged Asia and the Pacific. Manmade famines all over the world."

"It didn't work?"

Narine stared at the slowly tilting shadows that surrounded the church. "Often the consequences of meddling made the disaster worse. More lives were lost. More cultures were destroyed. More people suffering and dying." She looked at him. "And some of what you know as history is a better outcome than the original."

Jacob visibly shuddered.

"Time rolls over us, proving that we're powerless over and over again, but I have to believe that it can get better," Narine said. "Otherwise..." Her mind went to the darkest timeline. "I have to believe that despite people being... basically the worst sometimes, that human beings can get better. That real change can happen."

"Or what's the point of anything?"

"My mentor" —Narine's chest tightened when she thought of Abdi— "would often point out that what seems like a disaster in one time ends up being necessary in another. None of us knows how the story is going to end. We only see pieces."

He blinked. "Why not?"

"What do you mean?"

"You can't go forward? Time travel only works one direction?"

Narine took a deep breath. "In theory, someone could travel to the future, but we do not."

"Why not?"

"Because the past is known, the future is not."

"But our present is someone else's past."

"Yes. And they can travel to it."

His eyebrows were locked in a frown. "What if you meet yourself in the past? Wouldn't that cause some… I don't know, time paradox or something?"

She shook her head. "Time won't allow two of me to exist at one point in history. So my magic won't allow me to travel to any time I've been alive."

"So you can travel to before you were born but not after?"

She nodded. "Exactly. I could try, but nothing would happen. I'd stay in my native time."

Jacob muttered. "That's maybe the first part of any of this that kind of makes sense."

Narine grimaced. "There are people who can explain this a lot better at the order."

"So why did they send you?"

"Because they hate me." She huffed. "Long story. I'm not sorry they did. I mean, I was at first, but I told you, I think you're interesting."

Jacob held out his arm with the traveler mark. "Because of this?"

"Of course that." She shrugged. "But there are other things too."

He let out a rueful laugh. "And here I thought you were flirting with me."

"I might have been doing that too." She smiled a little. "I told you I thought you were handsome."

He nudged her shoulder with his own.

Her smile fell, and she turned her gaze back to the church pilgrims. "I can't make you go see them. And I'm not going to lie to you: Being a traveler will make many things in your life worse. If you start practicing magic, the timeline fluctuations you feel now will get worse. It's disorienting, but you have to learn to live with it. And you're going to be forced to ask questions of yourself you probably never wanted to ask."

"Tell me the good part."

She swallowed the lump in her throat. "I've saved lives. Despite everything, I have stopped tragedies. I've made a difference in history even if it's only a small one. And I've seen things that you can't even imagine right now." She blinked at the memory. "Waking up to the clearest dawn you can envision on the edge of a world you've only read about in history books." She met his eyes. "Seeing Eden."

His expression was a mix of caution and yearning. "Can they tell me where I came from?"

"I'm not going to make guarantees because I can't know for sure," Narine said. "But if anyone has the truth about your past, Jacob, the Seba Segel can find it."

# CHAPTER 15

*The Island*
*1920*

"Where did you go to school?"

Narine paused to catch her breath. "A private campus in Addis Ababa that was for mage families." Narine and Gideon were harvesting thistles on the mainland. They'd taken a boat early that morning, and Narine had covered herself from head to toe so the local people didn't ask questions.

They hadn't spoken of the kiss once since it happened the month before.

Gideon had tied a scarf around his forehead to keep the sweat from dripping into his eyes while he used a broad knife to cut the branches and stalks of the bristly plant. "You can use the whole thistle plant, so cut the stalks into the bags and chop up the main stem. I'll dig the roots once you've cut the stalk."

There had been a break in the rain and the clouds had unexpectedly cleared from the sky, leaving a bright blue expanse that warmed the soggy ground and lifted a low fog over the hills. The air was damp and warm, but the bright purple thistles along this stretch of hillside bobbed their heads in the humid air.

"These thistles are very sharp."

"Yes." He glanced at her arms. "You have your gloves?"

"I do." The sheepskin gloves that Tigist had given her that morning were Daniel's and they were large on her, but she could move her hands well enough to cut thistles and throw the stalks in the heavy canvas bags they'd brought from the island. "Why do you need them?"

"Thistles are good for liver problems and also the gallbladder. There are also healing spells and hedge spells that require ground thistle seed." He hacked at a stubborn stalk. "And when you strip the outer membrane, it's actually quite delicious. For plant eaters like me."

That was something Narine had noticed after some time with Gideon. He ate very little meat, which was unusual for Ethiopians, who ate their fill of beef, lamb, and goat on nonfasting days. It didn't seem to affect his well-being; the man was trim and muscled, and his skin and hair shone with health.

Narine asked, "Do you miss the food in Kenya?"

"Do you miss the food in your time?" He turned the question around on her. "What kind of food do you cook when you're home?"

She smiled a little. "I don't cook much, to be honest. Aster is the woman who keeps our house, and she does most of the cooking, mainly Ethiopian food. On holidays, my mother will take over the kitchen and make traditional family dishes."

"From Armenia?"

Narine nodded. "Yes, from Armenia."

"Where House Kayl was established." He paused in his thistle chopping and looked at her. "What does that mean? To be born into *House Kayl*?"

Why was he so interested in her house? Narine shrugged. "I suppose what it means to be born into any great house. Tradition. Duty to family. Obligations to the order."

Gideon raised an eyebrow. "You forget I wasn't born into a mage family. I was picked up and taken to an order training school in Mombasa. Mine wasn't the comfortable kind like your school in Addis."

"And your parents had no idea—"

"Students at mage training schools like mine are told not to share our magical studies with our parents."

"Even if they were mages?" Narine asked.

"Even then."

Narine knew what Gideon was talking about. While her school had the atmosphere of a privileged preparatory academy and finishing school, most order schools were run like military academies. They were the opposite of luxurious.

"Did your parents treat you differently when you were a child? Where there signs you were powerful?"

"No." He shook his head. "From what I can tell, alchemist mages don't have any early signs of magic like travelers or hedges do. All my parents knew was that some kind of charitable order—one that wasn't run by the British—wanted to educate their son and they wouldn't have to pay for my education. They were grateful."

Gideon worked in a rote fashion. Trim the tall thistle plants of short branches, hack at the large stalk, use the broad end of the knife to dig out the root.

Over and over again. Never stopping. Never flinching if the rough thorns touched his skin. He had a cut along his jawline and various pricks and slashes on his arms, but he kept going as if the blood meant nothing.

Narine couldn't tear her eyes away. "Your family doesn't like the British."

"Of course they don't," he muttered. "The crown took their family land. Drove them off and built tea plantations to make themselves rich." Gideon looked up, and there was a quiet fire in his eyes. "My grandfather went from being a respected landowner and elder in his village to being offered a job cutting tea leaves on territory his people had held for generations." He started chopping at the thistles again. "They moved to Nairobi rather than work as servants on their own land."

"That's infuriating." Narine wondered whether any of Gideon's family had been able to retrieve their land after the massive court cases at the beginning of the century. She had no way of knowing.

"Yes." He was breathing heavier. Whether from exertion or anger, Narine couldn't tell. "And yet the order of the Seba Segel and the old houses in Kenya have ingratiated themselves with the British."

"Because they're the government." Narine had been taught it was the same all over the world. The Seba Segel had an obligation to advise those in power no matter how that government had obtained power. It wasn't their place to withhold wisdom or advice if it could lead to the greater good.

It was what she'd been taught, but facing Gideon and his resentment, she knew how facile it sounded. It was a simple answer to an incredibly tangled problem.

Narine blurted out, "You asked me before if your country was still a colony."

Gideon froze and looked at her. "I did. And you told me—"

"It's not." Narine shook her head. "Kenya has had its independence for over one hundred years. It has a thriving democracy and one of the most successful economies in Africa. I can't tell you more than that, but you should know that it happens. And in my time, the order advises the Kenyan government just as it currently advises the British."

Gideon went back to chopping stalks of thistle and was silent for a long time.

Narine focused on the work—gather the tender branches and flowers, put them in one bag. Cut the larger stalks into smaller pieces and put those in another.

"What makes a great house in the Seba Segel?" Gideon asked her again. "Your House Kayl in Armenia. The house of Abay here in Ethiopia. The house of Mkisi in Mombasa." He straightened from his work. "Are they all still 'great houses' in your time?"

"It's hard to imagine a time when House Abay isn't a great house," Narine said.

"So it's like the aristocratic families here in Ethiopia? Or in Europe?"

"I suppose it is," Narine said. "In a way. My family isn't the owner of giant houses or land. We don't really have a lot of money."

Gideon kept his eyes on his work. "No, your wealth is in power, isn't it?" He paused and wiped the sweat from his forehead. "Your wealth is in magic, blood, and connections."

She nodded. "That's one way to look at it."

"So it's just like the aristocracy." Gideon kept hacking at the thistles. "My country may be independent in your time, but there are still aristocrats that rule the Seba Segel all over the world." He crouched down and dug his knife into the ground, plunging the sharp blade into the earth and prying up the gnarled white roots that held up the thorny plant. "So tell me, what has changed? One aristocracy leaves, but another moved into its place." He held up the roots and looked at Narine. "Unless I take out the root of this plant, it will grow back again and again."

Narine bristled. "You're saying my family is like a thistle plant?"

The corner of his mouth turned up. "Are you taking that as an insult?" Gideon cocked his head. "Thistles are useful."

And dangerous. Thistles might have a beautiful flower, but they could definitely make you bleed.

So maybe Gideon had a point.

Her head swam in the watery place between waking and sleeping.

His mouth was on her neck; she felt heat between her thighs. The sound of heavy breathing surrounded her. The pulsing grip of her body around his cock forced a cry of pleasure from her throat.

He slapped his hand over her mouth and didn't stop the relentless drive of his hips between her thighs even as the pleasure built to a level where tears leaked from her eyes and every inch of her skin was painfully sensitive. She felt everything: his weight pressing her down into the earth, the rasp of rough cloth against her thighs, the prick of stones digging into her back. The mix of pleasure and pain that rushed to her head in an intoxicating mix of desire, passion, anger, and addiction.

She shook her head to rid his hand from her mouth, then licked along his shoulder and sank her teeth into the hard muscle she found. She wanted the taste of salty skin on her tongue. His arm around her flinched at the bite, but he didn't stop.

His rhythm was relentless, and she bit her own tongue to keep from crying out when he plunged into her faster and faster, and then his own throat couldn't contain the groan of satisfaction as he found his release.

Her body was still shivering as his went still. He curled down and captured her mouth with a kiss, pressing his lips against hers, then moving the kiss to her cheeks, the line of her jaw, her eyes clenched shut in pleasure.

"The ground is rocky. I should have brought a blanket." He left her body, rolled to the side, and lifted her so she was lying across his chest. "You found pleasure twice that time."

The shivers made her skin prickle with goose bumps. "Yes."

"Good." He ran a hand over her bare bottom, then reached for the shirt he'd thrown in the grass. "You're cold."

"Not cold."

He nuzzled into her neck, then wrapped his shirt around her, his arms warming her as their passion turned tender and her racing heart began to slow.

A baby cried in the night, and she turned to the sound.

"Shhh," he whispered in her ear. "Don't. The baby is crying, but I think she'll go back to sleep if we don't move."

Every instinct in her rose and shoved her toward action, but she knew he was right. "I know she's fine, but—"

"But nothing." He ran a hand up and down her back. "You need a rest and the nurse is there."

She felt the heaviness behind her eyes. He was right; she was so tired. "Yes. The nurse will get her."

"Of course she will." He fluttered a kiss over the shell of her ear. "You've been tired for days."

"I know." But she was never too tired to make love to him. His energy fed her. He was passion, magic, and energy narrowly contained in human form. Sometimes when he brought her to orgasm, she felt a spark of static electricity from his kiss, as if all of his being was a channel for power.

The faint cry calmed, and the sound of the nurse's soft lullaby floated in the night air. The lapping water of the lake sang to her as she drifted in the liminal space between waking and sleeping.

"Narine, wake up."

She pressed her face into his chest and hid from the voice. "Don't want to."

"Narine!"

She blinked awake in an instant and sat up in the cold room where Tigist was banging on the door.

She tried to speak but couldn't. She cleared her throat and

took a drink of water to open up her voice. "What is it?"

"Daniel has returned from the city."

Narine looked around and realized that while it was dark outside, it wasn't nighttime or morning. It had to be late afternoon at most, and there was a journal beside her next to a pen. She must have been writing in her journal and fallen asleep.

That dream...

"I'll be right there." Narine swung her legs over the edge of the bed and rubbed her eyes.

Her dreams about Gideon were becoming more and more frequent. They had moved from being wholly sexual in nature to something more intimate and... nurturing.

What was that about a baby in the dream?

Narine scoffed. Not likely. She knew her family expected her to procreate eventually, but that was far off in the future. And the worry and fear she'd felt when the baby cried?

Dreams were strange.

She stood and read over the last bit she'd written in the journal Gideon had found for her when he went to the mainland. He'd brought it back two days after they harvested the thistles, along with a fountain pen and a bottle of india ink. She'd been writing furiously ever since.

*When I was fourteen, Jamila and I found three broken assistants left in a car off Lafto Road. We'd been going to visit her cousin at the health complex there and we were still in our school uniforms, though Jamila had changed into a smart pair of trainers her brother had brought her from Dubai.*

*The thieves had been arrested by the police, and Jamila said the assistants were already wiped, so it was pointless to try to find the owners. She was probably wrong, but I went along with it because she was so excited. She took them apart to figure out how they worked; then she put them back together again. That was how she taught herself.*

*We taught ourselves other things later.*

Narine was writing down as much as she could remember about her life, starting with her earliest memories of Genet, her mother, Aster, and her father. The story about the phones had happened just after she had started traveling for the order. Her mother and Abdi had trained her to be a silent spy at that age because who would take a child time traveler seriously? Better that she go along with her mother and learn how to listen.

After all, important people didn't pay attention to teenage girls.

She rose and washed her face in the basin with a small broken mirror hanging over it. She glanced at her reflection and barely recognized her own face. Her skin was brown from working outside, yet her eyes were sharper and her teeth whiter. She'd lost weight when she had malaria but had gained some of it back. Her cheekbones were still hollower than they'd been when she arrived.

Would Jamila be shocked when she returned to Addis?

The teenage phone theft was typical of their friendship. Jamila had been jealous of Narine's secrecy and increasing responsibility. While Genet saw her every day at home, Jamila missed Narine as she spent more and more time away from school, occupied with order business.

Was luring Narine into a secret life of petty crime Jamila's way of trapping her as a friend? Maybe, but Narine hadn't cared. She'd been afraid that Jamila wouldn't want anything to do with her when her own magic didn't manifest and Narine's did. She'd be her accomplice if it meant keeping Jamila as a friend.

Plus learning basic electronics was a useful life skill.

"Narine?"

"I'm coming!"

She wished Jamila was with her. Her best friend always seemed to bend reality to her own will. If she wanted to succeed in something, she did. If she wanted someone to notice her, they did. The only thing she hadn't been able to control was her own magic, and she'd even managed to work that to her favor.

As for Narine? According to the elders, she would eventually be even more powerful than her mother and grandfather. But with that power came orders. Her mother's orders. Abdi's teachings. The order's commands. The elder's wishes. It was a life of duty, and as she walked to the outhouse to relieve her bladder, she wondered if Jamila hadn't been right when she told Narine to run away.

*Can't run away now.*

A persistent drip of rain leaked through the thatch on the outhouse roof and dripped down Narine's back, crawling down her spine while she hurried to wash herself and get back inside.

Narine washed her hands with water and the harsh soap they kept behind the outhouse, then walked back to her room, threw her wrap around herself, and twisted her hair into a neat bun at the back of her head. Tigist had coated her hair and scalp with butter a few days before and—unlike her rough hands—Narine's mane of curls was soft and shining.

Daniel was standing in the courtyard, his white clothes stained from traveling but with a giant smile on his face. "Narine!"

She couldn't help but return the grin. The friendly mage felt like a brother now. Or at least what she would hope a brother would be like. "We were wondering!" She walked over, pressed her hand to his, and touched her right shoulder to his in a friendly greeting. "Did something go wrong?"

"Come inside," Tigist said. "It's cold and the girls are warming up food."

"It was all good," Daniel said, following Narine into the warm house. "All good. My love, the food smells as delicious as you do." He pressed a kiss to Tigist's cheek. "Thank you." They took off their shoes and sat around the low table. "It took longer because the prince agreed to see Tigist's mother, and I thought I would stay until after their meeting so you would know how it went."

Narine nodded. "You were right to wait, I would have gone crazy if I knew the meeting happened but had to wait for a letter to learn the outcome."

Daniel smiled. "She met with the crown prince, and according to her, he listened very carefully and was impressed by her mother's service in Taytu's household. He asked a number of questions that led our mother to believe that he was taking your admonition to press the British much more seriously."

Narine sat back and breathed a sigh of relief. "That's good. Questions are good. An audience with the crown prince was more than I could hope for, Daniel. Thank you so much."

His face glowed with happiness. "I believe he will heed your warnings, Narine. Your mission has been accomplished and your advice heard by the highest power in the land. No elders could expect more."

Narine felt a weight release in her chest. Whatever else happened, her first mission as a solo traveler had been a success. Hopefully she had made a difference. Hopefully the two hundred and fifteen people who would have died in that massacre would live. And who knows what those people might do with their lives?

*Whoever saves one life, it is as if she had saved all of humanity.* How many times had Abdi told her that in training? The tension in Narine's chest eased, and she felt a satisfying wave of peace.

Her mission was complete.

NIGHT FELL WITH A CELEBRATION IN TIGIST AND DANIEL'S household. None of the elder council knew of Tigist's letter to her mother, so to the rest of the compound, it was just another night.

But for Daniel, Tigist, and Narine, the dinner was one of celebration. She sang them a popular song from her own time, then another one of her grandfather's favorite folk songs from Armenia that they liked much better. Daniel played his *masinko,* and the cook came in to sing along. She had a light and lyrical voice, worthy of an audience, and Narine marveled at the extraordinary talent hiding in a humble rural kitchen.

*I will miss this.*

As desperate as she felt to return to her own time, part of Narine would miss being among others of her kind that had no relation to her, those who didn't know and didn't care who her mother was, where her family came from, or how much power she had.

She was furloughed in the past, her mission had been accomplished, and she had nothing to do but wait. Narine looked around the table and saw friendly faces. No simmering resentment, no disappointed expectations. To the people here, she was simply Narine who ground barley, boiled water, and was pretty good at catching fish.

For the first time in her life, she understood the allure of losing yourself to the past. She could stay here and remain as she was. She would lose her magic and become an ordinary person. She would never see another time than this one. She would fall into this current of time and simply… be.

*You are Narine Anahid Khoren of House Kayl. Your father is a diviner of House… You were born in the year 2043 of the Old Calendar. You are a third-degree traveling mage of the Seba Segel, ninth in your line of power. You were born in Addis Ababa. You have no siblings. You are the godmother of Gelile, the adopted sister of Genet, the daughter of Anahid. Your best friend is…*

*Your best friend is…*

*Your best friend…*

# CHAPTER 16

*Addis Ababa*
*New Year's Eve, 2071*

Narine programmed the electric crawler to pick up Jacob at his house the next day. It was New Year's Eve and the house where the AI brought them in Old Airport was sporting a bright yellow garland across the front gate. She parked the crawler on the street, opened the side door, and called to the guard at the gate.

"*Abati, tena yistilin.*" She greeted him in Amharic. "How are you today?"

"Sister, I'm doing well," he replied in kind. "How can I help you?"

"I'm a friend of Dr. Jacob's. I think he is expecting me."

"Dr. Jacob!" The old guard bowed a little. "Of course, of course. No problem, do you need the gate open?" He motioned to the high-tech electronic gate behind him. "I just press a button."

"Please don't bother with the gate, *abati*. We're going out this morning."

"Of course, I will tell him you have arrived." He tipped the edge of his cap. "Give me just a moment."

Narine slid her sunglasses on as the day grew brighter and the morning sun hit the windshield with a vengeance. The last day of the thirteenth month had arrived, and Narine could feel the energy of New Year enveloping the city.

A few moments after the guard had left to fetch him, Jacob appeared at the side door and waved. "Hey."

"Hey, yourself," she answered in English. "Am I early?"

"No, I'm late." He walked out and climbed in the wide passenger door. "I was still getting dressed when Fitsum knocked on the door. Thanks for picking me up." He looked around at the wide interior of the crawler. "This is… cool. I've never ridden in one of these before. I usually take the train."

"I've heard they're not as popular in the US. What do you drive there?"

"In Seattle I don't drive. My parents have an old electric truck though. It's good to take out of the city."

She hit the button and the door behind Jacob slid shut with a whisper. "Crawlers are really good on rough streets, and Addis always has so much construction. Plus they hold a lot of people."

They both waved at the guard, then Narine engaged the self-driving mode and the computer eased the crawler into the already bustling alleyway and toward the side road that twisted through the neighborhood.

"It's practical for the muddy roads, especially with kids. Genet uses it more than I do, but it's handy outside the city too, especially when it's rainy. We have a zip car, but you're tall. I don't think you'd even fit in it."

He glanced at the dashboard. "And it's completely self-driving?"

"Only in the city. Manual in the country. Believe it or not, there are still a lot of places in this country without paved roads."

The crawler AI spoke quietly in the background as they worked their way through traffic, chiming in on route changes that avoided holiday road closures. There were already neighborhoods that were setting up for the bonfires on New Year's Eve, and the road Narine would usually take was blocked.

"You said you didn't sleep very well last night," she said. "Because of our conversation yesterday?"

"Are you surprised?"

"No."

The crawler maneuvered around a clutch of market stalls that had popped up on the corner of the intersection, selling flowers, fresh and paper grass, and the spinning gold fireworks and popping wristbands that had become so popular.

"Any questions yet?"

"Only about a hundred." He kept his eyes on the windows, watching the city as it decorated itself for the holiday. "This is wild. Where do the all the flowers come from? Farms?"

Narine smiled. "Those are *adey ababa*. Meskel flowers. They still grow wild in the hills outside the city. A lot of those areas are protected now, so kids go out in the mornings and cut them. You'll see them all over from now until Meskel."

"That's the big bonfire holiday, right?"

"More light shows now than bonfires with all the air regulations, but there will be a central bonfire in Meskel Square. It's a protected historic event, so they can't outlaw the smoke entirely. People still do little bonfires at home though. You just take your chances with the drone tickets. You have Ethiopians in your compound?"

"Oh yeah. The couple who owns the house lives in Germany most of the time, but they live here part time. Both guys are great cooks. They invited me to the party tonight. I just need to bring whiskey."

"Good. If you didn't have anywhere to go, I'd have to take you home with me or my sister would have my head."

"Would that be so bad?" He glanced at her. "You've seen where I live now. Turnabout is fair play."

She frowned. "What does that mean? I've heard my father say that."

Jacob smiled. "Mine too. It means you have to be fair, I guess."

"I've seen your house, so you should see mine?"

"Exactly."

Narine raised her eyebrows. "That sounds like an American rule to me, and we're in Addis."

Jacob laughed a little. "Maybe for the Meskel holiday."

"Maybe."

They were passing by one of her favorite churches, Kidist Bole Michael, a little out of their way, but they could take the new airport expressway north and avoid some of the closed neighborhoods by diverting that way according to the AI.

Narine pulled over to the side of the road and beckoned to a girl in a messenger uniform perched on a zip bike near a small coffee stand. The skytrain clacked overhead, drowning out her voice for a second, but the messenger recognized the beckoning hand.

The girl strolled over and gave her a cool nod. "Good morning," she said in English. "Can I help you, ma'am?"

Narine quickly responded in Amharic. "You know the Harari woman who sells khat near the mosque? The one with the big transport with the blue sides?"

The girl instantly became more interested. *"Eshi."* She switched to Amharic. "You need directions?"

"No, I need to get a message to her." Jamila was going to be pissed, but there was no way Narine was making that air transport to Harar for the New Year. She dug in her pocket for a small plug-in drive. "What's your transfer number?"

The girl pulled out her assistant and held it up so Narine's lens could scan the code embedded on the side. "I'm sending you three thousand." She handed the girl the small drive. "When my friend gets this, you'll get another three."

The girl's face brightened. "I'll go right now."

*"Chigur yellem."* Narine waved a hand. "You don't have to rush. She won't be there until four at least, but I'm going to be busy today. By the way, the drive's encrypted."

The girl looked slightly offended, but only slightly. "I'm credited." She pointed to her badge. "You want my pass?"

"It's on your transfer receipt," Narine said. "No worries. Remember, *only* the Harari woman in charge of the truck. Not her helpers, okay? Only her. Tell her it's from Narine."

The messenger nodded and ran back to her bike with the drive clutched in her hand.

"What was that?" Jacob said.

"Nothing." Narine watched the girl take off on her zip bike. "I just don't trust the mail."

THEY ARRIVED AT THE ORDER'S GATES TO FIND A SKELETON crew, but Mesfin the Meticulous was still manning the door. Narine walked up to him, expecting to have to give him a complete biographical breakdown of Jacob, why he was at the order, and why he didn't have ID, but Mesfin glanced at him, took a step to the side, and gave Jacob a slight nod.

"Dr. Jacob Martin, welcome to the Seba Segel," Mesfin said in perfect English. "We've been expecting you."

Narine stared. "Really?"

"Thank you." Jacob returned Mesfin's nod. "I'm still wrapping my brain around all this. What's your name?"

"Mesfin Hailemariam, Dr. Martin. Please accept my welcome." Mesfin handed Jacob a business card. "I am a hedge mage here at the order, which means I guard the compound, but if you ever need any assistance, here or in the city, I am at your service."

Narine was frozen, her mouth hanging open. "Are you serious right now?"

The hedge glanced at her, and she finally saw a glint of humor in the man's dark eyes. "Sister Narine."

She narrowed her eyes and ushered Jacob into the headquarters, her eyes locked with Mesfin's. He was laughing at her. Externally she was glaring, but internally she couldn't help but be amused.

There was no one at the front desk because officially the offices were closed, but Narine walked Jacob back to Kebret's office where she knew the elder would be waiting.

She tapped on the door and heard his gruff voice on the other side.

"Enter."

Trust him to make a welcome a command.

Narine opened the door and poked her head in. "Elder Kebret?"

"Sister Narine, I trust you have brought someone to meet me?"

"I have." She opened the door wide. Jacob was beside her. "Elder Kebret, this is Dr. Jacob Martin from Seattle, Washington, in the United States. He's currently a visiting professor at Addis Ababa University and an uninitiated traveler mage belonging to no designated order." She turned to Jacob. "Jacob, I introduce you to Elder Kebret Afework Urgesa, third-order hedge mage of House Abay and the head of the elder council here in Addis Ababa." She leaned in. "Very important," she whispered.

"I can hear you, Narine." Kebret was sitting behind his desk, a gruff scowl decorating his face. "And if you'd done your job earlier this week and brought Dr. Jacob earlier, none of us would have to be working on a holiday."

"Sorry." Jacob stepped forward. "I'm a bit of a skeptic. I'm sure Narine was trying to ease me into the idea of... magic. And time travel. And all of it."

"The Seba Segel is far more than time travel," Kebret started. "In fact, traveling—though obviously important for *your* magic—is a relatively minor part of our responsibilities here." He motioned to the seat across his desk. "Sit. Let me explain."

Jacob moved to sit, but Narine hung back. "Elder Kebret—"

"Go." He waved a dismissive hand. "Come back later."

Jacob turned to her with slight panic in his eyes, but she gave him a reassuring smile.

"Don't worry, you're in good hands. Elder Kebret is far more knowledgeable about explaining things than I am. I'll come back for you in an hour or so."

"Two." Kebret was still shooing her out. "And tell someone—whoever is working today—that we need coffee."

"Of course." Narine backed out of the room and shut Jacob in with the elder.

She flagged down the first person she saw. "Elder Kebret needs coffee."

The man scowled at her. "I'm a clerk, not a coffee girl."

"And I'm a traveler who burns coffee," Narine said. "Just see to it."

She left him without another word and made her way out of the building and through the compound until she reached the unusually quiet archive building.

There was another bored guard at the door who nodded at her before he continued staring at something on his lens.

She entered the building and walked directly downstairs without asking for directions. She found Aida and Tadesse in the same room where she'd seen them the day before, only this time the long table in the archive room was covered by a multicolored tapestry, intricate and beautiful.

Nearly two meters wide and almost the length of the room, the Tibeb was woven with a rainbow of threads, different geometric patterns, and fine motifs that contained a detailed history of the Seba Segel in each year.

Tade looked up with alarm when she walked in, only to relax when he saw her. "Technically we're not supposed to be working today."

"Nonsense," Narine said. "Didn't the elders tell you to investigate the warp?"

The Tibeb in all its beauty was far more than decorative. It was a language that could only be read with magic and training. Aida had her hands over a section of the weaving at the very start of the tapestry, rich with reds, golds, and black.

"What it is?" Narine pulled over a tall stool and perched on the edge.

"I found the warp." Aida pointed to a small knot of red that was misshapen, out of place in the perfection of the weaving that covered the rest of the table. "If I hadn't been looking for it, I would have missed it." She pointed at a line of black that ran from the knotted section of the Tibeb to a dark-red-and-black block of pattern. "I can't tell what the original tasary was—the warp obscures the original pattern—but the threads that leave from that knot" —her finger hovered over the cloth— "lead directly to the Southern Mage Massacre."

Narine frowned. "The what?"

"That's what I said too." Tadesse grimaced. "Then I had this vague memory that it happened in the early 1930s, but nothing clear."

"And I told him," Aida said, "that was impossible because we all know about the Southern Mage Massacre. It's something we're taught as children as an important turning point in Seba Segel history."

"The Southern Mages are Abdi's clan," Narine said. "And that's what the warp leads to?" She turned to Tade. "That's it then. If his family was wiped out, that explains his disappearance."

"It's far more serious than that," Tadesse said. "Narine, the Southern Mages don't even exist anymore."

Narine turned to Aida. "How?"

Aida shook her head. "We were all taught this in school. The Southern Mages were a collection of free-mage clans in the south with no loyalty to the old houses who formed together as a band to share power and remain free." Aida pointed to the intricate weaving in front of her. "In 1934, at what should have been their spring festival, the Southern Mages were attacked. No one knows exactly who it was, but the council in Addis suspected it was another group of free clans. They were camped in the foothills of the Bale Mountains, and the massacre effectively wiped them out. There were a few survivors, but all the elders of the clans were killed."

Narine felt as if she'd been punched in the stomach. "Abdi's father and grandfather were elders in the clan."

"After the massacre, two old families—House Wensho and House Zuria—moved south and took over that territory to secure it from more violence and stabilize the region." Aida looked up from reading the Tibeb. "The Southern Mages don't exist anymore except in our history books."

THEY WERE IN NARINE'S OFFICE, AND TWO MORE MESSAGES had come through.

"…nothing in the archives here. It's like the Nomad movement never happened." Noura and Omar were twin travelers from Jeddah. "Two of our elders in Mecca have vanished."

"Not vanished from the timeline," Omar clarified, "but they're ordinary mages with no particular authority."

"We heard that something happened during Pagume. Let us know if you have any ideas. We're trying not to panic." Noura ended the call.

The second message was from Ander, a traveler from the Pyrenees in France. "…heard from Cyril that he'd contacted you. Don't know what's going on. Only my father and I have registered the change. Our local council is oblivious."

"It's spreading," Tadesse said. "The effects of the warp are spreading. We have to speak to the elders tomorrow."

Narine shook her head. "I say we jump first and find out what happened."

"This needs to be organized. If this massacre was so pivotal, the elders would want to help."

"Unless…" She didn't even want to think it, but it had to be said. "Unless the elders are the ones who planned it."

Tadesse's mouth dropped open. "How? Why?"

They had the door closed, but they still kept their voices low. "Tade, we both have the same memories. For now we remember them. Noura and Omar, Cyril. Ander and his father. The travelers remember the free mages, but for the rest of the Seba Segel, this massacre is all they know."

"So because the Southern Mages were killed, none of the rest of the free-clan movements happened?"

"They were the model all over the world. Free mages not associated with old houses banding together to gain power in the order? No one had ever done it before them. They were the reason the Rhone Valley Mages formed, that the Nomad movement in the Middle East happened. Think of every group of free-mage clans around the world, and you can trace their formation to the success of the Southern Mages."

"Not all of them. In the Americas—"

"Different history, different system," Narine said. "We both know that the power of the Seba Segel in Africa, Europe, and Asia has always rested in the old families."

"Until the Southern Mages." Tadesse stroked his beard. "If someone went back to wipe them out, their entire motive could have been to destroy the free-clan movement from the beginning."

"The free-clan movement was powerful in 2071, but in 1934?" Narine shook her head. "It was a thought. An idea. Not even a well-formed one at that."

"So you think the elders of the old houses—our elders—were behind this massacre? You think they altered that tasary?" Tadesse grimaced.

"Someone altered it, Tadesse, and it had to be a traveler. We have to find out who is behind this and what their goal is. Was it the massacre or was that just an unseen side effect? We can't fix the Tibeb, not without going back to Pagume in 1934—"

"Which would be committing one crime to fix another." Tadesse wiped a hand over his face. "The best we can do now is try to fix the massacre that resulted from the warp. We can take it to the elders—"

"I'm not taking it to the elders. They could be part of this."

"You know I don't have a clan, so I don't have a stake in this, but Narine, you're talking about your own people. You think they planned this? The council respects the free clans."

"Because they have to. Because they've been forced to acknowledge their power and their acceptance of clanless mages like you within their ranks. Abdi was the first free mage ever on the elder council in Addis, and someone wove him out of history." She shook her head. "I am *not* taking this to the elders."

"You can't go on your own."

"I'll figure something out." Her mind raced. "We know where the massacre happened, correct?"

"Yes. Aida has the location and the time."

"I'll give myself two weeks after the warp. If I can forge some letters, they'll believe I was sent by the Addis council. I'll go, find information, and come back. It won't be a long trip."

"You need a diviner for the calculations," Tadesse said. "Who—?"

"I can do them myself," Narine said. "I'll use my mother's algorithm."

Tadesse scoffed. "Your mother's algorithm?"

"She taught me how to use it, and it worked for her many times before…"

"Before she was lost to the timeline?" Tadesse continued. "Don't forget to add that part, Narine. She used it multiple times as some kind of test before she didn't return, and you haven't seen her in nearly four years. No one has. So I don't think—"

"I don't think you can stop me." Narine rose to her feet, the note burning with anger in her desk drawer.

*This cannot continue.*

He couldn't have had anything to do with this. It was impossible. His anger was justified, even Narine understood it, but it would never stretch this far. There had to be another explanation.

"I'm going, Tadesse. I'm not going to stop a war by myself, but I can at least find out more about what happened." She dropped her voice again. "Don't you think it's odd that in this timeline where the massacre happened, no one tried to stop it? No one saw that it resulted from this warp? Don't you think that's strange?"

Tadesse nodded. "It's strange, but Narine, the warp just happened. And in this timeline, Abdi's people were a minor blip in history. No one here realizes how important they became."

"They were important enough to learn about in school."

"Because the violence that happened then was a confirmation to the order that security rested in the old houses," Tadesse said quietly.

"Someone knows how important they become," Narine said. "Otherwise they wouldn't have been targeted. Whatever change happened, it happened in this Pagume. During *this* month. Because before this, Abdi was here and so were his people. This was only four days ago for us, Tade!"

He rubbed his temple. "I know it's important, but the memories are fading, Narine. This timeline—"

"Stop it." She cut him off. "Hold on. Whoever targeted Abdi and his people did it within the past five days. That means it's not ancient history; it just happened, and we can change it back."

"Fine," Tadesse muttered. "But if you're going back to 1934, I'm going with you. You're not going alone."

Narine shook her head. "You don't trust the algorithm, and if you don't trust it, your magic might not hold—"

"I don't trust the algorithm, but I trust you." His voice got even lower. "And we both know what you can do, Narine. Your traveler rank is not a secret."

She stared at him. "It's not something we talk about."

"Of course we don't." He smiled. "But we both know you're more powerful than I am, and I trust you to pull me along if my doubt trips me up, okay?"

As a second-tier traveler, Tadesse could take objects along with him when he traveled, a huge benefit over first-tier mages, who landed in their locations completely in the nude and had to find clothes. But Narine was a third-tier mage. There were only a handful of her kind in the world who could carry people when they traveled.

There came a tap at the door, and both of them stopped talking.

Narine glanced at her desk, but there was nothing visible that was incriminating. She sat down and struck a casual pose. "Come in."

Jacob poked his head in the door. "Hi. You left me."

"I'm sorry! I got talking with Tade about some... work stuff." Narine gestured to Tadesse. "Tade, this is Jacob. Jacob, a senior traveler sits before you—Tadesse Girma, darling of the Elder Council and the most competent and respected traveler in the country. Probably the world."

Tadesse's eyes were rolling. "Narine, you are being ridiculous." He stood and turned to Jacob. "Welcome, Brother Jacob. How are you feeling? Narine tells me that you had a meeting with Elder Kebret this morning. I hope he was helpful."

"I did, and it left me feeling…" Jacob let out a deep breath. "Confused. Overwhelmed. Excited?"

Tade smiled. "That's an understandable combination." He glanced at Narine, then back at Jacob. "You're very tall. Did you play athletics when you were younger?"

Jacob shot her a look, but Narine could only shrug. Tadesse was being intrusive, but he probably had a reason. Tade was a runner. Maybe he was trying to make Jacob feel at home.

"I did," Jacob said. "American football. I loved it, but I wasn't good enough to play professionally or anything like that."

Tadesse patted Jacob's shoulder. "You look like you still work out though. Do you have a gym here in Addis?"

"I do. I found a nice gymnasium over in my neighborhood, and I've been—"

"You're very strong." Tadesse sat down again and stared at Narine. "I bet you'd be good to have in a fight."

"Why are you asking about fighting?" Narine glanced at Jacob. He was a formidable man, and he carried himself with a level of confidence that other men would find intimidating. Narine saw the kindness in his eyes, so she wasn't put off by it, but others might be. "Don't be an ass, Tade."

"I'm just making conversation." Tadesse lifted an arm and flexed his biceps. "I've been thinking about working out more."

"I think that's great." Jacob looked confused, and he

crossed his arms over his chest. "But you should avoid fighting. That's not why I—"

"I only mean that, given your size, you'd be an intimidating opponent." Tadesse raised his eyebrows at Narine. "Should a friend find themselves in a threatening situation."

She narrowed her eyes. *Tade, you irritating son of a donkey. Don't you dare.*

"I guess I don't think about it much." Jacob sat in the chair next to Tade. "I know I'm a big guy; most people leave me alone. I'm lucky that way."

"Absolutely not." Narine narrowed her eyes. "Whatever you're thinking—"

"Narine and I are making a jump tomorrow." Tade turned back to Jacob. "A fact-finding mission only. We wouldn't be altering the timeline at all. Perhaps you would like to join us and get a taste of what all the Seba Segel business is."

"No," Narine said. "He's untrained. He couldn't never learn the spells in the time we have before the jump."

"We both know that won't be an issue." Tade's eyes bored into her. "We both know that your magic can help him along, and let's face it, having another traveler with us—one as big as Jacob here—would be a good thing, especially when we're going into an unknown situation. Or would you rather take a hedge who would report us to the elders? Maybe Mesfin is avail—"

"We're not taking a hedge, and we don't need to take Jacob," Narine said. "This is not going to be dangerous."

"Making a jump?" Jacob asked. "You mean actually traveling back in time?"

"Yes," Tadesse said. "Interested in finding out what it's all about?"

"Absolutely."

Narine nearly choked. "Tade, what are you doing?"

"I'm game for whatever." Jacob shrugged his massive shoulders. "I can't lie, I'm dying to know how all this works."

"If you don't know what you're doing, it can be very dangerous," Narine said. "You're not ready for it."

"He doesn't have to be." Tadesse turned to Jacob. "You don't have to be. Narine can take you with her. She can carry you with her magic. That's what makes her a third-tier mage. Surely Elder Kidist told you about the power tiers."

Jacob frowned. "Mostly he seemed… Let's just say he's not a big fan of time travel." He sat forward. "Did he just say you could take people with you? You mean you can carry other people along with your magic?"

Narine stared at Tadesse, who had a small smile on his face.

Troublemaker.

She took a deep breath. "Yes. I can take you with my own magic. If you really want to go. I still don't think it's a good idea."

"I do," Tadesse said. "I think it's a great idea."

"I don't want either of you coming with me," Narine muttered. "I'd rather go alone."

"Says the former spy." Tadesse smiled. "Too bad. You may be going rogue on this one, Narine, but you're not going alone."

# CHAPTER 17

*The Island*
*1920*

"We need to meet soon."

Narine whispered it to Gideon as he entered the meeting room, and he gave her a subtle nod before he took his place on the far side of the room, lined up with Tigist, Ger, Samuel, and the other two elders who had returned from visiting family to spend the New Year at home.

"Sister Narine." Samuel started the meeting. "Thank you for coming."

She nodded. "I serve the order, Brother Samuel." Narine looked at Tigist, who was glancing around, her eyes wary on the men surrounding them.

"Sister Narine, we have received a message from the capital city that we hope you might explain for us."

Shit, shit, shit. She didn't want to get Tigist in trouble with her fellow elders, but it sounded like someone had loose lips in the empress's household. Narine decided to play innocent.

"A message that needs explaining?" She smiled. "Of

course. Do you need a translation? I speak nine languages; I might be able to help."

She saw Gideon hiding a smile behind a subtle clearing of his throat.

Samuel was not amused. "We have been informed that the crown prince received information from a source that made it clear a 'massacre' would occur if he did not cut off negotiations with certain parties. We want to know how he got that information."

"However he received that information, I am only glad that he acted on it. It was my directive from my elders that sent me back to this time in order to communicate that information," Narine said. "If that information was received by those in power and acted on, then my mission has been completed."

Ger cast his eyes sideways at Samuel, whose face was turning dark with anger. "Sister Narine, I believe we communicated your message to those in power and they decided it was not information that was specific enough to pass along to the crown prince."

"Oh? I was told the crown prince wasn't interested in advice from the Seba Segel."

Ger blinked. "There may have been a miscommunication at some point, but what we are trying to determine is—"

"How I got my information into Ras Tafari's ear?" Narine sat up straight and didn't let her back slump for a second. Not one second could they see a hint of weakness. She had to be utterly professional. "It doesn't matter how I got the information to him; it matters that he received the wisdom from my elders, and I am happy that he acted on it. That action will save lives."

"That action could have consequences you don't even know," Samuel blurted out. "This is why traveling is an ancient practice that has no place in modern life."

*You call yourselves modern?*

Narine didn't say it. "With all respect due to you, Elder Samuel, I do not serve this local council. I am a scribe of House Kayl, and I serve the high council of the most ancient order of the Seba Segel in Addis Ababa. If they have a problem with my actions here when I return and give them my report, I will subject myself to their authority. But I was given a directive to share information, and it was shared. The manner in which it was transmitted is no business of this council. I am only here because of an accident of the timeline."

Gideon finally spoke. "I was told that time makes no mistake." He glanced up and his eyes met hers. "That all things happen for a reason. A tiny pebble can create a ripple that creates a wave that can swallow a mountain."

"Yes." Narine looked at him squarely. "And that ripple was what I was meant to create here in this time. The fact that I am still here—that the timeline saw fit to have me remain in this time until my mission was complete—is evidence that time is wiser than we are."

"Time has no will," Gideon countered. "It only is."

"The existence of the Tibeb argues against that statement."

Gideon leaned forward, his elbows resting on his knees. "The Tibeb is a record of wisdom; you are saying time is a god with a will and you serve it."

"I'm saying that whatever god we believe in, time is in service to it and we are in service to time."

Ger interjected, "This is all very interesting, but I believe Elder Samuel wants to know how you got your message to Addis Ababa and if it has anything to do with Daniel Kebede's recent trip to the city."

Narine glanced at Tigist but only for a second. She directed her answer to Ger. "I believe Daniel was carrying letters from Tigist to her mother. Is family correspondence now a subject for local council attention?"

"No." Ger turned to Samuel. "Brother, I know you're irritated by all this, but none of these political twists or turns reflects poorly on our village or our council. The information that the traveler was sent to share was shared. Surely you must respect that she has her mission to complete, just as we have our own."

Elder Samuel stood and looked down his nose at Narine. "She doesn't know her place."

"I know exactly what my place is." Narine lifted her chin. "The problem is, you really have no idea who you're talking to." She stood. "You have no idea who I am."

Elder Samuel scoffed. "Is that supposed to mean something to me? Are you supposed to be someone important? I know those of the old houses, even in the city, and House Kayl is not among them."

Gideon let out a sharp laugh. "In this *time*, Samuel. Have you forgotten she is of another?"

The curl of the elder's lip put Narine on guard. She didn't often pull rank or allude to her bloodlines or her family's power, but she was tired of these petty men thinking they had authority over her when they had none, and she was irritated that Tigist might become a target for their anger after she left.

"For now, you live under our authority," Elder Samuel said quietly. "And I expect you to show the proper respect."

*You are Narine, third-degree traveling mage of the Seba Segel, ninth in your line of power and scion of House Kayl. Student of Abdi Mulenah of the Southern Mages, daughter of Anahid, daughter of Khoren, son of Madlene. Your blood can be traced back to the Melkior, servant of the light.*

Narine curled her mouth into the sweetest smile she could manage. "Elder Samuel, I will always give respect to those deserving of it, as my mother and the elders of my house have taught me. May the sun, moon, and stars judge our actions this day and every day."

*And fuck you very much.*

215

Narine didn't wait for their permission to depart the meeting room. She turned on her heel and left.

SHE MET HIM THAT NIGHT BY THE FICUS TREE ON THE EDGE OF the lake. She was beginning to think of it as "their tree," and many of her sex dreams about Gideon seemed to be in this location.

But that night Narine wasn't thinking of her sex drive or her simmering attraction to the Kenyan mage. She was angry about the meeting and worried about Tigist.

"You handled that well." He stood on the jutting rock that hung over the lake. "They won't be able to blame Tigist for the leak."

"Leak?" She turned to him. "It wasn't a leak. It was vital information that they sabotaged because they don't like travelers."

He shrugged. "Some people here see travelers as meddlers who are unhelpful and only disrupt the timeline."

"But diviners are fine?" She pointed to the observatory on the top of the hill that gave the order on the Zay Islands its reason for being. "Divining the stars is respected. Knowing the future is desirable, but changing the wrongs of the past is not?"

"Didn't you say it today?" Gideon appeared amused. "'Time is wiser than we are.' That's what you said. So what is the use of changing the past?"

"What is the point of knowing the future?"

Gideon raised a finger, and it reminded Narine of a pompous teacher she'd had in school. "Knowing the future allows one to avoid mistakes. Changing the past is like... cheating."

"Cheating?"

"Yes, cheating. Humans didn't get it right the first time around, so they have a chance to edit? What does that accomplish? Haven't you ever wondered if travelers are running around history making changes that they only have to correct later?" He shrugged. "You can't seem to change the really important things, so why bother?"

"Two hundred and fifteen."

Gideon shrugged. "What does that mean?"

Narine stepped toward him. "Two hundred and fifteen lives were lost in a massacre that didn't need to happen. I know some things we can't change, and I understand how... *maddening* that is. Travelers talk about the Pagume prohibition constantly, questioning it, wondering if just this once would it be worth it..." She shook her head. "We don't break it because we know the consequence last time was a war that almost destroyed the order."

"Now you sound like all the rest of them." He stepped closer, and she could feel the heat of his body on her skin. "Travelers could stop the British from colonizing my country," Gideon said. "You could make their ships sink."

"We did." She blurted the words out before she could stop to think.

Gideon frowned.

"They sent more. We sank those, and they moved across the continent, stealing more, causing even more suffering." Narine shook her head. "Every time we tried to stop these kinds of tragedies, time gives them another route."

Gideon's expression didn't change.

"There will be war in Central America," Narine said. "There was famine in Ireland, and there will be more famine as the planet warms until previously fertile land turns into desert. There has been wave after wave of conquest in Asia." Narine felt small. Weak. Foolish for even trying. "Sometimes all we have is two hundred and fifteen."

He reached out and gripped her arm. "What does that even mean?"

"Those are the number of lives that can be saved if the crown prince listens to the warning that my council sent him. Those are the ones I can save."

The grip on her arm softened. "Why can't the diviners see it? Why won't it be prevented that way?"

"The diviners don't see everything; they have their limits too. But if the prince listens, two hundred and fifteen people who died for no reason will live. And from those people's lives, who knows what could happen? They could cure disease or write poetry. Their lives have meaning; they can be a pebble…"

"A pebble that starts a ripple that turns into a wave." He released her arm and stepped back.

"That's what I was taught." Narine felt cold. The wind from the lake whipped up and tossed water-laden air around her, creeping cold fingers up her skirt and teasing her neck with chilling breaths. "I know that may not seem like much to you, but—"

"I have feelings for you that are more than friendly." Gideon stared at her.

It was such an abrupt change that Narine nearly laughed. She didn't because she saw the intense way he was looking at her, and he didn't seem happy.

"I'm sorry."

His eyes were cutting. "I didn't ask for your pity."

"I don't pity you. I'm apologizing because clearly this isn't something you're happy about."

"We never spoke about the kiss."

"The kiss…" She tried to play it off. "That was a result of a bad night and an intense moment we shared. It doesn't have to mean anything, Gideon."

"I dream about you."

"So do I." The words came before Narine could stop them. "For weeks now."

Gideon didn't reach for her, but he stepped closer and she could feel the heat from his body again, blocking the cold lake air from reaching her. "What kind of dreams?"

She felt the heat in her cheeks. "Just dreams."

"I see." His voice went low. "And what if I said I'd dreamed about you the same way? That I want to kiss your breasts and have you under me. That I want to take you right now."

Narine closed her eyes because the images that came to her weren't in her sleeping mind. They were vivid and alive in front of her. She could feel his mouth on her skin. She could feel his desire like a furnace. She wouldn't fall asleep alone and cold in her bed if she took Gideon as a lover.

"This won't end well," she whispered. "It can't."

"You talk about the end when we haven't even begun." He cocked his head and examined her like a specimen under his microscope. "I want you, Narine Anahid Khoren of House Kayl."

She looked up at him, and he still hadn't touched her but the fire of his body heat stole her breath. She wanted him so badly and so intently that he had to see it.

"Kiss me," Gideon said. "Or walk away."

She put her hand on his chest, pressing her palm over his heart to see if it was as impassive as his face. It wasn't. His heart galloped under her palm, and she stood on her tiptoes to press her mouth to his lips.

Gideon made her wait for a few long seconds before he took control and wrapped one arm around her shoulders while his hand landed on her lower back, pressing her closer to him so she felt the intensity of his desire manifest in his reaction to her. He barely moved, but their bodies were aligned, his mouth with hers. Her breasts against his chest. His lungs breathing in as she breathed out.

The wind crested around them, but there was no room for it between their bodies.

*This won't end well.*

*It can't.*

# CHAPTER 18

*Addis Ababa*
*2072*

The traveling chamber was a black vacuum until Aida flipped on the lights. A blue-green illumination lit the floor and the pool with an eerie light, and the consoles that set the constellation pattern flicked on.

"I cannot believe I'm doing this." Aida took a deep breath. "But if you're going, I'm staying here to supervise. You need someone in the chamber if there are problems." She walked over to the corner and switched on the electric brazier for the incense.

"Why would there be problems?" Jacob asked.

Narine and Aida shared a look but said nothing.

"It's just better to have someone observing," Tadesse said. "To make sure that nothing goes wrong here. For Aida, it will only feel like a few minutes. For us, we'll be gone two days."

"Two days." Jacob took a deep breath and looked down at the clothes Tadesse had dressed him in. "And I look okay?"

"You look great. Very *habesha*." Narine liked the traditional white pants and long shirt that Jacob and Tadesse were both wearing. They had wound cotton wraps around their shoulders, tucking them closely around their body so they wouldn't weigh them down in whatever water they landed.

Narine wore a similar outfit but with a lighter shawl, a *netela*, that covered her hair and shoulders, a heavier gebi around her body, and a pair of slim pants beneath her tunic. She was also carrying a pack with extra food, some basic camping supplies, and clothes, just in case the jump stripped Jacob. There was no telling how her magic would interact with his once they were in the pool. Logic would say he was a first-tier traveler if he was a natural mage, but his power felt stronger than that. If he had mage blood, anything was possible.

"The Bale Mountains are cold this time of year," Aida said. "But I located a river that's not too far from a village where you should be able to find shelter. The spring camp that was attacked is around five kilometers from that human village. I didn't want to appear too close when these people have just suffered an attack."

Narine patted her pocket. "I have your notes and maps."

"Do you have any kind of credentials?"

"I borrowed Elder Kidist's seal and wrote a letter of introduction. I don't think the Addis council seal has changed much in the past few hundred years."

Aida and Tadesse stared at her.

"What? We needed something."

Tadesse raised both his hands. "I know nothing."

"And I'm going to pretend I didn't hear you," Aida looked at her clipboard. "It'll be a walk from your landing to the village, but it'll warm you up from the water."

Most of Southern Ethiopia had a mild climate, but the Bale Mountains were the rooftop of Africa with peaks that reached over fourteen thousand feet. Though they were only going to the hill country, the elevation was still high and the weather would be chilly.

"We're arriving two weeks after the massacre happened," Narine told Jacob. "People will be suspicious, so be prepared for that. The local people will mostly be speaking Oromo, though some of the elders may speak some Amharic. Tade and I both speak Oromo, so you can stay quiet. I doubt they'll question you."

"It may work in our favor if we tell them we're from Addis," Tadesse said. "Anyone from the order will know that there are foreigners on the elder council. Remember, we're only going to get answers about what happened. Just stand by and observe."

"Where will we sleep?" Jacob asked. "Do you guys have money from that time? Can we buy food?"

"I have gold." Tadesse smiled a little. "We'll be able to find food."

Narine glanced at Jacob. "Having second thoughts? You can back out if you want. You're not committed to this."

He took a deep breath and bounced on his toes a little. "Nah, I'm good. I want to do this."

"Okay. Don't worry about shelter. We'll stay at an order house if they have one, or at a local church," Narine said. "There will be room for travelers somewhere. It might be in a barn, but we won't be exposed."

Aida was looking around the room nervously. "If someone comes in while you're gone——"

"It's fine." Tadesse put a hand on her arm and she calmed down. "Aida, they won't interfere with a ritual that's already started. You'll be fine. If anyone asks, tell them you're helping me with an investigation from the elder council. Remember last month?"

Narine looked at Aida. "Last month? Have you guys been taking jumps without me?"

Aida rolled her eyes. "You're not the center of the universe, you know."

"I don't know that," Narine said. "All I hear is my friends

leaving me out of the fun. See if I invite you to my next barbecue."

The joking seemed to put Aida at ease, and she let out a breath. "Okay. Tadesse Girma, you better be careful."

"Just Tade?" Narine pretended to pout. "I see how it is now."

Aida shook her head. "You're a pain in my ass, Narine."

Narine winked, and her friend smiled.

"I'll be careful." Tadesse touched Aida's cheek. "And don't worry. I won't let her cause trouble. We'll be back in a few minutes."

Narine watched them, wanting the world to be different.

Jacob nudged her shoulder. "Are they...?"

"No, but they should be," she muttered. "It's a whole thing."

"Right." He looked down at his clothes, then to the blue-green glowing pool. "I feel something."

She narrowed her eyes. "Describe it."

"It's almost like this... effervescent feeling in my stomach. Not bad. But I've never felt anything like it before." He looked at Narine. "What if this doesn't work?"

"I'm pretty sure that's not going to be a problem." Narine could feel his power reaching for the pool. It wanted to grab on to the magic; she could sense the eagerness in his blood. She might have to revise her classification of his magic. It was definitely growing as they got closer to the pool. "But if it doesn't, all that will happen is that we'll disappear and you'll stay here. Do not worry about that."

If there was anything to worry about, it was the calcula-tions for their return, which depended on her mother's algo-rithm. But she wasn't going to mention that at the moment.

"I'm putting in the constellar pattern now," Aida said. "Are you ready?"

"Do you have the incense?" Tade asked.

Aida nodded; then suddenly the lights above them shifted

and the stars took on a new pattern, mimicking the sky when they were headed. Aida walked over and added incense to the brazier that was smoking in the corner.

Narine took Jacob's hand and pulled out a knife. "I'm going to start the spell, but be prepared, I'm going to have to offer both our blood to the pool for this ritual to work."

Jacob glanced at her bared arm. "Just a cut like that?"

"Yes, just a quick cut. It'll scab over within minutes of our arrival. Whatever you feel when we go under the water, just go with it. It's like swimming within a current, okay? If you fight it, the magic won't take you."

Tadesse joined them. "You have to give in and float, my friend." He took out his own knife. "Narine, I'm feeling very good. My power always reacts well to yours."

"Yeah." Jacob breathed out. "What is that?"

"That's old blood, my friend." Tadesse smiled. "That's generations of magic concentrated in one annoying little package."

Narine took Jacob's wrist and felt his power reach for hers. *Whoa.*

She almost said it out loud. There was no way—no possible way—that Jacob had been born with spontaneous power. His magic was too dominant. In fact, his power slid along hers more comfortably than any magic she'd ever felt.

She focused on starting the spell, pushing back the urge to blush. "Listen to my voice," she said quietly. "Even if you don't understand the words, focus on the cadence."

Tadesse was whispering his own spell. He brought out his knife, closed his eyes, and added to the starburst pattern he was forming on his forearm.

Narine whispered the words of power, made one quick cut in Jacob's arm, then another in her own, before she pulled him under the water with her and the magic took them both.

*Bale Mountains*
*1934*

THE WATER SURROUNDING HER WAS FREEZING AND RAGGED stones dug into her back. Narine sat up with a gasp and felt the biting wind of the mountains hit her face.

"Fuck!" Jacob's voice was a groan next to her. "What just happened?"

"We're in 1934." She stood in the rushing mountain stream and pulled at his arm. "Come on. Out of the water or you'll get hypothermia. Out, out."

Tadesse was already stepping onto the shore. "We were supposed to get here midday."

"Jesus, that water is freezing." Jacob shook his head and unwound the heavy cotton wrap around his shoulders.

Narine looked up at the sun, which was sinking quickly. "I miscalculated." Narine and Jacob struggled to the shore. "Sorry."

"Sorry?" Tadesse was furious. "This is why diviners do the calculations, Narine! It's almost nighttime."

And night in the mountains was dangerous. They had no firearms and only rocks to fend off any animals that might find them interesting. "We'll find a shelter."

"Do you see anything around here?" Tade waved his arms. "If we don't find something before the sun goes down, we're lion food."

Jacob froze. "Wait, there are lions here?"

"Uh…" Narine shivered in her sopping-wet clothes. "Some."

"More than some!" Tadesse picked up a long stick from a fallen tree on the side of the river and snapped it over his knee to make a rudimentary walking stick. "Jacob, grab a stick."

"For *lions*?"

"No." Narine looked at him. "Probably not. A good walking stick can save your life."

"Save my…" Jacob trudged over to the tree where Tadesse had obtained his stick. "I thought this was supposed to be a simple trip."

Tadesse said, "Me too."

"Did we land in the middle of a migrating wildebeest herd?" Narine gritted her teeth and sawed off a sizable walking stick with her ritual blade. Jacob was right, she was freezing. "No! No, we didn't."

"Did that actually happen to you?" Jacob stared at her.

"That happens to everyone," Tadesse muttered. "I think I see something." He pointed toward the south. "What direction did Aida say that village was?"

"South along the river," Narine said. "I put us up here to avoid any humans seeing us."

"I think there's a shepherd's hut over there." Tadesse looked over his shoulder. "Everyone have a stick?"

"Yes." Narine waved hers.

"Got one." Jacob lifted a branch that was the size of a small tree.

"Then let's go. We need a fire, and we need to get dried off before this wind makes us sick."

They trudged over deep green hills and damp grass to reach a rudimentary stone structure constructed from stacked grey rocks. Wooden poles and old brush covered the small hut, and a firepit had been built close to the entrance and into the ground to keep the wind from killing the flames. There was a small stack of wood next to the hut, so Narine knew it had been recently used.

"We can stay here." Tadesse took off his gebi and spread it over the low wooden roof, weighing it down with stones so it didn't blow away. "I don't see any grazing herds, so the chances of lions hanging around here are small."

Jacob took off his gebi and copied Tadesse. "We need to get warm. There's firewood here."

"You guys start a fire." Narine took off her own wrap and

hung it over a scrubby bush, tying one end to a branch. "I brought waterskins. I'll fill them in the river."

"Before you get dry?" Jacob asked.

"We don't have time; the sun's going down."

Tade sighed. "We don't have any way to boil the water. Shit. I usually take a week to prepare for jumps like this and—"

"I got it." Narine bent down and pulled out two small metal cups. "They're small, but it'll be enough to get us through until tomorrow. Don't you have a go bag, Tade?"

While Tadesse and Narine had intestines seasoned by years of traveling in unknown places, Narine knew better than anyone that your entire mission could be upended by a bad meal or tainted water.

Tadesse was already building a fire with some of the kindling he'd broken up from a piece of wood and a flint kit he pulled from his pocket. "I usually plan my jumps so I don't need one."

Jacob was standing at the edge of the hut, staring at the horizon.

Narine turned to look at where Jacob was looking and realized he was watching the sun set over the southern hills.

Jacob was a man born in the middle of the twenty-first century on a planet ravaged by a hundred years of warming temperatures, intense global pollution, and night skies bristling with satellites.

Nothing could compare to the first sunset on an unpolluted horizon.

Narine and Tadesse stopped their bickering and shared a knowing smile.

"Have you ever seen anything as gorgeous?" she asked him.

"No." Jacob blinked glassy eyes. "Never."

She left him marveling at the sky while she walked quickly to the river, filled up two skins of water, and hurried back to the hut where Tadesse had managed to build a robust fire. As soon as she reached it, she sighed in relief. Fire equaled safety. Safety from cold. From animals. In places like this, fire was life.

"Let me get inside." She crouched low and maneuvered herself into the hut, where she took off her sopping-wet clothes and wrapped the still-damp gebi around herself before she walked to the fire and spread her pants and tunic on a rock near the flames. She also spread out the wet clothes she'd brought for Jacob and the other damp supplies in her backpack.

Tadesse didn't blink twice at her near-nakedness, but she could feel Jacob staring.

"I can warm up my skin by the fire," Narine explained. "But if I stay in those wet clothes, no amount of campfire is going to keep me from getting sick."

"Right." He took off his shirt and shivered a little as he laid it on a rock. "Once my gebi is dry, I'll get my pants."

Tadesse nodded and did the same.

The sun went down in a flaming gold tapestry of light and night followed quickly, the stars a dancing symphony of light overhead. Narine sat on the rocks by the campfire and watched as the southern sky filled with the constellations she had memorized from the time she was a child.

The guardian wolf, every traveler's shining light that mirrored the birthmark they all shared. The archer stood proudly next to the wolf, the bow of the great sea vessel below them and the spear point that marked the hedge mages.

And of course, reigning over all of them, the queen, draped in her shawl, the symbol of the Tibeb, the intricately woven tapestry of the Seba Segel.

"What do you see?" Jacob asked her. "I don't really know the constellations much. I suppose I'll have to learn."

Yes, he would. He would have to learn all of them, their

movements and their meanings. Though he was no diviner, the stars were their map of history and time.

"What do I see?" Narine stared at the bow of the great ship and remembered a time when she'd felt more lost than any other time in her life. "When I look at the stars, I see the way home."

# CHAPTER 19

*The Island*
*New Year's Eve, 1920*

It was comforting to know that the preparations for New Year's Day hadn't changed much. The New Year had always been a special celebration in Narine's home growing up. Because no travelers could make time jumps during the thirteenth month, Pagume was always spent at home, surrounded by family, cleaning out the house and garden, making way for a fresh start. Narine's cousins would visit, Genet's cousins would come for the day, and the compound would be full to bursting with family, friends, and visitors.

It was the same on the island. The heavy rains had passed and the flowers were blooming, the bright yellow splashes of color filling the hills and fields around the village.

Narine returned to the compound on New Year's Eve with an armload of long cut grass, ready to spread it over her floor and the rest of the compound to decorate the stones and packed earth. She was surprised to find Gideon waiting at the gate, ready to open it for her with a smile flirting around his lips.

"Sister Narine."

She did her best to hide her delight. "Brother Gideon."

"You've gathered a lot of grass today."

She pulled out her curved ritual knife. "Well, it has to have some use at the moment, doesn't it?"

The amusement in his eyes fled. "Isn't it a nice break though? Staying in one time and not having to run around to play the order's messenger girl?"

"I don't travel every day." It felt good to speak openly with someone. "Sometimes I'll go weeks without a jump."

"A jump?" The amusement was back. "Now I'm picturing you as a school girl, splashing in puddles."

"It's more like jumping into a stream." She tucked her knife away before scattering the grass over the freshly swept stones of Tigist and Daniel's compound. "And getting carried away."

She could hear the cook singing in the distance and wondered if the woman would sing when they lit the bonfire in the village that night or if the priests were the only ones allowed to sing the New Year's songs.

"Jumping into streams?" Gideon leaned against the wall and watched her work. "So it's like swimming?"

Narine dropped her voice. "When we travel during the ritual, we're asking time to allow us passage. We tell it where we want to go, show it the stars we want to visit, and the water connects us to that time and place." She looked up. "Water is eternal, you know. The same water in this time is still there in my time. It moves, transforms, turns to ice or fog or rain, but it's all the same water."

"That's why travel is always via water," Gideon murmured.

Narine shrugged. "It's not a secret, but we don't talk about the specifics much. I suppose most other mages aren't interested. Every vocation of the Seba Segel has their secrets."

Gideon's eyebrows went up. "Do you want to know the alchemists' secrets?"

"Of course. I shared the travelers'."

"There are many explosions when we're young."

Narine burst into laughter, and it was the most free she'd felt in... She didn't remember. The grass smelled bright and green around her, and Gideon was laughing like he always did at New Year's. He was happy when the rains stopped; he didn't like overcast skies.

She blinked and realized that her memories were unclear. She didn't know that Gideon was always happy at New Year, did she? Who was singing? Was that Genet? The smell of sizzling beef wafted from the kitchen along with the smell of spiced butter and onion.

It was New Year. *Melkam addis amet.*

Yellow flowers and cut grass. The smell of food cooking and *aragash* bread in the stone oven.

She heard Genet's voice singing and smelled her mother's bread baking for the New Year table. The chopped beef for the dolmas was simmering in the kitchen and she was spreading grape leaves, unfolding them with delicate fingers so the edges didn't break.

"Narine?"

Someone touched her shoulder and she looked up. Gideon was there, and he'd taken the cut grass from her arm.

"Are you confused?" He kept his voice low. "Do you need—?"

"I'm fine." She put her hand over his heart and felt the steady thump of his pulse guiding her out of her memories and back to the present. "I was thinking about New Year's celebrations as a child and then they kind of.... merged with everything happening today, but I'm good." She nodded. "Thank you, Gideon."

"Are you writing in your journals?"

"Every day. Thank you, those really helped me."

He smiled, and his eyes creased in the corners. "Maybe I'll steal them someday and read all your secrets."

Narine smiled. "You better not. I put all my childhood crimes in there. I'm going to burn them before I leave."

His smile fell.

"Don't." She shook her head. "You said we had to live in the moment."

He shook his head, and the smile returned to his lips, but his eyes had lost their gleam. "And we will. I should talk to Daniel and see if there's anything I can bring tonight." He handed the bundle of grass back to her. "The compound looks beautiful."

She looked around at the spotless whitewashed walls that Daniel had touched up, the newly thatched roof of the main house, and the neatly brushed stones in the courtyard. She'd sprinkled grass all over the stones, and Tigist's two servant girls had gone to the hills early that morning and gathered bunches of bright yellow flowers to tuck in clay jars in every window.

It was beautiful, and for now it felt like home.

A TALL BONFIRE WAS BURNING IN THE MIDDLE OF THE VILLAGE, lit by every house of the order, the members of which brought long dried branches from their compounds to add to the bonfire and share the warmth. The priests of the order were singing the old songs, familiar hymns of praise to welcome the new year, along with some folk songs she knew and others that were unfamiliar.

Narine and Tigist followed behind Daniel as he carried lit branches to the village bonfire. Children were running every-where, excited to be celebrating after dark. Narine spotted

Gideon already at the fire, chatting with Ger, his arms crossed over his chest as he nodded seriously at something the other man was saying.

The smell of roasting lamb filled the air along with a faint waft of popping oil. She could see the women of the village piling fresh stacks of injera on a wooden table in the clearing.

Narine and Tigist clapped and sang along. The night air was crisp, and the smoke from the bonfire sparked and billowed into the sky. On the ridge of the island, the human village was celebrating too, and an echo of their songs carried on the wind from the lake.

"Sister Narine." One of the women from the spinning group greeted her. "Welcome. Happy New Year."

"Happy New Year."

"Blessings on your family."

"Thank you, and blessings on yours."

It carried from one person to the next. The press of hands, the touch of a shoulder, the familiar greeting and well-wishes for the new year.

Again and again, with every mage of the order. In some ways it was just like every human celebration of the New Year that was happening around the country.

And in other ways… not so much.

The alchemists had been busy, building sparkling whirligigs for the children that flew into the night sky and danced like colored stars before they dissolved in a shower of gold. It was a simple spell, but it delighted the children. The alchemists also treated the bonfire with spells, ensuring a light display no human village could match.

The archivists sat in a circle with traditional instruments, sharing stories of the past while young mothers, teenage sweethearts, and the oldest mages sat in the center, letting the wisdom of the past encircle them. It was a fine tradition for those looking for a quieter celebration.

The diviners had already spoken to the elders, giving their

best predictions for the new year, always a balance of caution and celebration, mixed with practical tips like what crops would grow best in the fields that year and where the rain would fall.

Hedge mages roamed around the perimeter of the village, keeping watch for any human intrusion and making sure no children strayed too far and no animals wandered in.

To Narine, the chaos was achingly familiar and new at once. She'd always celebrated New Year's in her own home with her own family and friends. They rarely kept all the village traditions that the island did, and Narine had only experienced them when she'd visited Genet's family village as a child.

Still, the magical whirligigs were a traditional favorite. Narine remembered burning her finger as a child when she'd held on to one a little too long. The voices telling the stories were familiar, and she clapped as the men circled the bonfire with their lit torches, singing the song her father had sung when she was small.

Her mother would sit with Aster, the two women leaning their heads together as they sat at the foot of the archivist mages and let the music wash over them while Narine and Genet ran around the village, playing with their friends.

She blinked. No.

No.

Her father had never sung that song. Her mother and Aster never sat among the storytellers. She'd never held a whirligig and burned her finger. Her memories were confused, and she was starting to merge her reality with the past.

Narine stared at the fire, trying to sort through her memories. She didn't know what was real and what was past. Where did she belong? In this village that welcomed her or with the family that waited?

Seconds dragged in the present as her mother sat in a corner, texting with someone while the incense burned and

Aida watched the constellar settings on the console, making sure they didn't waver during the jump. They were waiting for her to emerge from the pool. Time was frozen for them while it spun in Narine's head like a sparkling children's toy flying into the sky.

"Narine."

She looked up and Gideon's eyes were severe. His eyes were always severe, but his hand on her shoulder was gentle. Why was that? Why was he soft and hard at once? He was a man of contradictions. Was that why she loved him?

"Narine, you're forgetting." He kept his voice low, hooked his arm with hers, and shuffled her away from the hubbub of the village celebration. He waved at someone in the distance and ushered Narine along the path, moving her around the rock near the large acacia tree where she'd broken her foot when she was young.

"I hurt my foot on that stone." She glanced over her shoulder. "When I was a child. I was running home, and I took the corner too fast and—"

"No you didn't, Narine." He pushed open the gate to her compound. "You didn't hurt your foot on that rock because you didn't live here as a child."

She furrowed her forehead. She remembered the rock. Remembered the pain that radiated up her leg from the broken toe. Her mother had bound it so tightly when it swelled and turned purple.

He walked to her house and opened the door briskly. "Sit."

"Gideon?"

"Where is your journal?" He knelt in front of her and reached beneath her bed. "Where do you keep your journal, Narine Anahid Khoren?"

She pointed to the desk. Why was he so irritated? She didn't remember him ever being this angry before. "Did I do something wrong?"

He took a deep breath and sat back on his heels. He looked at her and then closed his eyes. "Maybe you did hurt your foot on that rock," he whispered.

"What?" She still didn't understand why he'd taken her from the party or why he was so irritated.

"No." He stood and walked to the desk, grabbed a thick journal, and flipped it open to the beginning. "'My name is Narine Anahid Khoren, only daughter of Anahid and Stefan. I am a traveler of House Kayl. My people were forced from their homeland and pursued by those who hated us and wanted to kill our magic, but we escaped and found refuge in the high order of the Seba Segel of Addis Ababa.'"

Narine heard her mother's voice repeating the words to her as if by rote, her voice holding none of the animation or emotion of the storyteller. She was reciting Narine's identity as if she were a soldier taken by an enemy.

"'I was born in...'" Gideon's voice faltered for a moment. "Born in the year 2043 in the Old Calendar and the year 2050 in the Gregorian year. I came into the world on the third day of Pagume, like my mother and my grandfather before me."

"My father is Stefan Boghosian of House Vana in California," Narine murmured, her world slowly coming into focus. "When I was fifteen, I went to visit my father and he took me to a park called Disneyland." She met Gideon's eyes and blinked.

"And you got sick spinning in teacups." He shook his head. "That sentence makes no sense. How can you spin inside a teacup? How big are these teacups?"

Narine smiled. "Quite large in fact."

"You were gone." He stood and set her journal on the desk again. "Are you back?"

She took stock of her memories.

*You are Narine Anahid Khoren of House Kayl. You are a third-degree traveling mage of the Seba Segel, ninth in your line of power. You were born in Addis Ababa, Ethiopia. You have no siblings and many cousins. You are the godmother of Gelile, the adopted sister of Genet, the daughter of Anahid. Your best friend is Jamila Sahid of the house Rajab. You have been stuck in the year 1920 for six months and are waiting for the day before Holy Week so you can travel back to your own time in the year 2065.*

"I remember who I am." She closed her eyes. "I think the magic flying around tonight combined with the celebration—most of which is the same—it triggered the confusion."

"Yes, it seemed like you were merging this timeline and your own." He stuck his hands in his pockets. "But you're fine now?"

She stood and walked to him, putting her arms around his shoulders in an embrace. "I'm back. Thank you, Gideon."

He returned her embrace, letting out a deep sigh as he hugged her and ran his hands up and down her back. "Did you really break your foot when you were a child?"

"Yes. The gate in our compound? It has this big block that the lock sank into and I always just cracked the gate open to squeeze through—"

"Because you were in a hurry."

"Yes." She looked up. "I was in a hurry and I slammed my foot into the block when I was nine. I broke three toes."

He tucked a piece of her hair behind her ear. "Maybe the stars brought you here because they want you to slow down."

"Maybe." *Maybe they brought me here to meet you.*

She moved her cheek against his, relishing the faint smell of herbs and oil that clung to his skin. It was something woodsy and fresh that reminded her of walking in a cedar forest. She began to nuzzle him with soft, fluttering kisses to his neck.

"Narine…"

"Why not?" She closed her eyes. "Everyone is at the bonfire," she whispered. "No one will miss us." It had been weeks of stolen touches and hidden kisses. She wanted

239

more, and she knew he did too. "Gideon, no one will miss us."

"Your mind wasn't clear." He might have protested, but he was kissing along her neck and his hands were clutching her buttocks, kneading the flesh there with eager fingers. "It wouldn't be—"

"I'm fine." She found his lips with her own and sank into a hungry kiss. "I'm fine."

He pulled back and met her eyes. "You know who you are?"

"Yes." She kissed him again. "And I know I want you."

He didn't hesitate any longer.

# CHAPTER 20

*Bale Mountains*
*1934*

"What did Tade mean: 'Says the former spy'?" Jacob glanced at her from across the firepit the next morning. "You were a spy?"

"I often still am," Narine said. "It depends on the situation. Some jobs need someone who can blend in, and often that's not me. It depends on where and when it is. I'm usually good to travel in North Africa because I speak the languages there."

"Arabic?"

"Arabic." She poked at the fire with a stick. "Berber. Coptic. And of course English and French depending on the era." She glanced at him. "Why do you ask?"

"You fooled me." He crossed his legs and put his feet nearer the fire. "I guess if you're a trained spy, I won't feel as bad about being fooled."

She blinked. "How did I fool you? I didn't fool you."

"You pretended to be—"

"What?" She shrugged. "I didn't lie to you, Jacob."

"No?" He narrowed his eyes. "It feels like you did."

"Omitting information is not the same as lying."

"It can be." He raised an eyebrow. "Sometimes it can be worse."

That's what she was afraid of. "You didn't tell me everything either."

The sun had risen in the east and was moving over the mountains, finally warming the small shelter where they'd slept through the night. Tadesse had taken off for the village to gather information and bring back some food before they continued on their journey.

"What didn't I tell you? I was an open book."

"You said nothing about playing American football."

Jacob burst into laughter. "Sorry about that."

"You should be." She glanced up from poking the fire. "I didn't want to lie to you. I didn't want to approach you at all, to be honest. I spotted your travelers' mark, but I assumed the elders would send a hedge. They're the ones who usually find and bring in natural mages."

"Natural mages?"

"People with power who are born to human families. People who don't know about our kind. I've never done it before—and for good reason, obviously—but the elders hate me."

"Why?"

She sighed. "Partly because they respected my mother and her house but resented her independence, and as much as I hate admitting it, the older I get, the more like her I become. Plus they don't like mages who ignore their summons."

"And you did that?"

She nodded. "About six years ago I took a sabbatical of sorts. I didn't work for a year. Personal reasons. They called me, and I ignored them. I figured that I had some time off coming since I'd been working since the age of fourteen, but they didn't exactly see it the same way."

"Did your family approve?"

"My mother did, and she is—she was—the head of our family. So in the end, they had to let me back."

"But they never let you forget."

"No." She raised her eyebrows. "Did Elder Kebret tell you about old families and houses and stuff like that?"

"He was very keen to point out that he comes from the oldest mage house in Ethiopia and probably the world. And that you were from one too. I assume Tade is as well. Which leaves me…?"

"Normal, like Tade." She smiled. "Not every mage family is from one of the old houses. The council…" She huffed out a laugh. "Never mind, they are all from old families now."

"Were they not always?"

She looked up. "The reason we're here is to find out about a massacre that occurred among the Southern Mages, who were a federation of common mage clans—people like you and Tade—who banded together. If you think of the old families—especially historically—you could equate them with aristocrats in a feudal system. There are old families with a lot of power and influence. Minor families with some. But they all kind of ruled over mages and magical activities in their regions."

"Okay, that makes sense. The Seba Segel isn't a democracy."

"Not even close." She sighed. "In many ways, it's incredibly backward. But the Southern Mages were the first to try to change that power dynamic. They were a collection of free-mage clans with no allegiance to any of the houses, and they banded together to make decisions and oversee this area. Eventually the old houses couldn't ignore their authority or their power. The Southern Mages produced very powerful hedges and travelers. My mentor was Abdi Mulenah of the Southern Mages. Only six days ago, I went to work on the first day of Pagume and time had shifted."

"Elder Kebret says that doesn't happen during Pagume."

"It's not *supposed* to because there are certain set points in history that cannot be altered except during the thirteenth month. They're called tasary. No mage is supposed to travel during Pagume. No one is supposed to alter the timeline."

"Except someone did." Jacob frowned. "And Abdi?"

"Abdi doesn't exist anymore, and a massacre of the Southern Mages was written into history, so all his people were wiped out." She shook her head. "It wasn't supposed to happen. We're here to find out who did it."

"And save the Southern Mages?"

"They became the model for groups of free mages all over Europe, Africa, and Asia." She waved her hand. "The Americas already have different power structures, but on this side of the globe, we were stuck in the past until the Southern Mages gained prominence."

Jacob nodded. "They challenged the status quo."

"Yes."

"Which is why you wanted to do this without the council knowing."

She nodded. "I don't need their permission to make a jump. But if we get caught, just make sure to tell them that it was my idea and not Tade's. Leave him out of it."

"Because you're from the crusty old families and you can get away with it?"

She smiled. "Something like that."

"So I don't know if you've heard this, but most countries on this continent have this shiny, fancy thing called *democracy*." Jacob smiled. "And the Seba Segel is still stuck in the past. How long do they think that's going to work?"

Narine shook her head. "Defenders of the old system will

tell you that democracies are still run by the powerful and that the old families are useful because they maintain traditions and maintain their connections to human governments and business."

"Is that true?"

She shrugged. "It's not *untrue*. Old families do usually have better access to those in power in human governments because they've been around a long time and maintain connections with the powerful and the wealthy in the human world. So if our job is to advise rulers and princes—which is why the Seba Segel was organized—there is definite value in maintaining those connections."

"Even if the rulers and princes are horrible people?"

She met his stare. "It's a hard truth of history that the best people rarely rise to the top. Do the best people run your country?"

Jacob laughed a little. "Hardly."

"That doesn't mean we can't use them for good when the opportunity presents itself."

He leaned back against the hut. "So that's how you grew up, huh? Maintain tradition and establish influence? Acquire money. Acquire connections. Doesn't strike me as very... you."

It was and it wasn't.

Narine shrugged. "Most old families, mine included, don't have much money anymore. We have our names and our traditions, but mostly they're obsessed with bloodlines and increasing their magical potential through arranged marriages."

He lifted an eyebrow. "So they're... magical breeding programs?"

She winced. "It sounds so horrible when you put it that way, but yes. That's pretty much what they are."

"Narine." Jacob was looking at her with pity and not a little horror. "Really?"

"My mother has tried to arrange my marriage for years. Aida's family too."

"Narine."

"I know!" She threw up her hands. "It's archaic!"

Jacob laughed at the look on her face, then stood and stretched his arms over his head. "Well, maybe one of those powerful old families had a black sheep they didn't want to claim or something. Maybe that's where I come from."

Narine didn't want to say it, but since Jacob was so powerful, that could be exactly where he came from.

She rose and stomped her feet to get the blood moving. "Let's start cleaning up the camp. As soon as Tade is back, we're going to want to move."

THE LOCATION IN THE FOOTHILLS OF THE BALE MOUNTAINS was little more than a summer meeting place for the pastoralists who made up what was left of the Southern Mages. By the time they got to the village, the scale of the massacre was clear.

Dozens of burned tents were scattered over the hillside, and fresh graves were visible lining the edge of the meadow. The belongings the clans carried had been tossed out of the tents before they burned, and dogs sniffed among the wreckage as herds of cattle and sheep grazed in the distance.

Two weeks had passed since the attack, but it was clear that the focus had been on burying the dead and not moving on.

Horses in colorful saddles and harnesses grazed on the verdant green hills, munching on grass and surrounding the remaining families. Every now and then, a horse would lift its head, look around for danger, then return to grazing.

"They didn't loot." Narine looked at the cattle and the abundant supplies scattered around the camp.

Jacob murmured, "It looks like they just came to kill people; then they left."

Bloody weapons and hide-covered shields had been gathered in a pile that two half-grown boys were guarding with wary eyes and long knives.

There were two hedge mages of fighting age sitting by the fire to meet them, one who had gone to the village to trade and another whose clan had been late to arrive for the festival. The only men of fighting age left of the Southern Mages belonged to his remaining clan.

Other than the single remaining group of thirty adults or so, there were some children, the elderly, and a smattering of younger women who had escaped the massacre by playing dead. The intruders had killed all the young men or fighting women they had found.

The hedges who greeted them accepted the letter they'd brought and sat down with them by the fire. They were welcomed with solemn expressions, but the young men of the village quickly erected a tent for them to shelter in, and the women warmed barley bread and vegetable stew to fill their bellies.

Both of the men they met with were dressed for a festival in bright white wool garments with horizontal stripes dyed in red and green. They wore heavy wraps over their shoulders, woven with family and clan patterns, and thick wool pants and boots suitable for riding. Both had deep brown skin and wore their hair in a common style of the mountains, a smooth, rounded clip that reminded Narine of a helmet with a sharp *V* carved into the front.

"My family came late because my wife was giving birth." The man's name was Obsa, and he was the leader of his clan and wore a green band around his head. "We didn't want her to move too quickly after the baby was born. When we arrived a week late, this is what we found." His eyes burned with fury. "You came from Addis to find answers? We want them too."

The other hedge's name was Kebek, and his eyes were hollow and grieving. "We were among the first families to gather in the meadow this year. My daughter was meant to marry this season." He cleared his throat. "Now my wife is dead, along with two of my sons. They were small." He glanced over his shoulder. "My daughter and my youngest son survived. I suppose that means the stars smiled on me, but I cannot understand it."

"Brother, now is not the time to find meaning in this violence." Obsa put his hand on Kebek's shoulder. "We must focus on protecting what is left of our people. The souls of your family may have been woven out of this time, but your sons will be reborn in another. They will be rewarded for their suffering in this short life."

Kebek lifted his chin and nodded but said nothing.

"We're trying to understand what happened," Tadesse said. "Do you have any idea who attacked you?"

"None." Kebek shook his head. "I was out of the village, and I met no one going to the camp while I was on the road. It's the end of the rainy season. The Southern Clans had come together for the spring festival."

Narine asked, "Is that your custom? Would outsiders know that this is the time the clans gather together?" She remembered Abdi talking about the spring festivals of his youth, but she wanted the men to share that information first.

"Yes," Obsa said. "We meet at this place every year. It's our main trading time and often when marriages are arranged. Business is discussed. The diviners need this time to consult with each other, and the archivists need time to share the stories of what has happened in the previous year."

"Hedges will usually meet to discuss threats against the clans." Kebek lifted his head. "But I am the head of my clan, and according to my people, no threats were on the horizon."

"I agree," Obsa said. "This has been a peaceful season.

Our diviners saw no warnings for our people. How could this be if the stars decreed this tragedy?"

"We cannot understand that," Narine said. "But I don't believe this was tasary, Brothers."

The men exchanged looks. "We expected word from the council that this act was written in the stars," Obsa said. "But if it was not, then a traveler could be sent to warn our people—"

"We cannot know if the elders will make that decision." Tadesse was quick to jump in. "My sister speaks from a grieving heart for your people, but she speaks too soon. Right now we're gathering information. We do not know if the heavens declared this tragedy or if it was the work of man."

Kebek narrowed his eyes. "We have travelers among our people. We may not have the city-educated diviners of the old families, but we are not without our resources."

"Wait," Tadesse said. "I know this is terrible, but I ask you to wait. We don't know what changing the timeline might bring. We must consult with the diviners."

Narine knew she'd said too much, but her anger was burning. "My brother is correct. Patience is the rule right now. If this is something we can prevent, you have my word we shall do it, and it will be as if this meeting never happened."

Both of the hedges nodded in agreement. "As the stars will it, Sister."

"Let the sun and moon show us their favor."

"For now," Narine continued, "we need to speak to those who witnessed the attack. Kebek, you said your daughter survived it?"

"She hid with her mother and her brothers' bodies," Kebek said.

"We need to speak with her," Tadesse said. "We know it might be horrible—"

"Southern women are not fragile blades of grass," Kebek said. "She will tell you what she remembers."

THE GIRL'S NAME WAS TEMARA, AND SHE HAD THE AURA OF A powerful hedge around her. She stared into the distance, leaning against her horse's shoulder as the animal waited in stillness behind her. Her face was a deep reddish-brown, and her dark hair was braided in two plaits that hung down her back. She wore a long white tunic with red stripes and a pair of cuffed pants that would allow her to ride. Her chin was lifted and her expression was stoic.

Narine asked her, "Are you in training as a hedge?"

Her eyes moved to Narine, and she nodded but said nothing.

"I started serious training when I was thirteen. How old are you?"

"Fifteen."

Narine nodded. "You're young and you weren't trained for battle yet. You were smart to hide."

"My mother was a diviner." The girl's mouth softened when she spoke of her mother. "Very gentle."

"Then the stars welcome her home." Narine kept her eyes fixed on the traumatized young woman. "It will help me find these people if you tell me what you remember."

"And who are we to you? This isn't your place or your people."

It was a familiar jab, but it still hurt. "Has a traveler been born to the Southern Clans yet?"

She narrowed her eyes. "How did you—?"

"His name is Mulenah, and one day the man who was my teacher will be born from his line. He will be respected among the wisest elders in the Seba Segel, and people all over the world will come to him for guidance."

The girl shook her head sadly. "There was a traveler born to the Warke clan. He was very tall, a good fighter. He was a cautious man."

*Was.*

He *was* very tall. *Was* very cautious.

Narine's heart ached. "He was killed, wasn't he?"

Temara's eyes flickered. "Yes, he was."

"Mulenah's family is important to me," Narine said. "Important to all mages. Are any of his family left?"

"I don't know. He was married last year. I don't think his wife traveled to the festival."

Interesting.

The girl challenged Narine. "So what can you do?"

"More than you might understand. Tell me who attacked your people."

"They were from the north, but not far north. I heard the leader speaking in a language I've never heard before. Not Oromo. Not Amharic. Hard, like foreigner language." She pointed her chin at Narine. "Like your language."

"Like this?" Narine spoke in English. "Was it a language that sounded like this?"

The girl nodded. "Yes, that sounds like what he was speaking."

"So the men who attacked you were white?"

"No. He was black."

Narine blinked. "Who?"

"The man who was leading them. He spoke in Amharic and that other language."

"And the men with him——?"

"It wasn't all men. There were women too. And they were our kind. Mages."

Fuck.

Narine swallowed the sudden lump in her throat. "Are you sure?"

"Yes, I could feel their power. They rode horses like our fighters. They told us they were travelers, so we welcomed them in the tradition of the Seba Segel. They surprised us;

otherwise they never would have defeated our hedges. They had guns too. The raiders had more guns than we did."

"The hedges here only use swords?"

"We have a few old guns, but our spears are more accurate. We use swords. Long knives," Temara added. "A few have guns, but they aren't common. We haven't needed them before."

"Tell me more about the man who was leading them."

"He was tall and very dark. He didn't look like he was from the south. Maybe the north. I don't know what people look like up there. He was wearing foreign clothes though."

"Farenji clothes?"

Temara nodded. "Yes. A shirt with a folded collar. The one with the points." She made two triangles along her collarbones. "That kind."

"I know the one you mean. What else? Did anyone use names?"

"No, they were careful not to use names. The leader, he told them to kill all the men. Someone asked him about the children and he said to leave them."

"What about the women?"

"I didn't hear him talk about the women, but they killed them. Even mothers with babies." Temara's hands shook with anger, and her horse turned and nuzzled her cheek. She patted the animal and seemed to calm down. "I have been training as a hedge."

"I know."

Temara shook her head. "This wasn't organized. If they had a plan, it fell apart. The leader was yelling at the people with him. I don't think he was in control."

Narine nodded. "Is there anything else?"

She frowned. "He had a scar on his jaw." She pointed to the left side of her face. "There. It was jagged, not a smooth cut as if from a blade. More like it was from a rock or—"

"Broken glass?" Narine was frozen.

*No.*

*No.*

*No no no no no.*

"Yes," Temara said. "Maybe it was from broken glass. That was the only thing about him that I remember. That scar and the sword in his hand." She shuddered. "I will never forget that sword."

# CHAPTER 21

*The Island*
*1921*

Narine was in Gideon's cottage, the tiny round hut built behind the medical clinic. There was no one sick, and the days were getting warmer. She'd come to him in the middle of the afternoon, brimming with anticipation and hoping he'd be alone. He'd spotted her in the distance and hung up the sign to close the clinic before walking to his house without a word and waiting for her.

As soon as she'd walked in the door, he'd pounced. She laughed as he caught her up, lifting her skirts and taking her against a wall as she stared at the sun glinting on the water over his shoulder.

Following Gideon's initial burst of passion, he loved her more slowly, helping her find pleasure as she lay in his bed, the rough cotton sheets warmed in the afternoon light. Afterward, he lay between her legs, still half-dressed and napping with his head on her breasts as she ran her hands up and down his back.

Their time together was scarce and secret, which made it

all the more exciting. Usually Narine stole out of the compound at night and ran to his cottage, or he slipped into her compound in the predawn light, sneaking into her room while the servant girls turned their eyes away and blushed.

They were foreigners. No one expected them to behave like others on the island, but Narine knew it wasn't a good idea to flaunt her affair in Tigist and Daniel's face.

"I like making love to you in the daylight," he murmured. "And I don't like hiding the truth."

"I know."

Gideon was a direct person. Secrecy of any kind annoyed him. He kept Narine's secrets, but that was because he considered all of them proprietary information.

"For now," Narine said, "I think it's smarter to be discreet."

"You mean secret."

She tugged on his ear. "I mean discreet. It's not like we're going to get married, Gideon. Like you said, this is living in the moment."

He lifted his head, met her eyes, and grunted.

Narine laughed. "What does that mean?"

"Nothing. I'm agreeing with you." He laid his head back down. "Scratch my back."

"Annoying man."

"Yes."

She smiled, amused that he was so honest about his faults. "You didn't even take off your shirt." She tugged at his proper European collar. "Why do you insist on wearing these?"

"Because I hear my father's voice in my ear, telling me that I won't be taken seriously unless I learn to play the European game." He sat up, tugged his white shirt over his head, and tossed it across the room. "There. Bare enough for you?"

His body was magnificent, and he knew it. She saw him running on the paths around the island, and he was a swimmer too. "Come here." She patted her breasts. "You favorite pillows are waiting for you."

"Ah yes." He nuzzled his face between her breasts and relaxed. "They're small but lovely."

She laughed. "I can't disagree with the small part anyway."

Gideon put his arms around her, embracing her torso as she ran her short nails up and down his back, scratching him like a purring cat dozing in the afternoon sun.

His skin was warm and smooth beneath her fingers, the angled planes of his shoulder blades rising up and down as he dozed.

Narine smiled. "You know, this is the first time I've seen you naked since the lake."

His shoulders shook a little. "Look your fill, but I'm not taking off my pants. With my luck a patient would come spying on me and all they'd remember is my bare bottom hanging out in the sun."

"Fine. Another day though. I'm going to take you swimming."

He turned his head and placed a gentle kiss between her breasts. "I'll look forward to it."

Narine was half asleep, her hands skimming over his back, gently massaging his back as he slept, when her fingers ran over the slightest bumps on Gideon's shoulder.

She looked at her hands, curious to see what marred his otherwise perfect skin. She was expecting a scar, but she saw a slightly raised mole instead. His shoulders were so dark she could barely see it, but it was there, a raised freckle on his shoulders.

Her pinkie finger hit another and she moved her hand, suddenly realizing that it wasn't a single mole or freckle but a series of raised moles that formed a pattern.

She blinked and stared.

He was an alchemist. What did it mean? If he was a naturally born mage then…

No, none of it made sense.

"Narine?"

"Sorry." She blinked and went back to scratching, trying to ignore the racing thoughts that pinged around her mind.

What could it mean?

Gideon was always perceptive. "What is it?"

"I just realized that I told Tigist I'd wash the bedsheets this afternoon and I forgot."

"Do you need to go?"

"No." She hugged him, a mess of confusion and affection making the time with him suddenly much more precious. "The sheets will wait."

*The mark on Gideon's shoulder is a traveler's mark. It's not as dark as mine, but it's definitely there and would have been visible when he was a child. Yet he is an alchemist. His magic is strong and clear. I would never doubt it if I hadn't seen that mark.*

*If he was born into a mage family, I would assume that one parent had traveler's blood and the other had alchemic magic and his magic followed alchemy.*

*But he says he is naturally born. Born mages never have more than one magic. At least not as far as I've ever heard.*

*For the first time since I've arrived here at the island, I genuinely miss my mother. Anahid would know what was going on.*

*Could Gideon's parents have been mages and not told him? That makes no sense. Could this mother have had an affair with a traveler? Possible.*

*This is all so confusing, and I probably shouldn't be writing any of this down.*

*I need to burn these journals, but they're the only thing keeping me sane. Well, the journals and Gideon. I can be myself when I'm with him. I can share who I am. I don't have to keep secrets. He wants to know about my life. Wants to know about my magic.*

*He likes me for being myself. Not because I'm Anahid's daughter or because I'm a powerful traveler. He clearly despises the old houses and thinks all the pomp and tradition is nonsense.*

*I can't blame him; I think the same way.*

*He wishes I wasn't white. I can tell that part bothers him, but he's obviously learned to live with it, and I can't blame him for the resentment. I know what the British did to his country. It doesn't matter what my own people did or didn't do in Africa when the face he sees is European.*

*It's better that I'm only here for another five months; he'll forget me when I'm gone.*

"NARINE?"

She shoved the journal away when she heard Tigist's voice calling from the courtyard.

"Are you in your room?"

She stood and gathered the sheets from her bed, busying herself so she had an armful when Tigist opened her door.

"Sorry!" Narine shook her head. "It's probably too late to start them now, isn't it?" She tossed them on the bed. "I'm so sorry. I'll wash them first thing in the morning so they have time to dry."

Tigist nodded. "It's fine. They're not that dirty. We all take baths."

Narine laughed. "Right."

"Are you okay?" Tigist pulled over a stool and sat down.

Narine sat on the edge of the bed. "I'm fine. I'm just homesick, I think."

"Of course you are." Tigist grabbed both her hands and squeezed them. "I feel like you've been distant since the New Year. Did the celebration make you miss home?"

No.

"Yes." She lied easily, as her mother had taught her. "So

much." She decided to share a little. "My sister—kind of my sister—Genet and her husband had a baby last year." Narine said. "And I know that when I go back, it will be like no time has passed for them, but I feel like I'm missing things. It's not rational, but I worry that I'm going to miss the first time she takes a step or the first time she says my name."

"But when you go back, it's to the same time you left, correct?"

"Yes." She shrugged. "I told you it wasn't rational."

Tigist laughed a little. "Well, I cannot imagine traveling through time the way you do, so I will take your word for it, but it makes sense that you're homesick." She leaned forward and hugged Narine. "You can talk to me anytime you need to."

"Thank you." In retrospect, Narine suspected she should have shared her life and struggles with the timeline with Tigist and not Gideon, but hindsight was pure and in the moment, Gideon had seemed a better choice.

"Narine?"

"Hmm?"

Tigist took a deep breath. "I know you're spending a lot of time with Gideon lately."

"We're spending… some time together. He's an interesting man."

"He is." Her friend nodded. "And he's a good man. But I should warn you…"

*Warn me?*

"About what?" Narine swallowed hard. Was Gideon married? Had he been sleeping his way through the village before she came? Did he have a secret family?

"I don't know much about his past," Tigist said. "But there is a root of anger in him, and I think you should be careful."

Anger? That was the dangerous secret? Narine felt like laughing. "Tigist, I don't think—"

"I know what it's like to be young and away from home and feeling like you want that connection." She blushed a little. "I was older than you when I moved here; I know what it is to be… lonely."

"Did you have a secret romance, Tigist?"

"No! I'm just saying that when you're young, anger and passion can sometimes feel like they're the same. But they're not."

Narine smiled. "I know that. And don't worry. I'm leaving in five months; I don't have any intention of forming permanent connections here."

Tigist nodded. "We'll miss you when you leave us. Daniel and I were just saying that we hope you come back to visit us again."

"Daniel's saying that because he likes the way I bake fish."

"Well, that's true." Tigist nodded. "But we like you for more than just the fish."

Narine smiled. "Good to know."

THE WATER OF THE LAKE WAS COOL AND THE DAY WAS steaming. An unexpected hot spell had fallen over the Great Rift Valley, and the days that were usually comfortable and warm were sweltering to Narine, who was more accustomed to Addis Ababa's cooler climate.

She fled to the lake with Gideon, jumping in and immersing herself in the comfort of the water. She floated on her back, the short tunic she'd donned floating around her in the shallows. It certainly wasn't as comfortable as her bathing suit at home, but she wasn't really swimming. All she wanted was the chill of the water to take the edge off the heat.

"You're very comfortable in the water, aren't you?" Gideon was wading waist deep, watching a few boats in the distance. Across the cove, a gaggle of boys from the village was playing in the water; their laughter echoed across the surface of the lake.

"My mother said that she never taught me to swim. She put me in the pool when I was a baby and it was as if I remembered swimming in the womb."

"Maybe you did."

"Maybe I did." She opened her eyes and peered at him. She hadn't told him about his travelers' mark. Maybe she never would. Everything about his magic felt like an alchemist, so if he had some traveling magic, it was minor. It added questions about his birth though. About his family in Nairobi and his upbringing.

"What age did you say the hedges found you?"

He raised an eyebrow. "I was told I was six. I have very scattered memories at that age though."

"But you remember the order school?"

"In Mombasa. At the beginning, I just remember that everything had to be a secret and it made me uncomfortable. I thought my parents would have questions for me when I returned home for holidays."

"They didn't?"

"No." He shook his head. "My father was always so conscious of how we were perceived socially, how he had to be the model Kenyan citizen because he worked with so many British, but when it came to my school?" Gideon shook his head. "Perhaps they suspected something. Perhaps they knew I was different."

It didn't sound like a happy memory, so Narine quickly changed the subject.

"So what was being home like?" She smiled. "Did you miss it when you were in school? Was your mother a good cook?"

"You always miss what you know." He lowered himself more deeply in the water, crouching down so his face was closer to hers. "My mother doted on me. And yes, she was an

261

excellent cook." He smiled. "She stuffed me full of food when I was home. She said they didn't feed me enough at the order school."

"They probably didn't. The order has some strange ideas about austerity."

"Yes, even for children." He shook his head. "Why do mages put up with it?"

"Most of us are born into mage families and we assume that's normal. We don't know any different. To be fair, most of us don't go to boarding schools either. They're usually for natural mage children or children who live in very rural areas like some of the free clans."

He cocked his head. "Free clans?"

"Yes. There are old families like mine and more typical mage families with three or four generations of mage blood. Maybe more, maybe less." She shrugged. "But there are old clans around the world where the mages have a more democratic structure. They usually come from remote areas that are far away from the large order houses. They could send their children to order schools, but they rarely do."

He frowned. "Why not?"

"Don't get me wrong, they're highly educated people, but not formally. My mentor came from one of those clans in the south, and he's a very powerful man."

"He's the one who taught you how to travel?" His eyes were intent on Narine, and she began to wonder why he wanted to know.

"I taught myself how to travel." She pushed away from the edge of the lake and swam away from Gideon in a slow crawl. "Like I taught myself how to swim."

"I don't blame the free clans for keeping their children away." Gideon stared at the boys jumping in the water across the lake. "I didn't have a joyful childhood."

# CHAPTER 22

*Bale Mountains*
*1934*

N arine was still in shock when they returned to the river the day after her meeting with Temara. They'd gathered notes about the massacre and documented as much as they could before they walked back to the river.

As Narine lay back in the stream, clutching Jacob's hand, she felt a familiar cold sink into her chest, but she tried to appear as normal as possible. Luckily both Jacob and Tadesse were as horrified by the massacre as she was. They took her silence for grief.

It was grief, but not one that she could name.

"I'm ready," Jacob said.

"Okay, don't let go." She could already feel Tadesse fading away.

Jacob's hand was warm as they sat in the stream and she started the incantation. She felt the gathering of magic buzzing in her chest and the water welcoming her home.

*Yes, come back.*

*Return to me.*

*Let me take you home.*

She held Jacob's hand and immersed herself in the river.

When she sat up, the room was dark and the water around them was warm.

Jacob blinked at her and swiped a hand over his face, wringing out his beard. "Wow. That felt faster than the first time."

"Returning is always easier," Narine said. "Your magic wants to be here, in this time. Not in the past." She looked around the room to see Tadesse standing on the steps of the travelers' pool, looking around the room. "What is it?"

She and Jacob stood and walked toward him.

Tadesse turned. "Where's Aida?"

Narine looked at the lit console and the blue-green lights of the pool. "She probably just stepped out of the room for a minute."

"She wouldn't do that." He grabbed a towel from the rack by the door and quickly opened it to look into the traveling chambers that surrounded the pool room. "Aida?"

Narine walked to the rack slowly, the cold knot in her chest becoming tighter and tighter. She took a towel and handed it to Jacob.

"What's going on?" He started to dry himself. "Is something wrong with Aida?"

She turned to him. "You remember Aida, don't you?"

He frowned. "Of course I do. She was here when we…" He paused and turned to the console. "No, what…? Did you set the console before we left?"

"Did I?"

He shook his head. "No, there was someone else here. I remember… Why is it so muddy?" His eyes went wide. "It was only two days ago. Only moments ago here. What's going on?"

Tadesse walked back into the room, and his jaw was tight. His eyes were furious. "Where is she, Narine?"

"Tade, you know as much as I do." Narine dried her ear and quickly locked her assistant in place. "Hey Ana, contact Aida, all channels." An alert would go through to her home, her office, and her mobile AI.

"Searching…"

The response that finally came back wasn't a surprise, but it was still devastating.

"There is no listing for an Aida in your directory, Narine."

She swallowed hard. "Contact Aida Mikel, all channels."

Tadesse was shaking his head. "No." His hand formed a fist. "No."

Jacob walked over and put a hand on Tadesse's shoulder. "Tade—"

"No!"

"There is no listing for an Aida Mikel in your directory, Narine."

She felt her lip trembling, but she tried one more thing. "Search Aida Mikel, all mage directories worldwide."

Tadesse was pacing back and forth. He'd stripped his wet shirt from his body and was clutching a towel to his chest as Jacob watched Narine with a solemn expression, finally realizing what was happening.

"There is no listing for Aida Mikel in the worldwide mage directory, Narine. Do you mean Aida Matthews of Atlanta, Georgia? Aida St. John of London, England? Aida Crenshaw of Sydney, Australia? Aida—"

Narine pulled the assistant from her ear, set it down with shaking hands, and stared at Tadesse, who was watching her.

She shook her head.

He let out a guttural roar that shook the water in the pool and punched his magic through the room. The lights on the console went out, and he lifted his hand to strike….

Nothing.

Time was a formless enemy.

Tadesse's face crumpled into a mask of agony and he fell to his knees. The tears that fell down his cheeks were silent, and Narine rushed to him, kneeling down and grabbing him around the shoulders in a fierce embrace.

"We'll get her back! Somehow we'll get her back."

Jacob began to pace, threading his fingers together at the back of his head and muttering under his breath. "Bullshit. This is bullshit. So much bullshit. This fucking magic…"

"Listen!" Narine stood. "There's no way that what we did caused this." She shook her head. "No way. The warp has spread. Somehow it spread to someone in Aida's family, but if we go back and correct the initial warp—"

"We didn't consult with the diviners." Tadesse's face was bleak grief. "There's a reason we consult with diviners before a jump, Narine."

"No, I'm telling you, this was not us." She shook his shoulder. "We go to the council tomorrow with the information we have. We can prevent this, Tade. We can send someone back to warn the Southern Mages. We can send one of the Southern houses to intercept the raiders. We know why Abdi is gone now, and once we reverse this, we bring Aida back too."

Tadesse was shaking his head and rocking side to side. "Aida."

"Everyone's coming to my house tonight." Narine suddenly remembered that she'd driven to the order that morning in the crawler, and she was ridiculously relieved. "Jacob, Tade, you're coming home with me. We have to keep our memories on this straight if we want to put this right."

Jacob frowned. "We're not going to just forget Aida. We all know she was here a few minutes ago in this time."

"No, that's exactly what will happen." Tadesse's face was blank as he stood. He moved like an old man with stiff joints. As if everything in his body hurt. "In a matter of days, our memory that Aida existed will fade and our minds will merge into this timeline. You didn't know her that well. Can you even remember what she looked like right now?" He looked at Jacob. "Think hard, American. Can you picture her face?"

Jacob opened his mouth, then closed it.

"Come on." Narine tugged both their arms and urged them toward the exit. "Let's get dressed and get out of here. We all need to keep our heads clear. We'll meet with the elders tomorrow."

GENET DIDN'T QUESTION IT WHEN NARINE USHERED TWO large men into the guest rooms of the house. She looked at Narine with a curious expression, then went to the kitchen to tell Samira to add more meat to the stew for lunch.

Both of the men took long showers, then retreated to the front sitting room that was furnished with *majlis*, the low Arab-style sofas that wrapped around the walls. They sat in silence while she put an old record on her grandfather's turntable and the comforting sound of Mulatu Astatke filled the house.

It was New Year's Day, and while their compound was small, the house AI rang with video messages from all over the country and the world.

"Hey, Geniii! Selamnew? How is everyone? Happy New Year!"

"Greetings from California, Narit. This is Dad. Message me back when you get this so I can talk with you girls. Just saw pictures of Gelile; she's getting so tall."

"Happy New Year, Geni and Narine! It's Cousin Zeke. I'm in London right now, but I'm flying back to Lagos tomorrow. Want to come for a visit soon. Let me know if there's room at the house."

Samira and Gelile were spreading flowers and grass over the hardwood floors and chattering about walking to the holiday market down the street. Narine's own assistant buzzed with messages from Jamila in Harar, but she kept her alerts silent while she served Jacob and Tadesse beef stew and chickpea salad with rolls of injera and fresh bread.

"What's going on?" Genet asked quietly in the kitchen.

"It was a hard jump."

Narine had completely forgotten about the holiday. For her, Jacob, and Tadesse, the New Year had passed two days ago with a massacre in the south.

Genet joined them and didn't ask questions of the quiet men but exchanged small talk with Narine about the state of the garden, what Gelile had done with her friends that day, and the holiday markets that were popping up over the city.

"Is there anything I can do to help?" Genet finally asked.

"I don't think so." She glanced at Jacob and Tadesse. "We lost a friend to the timeline, and we have to figure out how to get her back."

"You'll figure it out; I'll pray about it." Genet looked at Jacob and Tadesse. "I'm sorry about your friend."

Jacob asked, "Did you know Aida?"

Genet smiled softly. "I wouldn't. I'm not a traveler like you three. I'm not even a mage. If someone is woven out of time, I won't carry their memory."

"Right." Jacob looked more confused than grief-stricken. "Thank you for dinner. Are you sure it's okay if we stay here tonight? It's still afternoon. I can go——"

"It's fine." Genet waved a hand. "I think none of you is in the mood to celebrate. If you go back to your houses, people there will have questions."

Tadesse covered his face with both hands. "I don't want to see anyone right now."

"Then stay here," Narine said. "I may have another friend who's coming by later, but we're not having any big parties tonight."

Genet frowned. "Who?"

"I asked Jamila to come tonight if she can, and now she's blowing up my phone. She's probably pissed I didn't make it to her house last night, so she might not come." Whether she came or not, Narine needed to warn Jamila about sudden disappearances from the timeline. If this warp was growing, it could affect her family and friends in Harar.

Genet shook her head. "I haven't heard from her. She hasn't called the house."

"I was thinking I'd try to call her again. Jacob and Tade might want to nap this afternoon. We didn't get great sleep during our jump."

"How long were you out of time?"

"Only two days, but they were rough ones."

Genet nodded. "Sleep would be good then. All of you need rest."

Tadesse said nothing. He was jotting down notes in a small notebook he'd pulled out of his backpack, no doubt writing down everything he could about Aida to keep his memories fresh.

*Just like your journals.*

The journals she'd left in Tigist's home.

The journals that had become the writing paper for a message hidden in her jacket pocket.

"I think a nap would be great." Jacob rose and waved both hands at Genet and Narine. "If you'll excuse me…"

"Make yourself at home." Narine pointed down the hall. "If you need anything, just shout."

"I will."

Tadesse silently retreated to his own room a few moments later while Genet and Narine cleared the table from lunch.

The warp was growing, and the tangled threads of this mystery were getting even more snarled. Aida was gone, and a man wearing a suit with a scar on his jaw had led a massacre that had upended her entire world.

Her journals.

His messages.

The man with the scar.

Narine put her assistant back in and wrote down a particular list of names:

*Anahid* X
*Aster* X
*Abdi* X
*Aida* X
*Jamila*
*Bati*
*Sahid*


Narine could count the number of people who knew her secrets on less than two hands.

She put *X*'s by the names of people who were no longer here.

Aster had been first, her illness a swift and silent assassin.

Her mother disappeared next.

Abdi's people had been cut off.

Aida had been woven out of time.

Jamila and her parents were the only ones left.

Genet came back with two beers, a couple of glasses, and a bottle opener. "What's that?"

Narine folded the list before Genet could see the names. "A list."

Genet nodded silently.

"People close to me are disappearing."

Genet sat down. "Are Gelile and I in danger?"

"I don't know *why* you'd be targeted, but I don't know why anyone is targeting my family and friends." She pulled out the note she took from her desk before she came home. "This is from the man six years ago."

Not even Genet knew everything, but she knew Narine

had missed her window and had spent a year in the past against her will.

"Gideon?" Genet's eyes bored into Narine's. "You think this has to do with him?"

*This cannot continue.*

Narine spread out the note she'd taken from her desk. "It's his handwriting, and it was written on the journal pages I left. It showed up right before all this started happening, and I don't know how it's connected. I don't even know how he got my journals. According to the friend I left them with, she destroyed them."

"Maybe he took one or some of them without her knowing."

"That's possible." It was the only explanation. Tigist wouldn't have lied.

Genet looked at the note. "So someone from the order knows about that year. About him. Someone besides your mother."

Her mother, Abdi, Aida, Jamila. The list of people who knew her secrets was small and currently shrinking.

"My mother would never tell anyone in the order about Gideon."

Genet put a hand on Narine's arm. "He's in the past."

"And the past is what someone is changing." Narine put her assistant in her ear and called Jamila.

"You are on my shit list" —her friend answered immediately— "as the children say, but I'm on my way to your house."

"Don't."

"Why?"

She closed her eyes. "I need you to go back to Harar. Stay with your family. Don't talk to anyone from the order. I'm going to the elder council tomorrow and I'm looking for answers, but right now it's better if you don't know me."

The silence on the other side of the call was stark and

sudden.

Jamila spoke in hushed tones. "Give me the word and we disappear, Narine."

She nodded and held back the tears that wanted to escape. "I'll call you when I know something."

Her best friend hung up without another word.

*Give me the word and we disappear.*

It was the reason that Narine depended on her, but bitter fear sat at the back of her tongue.

No one could hide from time.

THEY DROVE BACK TO THE ORDER THE NEXT MORNING IN Narine's crawler. While most of the city was still in holiday mode, Narine knew the elders would be in their chambers and Tadesse had already called in a request to meet with them. As travelers, any petition to speak to the elders or the diviners was granted quickly.

"What do you want me to do?" Jacob was in the back seat, looking out the windows. "While you guys are with the elders, I mean."

"Stay in my office and don't talk to anyone," Narine said.

"Officially, you don't have a rank or any training," Tadesse said. "You shouldn't really have gone with us. Did they assign you to an elder to oversee your training?"

"Elder Kebret mentioned someone named Desta?" Jacob looked over his shoulder. "Do you know him?"

"Yes, Elder Desta is a competent mentor; he trained me." Tadesse said. "He's from a very old house and he's a snob, but his connections are good and if he likes you, he'll introduce you to the right people."

"That means if you get into his favor, you'll be the golden boy of the elder council like Tadesse." Narine smiled. "Not like me."

"Your mother trained you?" Jacob asked.

"And Abdi."

Tadesse said, "I'm having a hard time holding on to Abdi, Narine. In my memories. your mother was your only trainer."

"Well that's a terrifying thought, but it would definitely explain the council's hostility."

She pulled into the order gates and pulled out her ID as she approached Mesfin the Diligent. "Good morning, Brother Mesfin. How was your holiday?"

"Very pleasant, Sister Narine. I hear you have a meeting with the elders today?"

"We do. Have they all arrived?"

"I'm afraid I can't share that information with you."

She raised an eyebrow. "Discretion as well as caution?"

He smiled a little. "At least half the elders live in the order compound, Sister Narine. They come and go as they please."

Mesfin had a point. He checked both Tadesse's and Jacob's IDs, then showed them into the building where Njeri was back behind the desk after the holiday.

"Sister Narine!" She noticed Jacob. "And who is this fine young man you brought me as a New Year's present?"

Narine smiled at Jacob's dark cheeks. "Jacob Martin, this is administrator extraordinaire and bestower of all office supplies, Sister Njeri Kamau. She basically runs the day-to-day operations here." She turned back to Njeri. "Jacob is a new mage. He just discovered his magic, so he'll be training over the next few months."

Njeri's eyebrows rose. "Welcome to the Seba Segel, Jacob. How are you adjusting?"

Jacob glanced at Narine, then back to Njeri. "It's been interesting."

"Jacob is also a professor at the university, so you'll see him coming and going."

"And since he is with you two terrors," Njeri said, "can I assume that he's a traveler?"

"Unfortunately."

"Wait." Tadesse frowned. "When did I become a terror?"

"You've been hanging out with this one too much." Njeri winked at Tadesse. "What's that sad look on your face, my lovely?"

Tadesse forced a smile. "I'm fine, Sister. Just tired."

Njeri sucked her teeth and looked back at Jacob. "Young man, I am so sorry you have to spend time with these two. If they try to get you into some mischief, you come tell me."

Jacob smiled. "I will."

"Traitor." Narine started down the hall, but Njeri stopped her.

"You got something else from the mail room," the administrator said. "Was just delivered this morning."

Narine's heart skipped a beat, but she nodded and continued to her office with Jacob behind her.

Tadesse said, "I need to go over my notes before we go to the council. Jacob, I'd appreciate your ears if you don't mind. I want to make sure I haven't missed anything from the jump."

"Happy to help."

Tadesse looked at Narine. "Come to my office when you've checked your mail."

"I will." Narine continued to her office and saw the familiar seal of the letter sitting on her desk. She sat down and stared at it as if it couldn't hurt her if it just remained unopened.

*Foolish girl.* She could hear her mother's voice in her mind.

She broke the seal and opened the letter to find another simple message.

I will find him.

Fuck!

She dropped the paper as if it had burned her fingers.

274

Narine stood and put her hands behind her head, wishing there was something—anything—to punch.

She wanted to call Jamila immediately, but the smarter part of her knew that somehow a ghost from her past had found the secret she'd kept hidden for six years. Who knew whom he'd been talking to? There might be someone monitoring Narine and trying to provoke a reaction. She folded the letter with shaking fingers and put it back in her desk drawer, then went to Tadesse's office and knocked on the door.

He opened it, waved at Jacob, then joined Narine in the hallway.

"Elder Desta called me. The whole council is in session, and Yosef has appeared again."

"Great, so we have another elder back to check our work, only this one does it with cryptic messages and irrelevant questions."

"I don't think we can assume that any question Yosef asks is irrelevant. We just don't understand it yet." Tadesse pushed the outer door to the Elders' Chamber open. "You ready?"

"To find some answers?" She glanced at the inner doors. "You bet."

The hedges at the door greeted them, checked their IDs, then opened the chamber and waited for Narine and Tadesse to enter.

Narine took two steps inside the chamber and froze.

Sitting across from her, as easy as anything, Anahid sat chatting with Issa on her right side. Her hair was the same dark cloud, and the woman looked exactly as she had when she disappeared four years before in an ancient traveling chamber in the old city of Harar.

Tadesse froze, then crossed himself. "What is happening?"

Narine's mother met her eyes, shook her head slightly, then glanced at Tadesse.

"I don't know, but just go with it for now." She tugged his arm and walked into the center of the room.

# CHAPTER 23

*The Island*
*1921*

N arine didn't realize her menses hadn't come until two weeks after Christmas.

She'd always had an irregular flow, partly a consequence of travel that threw her body's internal clock into chaos on a regular basis. Her mother was the same.

She walked to Gideon's cottage after dark, her entire body tense with anger and panic. She banged on the door, and he answered with a furrowed brow.

"Narine?"

"Did you know?"

He lifted his chin and looked down his nose at her. "Ah. Yes, I did."

Of course he'd known. He was an alchemist; they always knew. In fact, her mother had told her that alchemist mages could know nearly at the point of conception when a woman was pregnant because of the change in her body's magical signature, especially if the child was also powerful.

"You knew? For weeks now?" She barged into his house. "How could you not tell me?"

He closed the door, crossed his arms over his chest, and leaned against it. "I assumed you would know soon enough. There's nothing to be done about it, Narine. What did you think was going to happen? We've been lovers for months now."

A startled laugh burst out of her throat. "Nothing to be done? I'm barely weeks into this pregnancy. You can make me a potion to end it, Gideon."

It was hardly uncommon, and she should have been more proactive from the beginning. There were herbs and spells to decrease the likelihood of getting pregnant, but Narine had been living in the moment, not thinking about magic or spells, and she was paying the price now.

His eyebrows went up. "I beg your pardon?"

"Please don't be so... *proper* right now. Gideon, I cannot return to Addis pregnant. I'm only twenty-two."

It was her first mission. Her first *solo* mission. Not only had she missed her window because she'd contracted malaria, but she'd started a relationship with someone in the past, which was never advised, *and* she'd gotten pregnant!

She could see the disappointment on Abdi's face without even closing her eyes.

Gideon's mouth twisted. "And I'm sure your very old family with their noble magical blood wouldn't want you bearing the child of a natural mage. God forbid."

Narine blinked. "What? That has nothing to do with it."

"Doesn't it, Narine?" He walked toward her. "You're an adult woman and I was hardly your first lover. You know how biology works, and yet you never asked me for a potion to prevent it."

"Gideon—"

"I was good enough to be your lover though, wasn't I? You came to my bed every night you could."

"I…" Narine felt her heart stutter. "I care about you, Gideon." *I think I'm in love with you.* "But I'm not ready to be a mother. I don't know if I'll ever be ready to be a mother. This child will probably be a traveler with my family history." She did the mental calculations. Even if she could manage to birth the child before the thirteenth month, the chances of bearing a traveler in her family were almost certain. "I can't do that to another person."

He scoffed. "And why not? I thought that was what your family wanted."

How could she explain to him the constant uncertainty of living when time was always in flux? Of never belonging to any place or time or people? Of never feeling home? "Gideon, I can't do that to—"

"Hypocrite." His eyes were cold, and all affection had fled from his face. "You're a hypocrite, Narine. I was good enough to be your lover but not the father of your child."

"This has nothing to do with your power or your family." She was starting to feel even more desperate. "Are you not going to help me?"

"Don't be stupid; I'll help you have the baby. I'll give you the best medical care I can. You're young and healthy, Narine. You'll be fine. And if you don't want the child after he's born, you can give him to me." He leaned down and spoke softly. "But if you think I'm going to help you kill a child—*my* child —that will be more powerful than either of us could ever be, you're fooling yourself."

"You want this child because it will be powerful?" She felt her heart breaking. "Our child would be hated, Gideon. In this place, they would be hated. Don't you see how they look at me? How the elders talk about travelers here? They don't trust me and they only accept me because they know I'm leaving."

His eye twitched. "Then we'll go someplace else. After you have the baby, we'll go to Addis or Mombasa. You can come to Nairobi with me. There will be other Europeans there. You'll be able to blend in."

She let his words sink in and realized that Gideon didn't envision her returning home. He didn't see her going home and having the baby and bringing him back; he expected Narine to abandon her life and stay with him. To marry him and raise her child in the past. Where children died of minor infections. Where women died in childbirth, had no rights, and she would be trapped.

She would be in prison with Gideon, and her entire life would be lost. She would sink into the timeline, and she wouldn't even be able to hold on to memories of her own family, her friends, or her home.

Gideon took her fear and horror as acceptance. He put a hand on her shoulder and stroked it. Then he kissed the top of her head and rubbed a finger along her neck. "You will have a beautiful life here, Narine. A *stable* life. Our child will be extraordinary. I'll talk to the elders tomorrow and ask for their permission to marry so that he won't be a bastard."

"My family..." She wanted her mother. For the first time since she was fourteen years old and her mother had thrown her into missions for the order, Narine desperately wanted her mother. She wanted her father. She wanted Abdi. If she was able to send a message forward, her mother could come and get her, but how—

"Your family will understand. We can send a message to them once the baby is born. Someday our grandchildren will meet your family and they will have a part of you back. It's a beautiful thing, don't you see?"

Oh God. Sun and stars, what a fool she'd been.

Gideon kissed the top of her head and shepherded Narine toward the door. "Go back to Daniel and Tigist's house. I'll come for you tomorrow, and we'll be married soon. Then we can be together. You need your rest, Narine; you're having a baby."

NARINE HAD BARELY LEFT HER ROOM WHEN TIGIST KNOCKED on her door the next night. She was numb from shock, fear, and panic.

"Narine?"

She recognized her friend's voice and went to open the door. The older woman took one look at her face, and tears came to Narine's eyes. Tigist stepped inside and put her arms around her.

It was the comfort she needed to loose the tears.

She cried for what felt like forever, but by the time she lifted her head, she felt calmer and her mind was clear. She could think the way her mother had taught her.

Practical.

Powerful.

Present.

"You're pregnant, aren't you?" Tigist's voice held all the worry and sadness that Narine had released.

"Yes." Narine looked at Tigist. "If I could give you this pregnancy—"

"Shhh." She put her finger over Narine's lips and crossed herself. "That is not what the stars have decreed. They have given this child to you, and there is a reason for it."

"I've done the math. It will be born during Pagume. With my blood and magic, it will almost certainly be a traveler." She wiped her eyes. "It's not a peaceful life. I never wanted to do that to another person."

"But this child came into being despite that, so the stars in their wisdom have decreed this child's birth. Honor that, Narine. Even if it is not what you wanted."

Narine closed her eyes and nodded. "After the panic passed, I thought about it, and I can make it work." Those at the order would look down on her for botching her first mission, but she could live with that. "My mother and Aster will be ecstatic even though it wasn't an arranged match. Gideon believes that I don't want the baby because he isn't from an old family, but I promise you, that never even came into my mind."

Especially because Narine was convinced that Gideon had mage blood in his lineage. It was the only explanation for the traveler's mark on his shoulder.

"The stars have willed it." The older woman nodded. "You are having this child. You're young and you're healthy, but if you have any issues, you must tell me. No more secrets, Narine."

There were *so* many secrets. "I'll tell you as much as I can, and I won't hide anything about the pregnancy."

Tigist took both of Narine's hands in hers and stared until Narine met her piercing gaze. "Do you *want* to stay here and marry Gideon? He spoke to the elders tonight, and the council gave their permission. They could hardly say no, especially when he told them it was what you wanted and that he would be moving both of you back to Nairobi and sending another doctor in his place."

Narine laughed a little. "They get rid of both foreigners at once."

Tigist sighed. "People here are... suspicious. It's a good place, but the caution about outsiders runs deep. Outsiders have not always been kind to the Zay."

"I understand that." She looked at her friend. "Did Gideon tell the elders that I was pregnant?"

"He didn't really have to. Asking permission like this—wanting to have the wedding so quickly—people assume." Tigist shrugged. "It's not uncommon. You and Gideon weren't doing anything that most of them didn't do when they were young. You still haven't answered me though: Do you want to marry Gideon?"

"No." Narine made her voice firm. "I've made my peace

with having this baby, but I *refuse* to stay in the past." She looked at her friend. "This isn't my home."

"I had a feeling you would say that. Will you lose the pregnancy if you travel?"

"No." She shook her head. "The baby and I will be perfectly safe. I promise you that. My family will help me. I have resources and a home in my time. A traveler born in the future will always be able to travel to the past, but if the child is born here, it will never be able to go forward in time."

"So you could bring the baby back?"

"Yes, but if it's born here, it can never go forward. Do you see what I'm saying?"

Tigist nodded carefully. "Surely Gideon will see reason if you frame it that way."

"I don't know." Nothing about Gideon's demeanor the night before told Narine he would be willing to compromise or lose control over her or the baby.

Tigist was staring at Narine's hands. "Medical care is better in your time. If the child was sick or had health problems…" Pain shadowed Tigist's face. "You wouldn't lose your baby to a fever." She blinked. "If my daughter had been born in your time, she'd probably still be alive."

She took Tigist's hand. "I don't think anyone can know that."

Tigist nodded and wiped her eyes. "I am your friend, Narine. Always. I wish you'd heeded my warning about Gideon, but the past is past. He has no right to keep you from your life and your family. I will make sure you get back. Gideon has no right to hold you prisoner here."

"But the elders are expecting us to marry now."

Tigist narrowed her eyes, and Narine could see the strategic hedge behind the friendly countenance of the nurturing woman. "I'd like to say that I could convince the elders that you have the right to return to your own time and it was in the child's best interest for you to go, but I don't know that they'll listen to me. I'm the only woman on the council, and frankly, too many of them think like Gideon. They will see the child as his before it is yours."

"So what do you think that I should do?"

"For now?" Tigist looked at her. "It will be difficult, but I think you must play along. Go along with Gideon. Don't defy him. I'll pretend to be excited and start planning your wedding." She sighed. "You may have to marry him because you've got three more months before your window, correct?"

Narine nodded.

"I wish I could speed time for you, but I can't." Tigist squeezed her hands and stood. "Let me go tell Daniel what's happening. Don't worry; he sees you like a sister. He will be on your side."

Narine knew her position was precarious. With Gideon determined to keep her in the past, she had no one with an incentive to keep her grounded in her own mind. She would have to reread her journals every day. She would have to write more, write between the lines, write to her mother, her child.

Narine put a hand on her belly, trying to feel the burgeoning power of the tiny spark that would become her son or daughter. "I'll do what I need to do to keep us safe," she whispered. "Even if it means marrying Gideon."

Her heart ached. She had painted a future in her mind where she and Gideon could stay together, if not in time, then in heart. Where she could come back and visit him. Where the man she'd come to love could remain part of her life.

But his sneering reaction to her distress would never be erased from her memory.

Narine would marry him, but in her mind, any vow she made under duress was no vow at all. He couldn't hold her to a promise that was coerced.

"I'll keep us safe," she whispered again. "I'll keep us safe."

# CHAPTER 24

*Addis Ababa*
*2072*

Elder Kebret looked over the report that Tadesse handed to him, then passed it to Anahid. "This conforms to my memories as well. We told you to investigate the warp, and it is apparent that you found answers."

The chief elder had not changed, but in place of Elder Desta, Narine's mother was sitting in the traveler's former seat. Yosef was next to her and Issa next to him, but Narine couldn't take her eyes off her mother.

In her mind, it had been four years since the woman had disappeared. She'd believed her mother had been lost in time, but now she didn't know what to believe. Had Jamila's mother lied to her? Had Anahid been in hiding all this time?

Anahid raised an eyebrow. "So last week I was woven out of the timeline?"

"Or hiding," Elder Kebret muttered. "With you, there's no telling, is there?"

Her mother smiled beatifically. "Brother, how well you know me."

Narine felt like her mind was spinning in three directions. All the elders—including Yosef—were acting as if her mother's appearance was nothing but ordinary.

What trick had time played on her?

Yosef looked at the report next. "Let me summarize for our brothers and sisters who have no memory of this. Six days ago, on the first day of Pagume, there was a warp in the timeline as a tasary was changed during Pagume. Abdi Mulenah, respected elder of this council and leader of the Southern Mages, was woven out of this time." He nodded at Tadesse and Narine. "We assigned these two travelers to search the Tibeb with one of Issa's archivists named Aida."

The senior archivist frowned. "Who?"

"One of your most promising young weavers," Yosef said. "Now lost to the timeline as Abdi has been, as more of us surely will be as the warp in the Tibeb grows and entangles more and more threads." Yosef looked at Tadesse. "To answer the questions you must have, Aida's grandfather was sent by the elders in Addis Ababa to investigate the Southern Mage Massacre. He was killed—we believe—by the same raiders who massacred the Southern people, who were then killed by hedges of House Zuria."

House Zuria.

"Elder Desta's house?" Narine asked.

Anahid looked at her. "Was Desta an elder? Interesting."

"Her grandfather was murdered," Tadesse said. "That is why Aida no longer exists."

"I'm afraid so," Yosef said. "And after that mage group from Addis was killed, the matter was left alone. No one investigated the Southern Mage Massacre any longer, and the matter was put to rest by the two Southern houses that took over their territory."

Narine swallowed hard. "So in this time, the Southern

285

Mages no longer exist? What about the Afghan Group or the Basque Mages?" She looked around the room. "The Arabian Cooperative? The Rhone Valley Collective?"

Yosef shook his head. "I'm afraid none of those free-mage groups exist except in your memories."

But not for long. If Narine and Tadesse didn't do anything to change the past and prevent the Southern Mage Massacre from happening, even their memory would melt away and she would fall into this reality.

"So who are the dominant powers in this time?" Tadesse asked. "Forgive me for asking, Brother Yosef, but who is in charge now?"

Yosef seemed amused. "The power of the Seba Segel rests as it always has rested, in the houses of the great priests' ancestors. Like your house, Narine." Yosef nodded at Elder Kebret. "Like House Abay." He looked at Issa. "House Chwezi in Uganda." He looked at Narine. "Or House Mkisi in Mombasa." He stared at the brightly painted ceiling. "House Mkuu in Zanzibar."

Why had Yosef looked at her like that? Why would he bring up Kenya and Zanzibar?

"The Southern Mage Massacre became a tragic footnote in history." Yosef smiled. "In this time."

Anahid was the first to put everything together. "So what you're saying is that five days ago, there was a growing political movement of free-mage groups across the Old World that had gained independence and political seniority in many places." She looked at Elder Kebret. "And now there are none? I think we have found the reason for the warp. Obviously it was someone's intention to stop this movement in order to retain political power."

One of the elders Narine didn't recognize huffed out a breath. "Sounds like the exact reason the Second Mage War kicked off, don't you think, Kebret?"

"And how do we know that the Southern Mage Massacre,

like so many other tragedies, was not tasary?" Elder Issa was clearly suspicious.

"I was with Aida when she examined the Tibeb," Tadesse said. "The tasary that had been altered led directly to the Southern Mage Massacre."

Elder Kebret's voice was curt. "Which five days ago had never happened. All the travelers here remember this Abdi and his people."

"So we must trust you only?" Issa looked at Anahid. "Five days ago, this report says *you* were gone."

Anahid spread her hands and glanced at Narine. "And so I must have been. I do not doubt my daughter's memories."

"There is a warp," Tadesse said. "I saw it with my own eyes. A knot that has probably only grown bigger or more tangled over the past five days."

Elder Issa narrowed her eyes. "I have never seen this warp, and it would have been a subject of study if it coincided with such a tragic event."

"Your memories have been aligned to the changed time-line." Narine stepped from behind Tadesse. "The Tibeb does not warp unless a change has been made to a tasary. Five days ago, this warp didn't exist because the Southern Mage Massacre was never supposed to happen."

Elder Issa rose. "My weavers and I must examine the Tibeb. If it is as you say it is, then this cannot stand. While threads of the Tibeb change as time shifts around us, tasary must never be altered."

*Except one has been.* Narine's frustration only grew. And she was forbidden from setting it right.

"I agree with Issa," Anahid said. "My sister speaks wisdom." She looked around the room, and all the other elders were nodding. "If the Southern Mage Massacre wasn't supposed to happen, we must find a way to stop it even if that means I disappear again."

ANAHID FOLLOWED NARINE AND TADESSE BACK TO HIS OFFICE, where Jacob was waiting.

He rose as soon as they appeared. "Hey, how did it— Oh. Hi." He held out his hand and glanced at Narine. "Who is—?"

"This is my mother." Narine wanted to run away, but she was stuck in Tadesse's office, her mind a whirl. She paced in the small space, unsure what was real and what were her memories in flux.

"And you are Jacob." Anahid looked up and smiled warmly. "This is the first time we meet, but not the last."

Narine burst out, "What the fuck does that mean, Mother? Who have you been talking to? Where have you been?" She flung her hand toward the door. "Is it Yosef? Is he telling you things about the future, because what the hell?"

Jacob stepped back. "Whoa."

Tadesse put a hand on Narine's shoulder. "Anahid, we're surprised to see you. Five days ago, you'd been lost for four years."

Narine shrugged her friend's hand off her shoulder. "You used your damn algorithm and a decrepit travelers' pool in that old temple in Harar, and you didn't come out of the water. Where have you been?"

"If I read between the lines of that very carefully worded report—well done, Tade—you all used my 'damn algorithm' to reach the past without the diviner's help, didn't you?" Anahid sat in Tadesse's chair and kicked her feet up on a stool nearby. "Does anyone want coffee? I'd give my left arm for a macchiato."

Narine shook her head. "I cannot believe you."

"I've been traveling, my daughter." She raised an eyebrow. "I had certain matters that needed to be attended to."

"On your own? With no help? No diviner?"

"I have Bati."

"Oh lovely," Narine said. "So Jamila's parents have been lying to me too?"

"Just Bati, and I swore her to secrecy, Narine." Anahid rolled her eyes and looked at Jacob. "She was always a dramatic child. You'll get used to it."

Jacob was leaning on the far wall and taking all the chaos in. He opened his mouth, then quickly closed it.

Anahid pointed at him. "I approve of a man who knows when not to speak."

Tadesse had his arms crossed over his chest, and his face was still bleak with pain and loss. "Elder Anahid, I know that I am not privy to your confidence, but we have lost friends—"

"Only temporarily, Tade." Anahid's voice was softer. "When I say that she is your destiny, please believe me. Aida will return, and this will all be set right."

Tadesse collapsed into a chair. "I don't know what is real anymore."

Jacob raised a hand. "Make that two of us."

Anahid rose and walked to Jacob. "You are an interesting conundrum, Dr. Martin." Anahid's eyes lit up. "How old are you?"

"Thirty-three."

"Too young for me to make the jump, but not for Narine. I do believe when this current chapter has passed, we'll find interesting things about your history, young man." She put a hand on his cheek. "I'm not surprised she was drawn to you and you to her. Your power is… rather extraordinary. Who are you supposed to train with?"

"Elder Desta."

She patted his cheek, then stepped back. "I outrank him. I'll train you."

Narine shouted, "Absolutely not."

"It'll be a great challenge." Anahid's eyes lit up. "And I love your American accent." She turned to her daughter.

"Isn't the American accent cute, Narine?" She turned back to Jacob. "That was one thing that charmed me about her father. We're still dear friends, by the way. But his accent." Anahid put a hand over her heart. "So adorable."

She started walking toward the door, but Tadesse stopped her. "Elder Anahid—"

"Nothing will happen until Issa examines the Tibeb." She turned to Tadesse. "They will have their meetings and debates, but in the end they will command a rather large group of travelers to jump back—I imagine we'll all be in on that—and organize either a defense for the Southern Mages or some kind of force to intercept their attackers." She glanced at Jacob. "For now, Tadesse Girma, you should start teaching Jacob the basics so he's not helpless. I need to speak to my daughter."

And with that, Anahid walked out of the office with Narine at her heels.

ANAHID CLOSED THE DOOR BEHIND THEM, AND ALL AMUSEMENT fled from her expression. She snapped at Narine. "Assistants."

Narine took the AI-controlled assistant from her ear and Narine took hers out as well.

"You have a dead box?"

Narine reached into her file cabinet and took out a small box the size of a tissue container. She opened the lid and held it out to Anahid, who dropped her assistant and mobile screen in the box. Narine did the same, then closed it and fixed the latch. Then she locked the door and turned to Anahid, who was already pulling out a small cone-shaped device from her messenger bag.

The sound-wave-dampening device was one of Anahid's most constant companions. Unlike many of her generation, she was keen to embrace technology and had customized this one to her precise vocal signature.

"Okay, we can talk." She pointed at Narine's desk. "Someone has been playing a very dangerous game. Show me the notes."

"How did you—?"

"Yosef told me the first one arrived during Pagume."

Narine went to her desk drawer and grabbed the second note. "How did Yosef know about them?"

"I'll explain Yosef later," Anahid said. "For now we focus on protecting our family and getting Abdi and Aida back."

"We can't fix that tasary. We can't travel back to Pagume in 1934. What are we supposed to—?"

"We can stop the massacre, and right now that needs to be the focus. That's what will contain the damage to the timeline."

Narine took the first note from her pocket and handed both to her mother. "The notes don't say much. I don't know why he sent them except to scare me."

"Bastard," Anahid muttered. "He would break the world because he couldn't own you."

"We don't *know* that it was Gideon behind all this. I mean…" She remembered the girl's description in Bale. "It doesn't make sense. He's not a traveler, so he can't have been the one to alter the timeline. And he hated the old houses. He hated the whole system. He wanted to pull it out by the roots. He said so many times. Why would he—?"

"Because he thought you belonged to him." Anahid stood. "And for some reason, that is all it took for him to start this crusade. We both know he put this in motion, Narine." She lifted the notes. "He told you."

Narine swallowed hard. "He's not evil, Mother. He hates me, but—"

"He's not evil? What do you call a man who would kidnap you and threaten your life to keep you? Who might have planned a massacre of innocent people?" Anahid looked at the second note. "He will find him? Good luck." She muttered, "You're dead now."

"What?" Narine felt her heart lurch in her chest. "Mother—"

"I mean *now*, Narine. Gideon is dead *now*. The man would be approaching two hundred years old; not even mages live that long. Relax, I didn't do anything to your former lover."

"My son's father," Narine said. "The man who lost his child. He has good reason to hate me."

"No, he doesn't!" Anahid stood. "If he hadn't..." She shook her head and raised a single finger in fury. "You carry this guilt about Gideon, and you should never have taken it on. I see it in your eyes when you whisper your prayers. I see it when you're with your son. You have spent the past six years living in regret, and I will not have it. Not anymore."

"I took Samson from him." Narine felt small and selfish. The bitterness was back in her mouth. "And I'm not even a mother to my own child."

"You *know* the reason for that. You know what he is. What he has the potential to be."

"I don't know because you never tell me everything! You say to trust you, and then you disappear for four years." Narine stood and paced, anger burning in her chest. "And now I'm *afraid* to see him. He barely knows who I am."

"That's not true."

"Isn't it?"

"No!" Anahid walked to her and took Narine by the shoulders. "Samson knows his mother, and I know my daughter. If Gideon had any honor, you could have been a family. He could have raised his son. None of us would have kept Samson from him."

Narine blinked her tears away. "How did he find out? Who told him the baby lived? He killed Abdi's clan. He killed

Aida's grandfather. Is he picking off the people who helped me hide? Will he go after our ancestors next?"

"No, because then his oh-so-powerful son wouldn't exist." Anahid stepped back and took a deep breath. "You've warned Jamila? He may have allies in this time we don't know about."

"Yes."

"He has to have allies." Her mother's eyes were going back and forth, looking at the notes, looking at Narine, the report she held from the Elders' Chamber. She narrowed her eyes on the report and skimmed it again. "The group that attacked the Southern Mages came from the north, they had guns, and all of them were mages."

Narine nodded and sat across from her mother. "Men and women, but they weren't only using magic. They had firepower."

"Who has firepower in the south in that age?" Anahid muttered in Armenian, and it was so fast Narine had trouble following. "Gideon hates the old houses."

"Yes. He always railed that they were just another form of colonialism."

"It's an old system and it needs to change. I don't disagree with him on that."

Narine snorted a laugh. "Says the woman who has tried to arrange my marriage to another old house more times than I can count."

Anahid waved a hand. "Marriage is useful, Narine, not romantic. We both know that. It's a strategic union, and I would be just as happy arranging a union with a powerful mage from a free clan as from an old house, there are just not enough of them yet."

"There are none of them now."

"Yes, you're right." Anahid cocked her head. "Someone is using Gideon. Someone who can travel through time. Someone who has a bigger plan."

"You mean someone put him up to this?"

"I think someone found out about your son, discovered what happened when you lost that year, and has decided that the best way to keep their power and influence in this world is to stamp out a quiet revolution in the past." Her mother met her eyes. "We're living in that timeline right now. If the Southern Mages don't emerge as a power—"

"Then the old houses of the Seba Segel retain all their authority," Narine said. "The free clans were too powerful to get rid of in the future."

"So someone ambitious found a way to trace them back to their roots, and they're using your husband to do their dirty work."

# CHAPTER 25

*The Island*
*1921*

Narine stood in a fine dress that Tigist and her friends in the village had made for her, decorated with bright threads and a *netela* so fine that the afternoon sun filtered through it like an alabaster window.

She stood in the sunshine next to Gideon while the priests spoke the words of blessing over the marriage she didn't want, asking for the abundance of God over the new couple, for their union to be one of peace and fulfillment. That their house be blessed by many children who would always walk in the light of God and the stars ordained in the sky.

Narine was silent throughout the ceremony. There were no words for her to say. Tigist handed her a simple gold ring, and she slid it on Gideon's finger. Then he put one on hers, struggling to twist it over her swollen flesh. The corner of her mouth turned up, but she kept her face down so no one could see that his frustration made her happy.

The wedding feast was hosted by Daniel and Tigist with the entire village attending, all of whom had seemed to forget

—at least for the day—that Narine hadn't always been among them.

"It's very strange." Tigist leaned over to her to offer food from her own hand while Gideon danced with the other men after the wedding feast. "I feel as if you've always been here."

"It's the inevitability of time," Narine said. "If I stayed, eventually everyone in the village would no longer remember a time I wasn't here. There would be some reason that a white woman was living with you. Time would create memories for them of how I got here and the life I've had with them. Eventually that would be normal to everyone here. That's the way human memory works."

A male azmari sang a bright wedding song, playing his fiddle-like *masenqo* on one side of the dance while a woman playing a stringed *krar* responded with the women. The song was wax and gold, teasing both the bride and the groom about the duties of a husband and wife in marriage.

"The people here are good," Narine said. "If I wanted to stay in the past, this would be a good place."

Tigist paused. "Are you changing your mind?"

"No." Narine shook her head. "But I don't want you thinking that I'm ungrateful to you for welcoming me into your home or for throwing this party. For being my family in this place."

Tigist gripped Narine's hand. "Do not think this way. If you remained here, you're right. I know people would embrace you, but you are not of this place or this time. You need your family and friends." She glanced at Gideon, whose face was glowing with joy. "Perhaps with time he will come to accept your decision. But you must go home first."

Narine nodded and folded a piece of injera to feed Tigist. "That's what I'm hoping. I will go back, have the baby, then return to make peace with Gideon. He can be a father. We can spend so much time here, and we won't even lose an hour in the present. But if I stay here—"

"It is not even a question." Tigist shook her head. "To lose your past is to lose yourself."

*And my magic.*

Growing up as a traveler, Narine never really felt like any place was her home, but in the absence of the present, she felt her longing for Addis Ababa keenly. She missed walking in the rainy streets and hearing the mix of voices and accents from all over the world. She missed the hundreds of languages and faces and customs. She missed the street fairs and the children who took over the street on Sunday to play football.

She even missed the traffic.

She missed her friends in the order. She missed Abdi. She missed her father. She missed Genet and Jamila. She missed Aster and her mother.

Especially her mother.

She didn't want her child to grow up in a small place where he or she would never see the world or learn about the stars. Where he would be an outcast who was misunderstood with a mother who had lost her memory and her magic.

She wanted to feel her power again, feel the embrace of the water as time pulled her along in its current, jumping to places and times that only a traveler could imagine.

"I miss home."

Tigist clutched her hand, her bright smile pasted on her lips. "Two months, Narine."

She nodded.

Two months.

GIDEON LOOKED OUT THE WINDOW, STRETCHING HIS ARMS over his head as he gazed at the lake. "There's a boat coming."

*Will it take me away?*

Narine didn't say it, but she'd thought it more than once.

Could she make it to Addis on her own? She was counting the days, and she didn't have to be in Lake Ziway to travel back. Any decent amount of water along the same latitude would work for the spell, even a bathtub.

But Gideon watched her constantly.

She sat on a stool in the corner, having finished serving him lunch. She was roasting coffee and focusing on the familiar smell, forcing her mind to remember how Aster shook the pan along with music playing from the speakers in the house. Joking about playing 'jazz buna' as if the coffee pan was a maraca and Genet and Narine were Spanish dancers.

*There was so much dancing in my home.*

"Narine?"

She blinked and looked up at Gideon. "Sorry, my mind was wandering."

He smiled indulgently. "The coffee smells good. It always tastes the best when you roast it."

She smiled but said nothing. He was doing this more and more. Showering her with affection and saying phrases like "you always" and "we always" as if Narine had lived in his time forever. She knew he was trying to make her forget.

"If you have patients coming," she said, "then I'll probably go up to Tigist's with the laundry to wash it with her."

"Why? You're right by the lake here."

Narine shrugged. It was a hike up to the village with their clothes, but if she was at Tigist's house, she could read and write in her journals. "I'd rather wash the clothes with my friends. Like I always do."

He smiled. "Of course."

Gideon put on his jacket before he walked to the door. He dressed like a British clerk even though he disdained them, and Narine pressed his shirts every morning before he woke up like a good country wife.

She watched him walk down the path to the clinic to greet the group of people landing on the rocks. There was a large group including an older man and two middle-aged women along with a gaggle of school-aged children.

Excellent. Seeing to that group would probably take him all day.

She ground the coffee after she roasted it, delivered a tray of small cups to the clinic where the patients clammed up when they saw her European face but thanked her profusely for the coffee. She went back to Gideon's cottage and carefully gathered a bundle of clothes, balanced them on her head, and started walking up the hill to the mage village and Tigist's compound.

When she was in shouting distance, one of the serving girls saw her.

"Narine!" They smiled and ran toward her, grabbing the dirty clothes from her and taking her hand. "We miss you."

"Is Tigist home?"

"She went to the order house to sit in an elder's meeting, but she should be back soon."

It was a harsh reminder that while most of the women in the village retained their mage duties and ran their households, Narine was powerless until she returned to her own time.

She ached to feel her magic again.

"We'll wash these for you," the older girls said. "Go and do your writing." She pulled Narine down and kissed her cheek. "We're so excited about your baby."

Another reminder. Pregnancy was never hidden in the Seba Segel. Mages of all kinds seemed to have an awareness of new life, especially if the child was powerful. If she had her power, she would have known far earlier that she was pregnant.

She put her hand on her still-flat belly. She'd lost weight living in the past, but so far she wasn't showing. She could feel a hardening in her womb though. Her stomach was firmer. Her body was preparing to nurture a new life.

*I suppose we're stuck with each other, kid.* Narine sighed as she walked to her room and took out her journals. *I'm sorry you're probably going to be a head case like me, but I'll do everything I can to make your life better than mine.*

She'd already decided that if she was going to be a mother, she wasn't going to be a mother like Anahid. No using her child for intelligence missions. No treating her baby like an adult when she could barely walk. She would hold off on her training as long as possible so that time wasn't so confusing and childhood memories stayed intact for more than weeks at a time.

Narine vaguely remembered what it felt like when the world wasn't in flux. She remembered happy times and a solid well of memories.

She still had those, but she also had the knowledge that all of them had been altered countless times over the course of her twenty-two years. Every little shift and every small blip in the timeline, she remembered until she didn't.

This child wouldn't speak her first spell until she was ready.

"Narine?"

She'd been writing down memories of her life for over an hour when she heard Tigist's voice. Her friend came into her room and quickly stooped to give Narine a hug.

"How are you?" the older woman asked. "Still sick in the mornings?"

"Not too much," Narine said. "That seems to be passing. Or at least getting better. What was the meeting about?"

Tigist rolled her eyes. "Politics, politics, politics. Samuel is hosting a hedge from House Wensho in the south. They're attempting to play the magistrate here, positioning themselves as authorities over the people on the mainland. They'd like the islands too, because they know how the crown prince respects the Zay people. It's symbolic but it's also intrusive."

"So they're trying to expand their influence?" In Narine's

time, House Wensho and their sister House Zuria were old but minor players in the political game, far outpaced by the burgeoning influence of the free mages in the south and the growing movement in the north to set up independent local systems. Neither house had any mages on the elder council and both were seen as 'rural relics' by the more senior houses in Addis.

"It's all that anyone talks about anymore," Tigist said. "My mother said they're talking about holding elections in Gondar for council positions. Can you imagine it?"

"Hmm." Narine nodded.

"Oh, I forgot! You can't say anything, can you?" Tigist shook her head. "It's probably normal in your time, isn't it? Elections are probably part of life, even for people like you from old houses." She shrugged. "Times will always change."

"It's the one constant in my life." Narine smiled. "Want me to tell you about artificial intelligence?"

Tigist covered her ears. "I don't know what that means and I don't want to know."

It was a month until Hosana when Gideon began to watch her. It was a week before Hosana when he hid all the knives. She pretended not the notice any of it, but she was marking off the days. She could barely sleep. He kept her busy in the house or the clinic. He hadn't let her leave his sight in weeks.

Gideon slept with one arm around Narine and one leg across her knees, weighing her body with his, caging her even as she slept.

When the morning before Hosana dawned, she felt her magic wake.

She breathed out a sigh of relief and hid the tears that gathered in her eyes. She'd almost wondered if time had forgotten her, but when she felt the power sweep over her, she knew she was going home. The magic in her bones rose up and suffused her body, making her skin prickle with goose bumps.

Unfortunately, Gideon felt it too.

"Gideon." She wanted to reason with him. Maybe seeing her power return would make him remember that she was more than just his wife, more than the mother of his child.

"No." His arm tightened around her. *"No."*

She made one final attempt to reason with him, mentally picturing the sharp rock she had already hidden at the water's edge under a root of the ficus tree where they used to make love.

"Gideon." She wiggled a hand free and put it on his cheek. "Some things are not meant to be." She opened her heart and pleaded. "I love you and I will love this baby, but if I stay here, my magic will choke and die."

His eyes wavered for a moment. His mouth softened.

"If I stay here," she continued, "I will be useless. Whatever power our child will have, I won't be able to teach him because I will have forgotten who I am."

He frowned. "You don't have to forget, Narine. I know you keep journals."

She prayed that Tigist would burn them when she left.

"It's not the same. I won't have any power anymore. I can't travel from this time." She struggled to sit up. "But if our son is born in the future, we can always come back. My magic will carry him with me. That's the extra ability, Gideon." She put a hand over his heart. "I can carry him with me. We can come back to you. It won't be like we're in another time, it will be just like we're over the lake or on the other side of the island, don't you see?"

His expression was everywhere at once. "You can't take my child from me."

"When he's older, he can decide—"

"No!" He batted her hand away and shook her shoulders. "You can't take him away!"

Her head snapped with the force of his shaking. "But you would take my life from me?" She couldn't stop the tears. "Am I nothing at all to you? You'd take my memories, my magic, my family?"

"It's not about you!"

She closed her eyes and felt the love that she'd held on to wither and shrink into pure determination.

Gideon would not steal her life.

Narine struggled out of his grip and fell to the floor. Gideon was on her in seconds, holding her arms behind her back while she screamed in rage and frustration.

"Let me go!"

"No." His hands were strong, stronger than hers, and her magic was barely waking. "I should have given you the drug last night." He dragged her toward his desk in the corner of the cottage. "Take it and I won't tie you up."

"No!" She screamed, willing her power to carry her voice to anyone who could hear her. "Help me!"

*I should have given you the drug last night.*

He had concocted something to steal her senses. Gideon was an alchemist and a powerful one. If he had created a drug to put her to sleep, she had no doubt it would last well through her traveling window.

There was no chance she'd last another year. Her child would be born in the past, and she would never be able to leave him. She wouldn't even remember who she was.

"Gideon, no." She let her body go limp; she made him drag her across the floor. "Please. Please don't do this. Don't steal my life."

"I'm giving you a life," he shouted. "Don't you see? That torment you feel every day? The confusion! The constant change. Have you felt it once since you've been here, or has time been steady? Think, Narine! Don't be stupid!"

"Gideon, let me go." The floor scraped her legs and her face. She felt a gouge in her wrist and smelled blood. Her shoulders felt pulled from their sockets. "Please don't do this."

He turned her over and caged her with his legs, sitting on her thighs and reaching for a vial on the desk. He'd turned off the rage and was speaking in a frighteningly calm voice. "I am doing this for your own good. You won't be confused anymore. You won't be burdened by time travel. You'll have a home. You'll have a normal life. With me."

*No no no no no.* She saw the vial glowing purple as he spoke over it, activating the potion with his magic.

She felt the panic in her chest. She had to get away!

Narine struggled, but he was so much stronger than she was.

The resignation crept into her heart like a thief. *You can't get away.*

Her tears were silent as Gideon shoved the glass vial between her lips, cutting her when she bit down and tried to stop the liquid touching her tongue. She spat it out over and over again, but he squeezed her cheeks and forced it down her throat.

"You won't leave me." His voice was eerily calm. "You won't."

Gideon pulled her to her feet, one arm locked around her waist. She'd done something to her ankle, and it ached when she tried to stand. She had to lean against him unless she wanted to fall.

He embraced her, stroking her hair as if soothing a child. "Not long now, Narine. When you wake up, you'll understand."

How long would it be? The magic was bursting to life in her blood; it was calling to the water. Her lips tingled and her skin felt like it was on fire.

*Find me.*

*Come to me.*

She could feel the water pulling her and the river of time beckoning her to its depths.

*Come back to me.*

She heard her mother's voice shouting her name as her head began to swim.

"Narine?"

There was a crash and Gideon dropped her; Narine tumbled to the ground, limp at Gideon's feet.

"Narine!"

"Get out!"

"What have you done?" Tigist's protective fury battered the air. "I will bring you before the council for this!"

Narine could barely move, but somehow she rolled onto her back. As Narine's head started to swim, she saw a group of women behind Tigist and Daniel. The women she'd washed with and cooked with and sung with. The women who had taught her how to comb cotton and spin thread. The archivists and diviners, her sisters in the order.

Tigist's magic was palpable in the air. She swung her arm out with an incantation and tossed Gideon against a wall. His body crashed against the brittle plaster, and glass shattered around him from the vials and bottles on his workbench, cutting his face, neck, and arms.

"Get away from me, witch! Let me go!"

Tigist's outstretched arm pinned Gideon to the wall even as the glass dug into his jaw and neck, even as he shouted and struggled.

"Daniel," she yelled at her husband. "Get Narine. She needs help; she has to get to the water."

"You can't take her!" Gideon roared in fury. "She's carrying my child."

"She is not your prisoner." Daniel walked over, and the hedge had never looked more furious. "What have you done? Have you drugged your own wife? What kind of man are you?" His arms slid beneath Narine. "Stars above, she's skin and bones."

Tigist kept her attention on holding Gideon back with her magic. "No more, Gideon. This madness is not love. Her power resides in her own time."

Blood poured down his neck and chest. "She is my wife."

Another woman spoke. "She is her own first."

There were more hands on Narine, soft hands—

*As Gideon's had once been soft.*

"Sister, wake up."

"Wake, Narine. It is your time to go home."

"Your family misses you, Sister."

They carried her out of the cottage and down to the water.

"How is it done?"

"Is she awake?"

"Sister, how can we help you?"

Daniel walked into the water with her, and the women of the village joined him, all of them putting their hands on Narine, one of the women fervently whispering a spell of awareness and clarity.

She felt the water welcome her, but she needed to offer it blood.

Gideon had been so bloody. Was he hurt?

"Narine?" Daniel patted her cheek. "What do we do? How can we help you go home?"

"Is anything written in the archives?"

She tried to speak, but her lips were frozen.

Her bleeding lips.

"Bloo..."

"She's saying something!"

"Narine, what do we do?"

The sacrifice had already been made. Her lip was still bleeding from the cut Gideon had given her with the glass vial, the same glass that had likely pierced his own flesh. All they needed to do was let her go so the water would cover her face.

She gathered all her strength, opened her eyes, and forced the words from her bloody mouth. "Let me go."

"Should we?"

Daniel's large hands left her first, but the women were still holding on.

"Look at the water!"

"Let her go."

"It's glowing beneath her. Do you see it?"

"She'll sink."

No, she would swim.

She smiled as the last hand tying her to the past let go of her body. Narine put a hand on her belly, cradling the spark of power that was reacting to her magic and dancing in her blood.

On the edge of the water, she saw Tigist in the distance, still holding Gideon back as he tried to jump into the lake.

She closed her eyes and sank beneath the surface.

"NARINE?"

She felt the warm embrace of the travelers' pool around her and saw the soft blue light; the scent of frankincense filled the air, but she couldn't open her eyes, not even when her face surfaced.

"Get her out of the water!"

Mother?

"Something isn't right. What did they do to her?" Abdi's voice joined her mother's. "What happened?"

Strong hands pulled her out of the warm water and onto the marble deck around the pool. She could hear Aida's voice, and her friend was frantic.

"There's nothing wrong with the panel. Should I call Calla?"

"No!"

"All the constellar coordinates are the same as they were when she went in into the jump. She was a few minutes late but—"

"My God." Her mother's voice cut through the chaos, and everyone fell silent. "Look at her. Look how thin she is. How…"

"She missed her window." It was Abdi, but Narine couldn't open her eyes to meet her mentor's comforting gaze. "Something happened and she missed her window. Anahid, do you see—?"

"My daughter." One of her mother's warm hands landed on her cold cheek and the other went to her abdomen. She sucked in a breath. "How time makes fools of us all."

Aida's voice was faint but clear. "Is that…?"

"We need to get her warm and get her home." Her mother's voice was the last thing she remembered. "No one speaks of this." A heavy blanket wrapped around her. "No one."

# CHAPTER 26

*Harar, Ethiopia*
*New Year's Eve*
*2065*

Narine turned her face to the side and pressed her nose into the saffron-scented blanket covered with gold flowers and twisting vines. The pressure of bearing down nearly overpowered her.

"Just a few more pushes." Jamila stroked damp hair back off her forehead and held her shoulders, the familiar blanket from home spread over her lap. "You're almost done."

"I can't."

Her mother spoke from the edge of the bathtub. "You have to."

She looked up and saw the flickering candles overhead in the ancient temple in Harar. The dome of the night sky was over her, candles forming the familiar signs of the guardian wolf who would watch over the child who was coming.

Her mother and Bati were on either side, hands cradling Narine's hips as the warm water in the old cast-iron bath lapped against her skin.

The old magic whispered to her, crowding out the pain that threatened to take over her mind. *Child of water. Child of time. Son of stars.*

Time whispered to her, urging her to bring forth the next generation. Her blood was in the water; the sacrifice had been accepted.

Her child would be born under the guardian wolf on the last day of the thirteenth month, a tasary if there ever was one.

"Push!" Bati urged her. "Know your strength."

"You can do this, Narine." Jamila braced Narine's shoulders with her thighs, sitting behind her as the pain tore through her abdomen.

She groaned and felt her muscles tense on instinct, her womb pushing the intruder from her body. Her head swam and she felt her magic take over, the current of power moving from her forehead, down her throat, into her abdomen and through her pelvis as she forced the baby into the water.

"I see him!" Anahid caught the baby in her hands and lifted him from the water, immediately setting him on Narine's belly. "A boy, Narine. Can you feel him?"

The child seemed to cough a little; then a mewing sound like a cat came from his throat. The mewing grew louder until a single full-throated cry erupted from his chest, making Jamila laugh.

"He's healthy." She wiped her forehead with the back of her hand. "He's fine. You're fine. You did it, Narine."

The baby cried louder, and the water in the mage pool churned at the sound.

Narine caught her mother's eyes; Anahid had noticed.

"Samson." Narine put a hand on the baby's back. "Shhhh."

The water calmed.

She started to shiver, and Jamila wrapped the blanket around her shoulders, encasing mother and child as Narine lifted the tiny child higher on her chest, bracing his bare bottom with a waterlogged hand.

"He's small. Is he supposed to be that small?" No child should be that small and vulnerable. "He wasn't early. Is he supposed to be so small?"

Bati smiled. "He looks like a normal, healthy newborn to me."

Anahid was whispering birth magic over Narine, and she could feel the power of her mother's spells touching her skin and drifting in the water. She looked at the travelers' pool, then lifted the little boy's arm to examine his left forearm.

There, as plain as her own, the mark of the traveler was already visible.

Anahid saw it and sucked in a sharp breath. "Already."

Jamila hugged Narine's shoulders more closely. "What does that mean?"

"Most of our marks develop during our first year," Narine said. "We're born with them but they're faint."

"Not his." Anahid stroked a shaking hand over the baby's cap of dark brown curls. "You will be stronger than all of us, won't you, little one?"

Narine looked up and saw tears in her mother's eyes. Their gaze met over the baby's head, and she saw Anahid's fear mirror her own.

*Samson Narine Anahid, first of his name.*

*Child of the sun and the stars.*

*Son of time and water. Born to the past and the present.*

The appearance of a traveler's mark so dark and so prominent fulfilled Narine and Anahid's suspicions and stoked their fear. Born of a third-tier traveler, sired by an alchemist with traveler's blood, tenth in his line of power, Narine's son would be the first fourth-tier traveler born in over a thousand years. The water already reacted to his voice.

Narine held Samson to her breast as she pushed out the

afterbirth, and Anahid and Bati helped her to her feet and out of the water.

"What does it mean?" Jamila whispered, holding the blanket around Narine and the tiny baby. "What does he mean?"

"I don't know." She stepped to the side, her legs quivering under her weight and the burden of motherhood she never expected. "No one knows."

Narine had never known of a child conceived in one time and born in another. As far as Anahid knew, one hadn't been born before. No one knew what his magic would do. No one knew what her son would be.

Gideon's son.

She felt a swelling of pain in her chest, and tears began to fall. Samson let out a grunting protest and twisted on her chest, searching for her breast. Narine cradled him, and her son began to suckle as tears poured down her face.

She didn't know if she was happy or sad. She was afraid and relieved at the same time.

He was here and he was healthy.

His power was frightening, but he was tiny, the smallest child she'd ever held. He seemed impossibly fragile in her exhausted arms.

Anahid walked to the travelers' pool in the ancient temple and filled a pitcher. "Jamila, take the blanket away."

"She's cold."

Bati cut her eyes to her daughter. "Do as you're told."

Jamila grumbled but moved to the side, leaving Narine and the baby naked and shivering on the edge of the pool.

The words Anahid spoke were harsh and guttural; it was a spell Narine had never heard before, spoken in a language that had died in the human world a thousand years before. She recognized a few phrases, the admonition to banish evil, a supplication to the stars and the river goddess, but most of it was foreign to her ears.

Her mother poured the pitcher of water over her head, and Narine was reminded that today was the final day of Pagume. The thirteenth month was closing its watchful eyes, and the new year would begin at dawn the next day.

"There will be bonfires tonight, but you will not go," Anahid said when the baptism was over. "You will stay in Bati's house and speak to no one but Jamila." She walked to the temple pool and filled the pitcher again, this time pouring the water through Narine's hair and over every inch of her body, cleansing her of the blood from Samson's birth.

Narine was shivering. "You want to keep him a secret, don't you? I'm not ashamed of my son."

Bati brought a towel to dry off her son, and Jamila wrapped a thick woven cloth around her, leaving her familiar blanket on a bench in the corner.

Anahid's eyes were cutting. "There is no shame in this child's birth. But I trust five people in the world, and three of them are in this room. Your father will be told, and no one else. Abdi has spoken to the girl in Addis."

"Aida is my friend and—"

"He's made sure she won't say anything. Aster knows, but Genet cannot."

Genet was her sister in everything but blood. "Mother!"

Jamila's mouth fell open. "Genet would never tell a soul. Why would you—?"

"If I could keep *you* from knowing about him, I would." Anahid looked at Jamila, then at Narine. "Both of you are barely more than girls."

"Stop." Narine clutched the baby to her chest. "He is my son, Mother. Not yours. Your authority only stretches so far."

"Do you know?" Anahid cocked her head and put a hand on Samson's forehead. "Do you know what I would do to anyone who threatened you or this child?"

Narine could see the truth and the fury in her mother's eyes. "We're not in danger anymore."

"It took every warning from Bati and every better instinct in my body not to jump to that man's time and kill him." Her mother pointed at the glowing travelers' pool; her hand was shaking again. "We don't know what the baby's power will be. And until we do, the order must know *nothing*" —she spat out the word— "about him. Do you understand me?" She looked at Narine, then at Jamila. "Do you both understand me?"

Narine reached for Jamila's hand. "I understand."

Jamila echoed her. "We understand."

Bati put her hand on Anahid's shoulder. "My friend, we must finish cleaning. The temple mages will be here in the morning to light the fire for the new year. Let's get to work."

SHE ROCKED SAMSON BACK AND FORTH, HER HAND NEVER leaving his small body. His belly was full of milk, and his cheeks had filled out in the week since he'd been born. He no longer felt quite so fragile to Narine, though he was still tiny to her eyes.

Her room in the compound in Harar faced the inside of the courtyard, and there was a single window that opened outside. Moonlight streamed through the open window, and slow shadows moved across the room.

The large square bed was piled with cushions and lifted only a few feet off the green and yellow tile of the floor. She lay among the pillows, Samson sleeping next to her and Jamila on the other side. Both of them were staring at the baby as he slept.

"He looks like you," Jamila whispered. "His nose."

"He looks like his father."

Jamila looked up. "What are you going to tell him?"

Narine had already told Jamila she was going back to the island after the baby was born. There was too much unfinished business to leave Gideon forever. She would need Aida's help though. Anahid would never allow her to go back to that place alone.

"I don't know. I suppose it depends on what he says when he sees me. I'm hoping he'll be more reasonable now that he doesn't have me under his control."

"You could tell him the baby died. That you miscarried during the jump."

"That's cruel."

"Narine, he drugged you and tried to kidnap you. The only reason you escaped is because your friends fought back and took you to the water."

Narine stared at Samson, seeing the echoes of Gideon's face. The broad cheeks and the angled eyes. His severe mouth had transformed into a soft pout in his son's rounded face. "I want him to see the good things, the parts I fell in love with." Narine blinked back tears. "I loved him, Jamila. I can't *not* love him, even after everything that happened."

"Your heart is too soft." Jamila ran a finger over Samson's head. "You have to think about Samson's safety now. You're his mother."

She looked up. "And you will be too."

It had already been decided that the baby would stay in Harar and be raised as Jamila's son. While Bati and Sahid were prominent mages, Jamila was their rebellious daughter who had already been married and divorced once. Though she was only twenty-three, she ran her own business and made her own decisions. No one would be shocked if she had a baby on her own.

There would be no way to hide that the boy had power, but the hope was that with Jamila assumed to be the mother, Samson wouldn't attract any more attention than the average child born in a powerful family. They would cover his arm and hope that Samson would be taken for just another one of the many Sahid grandchildren.

Narine and Jamila would be hidden for the first

month with the baby; then Jamila would emerge in public as Samson's mother and Narine the proud auntie. There would be questions about the father, but Jamila relished the idea of disappointing everyone with her silence.

Only their parents could know the truth.

"She doesn't even want me to tell Geni." Narine's heart ached. One day her sister would know about her child and she would be angry. "I have to tell her. He and Gelile will be cousins. I have to make Anahid understand."

"You know she'll tell Aster."

"She probably did as soon as I jumped back." Anahid and Aster were partners in all ways. They were two women with one mind. "How am I going to leave him?"

Just the thought made her chest ache.

Jamila reached over and took Narine's hand. "You will leave him knowing that I will love him with every cell of my being. I will protect him in every way, and I will shower him with all the love I have for him and for his mother." She placed their joined hands over Samson's round belly, the little one letting out a contented sigh.

Narine blinked back tears. "I never wanted to be a mother. I never wanted him to live with… all this."

"What are you always telling me? Time is wiser than we are."

"Right now I feel like the most stupid person in history."

"You can't think that way. You trusted someone you shouldn't have, but that's not your fault."

"Part of me still loves him, Jamila."

Her best friend was silent, but all Narine could think about was a different world where she wouldn't have had to hide her baby and where Gideon could have been a father.

"He would be happier in this time," Narine whispered. "He could live in a free Kenya. He could raise his child. He could—"

"It's not possible." Jamila's voice was flat. "Why are you even talking like this?"

"Because it is possible; it's just not allowed." Now she sounded like a child. There was good reason why travel to the future was taboo. "I don't know what I'm saying. I don't want him anymore. I can't forget... everything."

"Are you sure?" Jamila sounded suspicious. "Maybe it's not a good idea for you to go back to the island. You can wait. You could wait years and go back a week after you left."

"I'll be fine." She met her best friend's guarded eyes. "I'll be fine."

"I don't want to lose you. And Samson needs you. I can raise him and protect him, Narine, but even I can feel his power." She shook her head. "Your mother always says that a single pebble can make a wave that destroys a mountain. This child could be that wave."

"No." She laid her cheek on the bed, cushioned by the familiar velvet embrace of her childhood blanket. She looked at Samson, her nose almost touching his. "He's not a wave, Jamila. He's the sun."

*Six months later...*

IT WAS MONTHS BEFORE SHE RETURNED TO THE ISLAND. Months of secret planning with Aida, months of working to return her body to health, and months apart from the child who was quickly growing in Harar, safe in Jamila's house.

This time when she emerged from the lake, she could feel a difference in the air. It was months after she'd left, well into the dry season. The lake was lower and the sky overhead a brilliant, clear blue.

She waved at a familiar smiling face paddling toward her as she swam toward the landing in the cove.

"You came back." Abel, the old fisherman, greeted her like a friend and walked up the narrow beach with her. "Hasn't even been too long."

She eyed the cottage where so much had happened and the clinic where Narine could see people lined up outside. "Is the doctor here?"

Abel nodded toward the town on the far distant shore. "On the mainland today. His nurse is seeing people though."

She nodded and took her hair down, squeezing water out of the lengths until it wasn't dripping. "It's warm."

"It was a dry year." Abel shrugged. "Not too bad. Fewer fish than last year, but not too bad."

She eyed the path that led to the village. "The tall female hedge from the north. The elder. She's still here, right?"

Abel grinned. "How long do you think you've been gone? Of course she's still here."

Narine nodded and patted his shoulder. "Thank you, Abel. It's good to see a familiar face."

"No worries, Sister." He nodded. "Go see your friends. How long are you staying this time?"

"I leave tomorrow." This time she'd left no time for danger to fall. "But hopefully I'll be back."

"I hope so."

Narine walked up the hill in wet sandals, stopping to squeeze out the wrap she wore. By the time she reached Tigist and Daniel's compound, her clothes were almost dry from the warm breeze that wafted off the top of the hill.

She rapped on the outer gate of the compound and waited for one of the girls to answer, but it was Tigist who opened the door.

"Oh!" Her friend embraced her without another word, enclosing her in a fierce embrace and pulling her into the protective walls of the compound. "You're back. You came back."

Narine hugged her back hard and pressed her eyes closed so the tears wouldn't fall. "I came back."

"Did Gideon—? No, he's on the mainland today. Thank God he's on the mainland; I almost forgot." Tigist pushed her away and looked down. "How—? Has it been a long time in your time?"

She nodded silently.

Her friend glanced at the gate. "Gideon will be back tonight. Thank the stars you came here first." Her eyes fell to Narine's belly again. "What happened?"

In that moment, as much as Narine wanted to share Samson's birth with the woman who had saved them both, she knew from the woman's expression what she had to do.

Her mother was right. No one could know about Samson. Not even Tigist.

"I lost him," Narine whispered.

Tigist's face fell in grief, and she threw her arms around Narine again, holding her tightly. "I'm sorry." Her voice was rough. "The stars know why these tragedies happen, but I know you will be a mother someday."

She said nothing, holding Tigist's grief, feeling like a thief and swallowing her fury.

This was Gideon's fault.

She should have been able to share her son's birth with the woman who had saved her. Saved him. She should have been able to name Tigist as her child's auntie and brought Samson to visit this place.

They walked inside the house, and Tigist guided Narine to a low couch by the fire.

Narine asked, "So Gideon is still angry?"

"The admonition from the elder council cooled some of his anger." Tigist walked over and took some coals from the oven to roast some coffee in a brazier. "He won't make trouble for you again, but he still refers to you as his wife."

"Technically I am."

Tigist gave her a look. "Vows not spoken from the heart are no vows at all."

"But technically I *am* his wife." She took a long breath. "He's not wrong."

"He tried to keep you from returning to your family. No one in the village blames you for leaving." She caught herself. "Maybe Brother Samuel does and some of the older mages, but none of the women do."

"My mother thanks all of you," Narine said softly. "My whole family does. They might have lived their whole lives and never known what happened to me."

Tigist shook her head as she poured the coffee into a roasting pan. "I cannot even imagine. How long are you staying this time?"

"My window is only open until tomorrow. Can you stay with me until I go back?"

Tigist sat up straight, and Narine felt her power flex and spread through the room. "Try to stop me. I'm not letting you meet with Gideon alone."

"I wouldn't want to go without you." It was the only way that Narine had convinced Aida to help her make the jump. She'd promised that she wouldn't face Gideon alone.

"Coffee first," Tigist said. "We'll walk over tonight."

IT COULD HAVE BEEN EIGHT MONTHS OR EIGHT YEARS; THE hatred in his eyes hadn't changed. Gideon shook his head when he saw her but didn't try to lay a hand on her, eyeing Tigist in the distance where she was waiting at the end of the path.

"How long has it been for you?"

"The same as it's been for you. A little over eight months."

He stared at her abdomen. "You lost the baby, didn't you?" He curled his lip in disgust. "You stupid girl."

"I lost him, but it wasn't because of the jump."

Gideon walked away, giving Narine his back. He stared at the lake, putting his hands on his hips and letting his head fall back. He'd clipped his hair close to his head, and the afternoon sun glowed on his forehead.

He was as compelling as he'd ever been, and Narine ached to have him turn to her with a smile.

"It wasn't because of the jump?" He turned. "Of course it was. If you'd stayed here, my child would be alive." Gideon's voice was ice-cold. "He died because of your willfulness."

"Gideon—"

"Why are you here?"

Why had she come back? In a way, it was crueler to him, but she'd needed to know. She wanted to see if any softness cracked his heart, if any regret was evident in his eyes.

"We left things unsaid." *Because you drugged me and tried to keep me prisoner.*

"I think you said everything you needed to when you left me." He looked past her, over her shoulder to where Tigist waited. "And you turned the village against me. I'm being sent back to Mombasa after Christmas."

"Isn't that where you wanted to go?"

"No. I wanted to go back to Nairobi." His voice broke a little. "With you and my son. But you made that impossible."

Narine shook her head. "I'm not the one who was being unreasonable, Gideon. You were trying to keep me prisoner."

"I was trying to keep you safe."

"Safe?" She barked a laugh. "Is that what you call it when you drug someone?"

"How is it?" His eyes were piercing. "How's your mind, Narine? Still living in confusion? Waking up to a new reality every day? Traveling from one time to the next like the order's servant girl?"

Anger clogged her throat. "I took some time off. I'll be back to work soon enough."

"Good. You love the Seba Segel more than you loved me or our child, so I suppose that's what's best for you."

She stared at him and he stared back, unwavering in the expression on his face.

Narine looked away first. "I will do whatever I need to so you're free to marry again. I'll speak to the priests in the morning and—"

"You're still my wife, Narine."

She looked at him with narrowed eyes. "What are you talking about?"

He looked at her with a mix of hatred and satisfaction. "You will always be my wife."

She shook her head. "I don't accept that."

"You can accept it or not." He started to walk away. "But I'm still wearing my ring." He held up his hand. "And I have no plans to remove it." He paused, turned, and said, "See you in time, Narine."

She watched him turn and walk toward the cottage, his stride determined and his chin raised.

Narine walked away and joined Tigist under a spreading acacia tree.

"Are you okay?" She put a hand on Narine's shoulder. "He's a stubborn, angry man."

"He said I'm still his wife."

Tigist had known it by her expression. "He speaks of you as his wife to the council too."

"Is it true that he's going back to Kenya?"

She nodded. "The elder council in Addis received a request from House Mkisi in Mombasa. They are recalling him for some reason. He's not happy about it."

"Strange." She fell into step beside Tigist and took her hand as they walked. "At least after that happens, I'll be able to come back and visit you."

"That would be wonderful." Tigist patted her hand and smiled. "I would really love that."

# CHAPTER 27

*Addis Ababa*
*2072*

Narine was awake most of the night, ruminating over whom she could trust, what was going to happen, and what she needed to do. She wanted to talk to Abdi. She wanted to confide in Jamila, but she was worried that doing so could put her best friend in danger. She wanted to know the future, and that wasn't allowed.

She wanted her mother to not have disappeared.

When she asked Genet about her mother, her sister was confused.

"Your mother lives at the order. What's wrong? Do you want her to move back here? The two of you were fighting like cats, Narine."

Narine stared at the window, watching the shadow of the trees in the moonlight as they tracked slowly across the garden. The distant rumble of traffic echoed in the night as large trucks made deliveries across the city. She could smell rain in the air again.

She heard her assistant vibrating across the room and

walked to grab it. She glanced at the unfamiliar number on the lens and put the assistant in her ear.

"Who is this?"

"He's restless tonight."

Narine felt her heart melt. "Let me talk to him."

"Just a second."

She settled back into bed and waited to hear her son's small voice.

"Ema?"

She closed her eyes, still feeling unworthy of the title. *"Yene mar."*

"Are you awake?"

"I am." She settled back into her cushions. "Are you having an adventure with Ay?" Her son spoke Harari as easily as Amharic. "Don't tell me where you are, but tell me what you see."

"Uhh." He giggled a little. "I see very bright flowers. Aaaaand I see my breath because it's coooold."

"I'm building a fire right now." Jamila's voice echoed in the background. "We are not going to freeze."

"It's cold?" Narine suspected she knew where her best friend had taken him, but she didn't spoil the game. "Where is cold and also has flowers? That doesn't make sense."

He giggled. "The flowers are on the blanket."

"Oh, I see. Is the blanket very soft and warm?" Narine closed her eyes and saw the gold petals of the ancient blanket that had covered her bed when she was a girl, the same blanket her mother had brought to Harar to lay across her bed when she was recovering.

"It's so warm it's like a hug! Like your hug."

She closed her eyes. "I miss you so, so much."

"Are you going to come see us? You didn't come on my birthday like you usually do, and then I got mad and Ay made me go to my room because the glasses were breaking because of the water and it was boring. But I said I was sorry, and then I didn't have to be in my room anymore."

"I'm sorry." She never made excuses because she'd hated them when she was a disappointed child. "I'm so sorry I wasn't there, but I will see you as soon as I possibly can."

"Are you jumping a lot? Nani says we can't do that during Pagume."

Her eye twitched. "When did you see Nani?" Narine tried not to react. Samson had said similar things for years, and Narine had always put it down to an active imagination and hearing stories from Jamila and her parents. Now she suspected that Anahid had been visiting her grandson secretly. "When did she come to visit you?"

"Um… a long time ago." For a child his age, a long time could have been two days or two months. "Before my birthday."

"I'm sorry I missed it." She closed her eyes and thought of New Year's Eve. "I had to be here, and it was very boring here too. I would have had much more fun with you."

"Yes, I know. I'm taller than the last time you saw me."

"Are you?" She smiled. "Are you taller than Ay now?"

He burst into laughter. "No, I'm still your baby."

Samson Narine Anahid was six years old, the light of her life and Jamila's life, and their most closely guarded secret. To the rest of the world, he was Jamila's son. Only in private did Samson call her mother.

His traveler's mark was hidden by long sleeves Jamila forced him to wear, and his power was a sleeping lion, curled in his chest and waiting to rise. He saw things she didn't. He knew things he shouldn't. Her son was tenth in his line of power and the first fourth-tier mage born in over a thousand years.

When he had been born on the fifth day of Pagume, Anahid wept.

"Grandmother was gone and then she wasn't!" he said. "She came to see me, then she went away."

"Do you mean Umma or Nani?" Just like Samson used the Harari word for mother with Jamila, he used Harari to talk about Jamila's parents. Anahid was Nani, and Samson had been mentioning her more and more in the past months.

"Nani was here."

This time Narine knew it wasn't his imagination. "Does Nani come when you're with Ay?"

"No. She always visits me when Ay's at work. When I'm with Umma."

So Bati had been in on the deception as well. Leave it to a diviner to think she knew better than everyone. "I miss you, my baby."

He heaved a long, dramatic sigh. "I miss you too."

"I wish I could be with you right now."

"So come here. We're at the—"

"No." Narine stopped him before he could finish.

"Samson, no." Jamila's voice in the background again. "I told you, *ababu*. It's a surprise for Ema."

The little boy sighed. "I don't like surprises anymore. I want to see you."

"As soon as I can." They didn't keep secrets from the boy, but there were many "surprises" in his life that could only be shared with a few people. Her visits were always a surprise because Narine never knew when she would be able to slip away. Often, whole months stretched between her visits to Harar.

"Someday," he said, "I will see you every day. And when I wake up, you will always be there to make me *kuti* and sing to me and rub my feet when I am sleepy."

Narine couldn't help but laugh. "I think you are confusing your ay's voice with mine, because she is a much better singer."

"No," the little boy said. "I know what will happen."

The boy spoke about the future with a confidence that had always troubled Narine. No one really knew what a fourth-tier mage would be or could be. Any records of that magic had been lost long ago or, more likely, were never written.

It was late and the moon had moved behind the clouds. Narine could hear Jamila singing in the background, and somewhere in the house, flute music was playing. "My beautiful boy," Narine whispered, "are you sleepy yet?"

"A little bit. Are you sleepy?"

"Yes," she said, even though sleep was the last thing on her mind. "Is Ay finished building the fire? Is it nice and warm?"

"Yes, she's sitting in her chair now. Do you want to talk to her?"

"Only if you're ready to go to bed."

"Yes. I'm not cold anymore."

"Pull your blanket around you tight, okay?"

She could hear him shuffling in the background, and the assistant rattled as the little boy handed it to Jamila.

"Narine?"

"I'm here."

"He's all snuggled in now like a little worm."

Samson protested in the background. "I am not a worm."

"You are," Jamila said. "You're a worm in a flower cocoon."

"Ay!"

Narine laughed. "Good night, my beautiful boy. I will see you as soon as I can."

"Good night." There was more scrambling, then a loud whisper that filled her ear. *"Betam wedeshelew."*

Narine closed her eyes to stop the tears from falling. "I love you so much."

There was more rustling; then Narine heard a door open and close.

"I'm outside," Jamila said. "I think he couldn't sleep because of the cold. He was asking for you."

"Are you at Nash's place?"

"Do you want to know?"

"Yes. No." Narine thought of Jamila in the southern mountains west of Arba Minch, no doubt hidden in a village somewhere by a contrary Syrian hedge named Nash. "Have you and Nash kissed yet?"

"Oh! You know what? That's an excellent idea. My mother would love a surly, antisocial hedge in the family." She fiddled with something, and Narine suspected she was lighting a rare cigarette, which was something she only did when she was stressed. "Maybe I will ask Nash to marry me; his house probably wants him to get married too. It can be an absent marriage of convenience for us both."

"If I liked him more, I'd warn him." She swallowed the lump in her throat. "Are you safe?"

"No one will find us. You know how I can hide."

"My mother is back."

Jamila blew out some smoke. "Where did she go?"

Narine closed her eyes. "Right. Uh, glitch in the timeline, but she's back. Has she been over there?"

"Not that I know of, but you know how she and my mother are."

"Just be cagey with your mom for now. I don't know that I want Anahid knowing where he is."

"Done."

It had crossed Narine's mind more than once that it would be just like Anahid to stash her son somewhere "for his own safety" and not tell Narine. She was the definition of high-handed.

"So did you find your American?"

"I did." She looked at the door. "In fact, he's sleeping down the hall. Long day."

"That moved quickly, but I'll say it's about time."

"Not like that." Narine suspected that Jacob was awake

too. The music sounded Native American to her ears. "He's diaspora. Kind of. Raised in the US, but he's powerful."

"Huh." Jamila blew out more smoke. "And you found him?"

"I couldn't help feeling his power. He's a traveler."

"Really? How does that work when you don't know you have magic?"

"Most travelers don't really notice alterations in the time-line until we tap into our magic."

"Could have fooled me with Samson."

"Well, I've told you before, Samson is not a typical travel-er." She heard someone moving around in the house. "Jamila, I need to go."

"I'll have a different number tomorrow, so if you see an unknown contact, just assume it's me."

"Got it."

SHE TOSSED HER ASSISTANT ON HER BEDSIDE TABLE AND THREW a robe over her nightclothes, then went out to the kitchen where she heard someone moving.

Jacob was standing at the counter, staring at the electric wall unit to boil water. He looked enormous in her small kitchen.

"Need some help?"

He looked up. "No. Sorry, did I wake you up?"

She shook her head and pulled over a chair from the ornately carved dining table. "Are you trying to make tea?"

"Yes. I found some herbal here." He held up a paper box. "Genet said that I could help myself. Do you want some?"

No, but she wanted company. "Sure, that sounds perfect actually."

"Great." He frowned, opening cupboards, but quickly remembered where the teacups were kept. "You need mugs."

"Mugs?"

He held up his hands. "Big coffee cups for big hands."

"Oh, the big…" She smiled. "I know what you mean. You're right. We should get some for friends. It's mostly women around here these days; I tend not to think about people with big hands."

He put tea bags in two cups and put each cup into the unit to fill it with boiling water. "You said you live here with Genet and her daughter? That's all? It's a big place."

She reached for the mug he handed her. "I have a lot of cousins, and they visit a lot. Well… not as many lately."

He frowned and joined her at the table. "Any particular reason?"

"Life." She smiled. "Most of them are also mages, so they've been assigned to chapters all over the continent. A couple in Europe, but most have stayed closer to home. About half of them are travelers, so they're in demand."

Jacob traced the carved stars that decorated the table. "Is this Ethiopian?"

"Armenian. My grandfather carved it."

"Have you been?"

"To Armenia?" Narine nodded. "I have."

He smiled. "What was it like?"

"Uhhh." She narrowed her eyes. "Maybe what you felt when you came here. There's a connection, but it feels distant. It's not what you expect. I went with my grandfather when he was still alive, and I remember feeling…"

Jacob paused, his teacup halfway to his lips. "Resentful."

Her eyes met his and widened. "Yes."

"You wanted it to feel like home, and it didn't."

Narine nodded. "I was young. It took me a long time to realize that Addis was really my home. I went through a period of time when I was very angry with my family for moving away from Armenia. Or not moving back maybe, when it was safe. I didn't want to live in a place where I was different."

"I know the feeling."

"Even though I wasn't that different at all."

Jacob smiled. "Then you go to a place" —he looked out the window— "where you look the same as everyone, but—"

"It still doesn't feel like home."

He lifted his teacup. "Exactly."

"Yes."

He let out a long breath. "Yeah."

They both drank their tea in silence.

"So what does home mean for you, Jacob Martin?"

"Jacob Bekele Martin."

She raised her eyebrows. "That's probably your birth father's name, you know."

"I've been told that."

She set down her cup and allowed the heat from the dwindling tea warm her hands. "I kind of pulled you off track last week when I roped you into this, didn't I?"

He nodded. "You did."

"It's not too late, you know." She shrugged. "You haven't taken any vows. You haven't been initiated."

"There's an initiation?"

"Yes. It involves jumping over cows." She pursed her lips. "You're going to want to practice if you don't want to make a fool of yourself."

He froze for a second. "That's a joke."

She allowed the smile to escape. "Yes, that's a joke. Hamar people do the cow jump, and you're not Hamar. You're going to have to ride an ostrich."

"Honestly, at this point nothing would really surprise me."

Narine smiled. "It's magic." She met his eyes. "It's magic. There is an initiation, and after that, you will feel what Tade and I feel. Those fluxes in time? The ones that always felt a little murky or just tricks of your mind before? You'll remember more." She glanced out the window and saw Genet and Gelile's cottage on the other side of the garden. "You'll lose people. And even if you don't, you'll spend your life afraid of losing them."

He frowned. "What do you—?"

"Someone you love might cease to exist because someone fifty years ago turned right instead of left." Narine clung to threads that lingered in her mind, memories of memory that had already faded with the passage of time. "You'll remember them and grieve, but even worse, you know that eventually you won't even remember them anymore. Your mind will adjust to the timeline and you'll lose them all over again."

"Is it really that bad?"

"The more the Seba Segel changes the past, the more chances there are for time to flex and reroute. Part of the diviners' job when we make jumps is to find a path that will correct the wrongs of history while creating the smallest ripples of change, but there's no way to change the past without affecting the future. It's impossible."

"So why change it at all?"

It was a question that she'd faced before.

"Abdi used to tell me that the motto of the Seba Segel was to do the best we could for the most we could. That if I saved one life, it was as if I'd saved the whole world."

Jacob stared at her. "Do you believe that?"

"I used to." She swallowed hard. "My mother told me something else."

"What was that?"

"A tiny pebble can start a ripple that breaks a mountain."

He folded his hands and pressed his thumbs to his lips. "You're saying that you can change history, right wrongs."

"That's the idea."

"But what if those things, the tragedies and the wars, what if those are necessary for some reason? What if the bad things are necessary for the good things to happen?"

"There isn't a simple answer to that." She leaned her elbows on the table. "Is there nobility in suffering?"

"Is there? Maybe sometimes."

"I don't think there is. I used to, but not anymore." Narine took a deep breath. "Some tragedies we can't change." She touched the small scar on her lip where a glass vial had cut her. "Some suffering we can't avoid. But I don't believe that there's meaning in it. Lessons? Always. But suffering for suffering's sake?" She shook her head. "That's a lie the powerful tell to keep the powerless from revolution."

"So you want a revolution?"

"A tiny pebble?" Narine raised an eyebrow. "I don't think I've decided yet."

Jacob pressed his hands to his lips and stared at the table. "You asked me earlier what home means for me."

"Yes."

He looked up and met her eyes. "When I got in that pool with you, it felt right in a way I have never felt before in my life. When I felt your magic? It fit, Narine. And I want it. I want to feel that again."

"Then welcome to the Seba Segel." She looked at her hands. "I don't always paint a rosy picture of what we do, Jacob, but it's important. I think… I hope we make the world a more just place. And if that means that I have to live in a constantly changing reality, I'll deal with it."

"And it's worth it?"

Narine leaned forward. "Six years ago, I took my first solo mission. No one with me. All by myself. I went back in time and stopped a massacre of innocent people in the north."

"That's amazing."

"It was hard. That jump was… hard on me. But over two hundred people lived because of it." She stared at her hands. "Sometimes when things get confusing, I have to remind myself… two hundred and fifteen."

"You saved them."

"But I didn't. I didn't even have to do that." Narine shook her head. "I wrote a letter to someone with the king's ear. The ones who stopped that massacre were the ones I left behind. The ones who listened…"

"Narine?"

*The ones who saved them were the ones who listened to a stranger.*

It hit her then. Why she hadn't been able to sleep. Why she felt an urgency to go go go. "They did it, not me."

"What do you mean?"

She looked up. "We have to get to the order. We need to go back to the Southern Mages before the elders do."

Jacob and Narine squeezed into her zip car the following morning since Genet needed to use the crawler, heading to the order and then parking and nodding at Mesfin before they walked inside and straight to Tadesse's office.

He looked up from behind his desk. "The last I heard, Issa and the rest of the archivists found the warp in the Tibeb and were trying to figure out what the original tasary was supposed to be. Either way, the threads from that warp led to the Southern Mage Massacre, which was clearly *not* supposed to happen. The council will likely be putting together a team to jump within the next week and—"

"And go to Addis." Narine sat across from Tadesse. "Which is not good."

Tadesse looked confused. "Why not?"

"I realized last night that we can't wait for the elders."

"Why not?"

"Because we both know how they're going to deal with this."

Jacob sat next to her, and Tadesse put down the file he'd been reading.

"What are you talking about?" he asked.

"I couldn't sleep last night. I was awake for hours because something wasn't sitting right with me."

"So this is a plan conjured in exhaustion," Tadesse said. "What could go wrong?"

"I'm tired, but I'm not wrong."

Jacob shook his head. "She's not."

Narine kept her voice low. "This tasary cannot be put right. Not without breaking the Pagume taboo again. So the goal now is to mitigate the damage as much as possible, stop this massacre, try to fix the damage that breaking the taboo started."

"Obviously."

"To do that, the elder council in our time is going to communicate first with their counterparts in the 1930s. Then those elders are going to suggest a course of action. What action do you think they'll suggest?"

"Either building a defense around the Southern Mages or cutting off the attackers before it begins."

"And who will they get to help them do those things?"

Tadesse closed his eyes. "They'll defer to the old families in the south."

"You see the problem?"

"Yes." He rested his head in his hands. "Of course."

"They'll look to the old families in the area to defend the Southern Mages—remember what Aida said about House Zuria and House Wensho? They will do it." Narine held up a hand. "They *will* keep the massacre from occurring."

"But in the process, they'll take the victory from the free clans," Tadesse said. "So whether they defend the Southern Mages or stop the massacre before it begins, the free clans will be indebted to the old families for their survival."

"Which will change the power dynamic in yet another way," Narine said. "Leaving the free clans to be seen as a weaker party in the order."

Tadesse nodded. "And setting back their progress to attain equal status with the old houses."

"So we're not going to let that happen," Jacob said. "We're going back now."

Tadesse blinked. "To where? To when?"

"Back where we went the first time," Narine said. "Only we're going before the battle, not after. We're warning the Southern Mages so they can defend themselves and claim the victory."

"And who is going to help them get weapons? How are they going to match the firepower of the mages who attacked them? How can we possibly know they will win?"

"They can be ready," Narine said. "I looked into her eyes, Tade. I saw that girl's strength. These people are warriors; the only reason they were wiped out was because they were caught in a place they felt safe."

"And the calculations?" Tadesse asked. "We need to talk to diviners and see what the consequences of a battle will be."

"We can't. Any diviner is going to tell the elder council; then we'll be on ice."

"So how are we going to get the constellar settings to…?" He closed his eyes. "Your mother's algorithm again?"

"Do you know any rebel diviners willing to subvert the council to get us back to the past?"

"No." Tadesse blinked. "We all know they don't work like that anyway."

Jacob frowned. "How do they work?"

Narine and Tadesse both rolled their eyes.

"Diviners are…" Tadesse sighed.

"They're prima donnas." Narine fluttered a hand. "Guided by the stars. The true descendants of the Seba Segel."

"Let's just say that they don't work on command," Tadesse said. "But Narine's mother does."

"It was my mother's irritation with the diviners that

pushed her to develop the algorithm, so we'll use that." Narine stood. "I'm going to find her. Are you in?"

Tadesse didn't hesitate. "Will it get Aida back?"

There was no way of knowing that, and Tadesse knew it. What he wanted was hope.

Narine could give him hope.

"If we do this right, the massacre doesn't happen." She fixed her eyes on his. "Abdi's ancestors don't get wiped out. So Aida's grandfather never goes south to investigate it. Both Abdi's and Aida's lives should be woven like they were originally."

The cautious mage kept his eyes on Narine. "Should be."

Narine closed her eyes. "Someone broke the rules, Tade. I can't fix that part, but I can try to fix this."

"You know how I like my rules." He stood. "When do you want to leave?"

"You and Jacob gather what we need for the jump. I'll go find my mother."

# CHAPTER 28

Anahid clearly had her doubts. "What you're doing would never be authorized by the elder council."

"We know, which is why we're not going to the elder council; we came to you." Narine was already dressing in her traveling clothes, and Anahid was standing at the constellar console. She knew her mother would go along with them.

"We're preventing a massacre," Tadesse said. "It's not anything we haven't done before."

"This one has a little more consequence, considering it caused a knot in the Tibeb the size of my fist."

Tadesse and Narine exchanged a look. "Seriously?" he asked. "When Aida and I found it, the warp was around the size of a hundred-birr coin."

Anahid was punching numbers into the console, and the lights in the dome over their heads began to swirl and move. "There's a reason we don't change tasary. The ripple effects will keep compounding, and all we can do is clean up the mess. The cleanup efforts after the Second Mage War took decades."

"There's another reason we can't wait for the elders. If we

can stop this massacre, we might be able to contain the damage." Narine straightened Jacob's belt and handed him a pack. Now that they knew he wouldn't show up in the past naked, they could predict he was at least a second-tier traveler, which meant he could carry supplies.

"Weapons." Tadesse looked at Anahid. "Where are we going to find weapons in the south?"

Anahid blew out a breath. "Pre–World War II, the local lords will have armories, as will the old houses. The closest mage lords will be around Hawassa. Do you want to go there instead of the Bale Foothills?"

"No," Narine said. "Send us to the gathering place we left from. There's a creek at the base of the hills that I showed you on the map. We need to make contact with the Southern Mages first and make sure they spread the word. They may have weapons caches the girl we talked to didn't know about."

Tadesse added, "And we need to make sure they can get the word out to as many of their members as possible. Even if we can't find firearms for them, they need to ride into that meadow ready for war, not a spring festival."

Jacob took the heavy pack from Narine's shoulders and slung it on his. "Anything else?"

She looked up and smiled. "They're going to be happy to have you on their team. Can you shoot a gun?"

"Absolutely not. I am useless with firearms."

Tadesse grimaced. "Excellent."

"You know, I actually practiced archery with my mom growing up. She was a competitive archer, so that's probably a better choice for me."

Tadesse raised his eyebrows. "New gems of information about our American friend every day. Sadly, I don't think the Southern Mages are archers."

Anahid didn't seem impressed. "We'll teach you how to shoot when you get back."

Narine looked back to Jacob. "It's useful. She made me learn when I was ten."

"Jesus," he muttered. "We ready to go?"

They waded into the travelers' pool, and Narine could feel Jacob's magic already reaching for hers. Even with no training, his power was intuitive. That was good. He'd catch on to the formal training quicker that way.

Anahid had a hand raised. "Constellar coordinates are set. You've left all electronics here?"

All their assistants were in a dead box by the door. "Done," Narine said. "If there's an unknown-number call while I'm gone—"

"You'll only be gone a few minutes; she can wait."

Narine narrowed her eyes. "Just keep an eye on any calls please."

"Fine." Anahid glanced at the door. "Don't miss your window."

*Fuck you.* She wanted to say it; she held her tongue instead.

"Ready," Tadesse said.

"Ready." Narine reached for Jacob's right hand and knit their fingers together, her ceremonial knife at the ready. "Remember how to do this?"

He nodded brusquely. Jacob was jumping to go. His magic was buzzing and excited. Narine wouldn't have been surprised if the water turned effervescent.

"I'm ready when you are." He was trying to keep a calm expression, but a smile teased the corners of his mouth.

The lights overhead pulsed, and the glow of the pool intensified. She closed her eyes, and the smell of incense hit her nose. The spell whispered past her lips as magic welled up and spilled from her chest, diffusing through the water as the vibration at the base of her skull grew more pronounced.

She reached over and made the cut in Jacob's arm first, then a neat slice in her own arm before she pulled him underwater.

Time surrounded them, pulled them into its current, and they were gone.

*Bale Mountains*
*1934*

WHEN THEY ROSE FROM THE WATER THIS TIME, IT WAS TO shouts across the meadow and a clear, sunny sky overhead. Thundering hoofbeats approached, and as they reached the shore, half a dozen spears were aimed at them.

Narine lifted her hands over her head and shouted loudly in Oromic: "I am Narine Anahid Khoren of House Kayl, traveler of the Addis Ababa order of the Seba Segel! I seek an audience with my Brother Kebek, hedge of the Southern Mages."

She looked up and saw the girl Temara, whom she had interviewed after the massacre. In this time, the tragedy had not yet taken place and the traumatized girl was a proud young hedge mage with an angled chin and narrowed eyes.

Narine heard Tadesse and Jacob walking out of the water behind her. The older men on ribbon-clad mounts didn't take their eyes off the two strange men.

She looked to Temara. "You are Kebek's daughter, are you not?"

The girl looked to the side, exchanging a confused glance with her compatriot.

"If they're travelers, they'll have information about us," a young man to the girl's left said. "I am Bulluq of the Warke clan. We can take you to Kebek and the elders."

Warke clan. Abdi's clan.

Narine asked, "How many days until the spring festival arrives?"

"There is one week until the festival." Bulluq waved the

point of his spear in an upward motion. "Come, we will take you to the elders."

Narine checked over her shoulder to make sure both Tadesse and Jacob were with her. "Tade?"

"Good here."

"Jacob?"

"Cold but fine. Might have cut my foot on a rock in the stream."

She glanced at his feet and saw that his shoe had split open at the side. "We'll have to get that bandaged up as soon as possible. We don't want you getting infected."

Bulluq looked down from his horse. The young man couldn't have been more than twenty, but he led the party with Temara sitting across from him. The other four riders followed behind them, their spears held at the ready.

"What brings you to the Southern Mages?" Bulluq asked. "You look like a foreigner, but your Oromic is from the northern people."

Narine's boots squashed around her feet as they walked across the meadow she remembered from their first trip. This time no new graves marked the edges of the meadow, and the hills were covered in golden flowers instead of smoking tents.

She said, "I learned Oromic in Hawassa."

"Ah." The young man nodded. "So you're of the old families. I heard you say House Kayl, but I have not heard of it."

She knew that avoiding questions about her family would only lead to distrust. "House Kayl is of the far northern countries of the Seba Segel, but my great-grandfather was invited to Ethiopia by the elders here. I was born in Addis Ababa."

"He must have been a powerful mage."

"He was."

It was enough to set the young man at ease. "You know Clan Warke. I could see recognition in your face."

"In my time, I know them well."

"I see." Bulluq exchanged a smile with Temara. "I know

that travelers must keep close watch on their words in the past, but I am glad to know that our clan is known even in the capital city in your time."

"You are." She looked at Tadesse. "Which is why we were sent back to give you a warning."

There was a murmur of worried muttering from the riders behind them.

Bulluq glanced over his shoulder and silenced the men with a look. "Say no more except to the elders, Sister."

She saw a large meeting spot in the center of a circle of tents. Horses and children played in the nearest meadow, and young women were gathered around a cooking fire, exchanging happy shouts and calling to the youngest to watch their feet.

Along the backside of the fire near a neat row of tents, a group of older men and women sat, talking and tossing scraps of food to the dogs at their feet.

As soon as the riders approached, the dogs jumped to their feet, ran over, and stood at the edge of the fire. Lean, golden-haired canines with muzzles like wolves and wide, upright ears, they watched the strangers with silent attention.

Bulluq dismounted, and Temara joined him. They led Narine, Jacob, and Tadesse to the row of elders, and Narine immediately spotted Kebek. He was sitting next to a woman who resembled Temara. Her tunic was pristine white with black-and-red embroidery, and over her brightly wrapped hair, she wore a beaded headband. A toddler was at her breast, nuzzled into his mother but casting curious glances over his shoulders at the strangers in wet clothes.

Narine and Tadesse put their hands over their hearts and bowed to the clan leaders in front of them, Jacob matching their movements with quick perception.

Tadesse stepped forward and directed his attention at Kebek. "Brother Kebek, may the stars bless your family. I am Tadesse Girma, a traveler sent from the elder council in Addis

Ababa. This is my sister, Narine Anahid Khoren and our brother, Yacob Bekele."

Kebek seemed surprised that their attention was directed at him, but he acknowledged them with a polite nod. "We don't see travelers from the capital visit the Southern Clans, Brother. We welcome you, though I wonder why you honor us with such a visit."

Bulluq went to stand behind a tall, thin man with a narrow face and a silver beard. "Elder Rabbii, the sister says she knows of our clan in her time."

The elder of Abdi's clan sucked in a sharp breath and nodded. "Sister, do you carry a message for Clan Warke?"

"We carry a warning for all the Southern Mages," she said. "Brother Tadesse?"

"In one week, raiders from the north—mages we have not been able to identify—will attack your spring festival and kill your warriors, wives, and children while you celebrate peacefully."

Two elders jumped to their feet and cursed under their breath while the others exchanged looks and frowns among themselves.

Tadesse continued, "They will likely come in the guise of friends, perhaps travelers who want to celebrate the New Year with you. We don't know how they get past your defenses, but they will kill everyone they can find, even elders and children."

Now more elders were on their feet, and the chatter around the cooking fire had gone silent.

"We come from the elders in Addis Ababa with the message that this act of war is not the will of the stars or the true path of time," Tadesse said. "Nothing about this is tasary, and you need to prepare for battle."

"We were sent to warn you and help you prepare your defense," Narine said. "What kind of weapons can you get your hands on quickly?"

It was three days of hard riding to Hawassa with spare horses in tow, four mounted riders from the clans, Narine and Jacob riding with them. Leading the men was Bulluq, the young hedge from Clan Warke who had led the riders who met them at the stream when they arrived.

They reached the outskirts of the town by the lake at nightfall, but they did not approach. The four hedges organized watch and scouted the area while Narine and Jacob pitched the tents and started a fire.

They were setting up camp below a giant ficus tree, the tall roots creating a natural windbreak in the damp, chilly night.

"I think Boy Scout tents were easier to set up." Jacob was fumbling with the elaborate supports that one of the young men had shown him how to build the night before. "Either that or my brain is getting old."

Narine had already dug down to keep their fire as inconspicuous as possible. "Boy Scout training is better than nothing."

"You seem to have very good survival skills."

"Hmm." She added sticks to the wadding she'd made from shredded bark. "It wasn't really an option for me."

"No?"

"When I was fourteen, my mother jumped me to a place that was completely uninhabited. There was a freshwater spring nearby and a lake with fish. Some fruit I recognized. Then she left me there and came back two weeks later."

"Wait. How old did you say you were?"

"Fourteen. I survived."

Jacob cursed under his breath. "What would she have done if something happened to you? There could have been animals. You could have eaten something poisonous. There might have been—"

"I asked her the same thing, and she said she'd simply

have jumped back farther until she found me alive and well." Narine looked up. "That's my mother. She thinks time is her playground."

"Isn't it?"

Narine laughed ruefully. "I suppose it is. She has her little hidden temples and traveler outposts all over the world. She hid from me for nearly four years."

"How was it done before the modern technology?" He'd finally managed to build the wooden supports and was draping heavy wool blankets over the domed tent.

Narine pictured the elaborate grid over the temple in Harar where Samson had been born. "There have always been ways to create star temples. We make it look very complicated now, but all you need is a diviner to create the star map of the time and place where you want to go, then you have to find a way to re-create the position of the major constellations overhead. Water—a bathtub is sufficient—and our magic does the rest."

"Still a pretty elaborate setup." He threw a set of ropes over the tent cover, picked up a rock, and drove the tent spikes into the ground.

Narine fed more sticks into the growing fire. "That's one of the reasons the Seba Segel always stayed close to power. Temples aren't cheap to build, but leaders know how much power they can accumulate by having their own personal mages. It's always made sense for the elder councils to align with whoever has the most power in any given area."

"Even if they were a tyrant?" Jacob came to sit across from her and the growing fire. "Even if they were a colonizer?"

"Is it better to have a voice audible to a tyrant or no voice at all?"

Jacob's smile was bitter. "I suppose there is that."

"Ideological purity is a luxury of those who live in free societies, and despite the progress the world has made, many countries still aren't free." Narine cupped her hands over the warming flame. "The Seba Segel's role is to advise and create the most good for the most people as possible. Sometimes that means aligning with a tyrant or a dictator even if you only make things slightly less bad than they would be otherwise."

"And what if the tyrant wants information or advice on how to persecute people?"

Narine shrugged. "You lie when you need to. Mages obfuscate and play the politician as well or better than mundane humans. We're realists, Jacob. Anyone who's been close to power knows that sometimes finesse is needed more than honesty."

"Hmm." He rested his back against a jutting ficus root. "That makes a kind of sense, but it's still an imperfect system."

"I never said it wasn't." Narine stared into the fire, watching the flames eat the soft kindling and turn it to ash. "It's interesting to hear your perspective. It's good."

"I don't mean to be disrespectful."

"No, I'm not offended." She leaned back against the sheltering roots. "I grew up in this system. I don't know anything else, and I don't think I really started questioning the order at all until maybe… five or six years ago."

"After the hard jump?"

Narine nodded. "It was hard because… I was trapped in the past for an entire year. I missed my jump window."

"You were in the past for an entire year?" Jacob's eyes went wide. "How did your brain not…" He waved his fingers next to his temple. "You know, reset. That's way too long, right?"

"I was able to keep my memories intact by journaling and telling someone else about my life." She felt the lump harden in her throat. "I trusted the wrong person, and I barely made it home. I needed some time away, and they didn't want to give it to me, even with my mother arguing my case."

"That must have made you angry."

"I was hurt, I think, more than angry. I was only twenty-two, but I'd already done so much for the order. It was the first time that I felt like a pawn in their chess game. I mean, I always knew it was a game, but I thought I was a little more important than a pawn." Narine smiled ruefully. "I became a little more clear-eyed after that."

"But you still work for them."

Narine met his eyes across the licking flames. "I don't feel like I have a choice."

Jacob frowned. "Of course you do. They can't make you travel. If you wanted to disappear, I bet you could."

"I could." She nodded. "And I've been tempted. But it comes back to that question I asked you earlier, doesn't it?"

"Which one?"

"Is it better to have a voice audible to a tyrant or no voice at all?"

Narine heard the Southern Clansmen moving through the bush, though they were almost back to the fire before they made their presence known.

"I've had an idea." Bulluq spoke from the shadows. "Tell me what you think."

"This was a bad idea," Jacob muttered from the edge of the acacia forest where five of their party were watching the massive compound of stone and heavy wood that housed the leaders, the soldiers, and the armory of House Zuria.

"This was a good idea." Narine had to agree with Bulluq. "The faster we get the weapons, the faster we can head home and the less chance there is that anyone will spot us and report us to the human or mage authorities in the region."

Bulluq and his men had scouted out the boundaries of

House Zuria, and to say that they were not impressed was an understatement.

"The guards barely move from the gate." Bulluq spoke in Oromic, pointing over Narine's shoulder to indicate the fire near the front gate where two men were warming their hands.

"There will be hedge spells along the perimeter," Narine said. "Surely there will be spells."

"There are, but they're weak." Bulluq motioned toward a part of the wall that was shaded by a giant fig tree. "I think I can manipulate the spells along that part of the wall so we can jump over, then shore them up behind us. It won't hold them off forever, but it will buy us time to get away. We brought fresh horses, and Eba is readying the camp right now."

"And then we go in and find the armory?"

Bulluq nodded. "We go in, grab as many rifles as we can manage, and get out. We will need to move fast."

Narine related the gist of the plan to Jacob in English.

"And we know they have rifles?" Jacob asked.

Narine asked Bulluq.

"That will be the majority of what they have in their armory." Bulluq nodded at the compound. "House Zuria trades with the British in Kenya."

"When do we go?"

"We'll wait for the next watch to arrive. If they follow the first watch, they'll do one perimeter walk; then they'll go back to the gatehouse and they won't move."

"How long?"

Bulluq looked up and glanced at the moon. "An hour maybe."

Narine sat back on her heels and settled in to wait, but no sooner had she gotten comfortable than the sound of riders approaching the gate brought her up short.

She leaned forward and peered out of the brush. "Who—?"

"Shhhh." Bulluq took out a glass that looked like it had

come off an old rifle and held it up to his eye. "Three riders, all cloaked."

Were these the raiders who attacked the Southern Mages? Narine held out her hand. "Let me see."

"They have hood— Wait, one just took his off." He handed the scope to Narine. "Do you recognize him?"

She looked through the dark scope and managed to find the riders that Bulluq had spotted in the shadows of the main gate. She was half fearing, half hoping to see Gideon's face, so she wasn't prepared for the familiar visage she spotted.

"It's Desta." Narine stared through the scope. "I know him, and he's a traveler from my time too. What could he be doing here?" She turned and related what she saw to Jacob in English.

Jacob spoke quietly in English. "Maybe this is part of what the elders are doing. Remember what you said? The elders would go to the authorities in the region first."

"And they don't realize we've jumped." Narine felt her heart calm. "That makes sense. You're right."

"He doesn't change our plan, does he?" Bulluq asked. "If he is from your time, perhaps House Zuria is meant to help us."

"No." Narine's response was sharp. "It's very important that this victory belongs to the Southern Clans. The old houses must have no part in it."

Bulluq nodded. "Very well. Then we stick with my plan."

The arrival of guests from outside the compound seemed to only disorganize the watch around House Zuria even more. The men did a half-hearted perimeter check, then returned to the gates to enjoy the beer and food that was brought to them from the celebrating party inside.

As soon as the hedge mages were eating, Bulluq sounded a call that reminded Narine of a pigeon cooing; then he and his three men crept through the brush, approaching the perimeter wall with Narine and Jacob following behind them.

She could hear Jacob breaking the brush with his massive shoulders, but none of the guards seemed to notice.

They moved through the tall grass toward a section of the wall that was draped in the arching shadow of a ficus tree, then stopped at the base.

Bulluq whispered to one of his men, then the man nodded, stood, and spread his arms on the wall and began to whisper spells.

The crackling that filled the air made the hair on Narine's arms stand up. She could taste magic like the snap of ozone after a lightning strike.

"Come." Bulluq waved them over, hefted his man over the wall, waited for the answering birdcall, then helped Narine and Jacob over too. Finally he swung his legs over, nimble as a child climbing a papaya tree, and dropped to the ground beside them.

They had landed in a pasture where sheep were resting for the night, and a few of the goats among them bleated in protest of the newcomers, but Bulluq reached down, grabbed a handful of stones, and tossed them to the side, scattering the goats and distracting them from the strangers.

They walked as quickly as possible, keeping under the shadow of the trees as the moon rode higher in the night sky. They checked the first stone outbuilding and found grain storage; the second was a home for random furniture and old kitchen equipment.

"It will be near the main house," Narine said. "Or in the main house."

"Probably not *in* the house," Bulluq said. "No one will store their gunpowder where the master of the house sleeps."

"Good point."

Jacob wasn't following anything they said in Oromic, but he moved silently and without questions, surprisingly light on his feet for a large man.

"There." Bulluq pointed into the distance where a long,

low stone building jutted out from the main house in the center of the compound. It had a low roof and high windows; two men were guarding the door, watching the lights in the main house intently.

Bulluq silently motioned to his fellow clansmen, who broke off and ran around to the other side of the long building; then Narine held Jacob back with a hand while she watched the two men expertly and silently grab both guards around the neck, cover their mouth, and hold them until they stopped struggling.

Then they set them down in the shadows and waved for Narine and Jacob to approach.

"Are they——?"

"Not dead," Narine whispered. "Hedges have all sorts of spells to incapacitate opponents as long as they can surprise them."

"Come," Bulluq said. "We found it."

The armory of House Zuria wasn't as impressive as Narine had been imagining. There were mostly traditional weapons of the sort that the Southern Mages already had: spears and curved swords, heavy shields and leather armor. There were countless long daggers, and Narine saw the men grabbing two each and strapping them to their waist, so she did the same.

When they cracked open the wooden crates at the back of the armory, they found what they'd been looking for.

Rows of long guns made of wood and dark grey metal were packed in straw and lined up in four large crates. Each rifle was nearly four feet long.

Narine did a quick calculation in her head. "I think each crate will have sixteen rifles."

"We can't take all these," Bulluq said. "There are too many, and we need to move fast."

"Just take the rifles," Narine said. "As many as we can

carry. Wrap them like firewood, and we'll carry them on our backs."

"And the ammunition?"

"We'll take as much as we can."

Bulluq and his men started stacking the rifles on top of each other while Narine related the plan to Jacob. He started looking for rope to tie the rifles in bundles but found only flour sacks. He picked them up and tore them into strips, handing them to Bulluq and his men so they could be fashioned into bindings.

Each man was able to strap five rifles on his back with Jacob carrying double that. They found boxes of ammunition, and each carried one. Loaded down with guns and ammo, they left the armory and ran for the stone wall. Narine picked up as much ammunition as she could and followed.

Behind them, no one seemed to notice the six figures in the shadows with rifles strapped to their backs like firewood, carrying boxes of heavy ammunition out of the compound.

"How are we getting these over the wall?" Jacob asked.

"Same way we got in." Narine grunted through the pain in her arms.

Bulluq set down his cargo and scrambled up the wall, perching at the top as he called for his brother hedge to follow him, then go over the wall. Forming a chain, Bulluq called for his last remaining fighter to toss up the first bundle.

Five rifles over the wall, then a box of ammunition.

Another five, another box.

Another five, and another ten.

Two more boxes of ammunition, and Narine's arms were on fire. Jacob hoisted her up and into Bulluq's arms; then she dropped to the other side to see the two hedges from the Southern Clans strapping the firearms back on before heading toward the trees.

Jacob was the last over the wall, and while it could hardly be called a graceful crawl, it was at least silent. Bulluq patted him on the shoulder; then they picked up the remaining rifles and boxes of ammunition before they ran to the shelter of the forest.

They didn't hear a disturbance by the gate until they were already on their horses.

"Go!" Bulluq hissed. "Eba will be waiting. We'll ride through the night and into the morning. We can't stop until we reach the hills."

# CHAPTER 29

*Two days later…*

They came in the guise of friendship, twelve mages traveling from the northwest, weary from their travel and hiding among a group of humans. They had heard of the hospitality of the Southern Clans and hoped to celebrate the spring festival with them before they continued on their journey east.

Narine wore a face covering and veil over her hair, hiding among the women as the clan elders—all thirty of them—gathered around the fire and welcomed the travelers among them.

Despite their warnings, Narine and Tadesse could not convince these men and women to strike first; their laws of hospitality were sacred and they could not attack a guest without provocation. They would have to wait for these enemies to show aggression.

Narine waited with the older women and children in the tents along the ridge, watching the proceedings with her rifle loaded and ready, hidden in the blankets that covered the domed structure.

Among the hills, the best shooters were poised and ready to take out the enemy, waiting for the first strike. Among them, Mulenah of the Warke clan, cousin of Bulluq and ancestor of Abdi, waited. His young wife was next to him, holding his ammunition.

The leader of the visiting party sat down and lowered his hood, and Narine saw her husband for the first time in six years.

It had been longer for Gideon, well over a decade since they'd parted, and silver touched his temples, but his handsome face was still clean-shaven, displaying the scar left from their final fight. He wore a formal shirt and tie, and he appeared grateful to his hosts, smiling and charming as the Southern elders offered him food and coffee.

Jacob sidled over from where he was watching a group of boys playing in the rocks. "You know him."

"I know him."

He put a hand on her shoulder. "Did you know he was going to be here?"

"I didn't know for sure."

"Who is he?"

She didn't know why she said it, but the confession slipped out. Later, she could blame it on shock. "He's my husband."

Jacob was silent, but his hand fell away as a shout came from the meadow where some of the older boys were watching the animals. There was another shout, then a cry.

The elders turned their heads to see who was making the noise, and the guests waiting by the wagons pulled out long guns.

"Gideon!"

Narine shouted to draw his attention and saw Gideon's eyes go wide at the sound of her voice.

A shepherd boy stumbled up from the stream, holding bloody hands to his neck as scarlet red stained the front of his white shirt. He dropped to his knees at the top of the hill and reached a hand out before he fell on his face. Cresting the hill behind him came a pale female mage wearing a black cloak trimmed in red. Her dark red hair was braided down her back, and she was holding a long blade dripping with blood.

The first shots rang out from the ridge above them.

And everything happened at once.

Gunfire engulfed the meadow, pinging off the rocks over the ridge as the attackers quickly figured out there were snipers overhead, and the sound of iron clashing against metal cut through the sound of gunfire as armed mages of the Southern Clans attacked the mages who had pulled out weapons.

Jacob and Narine hustled the older women and children into the tents and handed each of the older women a spear or a sword. Then they both grabbed their firearms and took position behind two large boulders on the edge of the tents.

The elders of the village were already fighting off the mages in the circle, a combination of hedge magic and old-fashioned combat turning the previously peaceful meeting circle into a stage for battle.

Narine saw a Southern Clansman go flying through the air, blood dripping from his chest, and knew that Gideon and the mages with him were as lethal as had been reported. She felt the power building in the encampment, protective spells from the elders in the tents guarding the children, aggressive magic floating through the air from the snipers on the hill.

But no spell could stop a bullet.

"Dammit!" Jacob spun back, his shoulder bleeding.

"Jacob!"

"I'm fine. It's just a graze."

Narine handed him her empty rifle and took his. "I shoot, you load."

"Sounds good."

She braced her rifle over the boulder and looked through the scope, spotting Tadesse in hand-to-hand combat with a mage in foreign clothing sporting a closely shaved head. There were distinctive ceremonial scars on the man's face that looked familiar, but Narine couldn't place them in the heat of the moment.

The man was a skilled hedge and was fighting with magic and an arm-length knife that was throwing Tadesse off-balance. Narine kept her sights on the man, but they were moving too quickly to find a clear shot.

"Narine?"

"I can't get a clear shot at the one Tade's fighting."

"Then move to another target."

She blinked and swung her rifle around to see Gideon's face directly in the line of her scope. She gasped and pulled back, hiding behind the boulder. She slipped in a pile of horse dung, the grassy stink rising to her nose as she slid down the boulder and out of the line of sight.

"Narine!"

"I can't." She choked on the words. "I can't kill him."

Jacob grabbed the rifle from her and braced it on the boulder again, butting the stock into his bleeding shoulder. "Just get someone. Whatever power these guys are using is insane."

He fired off a shot and Narine closed her eyes, hoping and praying it wasn't Gideon.

*You foolish, stupid girl.*

She felt it again—heard his voice in her head—his hatred and derision creeping down her neck like ice-cold water. The clouds overhead opened up and rain started to trickle down, coating her face and sharpening the smell of blood, magic, and fire.

Narine felt paralyzed, hearing the battle around her without understanding what she was supposed to do.

Kill him? Kill her son's father?

Kill the man who had kept her sane?

Kill the one she'd loved once, even if it was a foolish love.

No.

She struggled to her feet and turned.

*This cannot continue.*

*You carry this guilt…*

*You cannot keep him from me.*

*You have to think about Samson now.*

Narine wiped the rain from her eyes and scanned the battlefield. The Southern Mages were winning, but not without significant loss. She could see a body hanging on the rocks that fell down the ridge. She saw Kebek's brightly colored cloak stained with blood, covering a fallen body in the meadow.

There were foreign bodies among familiar ones, and gunfire was still pinging off the rocks and over the meadow.

*Some day* —her son's small voice came to her memory— *I will see you every day. And when I wake up, you will always be there to make me kuti and sing to me and rub my feet when I am sleepy.*

She wasn't the girl Gideon thought she was. She was stronger. She was powerful even if she hadn't cloaked herself in hatred. Maybe she couldn't kill Gideon, but she could protect the ones he was trying to hurt.

*You are Narine Anahid Khoren of House Kayl. Mother of Samson, daughter of Anahid. Third-degree traveling mage of the Seba Segel, ninth in your line of power.*

She grabbed the second rifle, braced it on the boulder, and looked through the scope.

*You have no siblings and many cousins. You are the godmother of Gelile, the adopted sister of Genet. Your best friend is Jamila Sahid.*

*You are wise.*

*You are powerful.*

*Most importantly, you are loved.*

She swept her rifle sight over the field of battle and saw Gideon kneeling among the dead and rifling among the bodies to find another gun.

Do it. Fire.

Her finger curled around the trigger, but she hesitated.

Gideon picked a rifle up and turned to the side where the black-cloaked woman with the long red hair was standing. Her face was splattered with blood; she grabbed Gideon by the arm and pulled him, shouting something Narine couldn't hear.

"Narine!"

She turned and saw Jacob standing up, using the rifle as a club to beat one of the attacking mages.

She swung the rifle around but couldn't get a clear shot at Jacob's opponent. "You're too close."

Jacob ducked and tried to back away from the mage, but his foe was canny. He might not speak English, but he knew that Narine couldn't get off a shot if he stayed close.

The man grabbed Jacob around the waist, punching his fist into the larger man's kidneys.

Jacob cried out and fell to the side, leaving the man exposed, but before Narine could get off a shot, a spear flew through the air, piercing the man's back and lodging itself deeply in the mage's chest.

The attacker froze, and a line of blood dripped from the corner of his mouth. His eyes went wide, and he fell forward, revealing Temara, the young clan hedge, with an outstretched arm and a shield in her hands.

Jacob crawled to the rocks and braced his back against them while Narine swung her rifle around and looked through the scope, searching for any sign of her husband. She trained her eyes on the battlefield, the ridge above the meadow, and even the stream at the base of the meadow where bodies had rolled down the hill.

It didn't matter; Gideon was gone.

THE SOUTHERN MAGES HAD WON THE BATTLE, BUT IT WAS NOT without cost. Tadesse was wounded, with a large slice taken out of his shoulder and a gaping wound in his side. Jacob had a grazing bullet wound on his shoulder and bruised kidneys from the mage that Temara had killed.

Narine had a twisted ankle, a nasty knife wound in her hand, and ringing in her ears from all the gunfire, but other than that, she felt well enough to guide her two friends back to the present when they left.

She stood in front of the Southern elders, fewer in number but with their pride and status intact. "Thank you for what you did today."

Elder Rabbii of Clan Warke was the one who addressed them. "No, thank you. Not only did you come to warn us, you stayed to help in our defense, and we are grateful. These mages were powerful enemies. Without your warning, we could have easily been taken in and overwhelmed."

She looked at him and the fresh-faced warrior behind him, the young man who would one day become her mentor's father. Narine tried not to let her emotions overwhelm her.

"My friends are wounded," she said. "I hope you don't think badly of us if we travel back immediately. The water will heal them faster than any doctor or healer in this time."

"Of course," Elder Rabbii said. "Let us take you to the water.

"What you have done today is so important," Tadesse managed to say. "One day your children's children will read about this in the Tibeb."

"Thank you, Brother." The elders exchanged looks, surrounded the three travelers, grasped their hands, and walked with them down to the stream.

There was a woman next to Narine who looked familiar. It took her a moment to place her face.

"You're Kebek's wife." Narine stopped and spoke to her.

"Yes." Her chin tilted up. "He did not survive the battle,

but our children did, and they will tell their children of their father's bravery and sacrifice."

Narine swallowed hard. "Your daughter is a very strong hedge. He was very proud of her."

"We both are." The woman managed a slight smile. "May you be blessed with strong children and a clear purpose, Sister."

"Thank you." Narine turned back to the path that led to the stream. She could already feel her magic rising, feel the call of the water and the ready embrace of time.

She took Jacob's hand to walk into the stream. "You ready to go home?"

"So ready." He squeezed her hand and smiled down at her. "Never gonna forget this one."

"I won't either."

Tadesse was limping into the water, his face drained of its usual vitality, and Narine could see the relief as he sat down in the frigid stream and leaned his body back.

There was a flash of movement by the streambed, a shout from the crowd, and someone pushed past the press of elders on the water's edge.

"Narine!"

She turned at Gideon's voice, her eyes wide when she saw the arcing blade in his hand, raised and pointed at Jacob's chest.

He leaped over the rocks and launched himself in the air.

"No!"

She felt Jacob's hands on her shoulders as she jumped in front of him, blocking Gideon's blade from piercing his heart.

"No!" Gideon screamed.

Narine felt the burning slash of the blade as he tried to pull it away, but it plunged into her shoulder and ripped through her flesh. She fell backward, Jacob's arms firmly around her as they fell back into the water.

Her magic roared up, protecting her as she fell beneath

the surface, enveloping Jacob as she felt the world dissolve around her and time pulled her away.

*Addis Ababa*
*2072*

"THEY'RE BACK!" ABDI'S SHOUT FILLED THE CHAMBER. "Anahid, she's injured."

The knife wound was washed clean by the magic, but the blade was still embedded in her shoulder.

"Narine!" Jacob lifted her in his arms, and she'd never felt lighter.

"You're so strong." She blinked and saw Abdi's face staring down at her as Jacob set her on the edge of the pool. "Abdi." She reached up, tears in her eyes, and pressed her palm to his beard-covered cheek. "You're back. Tade, Abdi's back."

Tadesse was trudging to the edge of the pool, his injuries already healing and his color reviving. "Narine, who was that?"

"It was her husband," Jacob said. "Ex-husband? I'm not exactly clear."

"Gideon did this?" Anahid was furious.

"He was aiming for me and she jumped in front of me and I'm not sure what happened," Jacob said. "Who is this?"

"I'm Abdi Mulenah, elder of the Southern Mages." Abdi's voice was soft, and his hands probed the knife embedded in Narine's shoulder. "Daughter, I don't think this is going to leave permanent damage to your shoulder, but it is going to be very painful to remove."

Even with as much pain as she was in, Narine couldn't miss the irony. "Yet another thing Gideon left me with that's going to hurt a lot to get out."

# CHAPTER 30

N arine was sitting in the infirmary, a furious Elder Kebret standing over her, her mother once again sitting in the corner, working on her mobile tablet.

"What did you think you were doing? Anahid filled me in, and your actions were reckless, unauthorized, and rash."

"I was giving the victory to the ones who needed it," Narine said. "Has the damage to the Tibeb been contained?"

Elder Kebret glanced at Abdi. "This warp you told me about remains, but it's small and it doesn't appear to be spreading. Whatever tasary was altered, the damage to the greater timeline appears to have been minimal."

Anahid piped up from the corner, though she didn't even spare a glance at her fellow elder. "There was a knot the size of my forearm, Kebret! It was that big."

"And of course we have only the word of the travelers that any of this happened." Kebret crossed his arms over his chest. "Abdi, what do you make of all this?"

Her mentor sat calmly in the seat next to her bed, his long legs stretched in front of him and his hands folded elegantly on the arm of his chair. "Anahid and Narine have informed me that the victory I remember hearing about as a child growing up was a new course that time wove and that in this alternate timeline, my people had been wiped out. I don't find this hard to believe as I was raised with the stories of the three brave travelers who came from the future to aid the Southern Mages." Abdi nodded at Tadesse in the bed next to Narine. "Their names had been lost to history, but everything they have told you is exactly as I remember in the stories."

"And last week—according to all this—the Southern Mage Massacre never took place?" Kebret asked.

"No," Abdi said. "It appeared in conjunction with the altered tasary."

"Correct," Narine said. "Abdi was gone, and the knot in the Tibeb led to a massacre of the Southern Mages."

"Aida." Tadesse's voice was weak. "Where is Aida?"

Kebret and Abdi looked at each other, then at Tadesse. "Do you mean Aida Mikel?"

He nodded. "She's back. Thank God, she must be back." His face nearly crumpled in relief. "Where is she?"

"There's an Aida Mikel working in Bahir Dar right now," Abdi said. "But she's never worked in Addis."

Narine felt her heart sink. The altered tasary had still had consequences. The timeline had woven Aida back into their present, but not back into their lives.

"She exists." Narine caught Tadesse's eyes and held his devastated gaze. "She exists in the world, Tade. That means she'll come back to us. Her soul hasn't forgotten; I know it."

He opened his mouth, closed it, and shook his head. The cruelty of time wasn't lost on Narine. She'd lost a friend, but Tadesse had lost the woman he loved.

Abdi patted her shoulder. "The healers at the order are the best in the world," he said. "You should be on your feet in a couple of days."

Narine turned to her mother. "Can you let Genet know what's going on?"

"Already did. She says she's bringing some *kikile* for you and Tade for dinner."

Oh thank goodness. Her sister was bringing her lamb stew, which meant she wasn't going to have to put up with the cook who made the elders' food.

Jacob was napping on two small beds the healers had pushed together across the room. Other than the bruising on his lower back, he appeared to be fine. The bullet graze had closed during their jump back to the present, and Gideon's blade hadn't touched him.

He was more than a little confused about everything that had happened, but no more than Elder Kebret was.

"The mage who assaulted you—"

"My husband," Narine said. "Dr. Gideon Marangu. He is —was—a Kenyan alchemist I met during the year I was stuck in the past after I missed my jump window."

"During your first solo mission."

Narine nodded. "Yes."

"A mission you never recorded as lasting any longer than the scheduled week," Elder Kebret said. "Because?"

"Because I came back having been gone a year, having barely escaped from my husband, who was not a nice man, and I needed time to recover, which the elders never authorized."

"And yet you went missing for a year after that anyway," Kebret barked.

"I told you she didn't leave the order for no reason," Anahid said. "None of you wanted to believe me. It was for her own mental health."

"I had to recover," Narine said. "That's all."

"And now this man… You think he is the one who traveled during Pagume, who broke the taboo and changed a tasary, solely to get you back?"

"No." Gideon couldn't be that delusional. "He isn't a traveler. He could only travel if another third-tier mage brought him along. Somebody else must be behind this."

"Who?"

"I don't know." Narine took a slow breath. She was exhausted, but she knew the chief elder needed answers. "Gideon is an angry man, but I think someone is using him. I think someone wanted to discredit the free-mage movement to retain power in the old houses." Narine remembered the weapons raid in Hawassa. "Where is Elder Desta? He was in Hawassa when we were there. He was visiting House Zuria."

"Desta isn't in the city right now." Kebret frowned. "He went to Zanzibar to consult with the council there, but I'm sure there's a reason for his being in that time. No doubt he was investigating this warp on behalf of the council."

Abdi met her eyes and shook his head before she could say anything more.

Narine nodded. "I see."

Kebret cleared his throat. "No doubt some of the more *traditional* members of the order have… reservations about the free-mage movement, but change has come quickly and we're not accustomed to it."

Anahid piped up. "Change comes every day for travelers."

Abdi smiled a little. "But true change is frightening; we must be wise enough to offer grace."

"Don't," Narine said. "At least don't give these people grace. Even though they didn't win, Gideon and the mages with him attacked your people and killed dozens of innocents, including children and elders, in order to wipe you out." Narine shook her head. "Nothing excuses that."

There was a commotion by the door, and Mesfin rushed in, running straight to Kebret and Abdi. "Elder Kebret, Elder Abdi, we must see to your safety right now. The order is under attack."

"Narine Anahid Khoren!"

His voice echoed across the courtyard.

*This can't be happening.*

"How did he get here?" Jacob was at her back, roused by all the commotion in the infirmary. "I thought you said people couldn't jump to the future."

Abdi was the one who answered. "For one who would attempt to wipe out a people by breaking Pagume and warping the Tibeb, what is one more taboo?"

Her mentor was right. "Whoever is pulling Gideon's strings doesn't play by any rules. Where is he?"

Mesfin's voice was soft. "Sister Narine, you're injured. It's not a good idea for you to be here."

"He's calling for me." She turned to him. "Has he hurt anyone yet?"

"There are half a dozen mages with him. They broke into the order via the river and managed to injure a weaver and kill a hedge before we could react."

Two more lives lost.

"And now?"

Narine could hear fighting in the distance. To break into the Addis compound, Gideon and his allies must have been desperate.

And he was calling for her.

Mesfin's face was grim. "They have taken hostages."

"Let me." She pushed his concerned hand away. "I'm not afraid of him."

Mesfin's eyes cut through her bravado. "Yes, you are."

"Fine, I am." She looked at Jacob and Abdi behind her, Tadesse already bracing for another battle, though it wasn't his job. "But I don't want him hurting anyone else."

She pushed through the commotion of mages running here and there to make her way back to the archives.

Gideon was standing on the edge of a landing, rainbow lines of freshly dyed thread waving behind him like flags.

There were three mages on his right and two more on his left. Four men and two women in total.

All of them held weavers in front of them, knives to the mage's throats. Most of the hostages were young, but Narine recognized the oldest woman as one of the weavers who had been guarding the entrance to the archives days ago when she and Tadesse had first reached out to Aida.

She was plump and red in the face, wide-eyed and in shock. It looked like one of Gideon's allies had taken someone's grandmother hostage.

The entire order of the Seba Segel was frozen in shock.

Hedges were arrayed below the balcony, knives and stun batons at the ready.

Archivists who had escaped were milling around the courtyard, helped by whispering diviners in their ethereal-blue robes and wary alchemists in white coats.

"Narine Anahid Khoren!"

Narine pushed her way to the front of the crowd. She was exhausted, in severe pain, and felt like she was near collapse. She felt Jacob's magic come behind her, and when he put a hand on her unwounded shoulder, she revived a little.

"What do you want, Gideon?"

He took the knife from the young woman's neck and pointed at her. "Give me my son."

Narine shook her head. "You have no son."

"Liar!" He fumbled inside his ragged and mud-stained coat. "I know you're a liar."

All the mages with Gideon looked battle worn and wary, as if they'd come directly from the battle in the Bale Mountains to this invasion of the Addis Ababa compound with no rest in between.

The girl that Gideon had been holding fell to the ground and crawled away. Narine watched her go, and Mesfin whispered to a brother hedge over his shoulder.

Gideon held up a small photograph. "I want my son!"

Narine tried to keep her face impassive. "I don't know whose that child is, but you have no son, Gideon."

"Liar." He laughed, and it made Narine's stomach turn. "You are such a liar. Have you lied to everyone here? Do they not know about Samson? Have you kept him a secret?"

Jacob squeezed her shoulder, and Narine remained standing but said nothing.

Gideon began to pace back and forth, dragging his blade along the railing. "I thought you were different, but you're just like the rest of them, Narine. Arrogant. Superior. High-handed…" He shook his knife at the crowd. "All you aristocrats think the same way. You think you're better than us?"

He turned and ripped long hanks of bright thread from the lines and tossed them over the balcony. "You spin and gossip and record the doings of all the little people around the world, sitting in your towers and gated compounds." He jumped on the railing. "Well, I *am* the little people! You think you're above it all?" Gideon beat his chest. "What does your magic do? Nothing!"

Abdi stepped forward. "I am Abdi Mulenah of the Southern Mages, the people you tried to destroy. We are common mages, not aristocrats. We hold ourselves no higher than the most humble among us."

Gideon's eyes were wild, and his pacing didn't slow.

"And yet you tried to wipe our people from the Tibeb," Abdi continued. "You tried to erase us from history." Abdi frowned. "Why?"

"Because you lie!" Gideon squared his shoulders and shouted down at Abdi. "You think you're better than me— that there can be some negotiation with this order—but there isn't a middle ground!"

Abdi's expression was sad. "I disagree. Most vehemently."

Gideon waved his knife. "The Seba Segel needs revolution. That's why the Southern Mages needed to be eliminated. Because there can be no third way."

"So if one wins, another loses?" Abdi asked. "That is old thinking, Gideon. This isn't the philosophy of the free mages. We can rise together—the free mages, the old houses, and humanity alike."

"No!" He pointed his knife at Abdi and laughed. "You foolish old man. That's not the way the world works."

Narine took another fumbling step forward, bracing herself on the limb of a low-hanging tree. "Gideon, you're a healer. Why are you doing this?"

"Because I was nobody!" He gritted his teeth. "But then I had you. I had a wife. I was going to have a son born into *power*! But you took him away." His eyes were hollow. "You took everything from me. I wasn't good enough for you, and you took it all away to return to this." He curled his lip. "To return to them."

"To return to my family? My friends? My magic?"

"What magic?" He threw his head back and laughed. "The great order of the Seba Segel, counselors of kings! Protectors of the innocent." He reached over and grabbed the old archivist by the hair. "You can't even protect your own people!"

"Enough." Elder Kebret stepped forward. "We have heard enough."

The hedges stepped forward, raising their stun batons, but Kebret's hand rose. "Hedges of the Seba Segel, hold."

The pop of magic was audible.

Narine watched and saw Elder Kebret's eyes meet those of the senior archivist being held by Gideon's mages. Her head was twisted at an angle as one mage held her and Gideon yanked her braid.

But Narine saw her lips move as she cast a spell, and there was a soft whooshing sound that whispered through the air, loud enough that the mages with Gideon turned their heads to look.

371

Jacob put an arm around Narine. "You're going to fall over."

"What is that sound?" Narine looked around, but she saw nothing.

"Narine, if you don't bring my son to me, I will kill all of them!" Gideon let go of the old woman's hair and put his knife to the throat of the woman the mage next to him was holding.

The young woman had two blades at her throat, but she didn't look afraid. She was whispering too.

"What should I tell him?" Narine asked.

"Wait," Elder Kebret murmured. "And witness the power of the weavers."

The sound of wind sound grew louder, and Narine struggled to process what she was hearing. Nothing seemed to happen—the compound was still frozen—but the weavers and other archivists around the courtyard stared at the mages holding their sisters. All of them were whispering under their breath.

In one wave, the rainbow of colorful thread hanging to dry behind the attackers looped up like a flock of birds on the wing, flew through the air, and wrapped itself around the mages who were holding the hostages, then yanked them back from the edge of the balcony.

Every hedge in the courtyard rushed forward, some of them leaping onto the first balcony and climbing the face of the building.

The invading mages screamed, then fell silent as they dropped their knives and tried to wrestle the threads away from their necks.

The women they'd been holding turned and held up their hands, weaving the threads in the air and binding their captors.

Gideon fell over the edge of the balcony, the thick thread wrapped around his neck, and hung in the air, kicking and clutching his neck.

"He's going to die." Narine felt the breath leave her lungs. "Jacob, I can't let him die."

The courtyard had gone wild, mages and weavers rushing into the archive doors and making their way up to the balcony while other mages in the courtyard yelled in panic, seeing more attackers in every brush or unfamiliar face.

She looked up. "Can you reach him?"

Jacob strode forward and grasped Gideon's kicking legs before twisting the long hunting knife from his bound hand. He reached up, cut him loose, and tossed the bound man over his shoulder.

Narine made a split-second decision.

She couldn't let them kill Samson's father.

But she couldn't let Gideon hurt anyone else.

"Come with me." She took Jacob's right hand and led him through the crowd, pushing to the back and into a shadow of the trees. "Do you trust me?"

"I've jumped through time with you twice now," Jacob said. "I sure hope I can trust you."

"Get ready to jump again."

Jacob's voice went higher. "With this guy?"

"Trust me!"

Narine led them both into the traveling chamber, then quickly entered familiar coordinates into the machine. She didn't need a diviner or an archivist for this jump—she'd taken this journey countless times, though she'd never imagined taking Gideon with her.

"Get him in the pool."

"Can you take both of us?"

"If you weren't a traveler, it might be a problem, but you both have traveler's blood." She limped over after the constellar coordinates were set and she'd lit the incense. "I'm setting a very short window. We're not going for very long."

Jacob was barely holding on to the bound man, who was

twisting and trying to escape. "I really hope you know what you're doing."

Narine made her way down the steps and into the pool.

"Gideon." She grabbed him by the ear and forced his eyes to hers. "If you want to survive—and if you ever want to see your son—you better stop fighting us."

The thread was still covering Gideon's mouth, but he stopped twisting.

"That's what I thought." She retrieved her knife, reached for Gideon's arm, and met Jacob's eyes. "Ready?"

*The Island*
*Before time*

"WHERE DID YOU BRING ME?"

The weaver's thread hadn't survived the journey through time, and Gideon was swimming toward her with murder in his eyes.

Jacob was wading in the shallows, but Narine was barely treading water. Her shoulder was on fire and her ankle was killing her.

"You kill me" —she coughed water from her lungs— "and you're stuck here forever."

That made Gideon freeze.

Jacob spotted them. "Narine!" He swam in her direction.

"Where are we?" Gideon asked again.

"You know this place." Narine looked at the prominent fold of layered rocks that jutted into the water and the dense acacia trees that covered the island. "It's not *where* I took you, Gideon. It's *when*."

He turned and looked; then his eyes went wide. He looked to the top of the hill, but there was no church there. There were no small houses or wandering sheep.

"What did you do?" He swam to the shore, forgetting about his anger for the moment. "Narine, what did you do?"

Jacob picked Narine up and carried her to the shallows. "Tell me you're okay."

"I'm fine." She squeezed his shoulder and he put her down.

"He looked like he was going to murder you," Jacob whispered and pulled her into a hard embrace. "That nearly gave me a heart attack. We're going to have a talk about how reckless you are with your own safety when we get back to our time."

Narine was going to protest, but she could feel his racing heart against her chest. "I'm fine, Jacob." She hugged him back. "I'm okay."

"How's your shoulder?"

"Actually a little better for making the jump." She stepped away from Jacob and looked for Gideon. "He won't hurt me." She raised her voice to carry over the water. "You won't hurt me, will you, Gideon?"

Her ex-husband wasn't paying attention to her; he was climbing the rocks where a young ficus tree struggled to grow on the water's edge. The lake was higher than he was accustomed to, and most of the stepped stone that led down to the familiar shore was covered by lapping waves.

The birds were a cacophonous swarm, and Narine could see fish jumping in the water and a silent herd of hippopotamus floating in the grassy shallows across the inlet.

Gideon turned to her. "Where are we?"

Narine walked toward an easy beach farther down the point. "You know where we are. You're asking the wrong question."

The island that had once been her prison was now a refuge, the one place in the world where Narine could take Samson and they could be completely alone.

Gideon wandered from the point to a meadow just past

the edge of the trees, and Narine and Jacob followed him at a distance. Gold flowers swayed in the breeze, covering the hills that sloped up from the shore.

In the distance, she heard a hippo snort, and birds of every type and color filled the skies over her head. Monkeys swung in the acacia trees, watching the humans with curious eyes.

There was a small shack in the meadow, its walls constructed of tree branches and mud with a roof made of dried branches layered over themselves, sheltered by a massive acacia tree that spread arching branches over the clearing. Inside, there were comfortable, straw-filled beds, a few camping and fishing supplies, along with books and drawing paper.

Gideon stared at the hut. "What did you do?"

She stood behind him with Jacob at her side. "When the world became a threat, I made a refuge."

There was a firepit near the hut that the monkeys had destroyed again, and two large Nile lizards sunned themselves on the roof.

Gideon turned to her. "This is the island."

"Yes."

"Where is the village?"

"There isn't a village yet. There aren't any people or any domestic animals. Just some wildlife. No predators that we've ever run into, so don't worry about those."

"We?"

She walked around the hut, looking at the rudimentary patterns that Samson had pressed into the walls over time. He'd brought paints one day and painted the branches that made up the door, so the hut was decorated in green, yellow, and red.

Jacob never strayed from her side, taking everything in just as Gideon did.

Gideon knelt down and looked at the front step where a

child's muddy footprints were captured in the heavy clay. "My son has been here."

"Yes."

Gideon looked at the paint and the crayon drawings on the walls.

"This is his playground," she said. "Our safe place. He can do anything here. Be anything. Play however he likes."

Gideon was on his knees, staring at the door. "When are we, Narine?"

"You finally asked the right question." She turned and looked across the field of acacias. "About five hundred years before anyone inhabited it."

Gideon froze. "No."

"I can't kill you, Gideon. A part of me will always care for you too much." She closed her eyes. "And I don't know if that's a weakness or a strength anymore. But you can't be allowed to harm anyone else."

He stared at her in horror. "You're going to leave me here? For me to die? To lose my mind?"

"No! I'm not going to let you just…" She clenched her fists in frustration. "I won't leave you here forever, but for now it's all I can think to do. If I take you back to my time, the council will execute you."

He huffed out a bitter laugh. "It would be better to kill me."

"No."

"Why not?" Gideon looked up, his eyes raging with anger. "Why don't you just finish it?"

"I have questions, Gideon. And you're going to answer them."

He let out a bitter laugh. "Why should I?"

"Who told you about Samson?"

He shook his head.

She leaned against the little house, her shoulder and ankle still throbbing. "I didn't only keep him from you. I kept him

377

away from everyone. My friends, even some of my family. No one at the order even knows he exists outside a very few people."

"Why?"

She shook her head. "You have no idea."

"So tell me." Gideon's voice was dripping with resentment. "I am his father, remember?"

"Tell me who altered the tasary. It had to be a traveler. Who traveled during Pagume? What did they change? Why?"

Gideon laughed and sat on the ground near the hut, draping his arms around his knees and staring at Narine with delight. "I finally have something you want."

"The damage has been contained, but we still have questions."

He plucked at a blade of grass and stuck the end between his teeth. "I'll answer that when you tell me what's so special about my boy."

Narine debated. Talking about Samson felt like breaking a promise even if it was with her son's father. "Samson's power is unique."

"Of course it is. How?" He stared at her and didn't budge.

"He's a fourth-tier traveler mage."

Gideon raised his eyebrows. "Impressive. What does that mean?"

Narine huffed out a breath. "We don't know. Exactly. We just know his power is more than mine or my mother's or my grandmother's. It's more than any traveler in the written record. He connects with time in a different way."

"That sounds like a very valuable asset for your family."

"He's not an asset!" Narine shouted. "He's a little boy."

Gideon stared at her with an inscrutable smile.

"Would you have him taken away and trained by the order?" Narine demanded. "You want him stolen from his family and everyone who loves him? Because if anyone finds him, that's what will happen."

Gideon's facade broke and he whispered, "He's my son. I would have protected him."

The laugh that burst from Narine's throat was as bitter as her tears. "You don't have that kind of power. *I* don't have the power. The whole of House Kayl wouldn't have the power if the order wanted him enough. He's the first mage of his kind in over a thousand years, Gideon. You think if they know what he is, they'll leave him alone?"

Gideon stood and started pacing. "He— The... The mages who sent me on that mission didn't tell me anything about this."

"Because they don't know." She closed her eyes and shook her head. "The only thing protecting our son right now is that no one is supposed to know he exists. I didn't even tell my sister that I had a baby." She sighed. "I told you about Samson, so tell me who altered the tasary."

Gideon's eyes hardened. "No."

Such a liar. "Who gave you the orders to attack Abdi's people?"

He shook his head. "You may have me trapped here, but you can't make me talk. I have one ally in this world, and he's promised me a future with my child and a house of my own. Authority. Respect. I will do what I must to make that happen."

"Even kill innocent children?" Narine pictured the devastated faces of the Southern Clans. "Kill an entire people?"

"Some tragedies are unavoidable." His face was pinched and furious. "You taught me that, remember?"

"This was not tasary! Someone is using you, Gideon."

He lifted his chin. "Those people—the Southern Mages— they're nothing to me. You have your mission, Narine, and I have mine. I'm sure you think you're on the right side of history, but I *know* I am."

"So anything you do is justified?"

"You said it, not me. Mages have to look at the big picture."

Narine felt the last of her hope wither. "Then you don't deserve to know Samson, because he's better than both of us." She turned and felt Gideon's hand grab her shoulder, but Jacob was there, shoving him away.

"I don't think so," Jacob said.

Gideon stumbled back, his eyes fixed on Jacob. "You always did let others fight your battles for you. Tigist and Daniel. Now this one. Who is he?"

"A friend," Jacob said. "One that's here to protect Narine."

"He's your lover."

"No, Gideon." She sighed. "He's a friend. But if I had a lover, it wouldn't be your business."

"You're my wife."

"No." She felt it then, the severing in her heart. The final dissolution between the love she'd held for Gideon's memory and the reality of the man he'd become. "I am not your wife. In my heart, I never was."

Gideon turned to Jacob. "You should kill me. I tried to kidnap her. I drugged her and tried to steal her from her family. If I'd had my way, she would have never gone back to your time."

A muscle jumped in Jacob's cheek, but he didn't move. "This is between you and Narine."

Gideon turned away, let his head fall back, and roared into the emptiness of the uninhabited island. Then he turned and fixed his eyes on Narine. "You can't keep me here forever."

"I can't trust you, Gideon. I have to figure out what to do. Answer my questions so I can help you."

Gideon sat on a rock and folded his hands.

"Whose orders were you following? Who changed the tasary? Was it Desta? Someone in Mombasa? Who?"

He stared into the distance and said nothing.

"Who broke the taboo and brought you to the present to attack the order in Addis? Where are you meeting them? When?"

His expression didn't even change.

"Who are your real parents?"

That provoked a reaction. "What?"

"You have a traveler's mark on your shoulder," she said. "It's faint, but it's there."

"No." Gideon shook his head. "My magic is in alchemy. It always has been."

"Your strongest magic is in alchemy, but part of it is in traveling. I saw it on your skin and I felt it when I pulled you into the mage pool." She sat on a large rock at the edge of the clearing, giving her ankle a break. "If you don't know what that means, it means that you were born to a mage family." She met his eyes. "Natural mages only have one power. You are—at the very least—second generation."

His jaw set. "That's not possible."

"It's more than possible, it *is*."

She could see that the news surprised him, but his mask of indifference didn't crack.

"It doesn't matter," he said.

Jacob finally spoke. "Of course it does."

She stretched her ankle and felt her strength giving out. "I haven't allowed myself to be the mother that Samson deserves because I've been hanging on to this guilt I felt about you." She rubbed a hand over her heart. "But you could have prevented all of this. We could have been a family, but it had to be your way or war."

"There can be no third way. Not with you, not with the order, and not with my son. I *will* find him."

"Wrong. There has to be a third way, and I'm going to find it." She closed her eyes and let out a long breath. "And our son deserves to live in peace."

Gideon narrowed his eyes. "I could die here."

"I won't let that happen." Narine looked at Jacob, who nodded. She stood and he offered her his arm.

"Narine."

She limped toward the water, Jacob keeping her steady.

"Narine!"

They were in the shallows by the time he ran to the water's edge.

Gideon's face held the edge of panic. "You can't leave me here."

"I'll be back." She was exhausted and she needed to rest. "I won't forget this place, Gideon. I never could."

She clutched Jacob's hand, pulled him back under the water with her, and disappeared.

# CHAPTER 31

*Addis Ababa*
*2072*

Two days after the attack on the order, Narine, Tadesse, and Mesfin met in the anteroom of the Elders' Chamber to brief the elder council about what had transpired.

Mesfin submitted to an enhanced security screening, just as Narine and Tadesse did. He had a slice on his jaw and a bruise on his lip, but other than that, he and the rest of the hedges seemed invigorated by the attack.

"There are twice as many hedges at the gate as there usually are," Tadesse said. "Is that your doing?"

Mesfin raised a single eyebrow. "That breech of security wouldn't have happened if I had been in charge."

"So are you in charge now?"

He muttered, "Working on it."

Narine caught the determined look in Mesfin's eye and decided that maybe having a by-the-book hedge with an uptight personality wasn't a bad thing when someone within the Seba Segel had declared a quiet war.

"Their leader disappeared." Mesfin looked at Narine. "Do you have any idea where he went?"

"Yes."

"You knew the man."

Narine nodded. "I'm sure the elders will have questions too. I don't feel like answering them more than once."

He raised an eyebrow but asked nothing else.

"Where's Jacob today?" Tadesse asked her.

"I believe he had a staff meeting at the university," she said.

Tadesse blinked. "That's so... normal."

"I know." She smiled. "Cool, right? He's starting classes next week, but he's still going to teach."

"Good," Tadesse said. "Is Abdi training him?"

"I believe that's the plan."

The door opened, and a solemn East Asian woman with a curtain of waist-length hair and a red-and-black sash over her shoulder motioned for them to enter the chambers.

Narine and Tadesse went first with Mesfin at their backs. Narine was still limping, so she was relieved when she saw three stools in the center of the round chamber.

She sat on one and surreptitiously examined the room.

Elder Kebret hadn't moved from his position as the head of the council. Elder Issa was back in her chair, a newly woven shawl draped over her shoulder in red, yellow, green, and blue to celebrate the victory of the weavers over their enemies.

Abdi was back in the traveler's seat, and Elder Yosef was still present, his expression as satisfied as a well-fed house cat.

Added back to the Elders' Chamber was Elder Hawa, a regal diviner draped in azure blue who hailed from Clan Isaaq in Mogadishu. She had been visiting her family for the New Year and had missed all the excitement, though her eyes followed Mesfin with intentional curiosity.

And last on the council, representing the alchemists, was Dr. Majid of House Zaid in Zanzibar, who had also been out of the country during the New Year confusion. He was consulting with Abdi on his right, and they were speaking quietly as Elder Kebret called the meeting of the elders to order.

"Sister Narine, your mother has disappeared," he said. "House Kayl appears to have abandoned its seat in the capital again."

"As this is my mother," Narine said, "it can hardly be considered a surprise." As far as she knew, Anahid had taken an air transport to Arba Minch and was checking on Samson and Jamila before she returned to the city. "As my mother's only daughter, scion of House Kayl, I can assure you and House Abay that our family still owes its loyalty to the high order of the Seba Segel in Addis Ababa."

Elder Kebret nodded, but his expression was still sour. "Brother Mesfin, please brief the council on the events of two days ago."

"Gladly, Elder Kebret." Mesfin pulled out a tablet and projected a screen in the air. "As you can see, the incursion came via four travelers in the river who transported two other individuals with them." Surveillance footage from cameras on the roof zoomed in on a red-haired woman holding Gideon's hand and another traveler with a dull brown coat and curly brown hair holding the arm of the mage with the scarred face.

"I thought we had identified all the third-tier travelers working right now," Elder Issa said. "I don't recognize either of these mages."

Yosef leaned forward. "Because they're not working right now."

Issa pointed at the screen. "But they are."

"Are they?" Yosef cocked his head.

Issa's expression said that she was less than amused, but Elder Abdi picked up the thread.

"I believe what my brother traveler may be implying is

that these mages are not native to our time. They could have come from the future or the past."

"Not the past," Dr. Majid said. "Surely that wouldn't be—"

"Not permitted doesn't mean not possible," Narine said quietly. "We saw these mages during the Southern Mage Massacre. These could have been the same travelers who broke the Pagume prohibition and altered the tasary."

"And their leader, the one they call Gideon" —Elder Kebret spoke up— "is the same man who called you his wife."

Every eye in the room turned toward Narine.

She pointed back to Mesfin. "Doesn't he need to finish first?"

There was annoyed grumbling, but Narine could have sworn she saw silent amusement in Mesfin's eyes.

"As there is little we can do to prevent travelers from using the river to break into the compound—"

"Do we foresee this becoming a problem?" Dr. Majid asked. "When has the order ever had to protect itself from its own people?"

"Not since the Second Mage War." Abdi motioned to Mesfin. "Continue, Brother."

"Our mission is to be prepared," Mesfin continued. "Keeping that in mind, hedge spells on either side of the river have been strengthened and buttressed with alchemical traps to alert, slow, and hopefully prevent anything like this from happening again. Additional security has also been implemented along the perimeter of each of the buildings, particularly the weaving room and archives and the diviners' temple and observatory. This surveillance, combined with updated security algorithms designed to identify periods of increased system stress, should help to contain future threats."

Elder Kebret was beaming. "Thank you, Mesfin."

"Elders." The man gave a curt nod, minimizing the screen and tucking the tablet into his jacket. He stepped to the edge of the room near the woman with long hair, leaving Tadesse and Narine in the middle of the circle alone.

"Sister Narine." Abdi's voice was soft. "Can you relate the steps you and Brother Tadesse took to prevent the Southern Mage Massacre and minimize the damage from the altered tasary?"

Narine looked at Tadesse. "I think Tade would be better to explain all that."

Tadesse stood and carefully took the council through their jump, leaving out the bit where they didn't obtain permission from the elders for the journey. Since Abdi was the only one who knew the truth, they came out of it looking like "big damn heroes" as her father would say.

Tadesse recounted the bravery of the Southern Clans, and Narine couldn't help but notice that Abdi and Elder Hawa—who both came from federations of free clans—held their chins up just a little higher as Tadesse recounted their victory over the sneak attack.

"At the end of the day, all we really did was give the Southern Clans warning," Tadesse said. "Whoever plotted this massacre didn't count on anyone noticing in this time. Or they didn't count on anyone being able to stop it."

Elder Kebret rested his chin in his hand. "I can't help but think that—despite the use of travelers for this plot—whoever planned this has a fundamental misunderstanding of time travel."

Elder Issa said, "And a disregard for the Tibeb."

"I would agree," Elder Yosef said. "I would add, they also have a deep misunderstanding of Sister Narine's devotion to those she loves."

Narine's eyes met Abdi's and fixed on him. She knew the difficult questions were still coming.

"Speaking of Sister Narine…"

She closed her eyes and took a deep breath.

Elder Kebret waited for her to look at him before he continued.

"Sister, the man who led this attack asked for you by name and house. He demanded to see his wife and his son." There was a dark light burning in the back of Kebret's gaze.

"Dr. Gideon Marangu is a gifted alchemist whom I met on a jump over six years ago. His native time is in the early twentieth century."

She swallowed the lump in her throat and tried not to feel as if she were parading through the order hallways naked. "On that jump, I caught malaria and Dr. Marangu saved my life, but I was unable to return in time."

Elder Issa and Elder Kebret both sucked in a sharp breath.

"I had to wait a full year to find another matching constellar window, and during that time, Dr. Marangu and I formed a relationship. I did become pregnant, though I lost the child after my return jump." Not strictly a lie. In a fashion, she had lost Samson. "I went back after my recovery time—I'm sure some of you remember the period of time when I left the order's authority—and Gideon did not handle the news well." She kept her voice and her expression as blank as possible. "He was very angry and blamed me for the lost child. I think it is likely that someone is using his grief and inability to accept the truth as leverage. I believe someone else is behind these moves within the order."

"Why do you think that?"

"Because Gideon told me." She looked up at Abdi. "He told me that someone promised that if he destroyed the Southern Mages, he would have everything he wanted. Me as a wife, a child, a house, and status of his own. All of it."

"He mentioned a child by name," Dr. Majid said. "A child called Samson."

"A twisting of the truth," Narine answered smoothly. "Samson is like a nephew to me, a child of House Rajab in

Harar and the only son of a friend. I think whoever is behind this tricked Gideon into thinking that child was his."

Elder Yosef narrowed his eyes. "And where is Gideon now?"

"Yes, Sister Narine." Dr. Majid leaned forward. "The other mages who invaded the order groups were executed swiftly, but Gideon was not among them."

"That is because I took him away." Narine looked at Dr. Majid, then at Abdi, Elder Issa, Elder Hawa, and Elder Kebret. "I feel that there is more information he can give us."

"And where did you take him?" Dr. Majid asked.

"Someplace very safe." Narine folded her hands. "That is all I will say."

"This council demands the location of Gideon Marangu," Elder Kebret said. "This is not a debate, Sister Narine."

"Will you kill him for threatening the order?" Narine asked.

Elder Issa raised her eyebrows. "That is the consequence of his action. He broke two taboos and threatened the integrity of the Tibeb. Would you deny the Southern Mages justice?"

"Why don't you ask Abdi what he thinks I should do?" Narine turned to Abdi. "He can't hurt anyone where he is."

"And how do you know he's secure?" Abdi asked.

"Because someone would have to know exactly where and when I took him, and only one other person knows that."

"I see." Abdi sat back and folded his hands in his lap. "Then the Southern Mages are satisfied."

"And no doubt your mother is the other mage in possession of the knowledge of where this fugitive is." Elder Kebret was fuming. "Sister Narine, your actions leave you in defiance of this council, and we must determine your punishment."

Tadesse stood. "Elder Kebret—"

"Brother Tadesse, your loyalty to your fellow traveler is

admirable, but her reckless disregard for authority is not your fault or your weakness. Leave it."

He turned and looked at Narine, but she only shook her head slightly.

It wasn't worth it.

Narine stood and walked out of the Elders' Chamber.

"Sister Narine, think carefully before you leave."

She kept walking; she tried not to limp.

*You are Narine Anahid Khoren of House Kayl. Mother of Samson, daughter of Anahid. Third-degree traveling mage of the Seba Segel, ninth in your line of power.*

Narine walked past the hedges at the doors, nodding at Mesfin and his cohort as she passed, and out of the temple where the elder council met.

*You have no siblings and many cousins. You are the godmother of Gelile, the adopted sister of Genet. Your best friend is Jamila Sahid.*

She walked across the courtyard, under the softly waving canopy and past the sounds of the weavers singing as they wove the Tibeb.

*You are powerful.*

*You are trying to be wise.*

*Most importantly, you are loved.*

She met him in the coffee shop where she'd first noticed the travelers' mark on his left forearm. Narine waited at the round table near the entrance of the café, sipping on a macchiato and listening to the melody of languages in the café.

Amharic.

Oromo.

Chinese.

Hindi.

English.

She listened to the group of students at the next table, all with their lenses flipped down and a multimedia cacophony dancing around them. Two spoke in Amharic, another in English, and another in Hindi, but they all seemed to understand each other.

She closed her eyes and let the sounds of home wash over her.

*Addis, Addis, Addis.*

The smell of mud and synthetic oil from the misty sidewalk outside. The buzz of zip bikes and the racing blue minibuses as they climbed the hills going up to Shiro Meda. The distant clack of the skytrain and the floating smell of coffee and frankincense.

Narine felt his magic when he walked in the door. It felt familiar now, like a friend and something else that she didn't want to think about yet.

"Hey." He sat across from her and touched her shoulder. "How's it feeling?"

"Better all the time."

Jacob sat across from her, easy in his surroundings in a way that felt new.

Narine smiled. "What did you do?"

He leaned back and allowed the smile flirting on the corners of his lips to break free. "I accepted another year."

"They offered already?"

He nodded. "They want to extend the professorship for this year through the 2079 school year."

She leaned her chin on her hand. "You mean 2072."

"Don't start with me." He smiled and reached for her coffee. "You mind?"

"Go for it."

He sipped it, motioned for the girl taking orders, and asked for another, along with a piece of chocolate cake.

"Look who's feeling indulgent."

"My parents are coming next month for a visit," he said. "They've never been to Ethiopia before."

Her eyes lit up. "Do you think they'll like it?"

"I think they'll like that I like it." He took another sip of her coffee. "They want to meet you when they come."

Her eyebrows went up. "What did you tell them?"

"Just that I've made some really good friends since I've been here." He leaned forward and dropped his voice. "I didn't tell them about the time-travel thing. Or the magic stuff."

She leaned forward too. "Probably a good idea."

"I'm starting formal studies with Abdi next month."

Narine nodded. "Good. He's the best. Abdi will take care of you."

"How did it go with the elders?"

She lifted her right shoulder, the one that was still movable. "We'll see. They don't like me much right now because I won't tell them where he is."

Jacob sat back. "Why are you trying to protect him?"

"I don't know." She met his skeptical gaze. "I really don't. I just know he's Samson's father and I don't want him dead. That's what will happen if they find him. He also knows the answers to some questions, and there might be people out there ready to keep him quiet if they knew he was still alive."

"So for now?"

"For now he's safe where and when he is." Narine scrolled through the menu screen.

Jacob smiled softly. "You know, I'd like to meet the little man sometime."

Narine smiled. "The mystery man?"

"The mystery man."

"Hmm."

Jacob leaned back when the server brought his coffee and the cake to the table. "What does hmmm mean?"

"It's not Amharic, because we both know that you're still working on that. It's... an Armenian phrase. Actually."

He barely suppressed the smile. "Oh really?"

"Yes, it means... stick around and maybe what you want to happen will happen."

"That's a really complicated phrase for like, one sound."

"It's an intricate and ancient language, Jacob."

*One week later...*

SHE GLANCED ACROSS THE CABIN AND SAW JACOB SNOOZING ON the far side of the crawler. They'd decided to take a road trip while the flowers were still in bloom, so Genet and Gelile were in the back seat, taking pictures out the window as the southern landscape raced by and Jacob snored in the front seat.

"Akeste, where are we going?"

"We're going to see some new places and meet some new people," Narine said. "We're going to Ziway first, then to Hawassa. You remember Hawassa, right?"

"Yes, the place with the black-and-white monkeys?"

"Yes, that's the place. And after that we're going up in the mountains to a very special place." She glanced over her shoulder. "It's a surprise."

"Uuuugh." Gelile rolled her eyes. "I'm so tired of surprises."

She smiled. "I think you're going to like this one."

They made their way down the expressway to the bustling lakeside town of Ziway where pleasure boats and fishing vessels crowded the docks. They got rooms at a family-owned hotel near the dock, then ate fish goulash at Narine's favorite spot in town.

Gelile demanded to ride on Jacob's shoulders as they

walked home from the restaurant, and she squealed when she saw little monkeys in the papaya trees near the lake.

Pony carts moved up and down the main road, tourists delighting in the old-fashioned wooden transport and ribboned horses, and electric motorbikes zipped through the side streets while boys drove mechanized fruit carts laden with mangos and sugarcane across the road, and electric tuk-tuks ferried residents around the bustling lakeside town.

"Akeste?"

Narine was walking with her arm around Genet. The sun was going down, and the wind was picking up over the lake. "Yes, Gelile?"

"What are we going to see tomorrow?"

Narine smiled. "Who knows?"

SHE LEFT THE HOTEL EARLY, WALKING TO THE DOCK IN HER canvas shoes with a handful of cash and an old gebi wrapped around her shoulders.

The boat she wanted didn't take electronic birr. The old man would still want paper. She saw his horse cart tied by the pier, so she followed the concrete out to the end of the dock and searched for the bright flag of red, yellow, and green with a happy face in the middle.

She spotted the old man sitting in his boat, bobbing in the morning waves and watching the pelicans dive and dance in the shallows. Narine tapped on the frame of the old metal boat. *"Tena yistilin."*

The old man turned. "You're back."

Narine tossed her backpack on the boat and climbed onboard. "Do you have any passengers today?"

"I do now." He walked over, untied the rope, and hollered for the boy to push him away from the dock while he started the electric engine. "Same place as always?"

"Yes, the same place."

Narine sat in the center of the old boat, watching its bright flag flap in the wind and the water fly by as she made her way from the shore of the mainland to a very familiar island. They sped over the even surface of the lake, passing fishermen coming in from their early-morning catch. The birds followed them, swooping and diving into the churn of water and tiny fish that swam to the surface in their wake.

He let Narine off in the same place, the grey folded rocks that jutted out into the lake and the aging ficus tree that teetered along the edge.

"Back in an hour?"

Narine nodded and tossed the rope back to the old man. "See you then."

The old man held up a carafe of coffee. *"Buna?"*

She shook her head. "But thank you."

He looked around the boat to make sure she hadn't forgotten anything, then pushed away from the rocks and returned to the water, likely trolling around the islands to see if any of the small population of Zay people who still remained on the islands needed a morning trip to the mainland for shopping or other errands.

Narine walked to the old ficus tree, unfolded her gebi, and wrapped it around her shoulders, waiting for the sun to rise behind her as she looked to the west.

Her father had told her when she was a little girl that the east was her future and the west was her past. Narine stared into the past, watching the sky change as the sun rose, turning the clouds pink and gold. The air warmed, and all around her signs of spring life came forward.

There were bright yellow flowers scattered across the meadows and the tumbledown house that had once been Gideon's clinic. The acacia were blooming bright white in bunches that rode up the hill to the ridge where the church bells rang. And scattered among the trees, Narine heard the bleat of new lambs and kids in the herds the young boys watched from their perches by the water.

Narine sat at the base of the ficus tree and let her head rest in the curving roots of the old giant, her gebi pulled up over her shoulders to cut the bite of the wind.

"Are you there?" she whispered through the past, hoping that somehow he felt her presence from a thousand years away. "I'm sorry. And I'm not."

She looked over her shoulder at the rising sun and saw only more questions. The future was always uncertain.

"I don't know how this story ends," she whispered. "I just know I have to keep living it."

Narine let the memory of her hopes rise to the surface and flood her heart. She laid her head on the ground where they had first made love, and she finally allowed herself to cry.

# CHAPTER 32

*Gamo Highlands*
*2072*

The twisting back road that led to the Dorze village had been graveled over twenty years before, but it was still rough. The village had resisted the incursion of the central government into their territory, so the roads remained rough, modern convenience remained scarce, and the settlements at the top of the mountains remained independent.

"Where are we?" Gelile asked.

"We're in a very special place."

"My tablet doesn't have a signal."

"Nope." Narine smiled. "It won't have any kind of signal for a while."

They'd spent the night in Hawassa the day before, walking along the lakeshore, taking the zip boats out on the lake, and fishing with the locals at dusk. The resort town was a haven for the rich from Addis and Dire Dawa, with towering luxury houses lined along the lakeshore and private docks jutting into the tall grass that bordered the water.

Bird-watching was abundant, and Gelile squealed when they took the skycars over the city park, catching glimpses of the colobus monkeys and hornbills from a bird's-eye view. They ate dinner at another fish house, enjoying traditional dancing and the best coffee Narine had drunk in a long time before they returned to their hotel.

The next morning, they drove south into the Gamo Highlands to one of the last wild refuges bordering the Great Rift Valley. The villages to the east of Arba Minch were isolated and independent. Farmed terraces still lined the sides of the mountains, while animals roamed freely and a four-wheel-drive vehicle from the city was news that spread to the top of the mountain within minutes of their wheels turning off the paved road.

A fine, cool mist blew over the hills, hiding and revealing the valley below as they climbed higher and higher. Narine drove with her whole body, the crawler slipping and sliding in the mud as the electric motor struggled with the hills.

"Wishing you had Teddy's old diesel right about now?" Genet smiled in the back seat. "Though where we'd find diesel fuel anymore is a mystery."

"We'll make it." Narine set the computer to sport mode. "We just have to go slowly."

The road gradually evened out, and they drove through a village that appeared to be lost in time. Towering grass huts that resembled large round beehives lined each side of the road with lush inset gardens surrounding each house. A line of men were digging in an open field, turning over rich black soil while school-age children ran along the road, peeking in the windows at the visitors.

Narine stopped when she passed a woman carrying a backpack and a baby in a sling. "Good morning," she said in Amharic. "Is the road to the lodge clear right now?"

The woman looked amused. "Which lodge?"

"The Syrian's place."

"Oh." She waved toward the right. "Just past this field. You'll see a road going off to the right and uphill." She glanced at the vehicle. "You may have to push this one. The rain has just dried up."

"Thank you."

"If you can't reach that old place, try the next lodge down the road. Shangri-La. The husband is local and the wife is from Tibet. Nice people and very good food. My sister works there."

"Thank you," Narine said. "We'll check them both out."

She rolled up the window and ignored the curious glances from her passengers. "Okay, I know where I'm going now."

Genet said, "I thought you'd been to this place before."

"It's been a few years. Things change."

But not much changed in the mountains. Narine found the twisting road that led to Nash's lodge. It was overgrown but passable. By the time they reached the gate, children from the village had already run up the footpaths on the mountain and announced their arrival.

Genet leaned over the seat. "Is that Jamila?" Her voice pitched up. "And Samson? I can't believe how much he's grown!"

"Samson?" Gelile was bouncing in her seat. "I get to play with Samson?"

Jacob's eyes were fixed on the small boy jumping up and down on the grassy lawn in front of the lodge. He was bouncing on his toes, a brilliant smile lighting up his face. Behind him stood Jamila and Anahid, watching the car approach.

Jacob looked at her and he smiled, his eyes crinkling in the corners as he caught Narine's shining eyes.

Her sister and her niece only knew Samson as Jamila's son. Narine parked the car and turned to them before they could burst out of their seats.

"Okay, before we go say hi," she said. "I want to tell you both something I should have told you a long time ago."

Genet frowned. "What?"

Gelile sighed. "Can I go play with Samson though?"

Deciding that might be the better idea for the moment, Narine opened Gelile's door and let the little girl rush out to join her cousin.

Samson reached his arms out, shrieking in delight when he saw Gelile running toward him. "Lila!"

Narine watched them embrace and whisper to each other, already exchanging childish confidences and giggles.

Genet put a hand on Narine's wrist. "What is going on? Are you okay? Is Samson all right?"

Narine glanced at Jacob, who gave her an encouraging nod.

"Samson is my son." She didn't try to make excuses. "I was pregnant when I came back from that jump six years ago. The time I went away? It was when I was pregnant. Jamila raised Samson as her son, but he's mine. I mean biologically—"

"I know." Genet's eyes softened. "Narine, of course I know."

She blinked back tears. "You did?"

"His skin is darker and his hair is curlier, but he looks like you." Genet smiled. "Of course I knew."

Narine wiped her eyes. "You never asked."

Genet pressed her lips together and took Narine's hand. "I knew there was a reason. Especially with your mother, your family?" She squeezed her fingers. "I knew there had to be a reason."

Narine swallowed the lump in her throat. "He's a very special little boy."

"Of course he is." She leaned over and gave Narine a hug around the shoulders. "He's yours." She got out of the car, walked toward the celebrating family, and allowed Narine to collect herself.

She took a deep breath and let it out slowly. "Well, that went better than I expected."

"Family knows." Jacob was watching the three women and the two little kids already running around the garden. "So am I the only guy here?"

"Nash is probably around, but he has the disposition of an old donkey, so yes, it's probably going to be just you most of the time."

He smiled a little bit. "Sounds like Samson and I will have to stick together."

She turned to him. "Thank you for coming along."

Jacob's eyes met hers, and there was a light behind them that made Narine feel something like hope.

"Thanks for inviting me."

They got out of the truck, and Samson ran into her arms.

THEY SAT ON A CHAISE OVERLOOKING THE VALLEY AT SUNSET, the red orb behind them casting deep pink and purple shadows over the clouds in the valley below.

Samson lay back against Narine's chest, his fingers playing with the dry skin in the crease of her elbow.

"Ema, you have crocodile skin."

"Oh no. Does that mean I'm a croc now?" She leaned down and bit his ear.

Samson giggled from his belly. "Noooo." He reached up and put his arms around her neck. "I like this place."

"I do too."

"Jacob isn't my father."

Narine blinked. "No. Did you think that's why I brought him?"

"I don't know." Samson shrugged. "I thought you might bring him to me."

It was a conversation that Narine was expecting, but not for a few more years. It made sense that he would wonder though. Jacob was the first man she'd ever introduced him to, even as a friend.

"Jacob is my friend." She kissed the top of Samson's head. "He's a traveler like us, and he's a long way from home. Is it okay that I brought him?"

"Uhhh." Samson carefully considered the idea. "I think... *Yes*. His magic feels like a friend."

Narine smiled. "Do you think so? I think so too."

"And it's big power. Big like him."

She laid her cheek on her son's forehead. "Abdi is going to teach him magic. Do you think he'll be a good teacher for him?"

"Yes." He nodded decisively. "Nani wants to teach him, but he should learn from Abdi."

"Has Nani been teaching you things sometimes?"

Samson shrugged. "Just little magics."

"Like what?"

"Like... how to hide if I need to hide."

"Did you tell her about our island?"

"No." He turned his head. "You told me the island was a surprise."

Anahid would certainly get a surprise if she visited right now. "It is a surprise."

Samson turned, his small brow furrowed together. "Sometimes surprises are secrets, aren't they?"

Narine considered how to answer in a way he's understand. Her son was wise, but he was still a child. "I don't like keeping secrets, but sometimes I have to."

"Like me." He turned back to watch the drifting clouds. "I'm a secret now, but I won't always be. One day I'll be stronger than the people who make you scared."

*I hope you're right, baby boy.* Narine couldn't say anything, so she kissed the top of his head and squeezed him tight. "You are so precious to me."

"Is my abba alive?"

"Yes." Narine thought of Gideon, sitting and waiting in a wooden hut by the water. "He's alive." *Alive and probably fuming in anger, but definitely alive.*

Samson turned and rested his cheek on her shoulder. "Where does he live?"

"You know how Mommy lives in the now most of the time and in the past sometimes?"

"Yes. And when I'm big, I can live in the past too."

"For a little while, but always remember that the now is your home, okay?"

"Okay." Samson fiddled with the seam on his pants. "Does my abba live in the past or the now?"

"He lives in the past."

"Will I ever meet him?"

"I think you will. Someday."

He pushed his lips together in a small pout. "Do I have to be bigger?"

"Yes," Narine said. "That's probably a good idea."

"Okay." He turned and snuggled into her arms, pulling them around his thin shoulders and watching the eastern sky turn a brilliant, deep midnight blue as the sun slipped below the horizon. "Is the sun coming up on this side tomorrow?" He pointed at the eastern horizon.

"Yes."

"We should wake up to see it." Samson whispered, "We don't want to miss the beginning."

# Afterword

Thank you for taking the time to read THE THIRTEENTH MONTH. I sincerely hope you enjoyed it.

The second book in the Seba Segel series will be CHILD OF ASHES, coming Summer 2024, and the third book in the trilogy will be THE GOLD FLOWER, coming Summer 2025.

For more information about Elizabeth Hunter's work, please visit her website at ElizabethHunterWrites.com.

# GLOSSARY

- Ababa— Flower
- Akeste— Auntie
- Alchemist— Mage role characterized by magic that manipulates the natural world; a potions maker
- Ameseghinalehu— *Amharic*, Thank you
- Amharic— A Semitic language spoken in the Horn of Africa, the dominant language in Ethiopia
- Archivist— Mage role characterized by magic used to keep records via weaving, spinning, and writing
- Azmari— An entertainer who plays traditional instruments of Ethiopia
- Chechebsa— An Ethiopian breakfast dish made of fried batter
- Chigur yelem— *Amharic*, no problem

- Diviner— Mage role characterized by the use of magic and study to read the stars and predict the future
- Enset— A flowering plant in the banana family cultivated as a staple food in the south of Ethiopia; false banana
- Farenji— *Amharic*, foreigner
- Fasolia— *Amharic*, green beans
- Gebi— *Amharic*, a heavy cotton woven wrap used to cover the body as an over-garment or blanket
- Hedge— Mage role characterized by magic used in martial roles, defense, and strategy
- Injera— *Amharic*, the staple flatbread in Ethiopia made of teff grain
- Kemis— *Amharic*, a traditional dress
- Khat— *Amharic*, the leaves of an Arabian shrub that are chewed as a mild stimulant
- Kikile— *Amharic*, a boiled stew made from lamb or goat
- Masenqo— *Amharic*, a single string bowed lute instrument used in traditional Ethiopian music
- Merkana— *Amharic*, the high or "buzz" experienced while chewing khat
- Meskel— *Ge'ez*, word for cross; a major Orthodox holiday in Ethiopia that celebrates the finding of the True Cross
- Mesob— *Amharic*, a basket used to store injera
- Mezmur— *Amharic*, traditional sacred music of the Ethiopian Orthodox Church
- Netela— *Amharic*, a thin woven scarf worn over the hair and shoulders by women during ceremonial or church celebrations
- Pagume— *Amharic*, the thirteenth month in the Ethiopian calendar
- Selam— *Amharic*, hello

# GLOSSARY

- Selamnew— *Amharic*, informal, how are you?
- Sambusa— *Amharic*, a crispy fried dumpling filled with spiced lentils
- Seba Segel— An order of mages based in Addis Ababa who manipulate time and history by reading the stars, using magic, and time travel
- Tasary— Immovable points of history woven into the Tibeb
- Tenadam— *Amharic*, herb known as rue in English
- Tibeb— The sacred record of magical Seba Segel history woven by the archivists
- Traveler— Mage role characterized by the use of magic to travel through time
- Tuk-tuk— A three wheeled motorbike used as a taxi
- Wot— *Amharic*, a stew eaten with injera

# ACKNOWLEDGMENTS

It would have been absolutely impossible to write this book without the assistance, input, and knowledge of my incredible husband David Teshome. As a national guide in Ethiopia, his extensive travel, study, and experience make him something of a walking Ethiopian encyclopedia. While I'm happy I married him for countless reasons, he was absolutely integral to the writing of this book.

Also, he's super cute.

I also want to thank our family and friends in Addis Ababa who answer my many questions, always feed me more than I can possibly eat, and generally put up with my American weirdness when I lock myself away for hours in my "cave." (This goes for my family and friends in the States too.)

The idea for this book originated on a visit to Kenya when I was looking up at the stars. From there, the idea wouldn't leave me alone, even though I fought it. I always said I would never write a time travel book. They were too complicated, too opaque, too much of a nightmare for a plotter like me.

Well, I finally wrote one. It will be up to you if I did the genre justice, but whatever readers ultimately decide about THE THIRTEENTH MONTH, I love this book, I love these characters, and I cannot thank the following people enough:

Amy Cissel

Angela Houle
and Anne and Linda at Victory editing.

These incredible professionals are my editing team and I'm sure I tried their patience with this project. I cannot thank them enough.

Damonza created the cover for this book, and I think it captures both the magic and the mystery of the series so well. I am so thrilled.

I also want to thank friends like April White (who is far better at this genre than I am), Cat Bowen, Chevella Mack, Sinit Berhe, Didi, Teddy, Miki and Izzi, my niece Mistre, and all my sisters in Addis, Bisi, Hiwot, Elsa, and Tsegish.

When I say I was a bit of a basket case writing this book, it is not an exaggeration, but at the end of the day, I'm proud of it, I hope it's been a fun ride, and I hope you'll come back for the second chapter of this journey with me.

Thank you to all of you who took the time to buy this book.
Be well. Keep reading.
Elizabeth

# ABOUT THE AUTHOR

ELIZABETH HUNTER is an eleven-time *USA Today* best-selling author of romance, contemporary fantasy, and paranormal mystery. Based in Central California and Addis Ababa, she travels extensively to write fantasy fiction exploring world mythologies, history, and the universal bonds of love, friendship, and family. She is the author of the Elemental Legacy series, the Irin Chronicles, the Cambio Springs Mysteries, and other works of fiction.

*The Thirteenth Month* is her fiftieth book.

# Also by Elizabeth Hunter

The Bronze Blade

The Scarlet Deep

A Very Proper Monster

A Stone-Kissed Sea

Valley of the Shadow

The Elemental Legacy

Shadows and Gold

Imitation and Alchemy

Omens and Artifacts

Midnight Labyrinth

Blood Apprentice

The Devil and the Dancer

Night's Reckoning

Dawn Caravan

The Bone Scroll

Pearl Sky

The Elemental Covenant

Saint's Passage

Martyr's Promise

Paladin's Kiss

Bishop's Flight

(Summer 2023)

Vista de Lirio

Double Vision

Mirror Obscure

Trouble Play

Glimmer Lake

Suddenly Psychic

Semi-Psychic Life

Psychic Dreams

Moonstone Cove

Runaway Fate

Fate Actually

Fate Interrupted

The Cambio Springs Series

Long Ride Home

Shifting Dreams

Five Mornings

Desert Bound

Waking Hearts

Linx & Bogie Mysteries

A Ghost in the Glamour

A Bogie in the Boat

Contemporary Romance

The Genius and the Muse

7th and Main

Ink

Hooked

Grit

Sweet